Casting his
blinding glow.
roiling surface
and diving and
Black and re
The rising of   thing surfacing for a momen
Innova's breath fled him. He heard himself scream.

CHAOS WAR SERIES

The Siege of Mt. Nevermind

Fergus Ryan

For McGilligan
go raibh maith agai

THE SIEGE OF MT. NEVERMIND

Cover art by Glen Angus
First Printing: September 1999
Library of Congress Catalog Card Number: 98-88150

9 8 7 6 5 4 3 2 1

ISBN: 0-7869-13819
T21381-620

U.S., CANADA,	EUROPEAN HEADQUARTERS
ASIA, PACIFIC, & LATIN AMERICA	Wizards of the Coast, Belgium
Wizards of the Coast, Inc.	P.B. 34
P.O. Box 707	2600 Turnhout
Renton, WA 98057-0707	Belgium
+1-206-624-0933	+32-14-44-30-44

Visit our web site at **www.tsr.com**

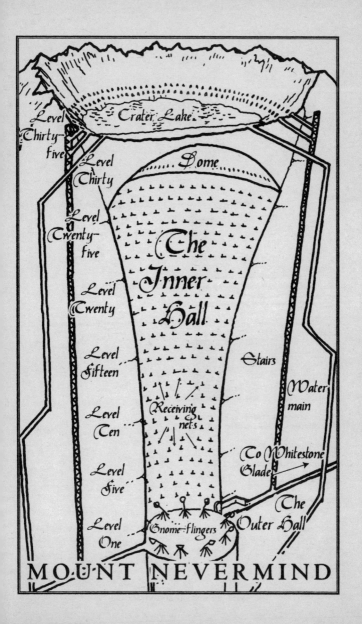

Level Thirty-five

Crater Lake

Level Thirty

Dome

Level Twenty-five

The Inner Hall

Level Twenty

Level Fifteen

Stairs

Level Ten

Water main

Receiving nets

Level Five

To Whitestone Glade

The Outer Hall

Level One

Gnome-flingers

MOUNT NEVERMIND

Chapter 1

It was the longest running event in Mount Nevermind, this High Tribunal of the Philosopher's Guild.

Established back in the Age of Might out of some vague yearning for justice, the Tribunal had been a good thing at first. On that, all historians agreed. But it was gnomish by nature, as gnomish as a thirteen-function can opener or a telescope designed for viewing the moon's reflection from underwater.

And like all things gnomish, it soon became involved.

Court cases, resolved in an hour anywhere else in Krynn, bogged down in paperwork, in barristers' arguments and counterarguments until a simple transaction—a transfer of deed, say, where both parties were ready and willing—took decades to complete.

Of course, a disputed claim might take centuries.

Cases of theft and industrial accidents would grind on until everyone—plaintiff and defendant included—had forgotten the charges. Nobody knew what the defendant's great-grandfather had allegedly stolen from the plaintiff's great-great-aunt, and all the eyewitnesses were dead of old age. Even if a case were solved quickly, often the steam scaldings had healed, the scars and abrasions as faint as

1

fossils under a millennia of rock, leaving no evidence for justices to debate or to worry into nothingness.

That was why Innova was surprised. It seemed his case was to be resolved with lightning speed.

Only six months after his arrest, final arguments were at hand. Rumors flashed through the corridors and levels of Mount Nevermind that the justices were about to reach a decision on his case, his crime, his future.

He had slept only fitfully the night before, aloft in his hammock and plagued by dreams of machinery grinding his legs into meal. When the Tribunal Guardsmen pounded at the door, Innova tumbled from the hammock, hit the stone floor of his chambers, and awoke.

Silently, he lay a moment between sleep and stupor, until Talos's voice brought him back to his senses.

"Wake up, you numskull! This is the day when all good gnomes come to trial and the best of the lot to grief!"

How can Talos be so cheery? Innova asked himself, as he dressed in the dark, fumbling with the stays and cords of his formal yellow jacket, turning his pale green trousers inside out so the judge would be less likely to see the food stains that speckled them from knee to buckle.

The guardsmen remembered to slip on the necklace of brass bells worn by all defendants in gnomish courts of law: *the better to locate bail jumpers*, and they were right.

A bright stocking cap, orange and red in a zigzag pattern that always reminded him of lightning, was the crown of Innova's apparel.

After all, this was a high occasion and demanded that he look his best.

He liked to look his best. After all, who didn't want to be the hero of his own story?

Pleased with his appearance, still drowsy, Innova emerged from his chambers into the blaring torch- and phosphorous light of Shaft Alley, the busiest street on the Twenty-Sixth Level of Mount Nevermind.

For a moment the light blinded him. A harsh whiff of cabbage and cayenne, of onions and ale and dwarf spirits, rose to meet him. So did a flock of beggars—gully dwarves mostly, mixed with a few industrially mangled gnomes, not to mention the abandoned old and the children.

Nothing on this level smelled good anymore.

"Please, sir!" the beggars clamored, as the guardsmen brushed them aside. "Please, sir, for charity's sake!"

I'm the one who needs charity this day, Innova thought, extending his hands for the ceremonial shackles in which all defendants were brought before the tribunal. Little more than jeweler's chains, suitable for watch fobs or medallions rather than restraint, they were all part of the finery of a court appearance.

His friends and co-defendants, Talos and Deddalo, were waiting for him. They, too, were encircled by a squadron of guardsmen and decked out in their own best attire. Deddalo smiled, lifted his manacled hands to display a particularly pungent onion.

"Breakfast?" he offered carelessly.

Innova shook his head.

So Deddalo wrapped the thing in his handkerchief and slipped it into his back pocket, where it would serve, no doubt, for lunch as well. Even for dinner, considering how the justices hemmed and hawed.

But the three friends looked splendid, with jackets and polished boots, with jewelers' chains and an escort of guardsmen. Splendid enough, they hoped, to influence the judges' verdict.

For it is a rule of long standing that a good gnome judge is influenced by everything short of evidence.

That accounted, of course, for the purses Talos and Deddalo, who both came from wealthy families, carried on their trouser belts. The leather pouches were so heavy with steel coin that the trousers sagged immodestly, and the Tribunal Guards were warning the lads to *hitch up them belts, please, that industrial miscalculation was a steep enough charge without compoundin' it with indecent exposure.*

Innova sighed as a guardsman manacled him between his companions. He was an orphan, had been so since his parents were entangled in the gears of a bottling machine eleven years ago. His inheritance had been ground up as well in the machinery of the very court to which he traveled now.

3

Innova had no money for bribery, and he consoled himself that the charges against him were lesser ones. No industrial miscalculation, which carried severe sentences—sometimes even banishment, but always the dreaded public service.

No, Innova's were simple misdemeanors. Two counts of guilty bystanding.

Which meant, quite simply, that someone thought he should have known better.

*　　*　　*　　*　　*

Innova had held back when the Barium twins caught fire.

Ignition had not been his idea, of course. In fact, Innova had never even seen the girls. Deddalo, bent on a confused revenge, had planned the whole nasty business: making the calculations from the silo atop which the girls were wont to picnic, then bringing the math to his fellows.

Numbers and physics, he had told them. *That will teach that trollop to take back her money.*

For Deddalo had been engaged to one of the girls—he could never remember whether it was Beryl or Meryl. Then, on the eve of the wedding, he had discovered that the promised dowry had been spent on dwarf spirits to lubricate the reception. Deddalo called off the ceremonies at once, and that should have marked an end to the whole deceptive business.

But putting an end to events before they spiraled into disaster had never been one of Deddalo's strengths.

Revenge was called for, he figured.

And revenge was best when sweetened with explosives.

Talos was all for his old friend's plan. He was in the midst of an unhappy courtship himself with whichever Barium twin did not interest Deddalo. He felt that *both* girls would learn from "vaporous instruction."

Beryl will learn from Meryl's greediness, he agreed.

Meryl, Deddalo corrected. For Beryl is my true love.

Phaistos, the dimmest of the four companions, nodded in outraged agreement.

So there, in Innova's quarters on the Twenty-Sixth Level

of Mount Nevermind, the lads had plotted the whole volatile business.

As usual, Talos was responsible for the chemistry. The spirits in the silo were aged well, he reckoned, evaporating almost instantly on the tongue. Revelers were known to pass out from fumes alone. And perhaps that was what the Barium Twins liked the most about their picnic spot atop the silo, where the essence of Thorbardin Red mixed with corroded copper, and the air itself was intoxicating.

All that was needed, Talos maintained, was something to lace the mixture.

That was where Phaistos came in.

The youngest of the group, and by far the most stupid, he would take the role of what Talos called *the catalyst*. Stationed in the bottom of the silo, knee-deep in mash, he would be stuffed with beans and lentils and cucumbers like a game bird fattened for a festival.

The mixture of fumes would be chemically unpredictable, Talos maintained.

Deddalo was not too concerned about predictions.

As long as one thing is certain, he maintained rather loudly, downing his seventh glass of ale that night in Innova's chamber, as the four of them put the final touches on a tipsy plan.

As long as one thing is certain, my heart will rest in peace. Meryl Barium must henceforth recall every detail of this day.

"Beryl," Talos had corrected. "For Meryl is *my* one true love."

*   *   *   *   *

Innova should have known, at the moment of planning, that things were headed toward disaster.

He knew now, but it was far too late to derail the foolishness.

Now, the three surviving conspirators walked down a torchlit corridor toward the pulley that, if it was still in operating order, should deposit them on the Twenty-Eighth Level of the huge, elaborate city.

Or that is what the guardsmen said. For his own part,

Innova was already lost.

At the Twenty-Ninth Level, a sergeant maintained, there should be yet another party of guardsmen to receive them. From there, it was only a vaultwalloper's journey up to the Thirtieth Level, to the threshold of a chamber virtually inaccessible to corridor and footpath.

The Philosophers' Tribunal convened in that chamber. The judges, four elderly gnomes chosen by weight, were seated in ceremonial thrones, which rested in the pans of an enormous steel balance. It was the duty of these judges to decide all cases—civil and criminal and accidental—through reference to an involved series of precedents and principles. In this, the Tribunal was like most courts of law anywhere.

But an accident two centuries past had changed the way that the court went about things. Most of the written precedents had been kept by the Barristers' Guild in the Great Library of Mount Nevermind; however, a shelf top-heavy with volumes of structural damage lawsuits had collapsed on a dozen librarians, leaving no survivors.

Since then, it had been impossible to find what you wanted in the labyrinth of cases and torts and amendments and codicils.

So the judges, Innova mused, as he rode past the Twenty-Seventh level in the creaking pulley, would rely entirely on principle.

And principle was a funny thing when it rushed undocumented through five generations of pampered and arbitrary justices.

In the centuries following the Great Library Mishap, justice itself had come to take into account not only the nature of the crime and the party's guilt or innocence, but also the style in which the crime was committed. A daring theft, filled with whistles and narrow escape routes and misdirections, could sometimes earn acquittal if the judges happened to admire its sheer complexity. There were occasions on which even murderers walked free because the homicide involved plenty of steam and laundry chutes.

And what made judgment even more unpredictable was its huge reliance on the whim of the judge. A Tribunal Justice would weigh both evidence and style in a subjective manner, as though he judged a ballet rather than a property dispute. It never hurt a claimant to come to a hearing laden with coin, for the scales of justice tilted for steel and gold.

All of this was not in Innova's favor. Unlike his comrade Deddalo—unlike most gnomes, for that matter—he was not good with a downpour of involved words and flattery. And unlike his wealthy friend Talos, his pockets, as usual, were empty.

Furthermore, his part in the whole venture lacked even the necessary style. He had seen disaster coming, and he had not tried to stop it. Caution on all counts, and to many justices, caution was a crime in itself. Seeing disaster coming made you as guilty as the next party.

If not more guilty.

So when the Guardsmen set Innova in the pulley and he was yanked past walls of rock and rubble, bound for a destination levels above, his thoughts were troubled. When another band of Guardsmen pulled him from the pulley bucket, tied him in the brown darkness and carried him through secret passages to the vaultwalloper room, the gloom had settled on his meditations.

Now, drawing him from the bag, they fixed him into the vaultwalloper—an enormous slingshot that would send him rocketing over forty feet in the air to the entrance of the Tribunal Chamber.

It worked most of the time, one of the guardsmen assured him.

Seated in the old contraption, drawn back as tightly as a nocked arrow in a bow string, Innova took a deep breath. All of his good sense—and he had more than all his friends, more than most gnomes for that matter—was focused not on the flight itself, not on the hard, glossy onyx that framed the too-narrow entrance fifteen yards above, but on the greater perils that would await him in the court.

Chapter 2

A sudden lurch in the great sling, and Innova was airborne.

Light and dark and glittering walls surged toward him, past him, as he tried to cry out a prayer to Reorx, but only a long, wailing "Yaaah" escaped him as he heard the snap of the sling behind him, as the walls and his breath seemed to vanish and he sailed through a narrow gap in the rocks, sliding in a bell-ringing heap to the threshold of the Tribunal Chamber.

Innova tried to stand up, slipped on the polished onyx floor, and jangled back again. All of his worry and anticipation had fled him, banished by aeronautics.

Where am I? he thought for a second, his jostled thoughts rising to meet him from over forty feet below . . . .

Then Talos came flying through the darkness, glancing against the smooth edge of the opening and tumbling into Innova, his own bells chiming and a handful of steel coins slinging from his purse and scattering down the corridor.

Rumpled, glaring at one another in the dim torchlight, the two gnomes struggled to their feet.

Because chaos always comes in threes, there was another cry, followed by a solid sound like a ham being dropped from a great height, as Deddalo hurtled by his comrades and crashed against the chamber door.

"Enter!" proclaimed a voice from inside.

"Knock again, and enter!"

* * * * *

The four justices were already seated, high above the onyx floor of the chamber. Dark meditation pools, replenished from above by Mount Nevermind's virtually inexhaustible water supply, reflected the torchlight and the bright underside of the scales in which they sat. Three of the judges—Harpos, Julius, and Ballista, if Innova remembered correctly—were piled together in one pan of the ceremonial balance. Julius, an ancient, almost doddering gnome, held an anvil between his knees.

It was all a question of equilibrium.

For in the other pan of the scales, his incalculable weight counterbalancing three gnomes and their ballast, sat Gordusmajor, the High Justice of the Philosophers' Guild.

The brass chains of the balance creaked ominously above him. He was drowsing now, enormous and hairy, dreaming no doubt of oatcakes and a morning barrel of beer.

Though the law maintained that each judge had equal voice in proceedings, every gnome in Mount Nevermind knew that this was not the case in practice. Because of his girth, it was Gordusmajor's opinion that would decide the case, and a smart defendant would do whatever he could to tilt the scales in the direction of the massive High Justice.

Innova gathered his hopes. After all, Talos and Deddalo would make smart defendants. And sure enough, as the bailiff began the lengthy process of announcing the names of the accused, Talos began the strategy of defense. He stepped forward, bowed ceremoniously toward the trio of judges, then turned to Gordusmajor. Speaking over the droning syllables of his own name, he addressed the bench.

"Reorx preserve the High Justice Gordusmajor!"

"Reorx preserve him," echoed Innova and Deddalo, as they had been taught to do by their counselor, the public defender Scymnidus, who was sleeping off a scheduled hangover on the Twenty-Ninth level and had sent his polite apologies three days in advance.

"Reorx preserve him from illness and untimely death," Talos continued. "From explosion and flame and too much immersion in oil—"

"Reorx preserve him from apes and panthers!" Innova added. Scymnidus had taught them well, mentioning with emphasis the High Justice's fear of wild animals.

"From powder and fuse," Talos said. "From industrial mishap and unforeseen holes in the ground. From the attentions of ugly females, from magic and assassins, from . . . from . . ."

9

"Hunger and thirst," the High Justice prompted. His eyelids fluttered open and a thin smile spread over his crumb-encrusted lips.

"From hunger and thirst. From chaos and unfortunate lunar convergences," Talos chanted. "From sour beer and those little currant cakes where the seeds stick in your teeth, from all monsters and from false lights and tunnels . . ."

"Great Reorx deliver him!" chimed Deddalo and Innova.

The High Justice closed his eyes. Began to snore.

"From bad dreams and from music," Talos said. "From pulley systems that cannot bear his inestimable weight, from Sargonnas and Hiddukel and all other gods who do not understand him, from lice and from spastic colon, from abstractions and from doctored dice . . ."

"From hunger and thirst!" Gordusmajor prompted as he dozed.

"From hunger and thirst," Talos repeated, moving slowly toward the High Justice, fumbling at his belt, hitching his pants and drawing forth a heavy pouch.

"And from poverty."

With this, Talos tossed the purse onto the scales. Harpos, Julius, and Ballista blinked as their seat rose, and the chamber echoed with the sound of steel on brass.

Gordusmajor's eyelids fluttered behind a layer of fat. "And what false charges," he asked, in a booming, judicial voice, "have been brought against these fine young specimens of gnomehood?"

*   *   *   *   *

It was fairly smooth passage from then on.

Before the recitation of Talos's name had ended, Innova knew that he and his companions would be free by the afternoon. As the bailiff began the seventeenth syllable of Deddalo's family history and heritage, Justice Ballista, speaking above the confusing account of revenge and trap-doors, asked the first hostile question.

"If the three of you are as innocent as you claim, how did the Barium girls undergo such . . . detonation?"

10

"A faulty heating system, it was, High Justice Gordus-major," Deddalo explained, his eyes never leaving the enormous judge, who was busy counting the steel coins in Talos's tendered purse. "It was innocent fun, I swear by all holy gods, except Sargonnas and Hiddukel, who do not understand you. Innocent fun, it was, turned suddenly tragic by faulty infrastructure."

"Infrastructure?" Judge Harpos asked, leaning dangerously over the lip of the balance pan. "Please explain, Master Deddalo. And remember that you are under oath."

Of course, they were *not* under oath. The Tribunal had dispensed with oath-taking years before, preferring flattery and bribery instead. After all, an overly scrupulous gnome *might* stick to the truth and thereby cease to be entertaining.

Deddalo was no lover of the truth and would not have balked at an oath to begin with. Encouraged by Justice Harpos's prompting, he launched into a lengthy account of the disaster that had brought them all here.

Innova sat back and marvelled. Rarely in the course of the telling did Deddalo stray from the facts. But those facts, like cogs in some immense, misfiring machinery, bumped and ground against one another, until, at the end of the day, the story resembled the whole truth and anything but the truth.

* * * * *

Almost at once, Innova noticed the eye.

It was a standing joke among his childhood friends. Deddalo's drooping left eyelid was his only truly unflattering feature, a flaw in an otherwise passable face.

If that had been the sum of it, the eyelid would have been nothing of importance, like Counselor Scymnidus's long nose or High Justice Gordusmajor's prodigious waistline. But it was a dead giveaway: for when Deddalo lied, hedged, or even colored the truth, the eyelid would snap open. He would take on a stunned, paralyzed look, like a deer caught in the hunter's lamp.

No matter how Deddalo fashioned his stories, his friends always knew when the fancy words were masking something.

11

"It was only a prank on the Barium twins, Most Eminent High Justice," Deddalo began. "You see, I was in love with young Meryl Barium—"

"Beryl," Talos corrected, rummaging within his coat for a second purse. "*I* was in love with Meryl."

Deddalo frowned. "By any name, she was a glorious lass, and even without a name our love would have blossomed, were it not for the thorns surrounding the rose of her heart."

The three lighter justices rolled their eyes, but Gordusmajor nodded and smiled, reaching beneath his outsized lapels and producing a neatly folded oatcake, which he stuffed in his cavernous mouth as the story continued.

"Two of those thorns were greed and gluttony," Deddalo said, then stuttered and caught himself. "Two qualities that are . . . distinguished signs of character in the male gender, but suspect in feminine hands."

The High Justice coughed a gobbet of oatcake onto his beard.

"And so it was with Beryl . . . Meryl. By Reorx, so it was with the both of them! My three companions and I learned this to our everlasting sorrow."

Innova scratched his head. He had never met or even *seen* either of the twins in question.

"Enough prelude and poetry!" Justice Julius commanded. "Bring on the circumstantial evidence!"

Gordusmajor shifted suddenly in his seat, lifting his three colleagues a good six meters into the air and sending them clattering back into the scale pan, their robes in disarray.

"Continue, Master Deddalo," he rumbled. "Three of the worthy gentlemen on this bench know little of love and its heartbreak."

Talos scurried forth and emptied another purse into Gordusmajor's lap.

"As I was saying," Deddalo resumed, his left eyelid rising to match his right. "I loved the girl with what the poets call a love surpassing all others. I rendered lard for her soaps and shampoos. Invented an oven that would pluck, clean, and baste a pigeon for her picnic suppers with her identical but strangely less attractive sister—"

"Meryl," Talos added, with a nod.

"By any name. And so it would have been, even unto our wedding day, after which I had sworn to be even less negligent than most husbands. Because I loved her so!"

Here Deddalo dabbed at a tear, and Innova remembered the onion his comrade had slipped into his handkerchief.

At some point in the telling, as Deddalo recounted old Incline Barium's spending his daughter's dowry on dwarf spirits and the "genuine sense of betrayal" that followed, Innova marvelled all the more.

For Deddalo had come to believe his own story. Tears pooled on the onyx floor, the notorious eyelid drooped once again, and the gnome squeezed his handkerchief and listed his own invented sufferings, in light of which the outright murder of the girls would have seemed justifiable or even necessary.

"But it was only a practical joke!" Deddalo emphasized, waving his arms frantically in the chamber, which was still echoing with the names of the defendants, as the bailiff finished reciting the last syllables of Talos's name and began on Innova's. "We knew that the top of the silo was . . . porous. So when we encouraged Phaistos . . . "

"Whose soul Great Reorx receive!" Innova and Talos chimed.

". . . to position himself in the bottom of the silo, fed on legumes and cucumbers and other gaseous vegetables, we only foresaw that the fumes escaping through the corroded roof would take on the more unpleasant odors of spirits and verdigris and elements more pungent. We had not taken into account, High Justice Gordusmajor, that the heating unit, whose cosmic function it was to render the climate of the distilleries more temperate and habitable, would fail as it did that fateful afternoon."

Now Deddalo was in full brilliance. The judges were silent, leaning over the tottering edges of the balance pans. They were caught up in the story, and for the first time in months Innova was sailing past worry.

All of the defendants, himself included, just might be home free.

In almost bardic tones, while the bailiff recited the middle of Innova's lengthy family name, Deddalo recounted the story's tragic end in a voice he should have reserved for chronicles and legends. How the girls must have become chilly in the vaulted room heated only by the small fires from the retorts at the base of the silos. How they probably wrapped themselves in heavy jackets, in quilts and linen comforters, and how it was no doubt still cold for them.

So cold that one of them—probably Meryl, considering she was the older by minutes—lit a fire atop the ramshackle silo. And then the fumes and gases . . .

"It was like a holiday!" Deddalo exclaimed. For a moment, his love of explosives transported him, and he described the blast in rich and fiery detail. Then, remembering where he was and the case he was pleading, he dropped one last onion-soaked tear.

Meanwhile, Talos shoveled yet another purse full of coins into the brimming scale pan of High Justice Gordusmajor.

"Horrible. By the gods, it was horrible!" Deddalo concluded magnificently.

Innova recognized Scymnidus's phrasing in the speech, the clever and disruptive tactics of Mount Nevermind's most brilliant drunken lawyer but the delivery was all Deddalo's. His was the voice and the drama that could make high theater of a recited alphabet and holy text of an instruction manual.

With a sidelong glance toward Gordusmajor, who had plucked one of the coins from the growing pile and was biting it to test its authenticity, Deddalo murmured the last words of his summation.

"I only wish that *our* little part, *circumstantial though it might have been*, had not contributed *in its completely accidental way* to the untimely departure of our good friend Phaistos—"

"Whose soul Great Reorx receive!" Talos recited on cue.

"—and to the tragic but equally accidental death by infrastructure of my one true love, Meryl Barium!"

"Beryl," Talos corrected, as the chamber burst into applause.

When he recalled that day in the dark times that were to come, Innova always returned to a single, quiet thought.

How Deddalo was a capable friend.
Who would make a dangerous enemy.

* * * * *

As the verdict was handed down in the Philosophers'
Tribunal, there were a few surprises.

Talos and Deddalo escaped rather easily. The one dissenting vote was cast by Justice Ballista who, it turned out,
was a distant cousin to old Incline Barium, the twins' father.
But Justice Gordusmajor dismissed this call for stern punishment on two accounts.

"One," the High Justice proclaimed, his stubby fingers
glittering with coins, "is undue influence. Distant though it
may be, the Justice Ballista's ties to the Barium family might
have swayed him from fair judgment.

"Two, perhaps more importantly, his judgment is pretty
near inaudible."

With the applause of the other judges and the loud droning of the bailiff as he recited the last of Innova's name,
added to the simple fact that Ballista's bench had been lifted
to the top of the chamber by the weight of the coins at Gordusmajor's feet, whatever he had to say was indeed quite
faint, virtually lost in the stone vault of the chamber.

Sentenced lightly to "clean up the mess"—a task that
would take no more than two months at the most—Talos
and Deddalo congratulated each other with handshakes,
pats on the back, embraces.

But the old High Justice was not finished.

"There remains," he pronounced, "the judgment in the
case of Innovafertanimusmutatasdicereformas—"

He would have gone on, reciting Innova's family name
to the end of his memory, but a cry from the rafters silenced
him. Justice Ballista, leaning far over the balance pan in
order to be better heard, fell to the floor of the chamber and
passed out, sending Gordusmajor's bench crashing down
and pinning Harpos and Julius against the ceiling.

"The case of Innova," Gordusmajor muttered, gathering
his dignity and coins. " 'Tis a special circumstance. Conduct
most ungnomelike. For it is alleged that *Innova saw it coming.*"

Innova took in a sharp breath. He was afraid he could see this coming as well. Wasn't there something in law about premeditation? Accident in the first degree?

A dire image passed through his thoughts: enforced labor in the depths of the mines below Mount Nevermind, his only company a band of gully dwarves who thought that premeditation was something you did before you took a pill.

He wished he could find the words to salvage himself.

"Some philosophers say," Gordusmajor continued, sprawled on the scale pan like an enormous, self-righteous spider, "that the process does not matter. That it is something called the *end result* that counts. They cite *history* to support them, and questions of good and evil.

"Are *you* one of *those* philosophers, Innova?"

"I . . . I . . ."

"Well, *I* am not!" Gordusmajor thundered, bouncing on the scales in anger. Harpos and Julius, wedged against the stone ceiling, squeaked in misery.

"Nor am I," Innova replied weakly. Nobody believed him.

"Cause and effect," the High Justice proclaimed, "is a disease. It corrodes the mind like a distillery silo, this worrying about end results and what will happen next. The only cure for it, I fear, is to work it out of your system."

"I expect that this whole sorry incident has banished such diseases from my mind, sir," Innova offered desperately. "I expect that the explosions and my deep regrets are . . . punishment enough?"

Gordusmajor laughed. "Oh, you don't get off *that* easily, boy! Nothing is punishment enough unless *I* decide so. Your sentence is six months of speculative labor. Tuning the gnomeflingers on Levels Five through Seventeen. Cause is your catapult. Effect is where it throws you. And since I believe that you're still a little sick with results, we might as well use your philosophical illness to our advantage, for the sake of all wayward travelers and the community itself.

"But still, none of you are a bad sort. Just unoccupied." The High Justice's eyes narrowed.

"So it is time to occupy you. After the conclusion of these sentences, I want the three of you to meet with me in my judicial chambers. There is the matter of a guild seat to set before inventive lads such as you."

He fingered the coins again.

"For the sake of our daughters," Gordusmajor continued, "for the sake of our infrastructure and our supply of dwarf spirits, the hands of our sons must not remain idle."

Chapter 3

Innova's sentence was stern, but not unreasonable. After all, it was giving him something to do.

Or so he thought as he tightened the springs on a rusty gnomeflinger, somewhere in the recessed chambers of the Twelfth Level. The gas lantern at his belt emitted an eerie blue light in which the shadows of the squat machine seemed stretched, almost monstrous.

For a month now, Innova had labored beneath the part of the city he called home. Squeezing through narrow passages, slipping on perilous inclines of shingle and shale, he had repaired somewhere around a dozen gnomeflingers—the catapults that served as a principal means of transportation here in the depths of the city, where neither handcart nor steam trolley had brought civilization or progress.

Most of these devices were at their expected places amid the vast underground complex: at the brink of the excavated central core of the mountain, the receiving nets intact above them to catch the hurtling gnomes in upward flight. Others were less easily explained—dragged to the center of chambers, positioned by stairwells or aqueducts in what pattern of design or accident or foolishness the gods only knew.

For a while, Innova had tried to strategize these oddly placed gnomeflingers, to determine where they truly belonged. But the complexity of the whole aerial transportation system baffled him finally, so he settled on repairing the machines where they stood, regardless of unreasonable sites.

On occasion, he had been forced to tightrope walk along the surface of the old wooden aqueducts, designed to irrigate experimental crops in the middle levels and to bring subterranean water to the ornamental fountains in the upper city. You had to boil this water to even think of drinking it, so thick it was with questionable salts and minerals.

But after the first week, it was what he had to drink. And it ruffled his bowels considerably.

He was glad *that* was in private. He would hate to be remembered for indigestion.

And the food did not help at all. Travel rations—dried fruit and dried fish.

It was a gully dwarf sentence Innova had been handed, and this was gully dwarf work—dangerous and thankless and, above all, unpaid.

But his apparently diseased turn of mind that delighted in cause and effect was satisfied by the work at hand.

After a hard day's work, it was great joy to sit quietly in the cupped basket of one of these ancient machines, to trip the lever at the base of the fulcrum—the lever that set the whole thing in motion, to rocket through dark space toward another destination, another contraption abandoned or disused.

Peaceful and gainfully employed, Innova would land, usually without injury, a hundred yards or so from the site of his launching. Then he would find the next gnomeflinger in the network and begin again, replacing spring or piston, cog or basket or dry-rotted leather thong, as Mount Nevermind's oldest transportation system slowly resumed its usefulness.

All of this without noise and chatter.

It was pleasant enough in a daily way. And yet he was glad that the sentence was only six months.

After all, this was no Life Quest for a philosopher.

* * * * *

The Life Quest was one of the oldest of gnome traditions through which the young of Mount Nevermind passed into adulthood and received a purpose for the rest of their days. Usually in late adolescence, each gnome appeared before the council of his or her guild to be assigned a mission, a project, a lifelong study. The Mathematicians' Guild, for example, might assign you to prove geometrically that a duck is different from a dragon or that two plus two makes either five or six, depending upon the

19

amount of resentment the calculator has against prime numbers. The Engineers might assign more practical projects, such as how to distill sunlight from cucumbers or silver from the lining of clouds. The Antiquarians looked for lost evidence, for archaeological sites that would prove all history was wrong except what they expected in the first place, and the Librarians . . .

Well, nobody knew or cared what the Librarians did, as long as it did not involve too much reading.

Innova, Talos, and Deddalo had always congratulated themselves that their families belonged by heredity to the Philosophers' Guild. It meant, of course, that their Life Quest would not involve heavy lifting. But membership in this particular guild was frustrating as well: the most complicated, even by gnome standards.

In the old times, a philosopher's Life Quest was simple: Young prospective guildmembers were assigned a definition of terms, a syllogism or a train of thought, and asked to present their conclusions in a way that nobody could understand. In recent years, though, this time-honored practice had fallen into ruin because the Guild Council had discovered a way to limit the number of new members and thereby assure their own continued power and influence.

They pretended to understand everything.

For example, say the test question was to complete the following statement: *A gnome lost in Mount Nevermind is like . . .*

The petitioner would contemplate the answer for months, years maybe. He might return to the examining board with an answer something like this:

A gnome lost in Mount Nevermind is like water flowing downhill.

One of the examiners would say, "I understand. A gnome lost in Mount Nevermind is like water flowing downhill, because both seek their proper level." The other examiners would applaud, and fail the petitioner, who perhaps all along had another answer:

A gnome lost in Mount Nevermind is like water flowing downhill, because both are in a situation of gravity.

The petitioner's answer, as good as the examiner's, would be lost in applause and the time-honored rule of etiquette that you could not, under any circumstance, disagree with the examining board.

The petitioner would return, then, burdened with another question, until the board decided, after a long period of hazing and torment, to admit or not admit the poor wretch to their number.

If admitted at last, the petitioner could console himself with one simple fact.

Later on, he could inflict the same frustration on others.

Needless to say, this situation could not last forever. The would-be philosophers had mustered a hundred challenges in the courts of Mount Nevermind, and countless coins and promises changed hands. But these lawsuits assured no future for prospective guild members. Fewer and fewer of the sons and daughters qualified, and those who did so had to wait later and later in life.

Innova and Talos and Deddalo had waited even longer. At an age when their fathers had been well embarked on Life Quests and courses of study, Innova and his companions were still without direction, spinning their cogs in childhood games they should have outgrown decades before.

It was prolonged youth and mild immaturity, but Innova and his friends were not the only offenders. It was happening with others throughout the city.

Mount Nevermind was raising a generation unable to grow up.

Or so the older gnomes maintained, blaming it all on *the chaos of the age*.

In ways beyond their knowing, the older gnomes were right. For across the straits that separated their island of Sancrist from the larger isles of Ergoth, and Ergoth from the continental mainland, *Chaos was* spreading over Krynn. There were rumors of new and powerful forces afoot— forces older than the gods themselves, allied with minions the like of which had not been seen since the Age of Dreams. Some said it had something to do with the Graygem of

Gargath, a legendary artifact of power, which had passed over Mount Nevermind itself, afloat toward its mysterious destination, a thousand years ago. Those who said this lived with the dread that whatever the stone had unleashed in this new age might well take its revenge on the coasts where it was last seen.

Most of the gnomes in Mount Nevermind, troubled by the laziness and ignorance of their sons and daughters, thought little of this. They thought even less of a danger far more real and immediate—the muster of armies in the western lands of the continent armies of knights devoted to the Dark Queen Takhisis, many of whom had fought in the War of the Lance. These veterans were more regimented than they were of old, more honorable in their service of the dark goddess.

They were said to be no friends to the gnomes.

And on the coast of Ansalon, a legion of them, led by a young commander named Halion Khargos, was preparing to set sail. They had cast speculative eyes toward the islands of the west, toward Ergoth and Sancrist beyond.

Toward Mount Nevermind itself.

But for now, the city sentinels, perched on stilts in the basin of Mount Nevermind's extinct volcano, saw no smoke of battle to the east, no sails on the straits between Ergoth and Sancrist.

If you could not see it, it was not there. Typical gnome philosophy. So the city accounted itself safe, far from even the rumors of war.

And Innova, a thousand feet under the Great Hall and removed from the city's news and worries, thought even less of global matters. Instead, he was fascinated by yet another gnomeflinger—one that, unlike some of the others, seemed in reasonable repair.

It happens now and then, he told himself, lowering his lantern to look at the wheels and body of the contraption. Deep scratches on the stone floor told him that the gnomeflinger had been moved some time in the past.

There were smaller scratches as well, on the underside of the catapult arm. In the dim lantern light, they looked like old runes or characters, strangely familiar and yet nearly illegible:

ᛉᛗ ᚱᛘᛚᛉᚨ ᚺᛉ0ᚦ

After a brief inspection, Innova thought little of them. Still, the parting advice of his cousin Scymnidus haunted him a little, as he turned his sights toward the business end of the flinger.

What was it Scymnidus had said?

Farewell. Serve your six months quietly, so they won't snatch you back on technicalities.

Believe nothing you see . . .

And everything you read.

He forgot such sound advice in his examination of the catapult before him. Fling basket inside out. Tensile cord, spanking new but absentmindedly reversed, or so it seemed, at the base of the gnomeflinger.

A simple problem. This one was neither worn nor broken, simply disarranged when it was installed.

Gully dwarf work, Innova thought. Can't live with it, can't pay a gnome to do it.

Quickly he slipped the cords into the proper notches, bent back the arm of the gnomeflinger, and locked it into place. Now the thing was aimed into a huge field of darkness at the top of the chamber, where no doubt a passageway or loft or adit would lead him to the next machine in the system. Climbing into the fling basket, he adjusted his iron helmet—protection against low hanging rocks or stalactites. He lifted his lantern in a last, tentative check, but the light bled away into the darkness above.

"Occupational hazard," Innova muttered. "'Believe nothing you see.'"

He set the lantern in the basket beside him, then pulled the release. In that moment, as he heard the arm of the catapult wrench free of its socket, in that moment before he vaulted into space, he glanced a last time at the mysterious runes.

23

Which looked more familiar from this angle.

POY↑ V↑↑R WY

" 'Poyt uttr wy'?" Innova asked himself as the arm of the gnomeflinger launched him into darkness.

And the translation hit him as the stale air rushed by, as Innova hurtled past startled bats. It hit him just before *he* hit the solid wall of igneous rock.

"'Point other way'!" he shouted, before the impact robbed him of his senses.

* * * * *

Stars pulsed above him.

Innova lay on his back, scanning an unfamiliar heaven for familiar constellations, trying to locate his whereabouts by reference to a sketchy astronomy.

Not even a moon in sight . . .

"Nor a star to steer by," Innova whispered to himself. "At least none I recognize. Should have listened in school."

It was a full hour before he realized that the stars were not in the heavens but in his head—a sign of obvious concussion. No doubt he had struck a wall in his flight, slipped down the rock face and fallen through a crevasse, landing the gods knew how many feet below. The wineskin he carried had spurted its contents around him, staining his leggings with what he thought at first was blood. He had dropped, fortunately, upon his rump, for the pulped apricots in his back pocket had cushioned the fall.

Will of the gods, he told himself gratefully, then laughed at the silliness.

Wasn't it Cousin Scymnidus who was supposed to have said that *the will of the gods is two inches up my nose*?

His slowly returning senses told him he would never find his way back. And gradually the stars faded, into the stone of branching corridors lit dimly by the glow of his guttering lantern.

Exhausted and still a little dazed, Innova sat down in an outcropping of faceted stones, tunnels spiraling off in all directions like the spokes of an incomprehensible wheel. The apricots squashed wetly over the seat of his trousers.

"It's the end," Innova muttered. "By Reorx, nothing could make this worse." Then his lantern sputtered and went out.

For a moment Innova sat in the darkness, laughing bitterly as the last mirage of stars winked out at his feet and a sea of black enveloped him.

Unguided and unarmed, he felt the entire weight of Mount Nevermind upon him. Oddly the words of the corrupt old High Justice Gordusmajor seemed to fall on him as well.

Some philosophers say that the process does not matter. That it is the end result that counts.

"The old fart didn't agree with them," Innova whispered into the blinding darkness. "And now I see what he meant, though probably not in the way he meant it."

For if the end alone was all that mattered, then all the possible ends that awaited him, here in these baffling caverns, would make all of his life that had gone before seem like . . .

Seem like what?

Well, like a bad story. Like a prelude to falling down a rathole. To eating mashed apricots, then trousers, then perhaps his own fingers until he weakened and died of starvation. To taking his place at the bottom of some mutated food chain, prey to whatever creatures the gods and toxic waste had created in these deep, unmapped recesses.

Far better to believe the corrupt old Justice. The truth lay in the process.

Innova laughed again. "I'm becoming a philosopher myself!" he proclaimed to the stones and the surrounding nothingness, to the monsters who inhabited the depths of the caverns and the depths of his imagination.

None of which seemed to care.

* * * * *

Innova decided that neither truth nor process was all that fun. Choosing one corridor at random, he followed it in the absolute dark, his left hand grazing the tunnel wall, his right hand clutching a steam-powered wrench that would serve as a decent weapon in close quarters.

The tool served a double purpose, providing a reassuring hissing sound that relieved his dreadful loneliness.

Once his hand brushed against moist stone. Hoping for water, he brought his fingers to his mouth, but the liquid, whatever it was, tasted vile—viscous and metallic.

The farther Innova went, the more hopeless it seemed. He tried singing to keep himself company. At first the echoes startled him, but then he began to enjoy them as companions, singing rounds and harmonies with his own returning voice. On occasion, the echo seemed distorted and estranged, as though someone else, deep in the caverns, had joined in the song.

"But it's no other voice," Innova told himself. "I'm here all alone. Or at least I hope I am."

For the prospect of what kind of people or things kept company with these depths and darknesses was a thought he would not consider.

So Innova continued, singing and groping and stumbling, bound for who knew where. Finally a faint amber light eddied ahead of him at the mouth of yet another branching tunnel.

"I refuse to hallucinate," he told himself, but his instincts got the better of him, and before he could reason himself past the opening, Innova was stepping toward that light.

What was hallucination, after all, but a fresh way of looking at things?

* * * * *

Innova's digression brought him into a little chamber, dimly lit by a lantern afloat in the midst of a glittering amber pool. The light was golden itself, and surprisingly steady considering the thin damp air. On the far side of the pool, an archway opened into further blackness.

Innova stood at the threshold, took a deep breath, and entered.

Whatever the liquid was at his feet, it had either spilled from the burning lamp, or the lamp had been set in it to draw fuel and flame. It was impossible to tell: lamp and oil seemed bonded together in a circuit of perpetual light. Not for the first time, Innova longed for his old friend Talos, whose chemical talents would have explained this business, even if the explanation made less sense than the truth.

Innova did not want to think that it was magic. He had a gnome's natural instinct for science and gadgetry. Magic would mean that something was amiss, beyond his understanding and control. And there was enough of *that* already, here in this maze of darkness.

Kneeling at the edge of the pool, he stirred its amber surface with his finger and brought the finger to his lips.

Viscous and bitter and undrinkable. Like the sweat on the corridor walls behind him.

He would never forget that taste. And these tunnels were filled with whatever it was.

With more curiosity than wisdom, Innova plunged his hand into the pool. Shallow. Scarcely deep enough to cover his wrist. Heartened, he began to wade toward the lamp and a closer look, but found himself gliding as though he were on skates, his feet skimming through the amber liquid like the prows of little ships.

Amusement changed to alarm as Innova slid by the lamp, out the other side of the pool, then kept on sliding, gathering speed, out the far entrance to the chamber.

The light faded behind him. He glanced off the corridor wall and kept sliding, the corridor sloping downward and his speed increasing. Desperately Innova reached out for the wall, but his hand, still wet with the unnatural oil, slipped away from the rocks, clutched at nothing. He was racing into the heart of the mountain—no brakes, no friction for brakes, and no protective padding.

This is the end, he thought. This is more sorry than I could have imagined.

27

The stagnant air of the corridor whipped by him now, and a deafening rumble shocked his ears as he suddenly passed the speed of sound. Friction tore at his clothes—the air itself was disrobing him.

He left the roaring behind. He plummeted into the silence, not slowing down at all.

Desperately, his jacket flapping behind him like a banner in a high wind, Innova passed from thought into panic with blind, gibbering instinct. He tried to lean back against his own acceleration.

A light behind him told him his clothes were on fire.

With a loud scream that vanished at the moment it left his lips, Innova toppled backwards and skidded, boots in the air, in a flurry of spark and smoke and ash. His unoiled backside caught rocks and dragged, braking the swift slide of his body.

Slowing now, Innova saw a green light ahead of him, a glowing at the end of the tunnel.

Still approaching at lethal velocity.

His thoughts returned, and for a moment he thought he saw his ancestors beckoning to him, fifty generations of gnomes chanting *Come into the light, Innova. Come into the light.*

"I will not hallucinate," he whispered again, but sheer momentum carried him toward that light, trailing sparks. He skidded into an enormous, empty hall, raced past an array of torches he glimpsed as a green blur. Then he crashed, still at numbing speed, into the far wall.

Where he lay, in tatters and cinders, for a long time.

Chapter 4

Miles above the repeatedly dazed Innova, miles across the narrow straits that separated Sancrist from Ergoth, a council was convened aboard a calmed ship.

Anchored off the southern coast of Enstar and Nostar, their dark sails taken in against yet another approaching storm, six ships awaited the rising winds and the will of their commander. *Cormorant* and *Shrike*. *Kestrel* and *Condor* and *Petrel*.

Aboard the flagship, *Peregrine*, bristling with guards and warding spells—the Knights of Takhisis pondered the next prize for their invading armies.

It was an unusual group assembled on these ships—an army composed almost entirely of Knights of the Lily, with only a scattering of Thorn Knights and a solitary Knight of the Skull thrown in so that all the orders would be represented.

The Commander had chosen his troops in accordance with divine Vision. And no voice had been raised against Commander Halion Khargos.

No voice, that is, until this hour.

"I know Lord Ariakan has set you at the helm of this venture, Commander Khargos," Subcommander Stormont conceded, pounding the table for emphasis, rattling flagons and bowls and candlesticks in his urgency," but by the gods, there is such a thing as overextending your forces, leaving supply lines and reserve troops vulnerable to whatever desperate resistance a conquered people might devise."

The younger man's steel-gray eyes betrayed no emotion. As the other Knights leaned forward to hear his response, young Halion Khargos seemed almost supernaturally at ease, slowly swirling the wine in his cup, staring into the red eddy as though he were reading auguries in the drink.

"It has happened before," Stormont cautioned. "I remember back in the War of the Lance, when—"

"Textbook strategies," Khargos interrupted. "With textbook examples from a war you helped lose, if I recall."

Stormont's face was scarlet now. Only the restraining hand of Subcommander Hanna kept the old Knight from rising and challenging this precocious upstart. For Halion Khargos's sword was as sharp as his tongue, and in the ranks of the Dread Queen's Knights, there were few who would choose to challenge him.

"But it's *history*, sir!" Subcommander Hanna protested plaintively, brushing a strand of gray hair from her eyes. "And it is said that 'those who heed not the lessons of history—' "

" 'Are doomed to a thousand lectures.'" Khargos's laugh was dry, intelligent. "Let my Subcommanders trade war stories. I shall set my thoughts to the future."

"Do not neglect the present, Commander Khargos," advised Subcommander Fleetwood, the cagiest of Khargos's subordinates. "While you set your sights toward the future, there is unrest among the brutes and uneasiness among the warriors."

Halion Khargos sighed. Always the brutes—the barbarian shock troops of the Dark Knights. More than half savage, they were brave in battle but a bother during the waiting times.

" 'Tis a consequence we learn to deal with," Khargos maintained. "We're on ship for months, and chaos is the mother of oceans."

"I am afraid that your theology is mistaken, Commander," the cleric Oliver, the solitary Skull Knight, observed slyly. "Zeboim is the mother of oceans. Lord Ariakan would frown at your . . . oversight."

"Figures of speech are not theology, Oliver," Khargos replied. "I was merely metaphorical, offering no dogma. Your confusion on this matter may become more than spiritually dangerous."

Subcommander Fleetwood glanced apprehensively at his fellow officers. Halion Khargos was a mystic of some note, famous for revelations carried from the Goddess herself.

Though the Vision was available to each and every Knight, Halion Khargos's dark communion was noted for its intensity and depth and frequency.

Some said it had made him half mad, others that it had made him prophetic. All agreed that in some incomprehensible way the Goddess had anointed him and that Halion Khargos, scarcely eighteen years old, was already one of the most dangerous Knights in her legions.

The cleric and the subcommanders fell silent. Wisdom was, after all, a fruit of their age and training.

And it was wise not to cross the Commander.

* * * * *

The rise of Halion Khargos was unusual only in its swiftness.

Of obscure origins somewhere in the western islands, a country that had for the most part escaped the worst ravages of the War of the Lance, he was said to be the son of a minor noblewoman, landless and poor, his father uncertain.

Other stories were less flattering: He was the son of a stone mason, or the youngest child of a hardworking family of peasants whom he had neglected and then forgotten in his breathless rise to power. In the old days of the dragon-armies there would have been other rumors, for the older Knights could scarcely have imagined such ascent without friends in the highest places, or blackmail or bribery.

No matter the talents of Halion Khargos—and there were many—he carried an excess of mystery. Those above him and those below him were uncomfortable in his presence, and only the most uninformed petitioners and supplicants trusted him entirely.

He had received the Call at thirteen, under circumstances unknown. Nobody knew his advocate—the Knight who had sponsored him through his training and tests—and it seemed to many that someone *would* have come forward to claim a prize student, to announce that *this prodigy is mine, this wonder I have sponsored.* But the Lords and the great commanders had been silent, and this silence had given rise to wilder speculation.

31

That Khargos's advocate was Lord Ariakan himself. That the great man was preparing the lad for a position high in the Order, perhaps as his eventual successor.

But influence and favor, no matter how powerful, stop at the Test of Takhisis, where it is written that the Goddess decides the worth of each Novice. It was said of Halion Khargos that whatever ordeal he had undertaken in the sight of the Dark Queen, he had passed through it without visible torment.

The older Knights took stock of their own experience, remembered the gaunt return from wastelands or tunnels or the unmanning country of their own nightmares. None of them had escaped unscarred, unscathed.

This one, this Halion Khargos, had passed through the test at fifteen, emerging as serene and boyish as he was when chosen for the Order. Something about him had sobered, yes; he had put away games and most outward signs of childishness. He kept to himself more than others.

And unlike any other Knight they knew, he *continued* to commune in the dark threads of the Vision the Dread Queen grants her servants.

He was Groupcommander in the Order of the Lily by the green age of seventeen. Now men older and more experienced than himself were expected to march at his order and die at his command.

* * * * *

This was the boy before whom they spread the western maps as a hard rain began to wash the decks of *Peregrine*, as the lesser Knights sought shelter in the crowded, humid barracks and the sentinels in the crow's nest wrapped their cloaks more tightly against the rising wind.

"We'll sail west, then," the Commander decreed softly, his eyes fixed on nothing but the faint light of the solitary lantern. "That much is in my bones and instincts. But the particular destination is cloudy at the moment. I shall consult Herself. She reveals all things. If all goes well, by morning we shall have an answer. Go to your quarters now. Go to your ships."

To these soft words and to their certainty, even the veterans deferred without question. Whatever the mysteries surrounding Commander Khargos, his path to the Vision was short and direct.

What Takhisis taught him was uncanny. Aided by the Vision, he knew at once the weakness in a line of enemy troops, the flaws in the most formidable fortifications. In the past month two fortresses had fallen to him, each on a single day, the casualties among his troops so few as to be negligible.

Indeed, there were a few among the Gray Knights who harbored the blasphemous thought that Takhisis had met her match in this boy, that their dark communion was almost a meeting of equals.

Most of the Knights would have scoffed at such a thought. But there was a surety about the Commander, a shrewdness and insight that could not have come from his years—not so much wisdom as a kind of prophetic instinct.

Which was why when ordered to their quarters, two of the three subcommanders, who might have questioned the tactics of a lesser mind, bowed dutifully before the lad and took their leave, along with the Thorn Knights who had been called to this council that was really no council at all.

The Bone Acolyte Oliver, alone in his skepticism, turned at the cabin door and looked back into the dimly lit room.

In a haze above the lantern he thought he saw the face of a woman, intent and savagely beautiful.

Like a lovely poison, Oliver thought. Like the breath of the Death Lily.

She had spoken to him once, as she had to all the Knights. During the long ordeal of the Test. On occasion—occasions such as this—Oliver thought he glimpsed her, but his senses were confused by memory and desire.

And knowing he stood on the threshold of something intimate, vaguely embarrassed like a clumsy intruder, he closed the door behind him and stepped out into the night and rain.

*   *   *   *   *

Khargos had learned to love the presence of the Goddess. He had come to her readily and eagerly, even before the Call. Before the arrival of his Advocate . . .

. . . he had waited for Takhisis, in bleak abandoned places far from the eyes of his puzzled guardians. On black coasts he had found her seated on rocks that spelled the death of sailors. In storm clouds her face had appeared to him.

Once also in a dungeon, and once atop a ruined tower.

Most often she came to him in a trance or a dream. Sometimes he thought he could remember the first time, a soothing narcotic voice from the shadowed corner of a nursery he could not quite recall.

She had always been with him, he supposed.

So his Call to the Order had been no surprise, but part of a thing so daily and accustomed that it was like food or sleeping. Like a drug, perhaps, because he longed for it past yearning, drew nourishment from her face and her voice.

Like a drug, but without the wasting away, he told himself, as now, once again, he met her, in the dark fire at the heart of the lantern glow, a darkness that expanded with the light until the walls of the storm-tossed cabin were twilit gray, and he breathed in a fragrance and a freedom he could not find in his waking life.

By all the assembled gods, and the chaos that fathered them all, he loved Her, and her night-struck seductions opened his waiting veins.

How is my love, my dear, my darling? asked the gray light at the heart of the fire.

Khargos sat silent, knowing from long communion that he was not supposed to answer, that something in the depth of that gray light cared not how he fared. Strangely, it was that indifference that he loved most of all.

He would wait. She would tell him how he was. Soon he would know what to answer.

Then he would know what to ask.

Stormont is a fool, the Queen observed. *But you know that.*

He sank into abiding stillness, and the walls of the cabin vanished. A cold rain bathed him, doused the light of the lantern.

He was inside the Goddess. He was home.

"Overextension of troop and supply line"? she asked mockingly. *"Strategic blunder"?*

You answered him well, my darling. And that night-grown mushroom Oliver, with his prattle of theology, you answered them both well, though perhaps too kindly, as is your sweet nature.

Let them stand in the storm. Make prayers to Our tortoise-shelled Sister for safe voyage and full sail. It is a courtesy I permit.

He felt a rush of blood course up the back of his neck. The hairs on his nape stood rigid and hot. Halion Khargos gasped, and his eyesight blurred.

Now She stood before him, Her dark and diaphanous robes open and inviting.

I have a plan for Stormont, she soothed. *He will not question you for long. Pay him no further attention. This is no time for diversion.*

For we are bound, you and I, toward a place where my darkness has failed before.

Will not fail again.

For I have found my one true Acolyte.

Invisible lips touched his own, traced a dry circle on his throat. The commander shivered in ecstasy, closed his eyes . . .

A sea stretched before him, black and calm and glossy as polished stone. Reeling, he bit his lip, tasted blood.

Now, at the edge of his visionary sight, an island came into view. A mountainous island capped by a smoldering volcano, the sky above it creased with lightning and the muted fires of sunset.

"Sancrist," Khargos murmured.

He knew the place at once. Remembered it, out of smoke and light.

And like an echo, like water coursing over his breast, pooling on his lap and thighs, a voice fragmented, only remotely feminine now, echoed his thoughts and words.

Sancrist. Sancrist it is, then.

With a shudder, Halion Khargos opened his eyes to the cabin room, to the table and lantern.

The rain hammered outside on the storm-lashed deck. His hand rested on the map still spread before him. Water dripped from his fingers onto the blurred silhouettes of the western islands. Dark ink smeared over the outline of Mount Nevermind.

Chapter 5

Innova dreamed of storms.

He was rocking in darkness, back and forth in an unbalanced balance. Somewhere at the edge of his hearing, a roaring sound—perhaps the sea, though he could not tell in his dreaming—disrupted the steady flow of his sleep.

Now the sound grew louder. He awakened in a dimly lit room, suspended by cords from an old aqueduct. Far out of reach above him, a rope ladder dangled from a hole in the chamber ceiling. His hands and feet were above him as well, trussed. Water, leaking from the rotting wood of the aqueduct channel, dripped on him like some old draconian method of torture.

It was like being caught in a web. And a web meant . . .

"Spiders!" Innova whispered. He closed his eyes, praying that this, too, was a part of the dream.

For spiders were his worst nightmare.

From earliest childhood, his imaginings were infested with the wretched things. Spiders that crawled from the masonry of his dreams, hurling thin but resilient silks from a corner to entangle him, to draw him toward their clacking, venomous jaws . . . .

Thunder and storm rolled loudly below him. He opened his eyes and looked down . . . .

Into the bed of a steam-powered handcart, a good drop of twenty feet onto the cavern floor, its rusty valves opened full throttle though the vehicle stood still.

A strange, ungainly figure labored in the cart, shrouded in sparks and billowing steam, all squat and spindle-limbed and waving energy.

Innova blinked. It was no spider.

"Where . . . " he tried to ask. "Who . . . "

"In the lowest levels!" the creature below him shouted. "And Lucretius Climenole!"

"I beg your pardon?"

Now the steam seemed to dissipate, spiraling on an updraft through a ventilating hole in the ceiling of the chamber, and the figure emerged from the cloud, revealing itself as a gnome, the oldest, most disheveled gnome Innova had ever seen.

"I knew that duct would come in handy!" the old creature shouted, triumphantly and much too loudly. "Pretty near broke my fool neck installing it, but it's worth the risk to see steam rise like that, isn't it?"

Thick with a dozen layers of tattered clothing, the old fellow was a shimmer of colors. Layers peeked through holes in other layers, shone faintly where the fabric was thin. Patches sewn upon patches glowed in the green light of phosphorous lanterns, and the sparks from the handcart smoldered on a shredded purple cape. The gnome stepped away from the flames, dusted himself off, and scraps of burning cloth floated into ash, rising with the steam through the humid air of the chamber.

"Now, as to your *wheres* and *whos*," the creature announced, "in order to answer your questions, we must first define the terms. Discussion cannot continue until terms are defined, unless you're a politician. You were asking, I assume—or let us say, you were *about* to ask— where you are and who I am. Now these are weighty questions, the abstract fuel of philosophy, but I suspect that the answers you seek are more arithmetical than geometric. So until my ventures at this confounded machine are complete . . . "

He stooped, picked up a hammer, and brought it crashing down upon one of the valves of the handcart, never stopping his lecture for breath or for leverage.

" . . . I shall tell you simply that you are on the Fourth Level of Mount Nevermind, and that I am Lucretius Climenole."

Lucretius Climenole? Innova struggled in the cords.

Lucretius Climenole. It would come to him. Meanwhile . . .

"What am I doing up here?" he rasped.

Lucretius Climenole craned his neck, squinted at Innova. "Squirming and thereby further entangling yourself. Those are slip knots, and your weight's on the wrong side of the slippage."

"That's not what I meant! I demand that you—"

But the old gnome had returned to his business. First he climbed up a rope ladder to the very top of the chamber, where he tinkered with some sort of ventilating duct.

It made Innova shudder. All this clambering and scuttling reminded him of spiders—this time a particolored spider with a long beard, smelling of a bathless decade and swearing as he dropped a wrench clattering to the stone floor.

Safely on the ground again, puffing from exertion, Lucretius set an outsized boot against the side of the cart and wrenched free one of the pipes. The chamber clouded and sparkled with hot vapor. The old gnome swore and leapt free of the cart, which burst into blue electric flame. Then, as the steam surged over exposed wire, the whole contraption sputtered and shuddered and fell silent.

"Great Reorx be praised," Lucretius exclaimed, "for the Second Law of Conjectural Dynamics!"

"Great Reorx be praised!" Innova echoed automatically. "Would it be possible to let me down from here?"

"Not in your best interest!" Lucretius shouted. " 'Tis provisional traction you're in, boy. For your broken coccyx, a malady that demands suspension or bed rest on a doughnut-shaped pillow, a therapeutic device not easily located in the magma fields."

"In *what*? *Coccyx*?"

"Your tailbone, blockhead! The seat of your wisdom, point of contact with bench or stool! The fundamental thing! The last we see of you! Need I be more plain and say, in the vernacular, that your arse is broken?"

* * * * *

"A *month*? A *month* before I'm down from here?"

Innova could not believe his ears. For an hour old Lucretius had rattled on, ignoring the questions of his entangled patient, struggling with the handcart, hammering new valves and appendages on the vehicle until it looked like a pipe organ on wheels.

Lucretius was ranting about the Laws of Speculative Dynamics, in a language both metaphysical and ancient. It sounded like some kind of pre-Cataclysmic dialect, the way, Innova supposed, that his great- and great-great grandsires had spoken before this old coot had bottomed out here at the base of the mountain. Lucretius recited these laws almost religiously, marveling that his captive audience knew none of them.

"First Law, first corollary: 'Matter and energy are indestructible.' Second corollary: 'but if you don't have the energy, it hardly matters.'

"Second Law, first corollary: 'All machines run down eventually.' Second corollary: 'unless they don't.'"

Lucretius paused, regarded his captive warily.

"Are you *sure* they never taught you these laws upstairs? What are you learning? Psychology? Animal impersonations?"

Innova shook his head stupidly.

"And then there's the Third Law," Lucretius continued. "First corollary: 'Less is more.' Second corollary: 'except when applied to liquor and sleep and how far you fall.'"

Innova tried to interrupt, to change the subject back to his own suspension, but the old gnome was off again, ranging over other subjects, from things scarcely imaginable to things best left unimagined.

How, at Innova's great height in the room, twenty feet above the proceedings, whatever he said must be consciously ignored because the words gathered weight as they fell.

How the number six recurs in all natural forms, from the number of leaves on two shamrocks to the number of seasons in a year and a half, from the exact number of toes on the left foot of Great Uncle Prodigious Climenole to precisely three quarters of the legs of a spider.

At the mention of spiders, Innova looked about anxiously, but old Lucretius was off on another subject.

How, if the Song of Huma was translated into Gnomish and every sixth character in every sixth line taken into account, you could come up with an anagram for the gully dwarf phrase, "Huma is a cheese."

All of these theories floated up to the suspended Innova, along with a deluge of irritating, rhymed proverbs that the old fool had apparently composed himself. None of it made sense to Innova, but after all, the bindings on his hands had loosened considerably and he was dangling ankles up. The blood was rushing to his head, creating all kinds of philosophical confusion.

Lucretius Climenole. It finally came to him.

The Climenoles were the most vanished of the vanished clerical families.

*   *   *   *   *

The long history of Mount Nevermind had followed its own version of the Second Law of Speculative Dynamics. Guilds ran down as often as machines, and families who had devoted their lives to a single pursuit were forced to find other things to do. And the Clerical Guild was a prominent example: it had lost its energy, and no longer mattered in the intricate gnomish society.

At the time of the Cataclysm, when clerical spellcraft disappeared from the face of Krynn, so did the clerical families of Mount Nevermind. Five of them—from the theologically minded Laputans to the Sardonicans, whose specialty was healing—dissolved in the usual gnomish ways: They married into other families and joined other guilds. Nowadays you might find contemplative Lagados among the Mathematicians, prophetic Malonados among the Mechanical Engineers or the Meteorologists. All of these families were pretty much indistinguishable from those with more secular backgrounds, except for a tendency to fall asleep over a project and suffer disturbing dreams.

It had been the duty of the Climenoles to "ground" the other clergy—to ask the Laputans simple questions and monitor the spells of the Sardonicans. They grounded the Malonados literally when that most honorable family stood in the midst of thunderstorms in order to prophesy. The idea of this grounding was simple: to make those who were in the clergy understandable to those who were not.

41

When the Cataclysm shook the foundations of Mount Nevermind, some said that it jostled the meditation clean out of the Clerical Guild. The Climenoles were left with nothing to do. Within a year, they had packed their belongings and departed—some to the continent, some westward in yet another hare-brained search for the Graygem.

Some, it was clear now, had simply gone downstairs, into the bowels of Mount Nevermind.

But all this history was of little importance to Innova. He was tethered to an aqueduct in the here and now, swinging back and forth like a pendulum above a slate floor, a sputtering handcart, and the last heir of the great gnomish clerical lines.

Chapter 6

If he had been thinking clearly while he dangled from the aqueduct, Innova might well be hanging there still. But the blood that had rushed to his head had somehow met with the rising steam from the handcart, and his brains were not only addled but temporarily poached in the process.

That was how he explained it later—to himself, to his friends, to anyone who might listen. Which is not to say that the explanation was right.

At any rate, it must have been something Innova said that unleashed him. He remembered babbling about steam and explosions, about the silo and the Barium girls and the eminent Gordusmajor.

Something about cream and potatoes as well, which didn't fit with the rest of his gibberish.

Meanwhile, Lucretius Climenole spouted on. So did the steam pipes on the handcart he had at last repaired. The whole chamber echoed with pronouncements and whistles, with rushes of steam as they swept through the vent far above.

In the middle of this confusion, Innova must have passed out. The clamor receded around him, and he forgot what he was saying, trying vainly to recapture the words and thoughts.

The next thing he remembered was sitting in the steam-powered handcart, riding along slowly to the discordant music of valves and exhaust pipes. Lucretius stood over him, once again busy amidst levers and copper tubing.

Painfully, Innova pulled himself to his feet. Lucretius was right: Something around his backside was broken, and it hurt less to stand than sit.

The cart struggled up a steep gradient, the rapid, irregular pounding of its pistons mixing with the whistle of the pipes to make a sound halfway between a wheeze and a death rattle.

"Where are we going?" Innova shouted.

43

But he received no answer. Instead, the old gnome guided the handcart through the slick strata of rock, deep into the heart of Mount Nevermind.

Innova could tell by the rising heat and the faint smell of the garbage dumps that they had reached the lowermost point of the known city, beyond which most reliable gnome maps trailed off into white space with a single scrawled warning:

Here be magma.

*   *   *   *   *

It was in these depths of Mount Nevermind that Innova's brief instruction began.

Old Lucretius, it seemed, had persuaded himself that his own Life Quest was a constant effort to keep the mountain from collapsing. Centuries of rain had trickled down through the fissures of the dormant volcano, through the porous pumice in its lower regions, and there were spaces in this underworld where water that had poured from the skies centuries ago now pooled and bubbled on hot stone, scarcely ten feet above red-hot deposits of magma.

It was like walking on the second floor of a house while a fire raged downstairs.

Equipped with thick-soled boots, the pair of gnomes passed the time hauling stone from the middle levels, stacking it on the flawed and steaming floor, creating a barrier between the rising eddies of magma and the endangered chambers above. Needless to say, it was uncomfortable work: After a day's labor, they would search out the nearest aqueduct and bathe for an hour in the foul but cool waters, trading steam for stink.

What made things worse was Innova's fear that the whole damned process was useless. After all, there *would* come a time when the magma burst through the thinning stone, and whatever was stacked above it—stone or metal or even the strange fibrous cloth that Lucretius insisted be spread across particularly damaged chambers—would serve only as fuel for a rising flame.

Innova tried not to think about it much. He steered himself by the words of old Gordusmajor: *Cause and effect is a disease, and process is all that matters.* Slowly, he forgot about the terms of his sentence, and his worries about unrepaired gnomeflingers faded to the back of his thoughts.

Meanwhile, in the course of a month or so, he learned a few things from Lucretius Climenole.

It was hard for Innova to tell just exactly how long he followed the old gnome up and down abandoned shafts and along the edges of the brimming aqueducts, retrieving rubble from the middle levels and carting it lower, deeper. Lucretius, beset with the insomnia of old age, kept irregular hours, and they were so removed from the cycle of day and night that the only clock was their own guesswork.

Innova thought at first that being paired with the last of a clerical family would be an advantage. Surely in the darkest corners of the caverns, Lucretius would haul out a perpetual light spell or draw on some mysterious spiritual source so that the two of them, tunneling as blindly as moles, would be able to see where they were going.

It never happened. Lucretius, it seemed, had no more spellcraft than a cat or a duck, than the blind creatures that scuttled into fissures and crannies when Innova lifted his lantern in an uncharted room. Eventually, Innova asked about this lack of magic, and received the sorry truth.

"Not even my grandfather remembered spells," Lucretius confessed with a wistful laugh. "Sure would come in handy down here, now wouldn't they?"

So, in a score of dim chambers, unaided by anything except the strength of their own backs and Lucretius's subjective science, the two of them piled stone upon stone.

Seldom was their task interrupted. However, they *would* pause on occasion when Lucretius discovered shiny things in the darkness. He called them all "jools," and indeed, a few were. On one occasion, the old gnome plucked a sapphire—already cut and beveled by the gods knew whom—from a crevasse in the wall where some long-ago traveler had secreted it, no doubt intending to return for it later. Some of the "jools" were uncut gems, ranging in size from the width of a fingernail to the fist of a hefty human.

Most, however, were simply broken glass, scattered around the greened bronze base of a lantern or clinging sadly about the frame of a discarded mirror.

Lucretius, it seemed, was no jeweller. When Innova asked him why he collected so indiscriminately, the old philosopher replied with one of the few short answers his student would hear in their long time together underground.

"Trust me, Innova," he said. "I *know* the difference. But don't they all reflect a gorgeous light?"

Nor were the daily aspects of Innova's time under the mountain all that bad. The food was roughly the same, but the old fellow seemed possessed of an inexhaustible source of distilled water. It was a mystery where he got it, but Innova learned to live within that mystery, grateful that drink was there when he needed it and that one of his worst discomforts was gradually relieved.

Only to be replaced by another, for Lucretius would not be quiet.

When he looked back on it later, Innova admitted that a typical lecture from the old cleric lasted no longer than three or four hours, though it seemed to go on for days. Framed in sputtering lantern light, Lucretius babbled on about solid geometry and hydraulics, while Innova, who had never cared for school in the first place, retreated to dark corners. There he would drowse standing up—a trick he learned early on in his friendship with the last of the Climenoles.

It was as boring as the Academy, and just as eternal.

On rare occasions Innova was allowed to ask questions. Then, if he was lucky and Lucretius was lectured out, he stood half a chance of learning something interesting.

Soon he found out something about the strange, viscous pools he had encountered not long after his accident with the gnomeflingers.

*   *   *   *   *

"Nobody's ever made use of those pools, as far as I can tell," Lucretius told him, hoisting a stone twice his weight and staggering toward a darkened corner of the chamber they were repairing. On the way, he stooped, picked up an amethyst button, and slipped it into a bag at his belt.

Somewhere beneath them, a shift in the rocks rumbled a warning.

"But I *do* know where they came from. I can tell you that much. Have you ever heard of the Graygem of Gargath, boy?"

"Of course!" Innova snapped. Ever since Lucretius had discovered his ignorance of the Laws of Speculative Physics, he had treated Innova like an imbecile, underestimating his schooling and intelligence, explaining the simplest principles of mechanics.

Spelling "pulley" for him, for the gods' sake!

"Well, in case your history is more rusty than you suppose, the Graygem was an artifact, created by Reorx in a cloudy time—"

"I know."

"Said to house something called 'the essence of Lunitari' at the heart of its many facets."

"I *know*."

"Then you *also* know," Lucretius continued serenely, "that the early history of our race involved heroic attempts to recover and harness it."

"I *know*!" Innova insisted. "The building of the Great Invention, to be powered by the Graygem. The construction of the Self-Propelled Lunar Extension Ladder, to pluck the stone from the heart of Lunitari. The siege engines at the walls of Gargath, designed to retrieve the great artifact when the barbarians stole it—"

"All of which may or may not be true," Lucretius said. "And at any rate, you're missing parts of the story."

Innova snorted, helped the old gnome lift another rock.

"One thing I know for sure," Lucretius continued. "All this business of the Graygem has something to do with the pools on the middle levels. For in its last passage over Ansalon, it floated over Sancrist and Mount Nevermind—"

"I know I know I *know*!" Innova shouted, his voice echoing back over the soft rumble of magma and shifting rocks, until the whole chamber reverberated with *I know*s. "It passed over us, hauling Chaos in its wake, and many of its pursuers stopped here, at the westernmost edge of the continent, digging the first tunnels of our great city as the Graygem floated out of sight over the western seas."

For a moment Lucretius was at a loss for words.

"You didn't think I knew that, did you?" Innova asked triumphantly. "Thought I was some gully dwarf, still marvelling that water runs downhill!"

Lucretius paused, glancing slyly at his assistant over the fluttering light of the lantern.

"There are some things you do not know, Innova," he said mysteriously, "and water has a lot to do with those things."

* * * * *

"You see, part of the chaos that the Graygem brought upon Ansalon was something more than firestorms and mutated rabbits. More than misfired spells and the moons knocked off kilter.

"For when the Graygem set out over the western shores of the continent, a soft rain rose to meet it. 'A soft rain out of nowhere,' the chroniclers called it, but when the stone reached Sancrist, the ocean had gathered her might. The winds picked up, the rain fell harder.

"It was no longer a shower, no longer merely a deluge. It was an out-and-out tempest: rain on the horizontal, ships hauled into the air by their sails, and the cliffs along the coasts of Ergoth shearing away, crumbling . . .

"A rain against which nothing wrought by gnome or nature could last. A rain that even the work of the gods could not weather unchanged."

Innova was silent now. The last of his echoes had tumbled into uncanny quiet. The only sounds were the soft rustle of Lucretius's robes and his grunts as he shifted the boulder on his back.

"For six days, they say, the Graygem hovered over this island. Zeboim, the poets think, was trying to steer its passage back toward the land, back toward her own veiled purpose. But the will of stone overpowered the will of the sea at last, and on the seventh day the Graygem sailed westward again and the skies cleared. The pursuing gnomes began the first tunnels into the crater of Mount Nevermind.

"The will of the stone had triumphed. Or that was the legend among my priestly ancestors. But a more secret part of the legend also says that the power of the storm eroded, if only slightly, the surface of the Graygem. That if one were to find that stone today—great Reorx forbid!—he would discover that the facets were worn, the edges smoother than in the faraway time of its creation."

"'All things wear down eventually,'" Innova whispered.

"'Except when they don't,'" Lucretius replied. "And the eroding rain that dripped from the stone onto this mountain trickled down through the cracks and fissures, found passage into tunnels scored by lava in the creation of this island, and settled in pools deep in the middle levels of Mount Nevermind. The solution is a kind of silt—part sediment, part oil. I haven't the tools to reckon its chemistry, but experience tells me that greasing a mile-long joy slide through the recesses of those levels is the only thing we can be sure it is good for."

"Useless?" Innova could not believe it.

"I didn't *say* 'useless.' If its source was the Graygem, there's no counting its uses. I said 'good for.' There are dozens of things it might be *bad* for. Drinking would be my first guess. I wouldn't trust it as lamp oil, as pomade or for cooking. Again, if its source is the Graygem, who's to say that it'll be good or bad for the same thing repeatedly? Or even *twice*?"

Innova shrugged. The old philosopher had a point. Apparently, when it came to the Graygem oil, Lucretius had set aside his natural gnomish curiosity.

Innova, however, found it hard to follow suit.

Still, all thoughts of the Graygem and the great rain fled Innova's mind in the weeks of labor that followed. Slowly, the abrasions on his rump and on the back of his legs began to heal. Eventually, his backside had recovered enough that he felt the constant company of cavern drafts across his buttocks.

For after all, the friction of the last hundred unoiled yards of his slide had tattered his trousers beyond repair.

It would have been embarrassing upside, in civilized districts. But here in the darkness and in the presence only of an old gnome who knew next to nothing of etiquette and proper attire, Innova could work with his anatomy open to the shifting subterranean air.

In fact, he was thankful for the ventilation by the time the dull pain in his lower back began to fade.

Chapter 7

In the first three months of Innova's sentence, important things had begun to happen in the larger world beyond Mount Nevermind and Sancrist.

The season of storms had passed. The seas were still choppy, the clouds low on western horizons, but now steady winds blew out of the east, and all along the coast of Ansalon the sails were aloft and the ships were moving.

The season had treated ill the flotilla of Commander Khargos. Battened south of Ergoth, the ships had rocked at anchor through tempest and unpredictable calm. Half of the Knights of Takhisis were seasick, and the brutes were restless and surly in the holds.

In his bare cabin, the maps spread once again beneath a pale lantern, Halion Khargos plotted a western path, an invasion whose time had come.

He wondered what it was about the sea that invited chaos. Now, even with the prospect of smoother sailing, old hostilities and insubordinations lingered in his command.

He had stumbled across a conclave of Thorn Knights, absorbed in some whispered debate with his two subcommanders, and the whispering had stopped when Stormont noticed his approach.

Soon afterward, in a brief calm amid the winds and the driving rain, he had ordered the fleet to land in a sparsely populated area of the Ergoth coast. It had seemed practical at the time, but within hours after the landing, a company of brutes had vanished into the surrounding forest, and the Knights had wakened in the dark morning to the distant sound of screams, the glow of fire from somewhere off in the woods.

He had sent out a Talon of Knights of the Lily, at their head a warrior by the name of William Naranja. Hours later, the Talon returned with bad news and the brutes in tow. The barbarians had raided a coastal village, massacred its inhabitants, and had been in the first stages of looting the burning huts when Naranja and his company had overtaken them.

Commander Khargos's justice was swift and merciless. That afternoon he had set the chief marauders on the beach at low tide, spreadeagled on the sand and bound in old backstay rope.

In the calm the tide had come in slowly. The rest of the brutes, circled around guttering campfires and guarded by a Wing of Knights, had listened in witless horror to the cries out in the darkness.

The cries eventually gave way to the rush and crash of breakers.

The next morning, as the company prepared to embark, the barbarians were most helpful, most cooperative. With a bleak satisfaction, Khargos noticed their secret glances at the half dozen bodies strewn along the beach, the blue paint already washing away in the surge and retreat of the waves. The bodies were covered with kelp and the flicker of amber and brown over their dead limbs signalled that the scavenger crabs were already at work. Faced with this spectacle, even the grumbling Stormont fell silent.

But out at sea, the grumbling began again. It grew louder as the ships turned away from Ergoth, then sharply to the starboard and west. The Thorn Knights that Khargos had ordered to predict the weather became sullen and uncertain, failing to inform the commander of yet a final gust of storm that rose from nowhere out of the south, bearing an icy wind and a rain that stung like nettles.

One of the ships—the *Cormorant*—went down in this last storm of the season. Only brave ventures by the Knights, lifeboats, and ropes flung out from the nearby *Shrike*, had saved the *Cormorant*'s crew and the warriors it transported, but as the vessel went down in turbulent water, the survivors swore they heard screams from the hold, rising above the clamor of the storm.

They swore as well that the ocean reached forth black tentacles, formed of saltwater and spume and something dark and indefinable that tugged at the *Cormorant's* bow and hauled her under.

Or that was what the Knights *claimed* they saw. Still, who could be sure?

Commander Khargos had saved those Knights, but the brutes had drowned. And now the Goddess hovered at the edge of his dreams, her sweet soft voice unintelligible, troubling his sleep.

His waking hours were troubled as well, by the rising discontent and the long voyage ahead.

"Evil turns upon itself," Khargos thought with contempt. It was a smug proverb of old, smug philosophers. The victors in the War of the Lance still used it to explain their victory, while the losers—even some of the veterans he now commanded—used it to explain their weakness and incompetence.

Lord Ariakan had dismissed that philosoph and had established the Blood Oath and the Code as a dark reflection of the old Solamnic nonsense. The new laws worked: it had become clear on the continent, where Ariakan was marching to triumph after triumph, and the world was bending to the will of the Dark Goddess.

But here on discordant seas, in the midst of sniping and intrigue, Khargos had come to see the frailty of this Code. It was still a young thing, still in need of nurturing and care, for at the slightest setback, many of the Knights who followed him seemed inclined to greed and resentment. To deception and double-dealing, regardless of the oaths they had taken.

It was in their blood, he thought. Thanks be to Takhisis for Visions and signs, and for the presence of Lord Ariakan.

Even that presence seemed remote on the high seas, as the ships scudded now along the eastern coast of Sancrist.

They had given up a southern landing entirely. Those shores were the old haunts of Gunthar Uth Wistan and his Solamnic legions. Even if Lord Gunthar had taken his companies elsewhere, to battle on Ergoth or the continent, it would be unsteady going for the Knights of Takhisis in unfamiliar forest. The Solamnic reputation alone would have sent Khargos's troops starting at shadows, imagining bright armor within the thick stands of evergreen.

So they had sailed north, keeping the lights around Gwynned faintly visible to the starboard and the beaches of Sancrist to the portside. Where the straits widened into the open sea, they took a westward route, bound for a landing on the island's northern shores.

It was not familiar country to Halion Khargos. Not yet.

The Knights encountered their first resistance near the reef that guarded the island's shallow bay. A strange, steampowered craft no bigger than a lifeboat, manned by a halfdozen gnomes, chugged out bravely through the maze of coral.

It was curiosity that had brought the steamboat out. The gnomes onboard were scantily armed, more busy peering through spyglasses and tinkering with their own unsightly vessel than marshalling any kind of attack or defense.

Halion Khargos found himself smiling at the boat, at its metal wings spread just above the waterline and the single mast that bore hooks instead of sails. It charmed him, as it had done long ago. He could have spent hours speculating on just what the crew thought these devices would accomplish and what they would *really* do.

Despite himself, he had always been fascinated by the gnomes, by their constant courting of a disorder he could not permit himself, and by the joy they derived from courting that chaos.

Yet these gnomes had to be silenced. Intelligence back to Mount Nevermind would be a small disaster, preparing the city for siege or invasion. No telling what traps and snares and elaborate machinery the Knights would encounter if they allowed these fellows to escape.

Reluctantly, Commander Khargos mustered the archers aboard his flagship *Peregrine*. Skilled bowmen from Neraka, they were a necessity for siegecraft. They gathered swiftly and efficiently, and within minutes a rain of arrows arched across the water at the steaming boat.

But the gnomes onboard rushed into action. Two of them leapt to an enormous crank at the base of the mast, and the metal wings folded above the boat until it looked like some kind of floating shed. The first arrows struck the water around them; those better aimed clattered harmlessly against the raised metal roof of the craft.

It was then that Stormont, in command of the *Kestrel*, ordered his ship to ram the gnome contraption.

From on board the flagship, Halion Khargos shouted fruitlessly. At his orders, the blood-red warning banner shot up the mizzenmast—a signal that all ships should with-draw into deeper waters. But the *Kestrel* was heedless, obey-ing the whim of its commander or some dark, contagious impulse from the heart of the sea.

Swiftly, the ship bore down upon the sputtering little boat, the iron dragon's head ram on her prow lowered to drive the gnome craft into the depths. Crewmen leapt from the stern and the portside, suddenly aware of the dangerous course of the ship. Stormont himself stood at the bow, and from a great distance Khargos could see him lift his sword.

Some faint cry—command or oath—floated incoherently over the crash of the waves.

The gnome boat turned tail and, with a taunting whistle, steamed through a narrow passage of the reef. The *Kestrel* fol-lowed, slipping safely through the passage as well. Now the water was green and amber around her, and the gravity of Stormont's error dawned on the headstrong Knights.

A great roar passed over the water, a fluster of sails being raised and lowered. The helmsmen turned the rudder vainly as though sheer desperation could reverse their course. Someone cast a hopeless anchor, which caught on a reef's edge and broke free under the *Kestrel*'s momentum.

Then came the sound, the wretched sound of the keel boards shearing as they scraped over the serrated peaks of the reef. The *Kestrel* rocked, tilted to starboard, and lay still in a jungle of coral.

Free of the reef now, halfway into the bay, the gnome vessel spun around wildly and exploded under the pressure of its own steam. Vapor and wood and tin leapt to heaven in a small geyser, and the folded wings of the steamboat fluttered over the water and landed harmlessly in the incoming tide.

Rescue work was heroic but short-lived. Most of the Knights aboard the *Kestrel* were wearing armor against the possible return of fire from the gnome vessel. Their breastplates weighed them down as the shallow waters closed over them. The brutes had been bolted below deck so as not to risk chaos aboveboard, and as the *Kestrel* sank, they were lost as well.

The big ship took in the sea like a conduit. In a matter of minutes the water had rushed over her decks. Swiftly, as though the ocean had opened its maw to swallow her, the *Kestrel* sank amid the coral ranges. The desperate cries from her decks and holds were even louder and more wretched than those from the vanished *Cormorant*, for calm waters and gentle winds could not mask the agony of the drowning.

* * * * *

There was not much that Halion Khargos could do, he reasoned in the privacy of his cabin.

Most of the *Kestrel*'s crew had been plucked from the waters, and a handful of Knights settled within rescue, marooned among the sharp notches of the reef, but it was small solace: Khargos had lost half a Wing to a sternwheeling rattletrap, along with a veteran subcommander—man, when all was considered, whose surliness and envy surpassed his usefulness on the field of battle.

After all, had not the gnomecraft exploded, taking with it all danger of reconnaissance?

Why, it was more convenience than disaster.

Slowly, there in the privacy, Halion Khargos smiled. He told himself that accident had preserved the order in his ranks, thanked Takhisis for her guidance in calm waters. When the sentries outside the door heard the faint sound of laughter from inside the cabin, they assumed that the Commander had entered the country of Vision, that communion with the Dark Queen had soothed his distraction and jangled nerves . . . .

Drowning out the chaotic song of the ocean.

Chapter 8

Innova's stay in the lower levels could have gone on for months. He could have lingered in the lower levels, stacking stones and bathing in fetid water, learning odds and ends from Lucretius Climenole up until the day that his sentence ended.

Even longer, if he liked.

There was something serene about the darkness and quiet there in the deepest recesses of Mount Nevermind. It soothed him, restored his balances. Even the lectures from the old gnome ceased to irritate him, though the proverbs still bothered him now and then, and the fear of spiders never left him. Innova began to think he was past major annoyance—bound for some strange and spiritual state in which all wrong and hardship paled before the peace of stacking stones, of shoring the levels against the undermining magma.

He continued to repair the gnomeflingers, of course, not so much out of a duty to his sentence as with a sense of quiet enjoyment. These repairs, too, were something to do as well, and he could never recall later which of the machines, spread throughout the lowest levels of the mountain, he had set his hands to in the idle times.

He would come to regret this lapse in memory . . . but not then, not in that peaceful time.

Two weeks into this harmony, somewhere around the Seventh or Eighth Level amid rubble and layers of shale, Innova and Lucretius came across something—or *someone*—who changed all this.

It started with voices behind a stone wall.

As Innova passed by a section of tunnel rubbled and bowed out like a bay window of shale, he heard a smothered cry from somewhere amid the depths of piled stone.

"Lucretius!" he hissed, but the old gnome was rattling on about the gardening he had done in a little glade at the foot of the mountain, about how a trough of mirrors might be made to funnel light into furrows seeded with sunflowers, thereby assuring . . .

"Lucretius!"

The old fellow blinked and staggered. Dropping the stone he was carrying—a piece of onyx so heavy that its fall made the tunnel shudder and rubble slide slowly onto the corridor floors—Lucretius approached the wall. He leaned into the debris, still whispering to himself and deaf as a post to boot.

Insisted he heard nothing.

Innova began to dig. Five minutes' scrabbling amid stones and collapsed beams produced a small crawlspace into a dimly lit alcove. And five minutes more had opened that space enough for Innova to crawl through.

He entered a little room, quite tastefully appointed with tapestries and dressers, with a canopied featherbed spread over with quilts.

Upon that bed sat a gnome girl, clutching a hand mirror and straightening her hair to receive visitors. She was golden-haired, appealing in a tall sort of way. Immediately, Innova was at a loss for words.

Unlike his companions Talos and Deddalo, he was no ladies' man. The prettier the female, the more fool he made himself, and though this one was only moderately attractive, he had been in the lower levels for some time, his only companion a smelly old metaphysician.

He saw it coming from long off. Tried to speak and only bleated.

The gnome girl glanced at the tattered intruder who had tunneled through her walls, threw down the mirror, and emitted a curious piping sound, like a teapot starting to boil.

Innova could have backed out of the room even then, could have jostled by Lucretius and hastened on up the corridor, writing it all off as hallucination, as some kind of rapture of the mineral depths. He could have remembered his pulverized father's advice: *Never trust a tall girl, for she'll always look down on you.*

Instead, he smiled, mustered his courage and charm, and courted her with words.

"H-hullo," he stammered. "Sorry to bother you."

"Who are you?" shrieked the moderately attractive creature, falling back onto the bed and covering herself with quilts.

"Innovafertanimusmutatisdicere . . . " Innova began, but his own name trickled off into oblivion, and he gaped and snorted.

A nose—a powdered and not unseemly one—poked out from the mantle of blankets.

"I *know* that name!" the girl exclaimed. "Where have I heard that name? Are you a friend of my father?"

"I . . . I don't know," Innova replied. "Who *is* your father?"

Sitting upright, emerging from the quilts like a tall sprite rising from water, the girl regarded him scornfully.

"And who are you," she cried, "not to have heard of Incline Barium? And of his daughter Meryl?"

*   *   *   *   *

She had survived the silo explosion by nothing short of a miracle. Wakening in unfamiliar corridors, for a while she had even forgotten who she was.

She took up with a band of beggars, she said, bound for the lower levels. It was something she did not want to talk about. Eventually, after long and aimless wandering with the outcasts of gnomish society, Meryl Barium's memory had returned to her when a beam in a crawlspace broke above her head and rained down rock and a three-day coma.

"I tried to return upside," she maintained. "Father would be half-crazy missing his elder daughter."

"Elder?" Lucretius asked. "I thought young Innova said you were a twin."

"A twin, yes, but two minutes older than my dear, departed sister." A tear brimmed on her eyelid, glistened like a half-hidden gemstone. "Not that it makes any difference now. Vaporized, she was, atop a distillery silo. I'm all alone, a solitary. But my father misses me, I am sure, more even than my unraveled sister. After all, an accident of birth made me the elder, the green apple of his eye.

"Silly girl that I am, when I tried to return to Papa, matters only got worse. I left the beggars bound toward the Second Level—I do not want to talk about them—and found my way to a gnomeflinger. I had seen it done before—how the lads climbed into the machine, pulled a thing at the side—"

"A lever," Innova added helpfully.

Her smile was mildly fetching.

"A lever, then. And when they pulled that lever, it would send them to the upper levels, would it not?"

"For all intents and purposes," Innova replied. Then kicked himself for sounding like Lucretius.

"Well, this one didn't work like that at all," she explained, casting a sly glance at Innova. "I suppose it was in . . . a state of disrepair."

Innova shrank into the shadows so the girl would not see him blush. Cheerily, her story by no means derailed, she turned to Lucretius, who was just now climbing into the chamber.

"That gnomeflinger catapulted me here, or around here. I was injured in the fall. Only in the last few days have I been able to put weight on this ankle. Fortunately, I found this furniture and these quilts at a garbage dump—what a blessed find!—and have waited here until my injuries might heal. Through the rubble I heard you passing and called out, hoping I might find escort back to the upside."

She batted her eyelids alluringly. "I am still rather weak, you see."

To all of this, Innova nodded enthusiastically. Of course, there were things he did not understand. How had she fed herself? Why would someone throw away a perfectly good dresser?

And why was Lucretius staring that way at *him*?

For the old gnome regarded him skeptically, black eyes darting from Innova to this Meryl Barium and back.

Lucretius knew something, or had hallucinated something.

For the life of him, Innova could not figure what.

* * * * * *

For the next day or so, the old gnome seemed subdued, lost in thought.

In fact, Lucretius had been moody since the girl had first told her story down in the caved-in chambers. He went about his business as usual, stacking stones and tinkering with the handcart, which had an irritating habit of always needing repairs.

But the lectures were less frequent. And when they came, they were much shorter and, for the first time, relevant to the subject at hand.

Still, Lucretius's moods were never hostile or dark as much as quiet. He ranged from his old cheerfulness and high volume—where you would think nothing had changed—to this new abstraction. Lucretius had stepped away from things when the two younger gnomes had met, much like a discreet friend will do when he discovers that he makes an unnecessary third to a courtship.

Not that Innova was courting the girl. Nor even all that interested, he had told himself, a little disappointed despite his desire to be proper and honorable. After all, this was Talos's one true love. Or that was what Innova's friends had told him.

Yet he wished that the girl found him more interesting.

Despite the attraction, Innova swore silent loyalty to his old companion. Though something about this girl continued to trouble and haunt and compel him, he would answer no call except that of his friendship with Talos. He would take the girl back to the upper city, and keep both his hands and his indecent thoughts away from her.

It was almost as though Lucretius had read those thoughts. In the week that followed, he stood at the margins while Innova and their new companion acquainted themselves with each other and realized how their stories intersected somewhere in the recent past and the upper levels.

Innova was a little disappointed that she had never heard that much about him. After all, he had fancied himself a major character in the whole Barium business.

"Oh, yes," the girl maintained when he asked. "I miss Talos immensely. But d'you think it's *safe* to go upside?

After all, it's all so *confusing* up there, with the High Justice sentencing all of you right and left, and the gods know what other business afoot. Maybe I'm silly—'ungnomish' my dear and darling father would say—but politics and law are as much a mystery to me as all these contraptions you boys seem to understand so readily."

She batted her eyelids at Innova.

"A poor little thing like me," she concluded, "would find it rough going up in the city."

Innova took her hand. This kind of talk made him feel larger, braver, and more protective. He wanted to explain to her that *he* would watch over her. He would stand between her and the roughness of the world. But something within him drew back. Maybe it was only that she was Talos's sweetheart.

Lucretius drew back as well. He sniffed and grumbled, and shook his head. Not ten minutes after the girl had finished her story, the old gnome was back in the handcart, reading the valves, adjusting the pipes and throttles.

Something has happened, Innova told himself. And it's something mysterious, because he's not talking this time. This time, he's thinking himself away from words.

"Get in behind me!" Lucretius shouted at last, as the makeshift vehicle shivered with steam and strained against its brakes. "We're bound for the upper levels!"

"Upper levels?" the girl asked. "So soon?"

Innova thought she seemed disappointed at the prospect.

"I'm taking you home, children!" Lucretius crowed. "Home for a little . . . *context*! Now come afore here, or we'll never top the first incline! And bring both those jugs with ye!"

The ceramic jugs that lay in the back of the handcart had been a mystery to Innova. He had asked about them before, received cryptic answers, and decided early on that some things about Lucretius Climenole's work remained and would remain none of his business.

He handled the vessels carefully, expecting some kind of explosive, and with Lucretius's careful turn of a switch, the handcart shrieked forward on the tracks.

The girl shrieked in harmony with the grinding wheels.

As the cart hurtled up the first of two dozen inclines, Innova wondered if he had done something wrong, had displeased Lucretius in some obscure way. After all, he had become settled in these daily labors, he even enjoyed the slow, comfortable dozes brought on by the old fellow's lectures and the strange peace of doing simple tasks far away from the bustle of gnomish business.

Then here comes this Meryl Barium, and the whole world changes.

Suddenly it dawned on Innova.

The old gnome was jealous.

The two of them had explored these caverns in a sort of lonely male teamwork. When a female stepped in, they had become rivals, like it or not.

And he was younger than Lucretius, more lively, more handsome.

Why, it all made sense now. It all fit. And part of it felt good.

He started to explain to his old mentor how the girl was betrothed to his closest friend and that he, Innova, had no designs on her. How he would not be interested, even if she were free and clear of attachment . . . .

He knew *that* was a lie, but now was not the time for lies or truths. The cart careened up a steep gradient, flew over a narrow but dangerous break in the tracks, caught traction and sputtered around a tight corner, racing for the upside and for a way of life Innova had nearly forgotten in his lonely and deep pursuits.

On the way they passed the pools of Graygem oil. Noticing the long glance of her companions at the glittering pool, the girl asked what was so fascinating.

Innova told her. Recounted his long slide through the deep corridors, he speculated on the prospect and power of this uncanny liquid, ending with Lucretius's warnings.

He was boasting in a way, displaying his knowledge.

Up through the Twelfth and the Thirteenth Levels the vehicle raced. A legion of bats scattered in panic as it raced by, and once Innova thought he saw a cluster of lights—a settlement down a wide straight corridor, which vanished almost as he glimpsed it.

Now yet a steeper incline approached, and Lucretius looked back at his passengers, his white hair matted by steam and sweat.

"Pour the first jug into the secondary expansion tank!" he commanded.

"The *what*?"

"Right next to the vertical articulator, Innova. No! Not *that* one! That's the claxon valve, you utter idiot! Right there beside—No! That's the pneumatic defibrillator!"

Absently, gaping at terms he did not understand and the prospect of sliding back into darkness and accident, Innova fumbled with the stopper of the jug.

The girl pointed to a funnel, shrouded by steam, in the side of a canteen-shaped tank.

"I'm a ninny around machinery," she said, "but perhaps . . ."

"That's it! That's it!" Lucretius shouted.

And Innova opened the jug. The smell of its contents washed over him at once—the familiar mixture of rust and grain and cayenne he had caught many times in the tavern alleys of the disreputable Nineteenth Level . . .

"It's . . . it's *dwarf spirits*!"

"Thorbardin Oeconomy Malt, to be exact," Lucretius yelled over the hissing steam. "What the gully dwarves call 'Old Tom' and the civilized world calls 'Widowmaker.' I discovered—and do not ask me how—its virtues as a supplementary fuel. Pour the contents of that jug into the funnel designated by . . . Miss Meryl, is it?"

Innova poured dutifully, and the handcart screeched like squirrels on fire. The jury-rigged vehicle shuddered and lurched forward, casting blue sparks across the buckling tracks behind it. The smell of boiled cabbage and pepper surged down to meet the cart and its passengers, mixed with the other familiar and forgotten smells of Innova's childhood.

They were nearing the upper levels.

They were approaching home.

"Now for the second one!" Lucretius proclaimed. Innova opened the jug, leaned toward the funnel, but the old gnome snatched the Old Tom from his hands and took a long, courageous draw of the noxious stuff. "Drink up, young fellow!" he shouted, proffering the jug to Innova.

"The last leg of the journey is on us!"

It tasted like magma. Innova could have sworn there was cabbage afloat in the stuff—cabbage and ginger. Cayenne raced down his gullet as though some hostile god was funneling spite into his stomach. Joining Lucretius at the helm of the handcart, all thoughts of safety and the girl cast aside, Innova pumped the primer with renewed energy, oblivious to fear, to his own pain and to the rush of light as yet another tunnel opened at their approach.

By Reorx, the spirits worked quickly! It seemed that the cart coasted up the incline, and Innova wanted to sing to the swift clatter of the wheels. He was almost home, back among friends and corridors he knew. He heard the far-off whistle of a guild hall signaling the end of its working day, and the shrill, staccato buzzer of a nearby emergency kiosk.

Talos would be here, be eternally grateful for his rescued sweetheart. Deddalo would be here as well, as would the old pulleys and alleys that mapped their ways through the upper levels.

Innova was home, unscathed except for the dull pain in his backside. With a long life ahead of him . . .

With a girl who was somehow inveigling his feelings . . .

And with three months yet to serve on a court-ordered sentence.

Chapter 9

Lucretius had deposited Innova and the girl as high in the city as his steam cart could take them. The volume and delight of the perilous trip upside had vanished, and in its stead was that recent and curious quietness that Innova had come to know and resent.

Both Lucretius and his vehicle puffed and hissed, as though a goodly power had left them.

"Well, then," Lucretius began, "if you're ever in need of me, look for me where you first found me. I like it when things go in circles: It feels like they've been planned."

He started to say something else, then seemed to think better of it.

"Thank you for . . . " Innova said, but the old gnome waved away the rest of his words with the soft swipe of a grubby hand.

It was just as well. Innova was not altogether certain how much he should thank Lucretius or how much he should blame him. The first, painful entanglement and the long, boring lectures were set in a scale against the old gnome's clumsy kindness and the basic fact that Innova would have died without his care and guidance.

All in all, the balance tipped toward gratitude, and Innova told himself he would miss the old fellow, steam and hogwash and bad breath and all. So he waved, balanced between sadness and relief, as the handcart backed into the darkness, trailing a cloud of acrid vapor. Soon, all he could see was its ridiculous little lantern, rocking back and forth in the depths of the tunnel.

"You're quite indecent, you know," the Barium girl declared.

"I beg your pardon?"

"This attire may be all well and good for stone-wrangling down near the magma, but we're back in the civilized part

of the city, and I will *not* be seen with you in such tatters.
Look behind you, Master Innova.

"Your ultimates are unveiled."

Innva blushed, was sure he had reddened fore and aft.
Blushed some more at the thought.

"Haven't you a . . . *scarf* or something?" he asked desperately, knowing from a glance that the girl carried nothing but a solitary travel bag, her clothing, and her
attitude.

She regarded him skeptically. "I've an extra skirt in my
portmanteau," she said, "but I expect that would deepen
rather than solve our problems."

"Then it's to Talos's quarters!" Innova urged. "I know
where we are, and it's not far from his family rooms. He'll
have something to drape me, and he'll be mighty glad to see
you."

"Not yet," the girl replied. She stepped away from the
tracks, out of the lamplight, and began some lengthy explanation about how it was too early to see her old beloved,
how the news needed breaking to him gradually. How Deddalo was after all more clever and could find a way to
smoothe the turmoil of their return to the upside.

An army of reasons, to which Innova paid little heed,
embarrassed as he was by his exposure.

At any rate, the two of them passed through tunnels and
down slides, up a torchlit ladder where the girl, following
her mortified companion, made jokes about the "new moon
on the rise." When they reached the Twenty-Fifth Level and
its confusion and tangle of tunnels, she seemed to know
even better than Innova the way to Deddalo's quarters, and
so she took the lead on the journey.

Much to Innova's relief. He preferred those sharp eyes
before him rather than behind him. It was a simple question
of dignity.

Soon the tunnels became more familiar. The old Chemi-
cal Engineers' Guild Hall appeared on their right, its foun-
dations still smoldering and glowing after seventeen years.
Then they passed the level's famous row of taverns.
Abstract Yearnings was first, its windows shut and a
"Closed" sign on the door. The Hell With Dinner was

closed as well, though the lights from behind the boarded windows suggested that it was closed only to indefinite drinkers. Delirium Tremens, the third pub, seemed rather busy for this time of day, as did the fourth and final establishment, the Hair of the Dog.

"Turn left at the Hair—" Innova began, but the girl had already turned. She turned again by the collapsed arch of the Masons' Guild Hall.

Now she stood at the threshold of Deddalo's stairs. Innova started to tell her about the warding trap—the chute that opened at any weight on the third step, sending trespassers down onto a brass gong that would awaken the household and knock out the burglar simultaneously.

She knew about the device as well, stepping carefully over the triggering stair, and whispered a warning back to Innova as she climbed to the doorway on the shadowy landing.

Innova scratched his head. There was a lot this Meryl Barium knew. For barely a minute more, he wondered how she knew it.

Her rap on the door summoned Deddalo, clutching a candle. He squinted into the darkness, and then cried out, "Beryl! But you were supposed . . . "

"The darkness plays tricks with your sight, Master Deddalo," Meryl replied hastily, beckoning Innova into the candlelight. "'Tis *Meryl* Barium, older sister of your late and lamented affianced, and you remember, I suppose, your old friend Innova?"

Deddalo glanced at Innova. He gasped, smiled sheepishly and bowed in welcome. His drooping left eyelid snapped to wide attention and Innova understood.

How could I be so thick-headed? he thought. How could I miss the slips and signs?

For it was obvious that this was Beryl Barium, masquerading, for some mysterious reason, as her own twin sister.

*　*　*　*　*

Innova was ungnomishly bad at the sly and roundabout. He had enough sense to know that it was somehow safer to pretend ignorance—not to let on that he recognized this exchange of twins. That was not difficult, he told himself. He'd been genuinely ignorant so many times before that it should not be hard to counterfeit.

The tricky part was finding out the *why*s and the *wherefore*s.

Part of those *why*s touched him sorely. Had not the girl flirted with him, back there in the lower levels? Could it be that all that eye-batting and dazzlement was just another contraption—a device to get her safely to the surface? Despite himself, Innova's pride was wounded.

At first he kept the conversation on trivial things, as Deddalo ushered them into his quarters, sweeping away blueprints and bottles and melon rinds in order to blaze a path to his rickety wooden table.

"Noticed the Hell With Dinner's closed," Innova observed innocently.

"You know how it is," Deddalo answered eagerly. "No dwarf spirits before noon, and since the place doesn't serve a passing lunch . . ."

They nodded at one another, having tracked and cornered *that* conversation.

"There's also talk of some kind of invasion," Deddalo added. "A flotilla of gray sails, circling the north and west of the island. It may amount to nothing—after all, the troubles of the continent are seldom ours any more—but there's a watchfulness abroad in the city, and even the hardest drinkers are staying away from more stupefying extracts."

Innova nodded. It made sense, though judging from Deddalo's eye it was hard to separate gossip from fact.

Best touch on other matters.

"And Talos?" Innova asked. "How's my lad Talos doing these months?"

Silently he swore at himself. Mentioning Talos only brought up the subject of the switched twins.

But Deddalo had almost recovered his poise. Like a chessmaster aware of an opponent's aggressive move, he

69

kept a firm, opaque expression and hastened to the pantry for ale and tankards.

"Talos is well," Deddalo said, his back to Innova. "Rattling around in his family treasuries up on the top Level. "We'll have to take Meryl up to see him soon," he added, a note of playfulness in his voice. "Like as not, he'll grant it a miracle that his sweetheart survived the accident."

The Barium twin glanced away hastily.

Now Deddalo stepped from the shadows and handed a brimming tankard to Innova, who sipped daintily at first, then greedily. After all, it had been three months since his last beer.

But what was afoot here? Why these suggestions and this camouflage?

"First of all," Deddalo said, more and more his old self, calmly calculating, "we'll have to get you into trousers. Remember the Decency Ordinance in the top five levels. A bare arse could get you another month among the gnome-flingers. Speaking of which . . . your sentence isn't served, is it?"

Innova hastened to explain that returning the girl was foremost in his thoughts, that he'd risk even a doubled sentence for her safety. Lofty thoughts, but a small warning voice in the depths of his mind urged him to *be silent!*

Be silent, stupid!

If they're hiding things from you, then they're somehow against you, and it's best to figure that out before you go off yapping.

"I'm sure the justice will take into account your motives," Deddalo replied pompously. "If you like, I'll speak on your behalf."

Yes, that would be fine, Innova assured him. That would be fine, indeed.

Deddalo was off on another errand, drawing a pair of purple trousers from a chest beside his bed—ungainly things, patched in red and orange, too wide in the bottom for Innova and too long in the leg.

They would do for now. Innova nodded gratefully and ducked into the pantry to change, as though three months with his buttocks dangling had left him any modesty.

Modesty, no, he thought, slipping on the pantaloons in the midst of discarded blueprints, beer barrels, and beside a strange device of cogs and turnkeys that looked like an overgrown corkscrew. He started to open the door, to ask for a sash or suspenders.

He heard them whispering, there in the far corner of the room. Snatching up a tankard, he pressed its mouth to the door, listened at its base.

Something about a *contest*. About *the guild*.

The end of a question in the high voice of Beryl/Meryl.

. . . *tell him?*

"Tell him," indeed! By Reorx, he was going to find this business out! This much he knew from the dodging and whispers in the front room: Deddalo and Beryl (or Meryl or whoever she was) would not be free with information.

Just what was Deddalo brewing besides beer?

Innova picked up one of the blueprints, crumpled and apparently cast aside in disgust. The narrow window near the ceiling of the room permitted not enough light to read, but a pair of good eyes could make out a diagram or drawing at the least.

It was a complicated plan he held in his hands—a map and some kind of sketched machinery. He held the paper higher for a better view and suddenly recognized the map.

Thirtieth Level. Wealthy residential chambers. Was some burglary in the offing?

These particular quarters were familiar: Talos's dwelling. The many rooms of a subterranean mansion, complete with laboratories, greenhouses, and bathing lagoons.

The sketch, on the other hand, was less detailed. It was some bastardized machine, part catapult and part hammer. Innova was not sure how it worked or if it would work at all. Two things, however, were clear: It was no gnome-flinger, and its design was dramatically lethal.

His first thought was an obvious one—that Talos was in danger—but even with all the revelations and surprises of the day, that seemed improbable.

Deddalo and Talos were friends. Surely that counted for something.

The conversation outside the door grew louder. Either Deddalo and the twin were coming closer or they were arguing. Under either circumstance, the possibilities were explosive.

... your father, Deddalo said, his voice creaking with concern.

But whatever it was, the girl laughed it off.

"Don't worry," she said. "I will take ... "

Her voice slid down to a whisper, and Innova could no longer make out her words.

Quickly, almost without thinking, he stuffed the blueprint in the back of his oversized trousers. Something in him kept insisting that he warn Talos, but that voice was drowned out by rising confusion—by the girl with two possible names, by the addled machinery, the strange behavior of his old comrade, and the whispers outside the door.

He would have to piece this together before he acted. He had to be sure, and right now he was sure of nothing.

* * * * *

Deddalo seemed relieved when his old friend announced his departure.

"I—I really must be going, old boy," Innova explained, trying for a note of cheeriness but settling for vague agitation. "After all, I've months to go on my sentence, as you said. Best go back and finish it, or at least hide out in the lower levels until ... until more appropriate times."

He was stammering, completely unconvincing to anyone with sharp ears and judgment.

Deddalo, it seemed, possessed neither at the moment.

"Where will you be staying, old fellow?"

"At my Aunt Tedia's, I suppose," Innova lied. "She's as close to family as I have, and she'll probably have a loft where I can bed down."

There was no bed, no loft, no Aunt Tedia, but Deddalo would not ask. He was more eager to be rid of Innova than Innova was to break free of that web of confusions.

Deddalo nodded, cast a sidelong glance toward Meryl or Beryl, who had something else on her mind.

Free of their skeptical stares, Innova backed toward the
door. Not for the first time he was glad that the always-
scheming Deddalo regarded him as a fool, as a naïve gnome
who would trust his friends to the brink of disaster.

A good heart was so often a disadvantage, it was pleasant once in a while when it was a reward.

"I'll talk to the Justice," Deddalo called after him as he
stepped out the door onto the landing. "Honest, I will. You
can return those trousers later—not tonight, mind you, but
at your leisure. Watch out for the third step."

Standing outside by the ruined facade of the Masons'
Guild Hall, Innova gathered himself, took his first deep
breath in an hour.

The something that was afoot was definitely complicated
as well—an involved contraption of disguises and maps
and machinery.

He was too unadorned for the likes of Deddalo, a babe in
the Barium woods. He wished he *did* have an Aunt Tedia—
someone older and wiser.

Someone more intricate and corrupt.

Innova was simple, but he was no fool. There, amid
crumbling bricks and the sharp smell of dwarf spirits rising
from the Hair of the Dog, the answer rushed over him.

He had an advisor, a barrister, a distant cousin as wily as
a fat water rat.

Providing he was sober, Scymnidus would have his ear
to every wall.

Chapter 10

It was not a bad choice, Innova's decision to seek out the public defender.

Scymnidus was a distant cousin, ten years older than Innova, and one of the few public figures in crowded Mount Nevermind whom folks thoroughly left alone. He lived in wealth and seclusion on the Twenty-Eighth Level, by the old silver smithy, and his purchase of that property near the end of the War of the Lance had brought him a small fortune to add to a sizable inheritance from his father's steamboat company.

But Scymnidus was more famous as a barrister, a renegade philosopher, a gadfly to the gnome state. It was a long story, beginning when Innova was only a child.

Nobody could have asked for a better student than Scymnidus. He was the kind of lad who seemed to remember rather than learn things—as though he had known them all along and only needed his memory jogged. Though he was the darling of many on the Philosophers' Council—Gordusmajor included—his sheer excellence had bred jealousy among those who would review his petition for membership in the Guild.

Everyone knew what would happen. The philosophical question Scymnidus would receive would be more difficult than most, and almost everyone on the review board would follow the old strategy: They would pretend to understand his answer, would dismiss it right away, and would set him on a process of several years, in which he would be assigned subjects and problems to which his answers would never be adequate. Finally, humiliated sufficiently after a long apprenticeship, Scymnidus would be allowed to sneak in the back door of the Guild, where he would serve as a minor functionary for decades and then, if his behavior was bureaucratic and slavish enough, would sit upon the

Council in his dotage, far too old to pose any danger to the way things had been for years.

That was simply the way things happened in the Philosophers' Guild. Nor would Scymnidus's special talents make him an exception. So the review board told itself, as the day of his first examination approached.

They convinced each other, but not Scymnidus.

His question had been a difficult one. "Complete this sentence: 'The will of the gods is _____.' " It was question abstract and open-ended enough to draw all kinds of fire from trained examiners.

But Scymnidus's answer surprised them all. It was said that he returned to the Guild Hall with the simple response that "The will of the gods is two inches up my nose."

There are some versions of the story in which the answer involved a nastier orifice, but most accounts agree on the nose. Otherwise the questioning that followed would have made no sense.

Justice Ballista, always vocal and always ignored, headed the review board. After the long, stunned silence of his colleagues, he took it upon himself to respond.

"I understand," he proclaimed. "The will of the gods is, by your metaphor, deep in the head of all philosophical thinkers."

"Not at all," Scymnidus replied. "For if the will of the gods were deep in the heads of *all* philosophical thinkers, I should be wiser than you because my nose is longer."

Ballista stammered. Fortunately, Judge Harpos was there to fill the breach.

"I understand," Harpos declared. "You are saying that the will of the gods contains mysteries that are best not brought to light."

"Not at all," Scymnidus replied, drawing a handkerchief from his pocket and blowing his nose loudly in front of the assembled board. Displaying the contents of the cloth to his examiners, who quite properly turned up their noses and averted their eyes, he proclaimed triumphantly, "For if that were the case, it would mean that the will of the gods revolts the Philosophers' Guild."

On and on the examiners posed their arguments. One said that the will of the gods *filtered and shaped the air that surrounds us*. Scymnidus admired the poetry of this, but maintained that most philosophers were mouth-breathers.

Another said that the will of the gods *was a humble place at the foundation of all spectacles*. Scymnidus admired the pun, but explained that, logically extended, such an answer would imply that there was nothing spectacular unless you were nearsighted.

A last desperate examiner suggested that the will of the gods *was a home for snuff*.

Scymnidus said he could not dignify that answer with a question, which created even more confusion on the review board.

Finally, exhausted and irritated and thoroughly flummoxed, arguing among themselves rather than with the petitioner, the philosophers had come to blows. Justice Ballista was carried from the room on a stretcher, his broken nose taken by some as a prophecy that he would lose his wisdom. Finally, when order was restored, the examiners left standing turned to Scymnidus, and asked, in unison,

"So what is the answer?"

"The will of the gods is two inches up my nose," Scymnidus repeated serenely. "Nobody can touch it but me, and I am too polite to do so in public."

He spun on his heels, left the Guild Hall, and walked out of philosophy and decent society forever.

*   *   *   *   *

He did not, however, walk away from public life.

Or maybe he did, because even that was subject to dispute.

Scymnidus never again had appeared in public. He sat alone in his quarters, amid his substantial library and a vast collection of gadgets and bells, conducting all his business by correspondence.

He was a public defender who never appeared in court, preferring to brief his clients on what to say before the various tribunals, then delighting in seeing his words take action. There were gnomes acquitted for theft and for poverty, completely guilty parties in a lawsuit going scot-free and then, having been declared completely innocent, receiving a fortune in reparational damages from the tribunals themselves, who, when they had been argued into a corner, had been known even to sentence their own members to lengthy jail terms.

There were rumors of plots on his life and property, of threats veiled and unveiled in his daily correspondence. Many said that Scymnidus started the rumors himself, but eventually the word in Mount Nevermind was that he was too nervous about his powerful enemies.

But it was more than nervousness. It was a kind of quarrel with the world.

Some blamed it on dwarf spirits, bthers on his isolation. But there was another story—one nobody but Scymnidus knew. Not even his family or the old High Justice who remained his friend.

It had to do with a time near the end of his father's days.

* * * * *

In the waning years of Lamnidus Carcharias's life, his son Scymnidus had taken time from his legal practice to help the old gnome on a hare-brained venture: organizing steamboat saltwater fishing cruises.

Of course, the puffing and whistling of the vessels, the constant churning of their wheels in the water, had scared away any sporting catch, so the venture had beached almost as soon as it began.

But not before a night on the western coast of Sancrist, when, at the helm of his wheezing vessel, the old gnome had run ashore in anticipation of a huge storm that never came.

Lamnidus had followed a faint light on the beach, using it as a kind of guidance in the midst of dark waters and a cloudy sky. When the keel of the boat scraped sand, the only soul who was surprised was the wealthy banker from the Thirtieth Level, who immediately called for his money back.

While Scymnidus argued with the banker, his father waded up the beach toward the light—a campfire up by a ramshackle shanty. Just when the young lawyer had almost persuaded the client to pay double for the prospect of adventure, the old gnome returned. He urged his son to follow, for someone needed aid.

It was a Solamnic Knight, nestled near the campfire, nursing the wound of a ragged beachcomber. The son of this peasant, apparently, had stabbed his father for what the old man claimed was no reason, and had fled into the night.

Judging from what the Solamnic Knight told them, the boy was barely eleven when the Knight offered to go after the lad, the old beachcomber had shaken his head.

"Nossir," the man said, fingering the nasty, shallow wounds on his side and throat. "No, by all the gods. Don't hurt the boy.

"It were an accident."

Old Lamnidus had spoken of the event as they waded back up the beach toward the grounded boat and the fuming banker. He said it showed a father's unconditional love for his son.

Scymnidus had seen it otherwise. Upon his return to Mount Nevermind, he bolstered the doors of his chambers with an elaborate series of locks, suffered insomnia, and then took to dwarven spirits to help him sleep.

We are raising monsters, he told himself. And the forgiveness we offer them makes them more monstrous still.

It was even worse when he mulled it over in the dark, whiskey-soaked hours of morning. For it was then he took his thoughts to their logical conclusion:

It is the monstrousness in our laws, our authority, and at the heart of our very nature that makes monsters of the young. When they steal, or vandalize, or even stab a parent . . .

They are living out their destiny.

* * * * * *

So Scymnidus took to his quarters, confronting from fearful distance all the powers of the city.

By now only High Justice Gordusmajor, who oddly had escaped the lawyer's cleverness, spoke kindly of the barrister in absentia. Nobody knew why, but relations between the Justice and the renegade barrister had always been friendly.

Indeed, there was a portrait of the old judge, high on the wall of Scymnidus's study, who glared down at visitors with a look of corrupt benevolence.

Standing at the threshold of Scymnidus's offices, Innova looked into the eyes of that portrait. Beneath it the barrister snoozed behind a rolltop desk, a heavy, leatherbound volume of law gabled over his face like a tent. All around him an array of machines chugged merrily, and atop the desk, in a place of honor, a lever carved to resemble a long-necked goose rocked back and forth like a metronome, with each rock dipping its beak into a brimming glass.

It was not a scene that promised security.

Innova knocked on the door frame, cleared his throat, knocked again.

"Counselor Scymnidus?"

"Who wants to know?" Scymnidus shouted, lurching suddenly into action. The book tumbled from his face, and before it hit the floor, the barrister had leapt into the desk and rolled the cover over him.

The dipping goose rocked precariously, then righted itself, and the chamber filled with the sound of clicking locks.

"It's . . . it's Innova, sir."

"*Cousin* Innova?" The voice inside the desk was faint. "Innovafertanimus?"

"The same, sir. Come for your advice."

A faint light flickered beneath the canopy of the desk.

"That's different. Never can be too cautious, you know. Death threats and omens of dismemberment."

"I beg your pardon?"

"I am not the most popular figure on this level, Innova."

A faint, rolling sound rose from the desk, rushed beneath the floor like a burrowing thing on wheels, then came to a creaking stop behind the wall on which Gordusmajor's portrait hung.

A suit of armor pivoted in a far corner: It was draped on a dressmakers' dummy, whose plaster arms now leveled a wicked-looking crossbow at Innova's chest.

"Aren't you supposed to be patching gnomeflingers ten levels down?" Scymnidus asked, his voice emanating from behind the portrait of the old High Justice. Innova looked into the eyes of the painting, which suddenly blinked at him.

"Indeed I *was*, Cousin Scymnidus. But . . . unforeseen circumstances brought me upside."

The portrait's eyes regarded him skeptically.

"Are you the *real* Innovafertanimus? Or are you a cleverly disguised impostor, intent on seizing me and dangling me above a cauldron, hearing my last desperate cries with cruel glee before you drop me into bubbling water or hot tea or magma or worse?"

"I'm only Innova. I have no designs on your life."

"Prove it!"

The portrait shook on the wall. The bill of the dipping goose struck the lip of the cup with a single, soft *click*.

"What's that?" Scymnidus shouted. His eyes darted to the desk, and for a moment it seemed as though Gordusmajor's painted eyes had turned around in his head, that the old judge had fallen into a seizure or religious ecstasy.

It was all Innova could do to keep from laughing. But laughing could be dangerous, given his surroundings and the hair-trigger impulses of dressmakers' dummies.

"Prove it," Scymnidus repeated. His voice was softer now, less hysterical.

How do you prove you are who you are? Innova pondered the question for a moment, but as usual, the philosophy made him dizzy.

"How are your parents, Innova?" Scymnidus asked.

"Dead. And yours?"

"Dead as well. And your good friend Phaiston?"

"Phaistos. He's dead, too. You know these things, Scymnidus."

"As does anyone in Mount Nevermind." The lawyer's paranoia was thorough. "Have you seen your other two friends—what are their names?"

"Talos and Deddalo, sir. In fact, I just left Deddalo and plan to visit Talos shortly."

The portrait fell into silence. Thin smoke began to rise from the desk, and the inner light flickered.

"I believe, sir, that . . . your papers are on fire," Innova said.

"Never mind that. What were you sentenced for?"

"Inappropriate causal analysis."

"Which means?"

"I saw things coming."

Again Scymnidus was quiet. From somewhere in the room—high up on the wall, judging from the sound—something creaked and shuddered. Innova did not dare to look, one eye fixed on the portrait, the other on the nasty crossbow in the mannequin's hands.

His gaze was so divided that soon his head hurt.

"Matter of public record, your sentence," Scymnidus said at last. "Easily looked up in the library, if you know where to look."

"Most people don't, sir."

"But a conspiracy of judges *might*. Julius and Harpos have been after my pelt for months."

Again, the creaking sound. Innova flicked his gaze around the room, but could see nothing moving, nothing menacing. The smoke from the desk was thicker now, blocking his vision and making his eyes smart.

The portrait wheezed and coughed.

"I believe that your desk . . . "

"I'm not studying my desk!" Scymnidus snapped. "We have yet to determine your intentions. Your *identity* for that matter."

The creaking became a whirring sound, like a clock preparing to strike or a reel unwinding. Something brushed against Innova's shoulder, and he turned . . .

To see a dark thing, half obscured by smoke and dangling from a cord before him.

A squat, knotted thing with a splay of legs.

"Great Reorx!" Innova exclaimed. "Spiders!"

The smoke and his fear choked his senses.

* * * * *

"That's what I call sufficient evidence," Scymnidus explained, as he pushed a reviving cup of dwarf spirits under his cousin's nose. "Can't be too careful in this day and time."

The smoke, lifting through an open, barred window at the top of the chamber, left a musty smell behind, but other than that, the room was surprisingly unharmed, very much the way it had looked from the doorway.

The portrait of Gordusmajor stared empty-eyed across the room, and the mannequin had been turned toward the window, its crossbow raised against burglars and assassins.

The supposed spider, a halfhearted collage of wires and sticky gray tape, lay atop the smoldering desk. Beside it, the dipping contraption continued cheerfully, as though it was set on a course through eternity.

"Just how does that thing work?" Innova asked, his curiosity finally having overwhelmed him.

"Weight of the water tilts the balance," Scymnidus explained, "and when the water on the beak evaporates, it tilts back. The lever is hollow, and the water inside preserves the steady motion. It's surprising how much of hydraulics comes down to evaporation."

Innova smiled. It sounded like one of Lucretius's proverbs.

"So what can I do for you, Cousin?" Scymnidus asked. "What do you want?"

Innova explained the circumstances, why he had returned from the depths so early, and what he had discovered upon returning. He did not tell the whole story, his suspicion that Beryl Barium was masquerading as her own sister.

He figured that Scymnidus harbored suspicions enough.

After the public defender stared long and hard at Deddalo's maps and sketches, those suspicions came tumbling out, as Innova had expected they would.

"First of all, it's odd that he's working on a booby trap rather than something more philosophical," Scymnidus began. "After all, winning the contest would serve his ambitions."

"The contest?" Innova asked. "*What* contest?"

Scymnidus's eyes stayed fixed on the blueprint. "I'm not surprised he didn't tell you. About a month after you began your sentence, he and Talos went before Gordusmajor again. I think it was the prospect of more money that made the Justice summon them.

"Well, rumor has it that a place on the council of the Philosopher's Guild is opening up since Belisarius's balloon ride out to sea. . . . "

Innova nodded.

"And rumor has it as well that Gordusmajor wants younger blood on the council—someone naïve whom he can guide in matters of policy."

"Deddalo is not naïve," Innova objected.

"Perhaps not." Scymnidus lifted his eyes, regarded his visitor curiously. "But I might name some who are.

"At any rate, the terms of the contest are simple: to create a machine that best represents the gnomish outlook. The *essence of gnomitude*, as the old bounder called it."

He looked up at Gordusmajor's portrait, smiled almost affectionately.

"Deddalo thinks he has the inside track. Talos has good ideas, but putting him on the council would dry up an obvious source of bribery.

"And you? Well, out of sight, out of mind. You're a wrench in the works for Deddalo, and I'd watch your back if I were you."

Innova shuddered. Perhaps he should tell Scymnidus about the switched twins. And yet Deddalo was his long-time friend. Whom should he trust? Or should he trust anyone?

"All of this," Scymnidus continued, "makes this blueprint that much more curious. Why is he setting some kind of lethal device outside Talos's quarters?"

"To get Talos out of the way and assure a better chance at the contest?" Innova hated to bring it up, hated to imagine dark things of his old friend.

Scymnidus shook his head. "Too easy. If an anvil fell on Talos, the first one to be blamed would be Deddalo. Even someone unspeakably naïve would figure that one."

Innova blushed.

"No," Scymnidus said. "The answer is more complex and deeper. I think that the so-called Meryl Barium is *really* her sister Beryl. Together she and Deddalo are plotting the demise of old Incline Barium to hasten her inheritance . . . just as, a few months ago, they plotted the fragmentation of the *real* Meryl Barium, to establish the aforesaid Beryl as her father's only heir."

Innova gasped. "That's—"

"Ridiculous? Far-fetched and paranoid? Too diabolical? Well, you asked. And you're fully entitled to think what you like.

"But I have seen worse between child and parent."

Scymnidus glanced toward the smoldering desk, took a long draw from the dwarf spirits.

"Setting the lethal engine near Talos's dwelling will naturally cast suspicion on him, thereby eliminating Deddalo's chief competitor for the council seat. And once on the council, Deddalo can bury all the bones, destroy all the evidence, and Talos will be out of the way."

"But you said Talos doesn't have a chance," Innova objected. "That his money is worth more before the bench than upon it!"

Scymnidus shrugged. "Deddalo doesn't know that. He tends to overplan and think about things too much—a common failing of our people. But you're the wrench in the works, as I said. Don't be surprised if Deddalo has plans for you as well."

"What should I do, Cousin?" Innova asked meekly.

"Whatever you can," Scymnidus replied. "You'll be in danger wherever you turn, so I would do what I could to disrupt his schemes. Starting with the contest.

"I would do my best to keep him off the Philosophers' Council."

It was enough said. Stunned and confused, Innova stared off into space as Scymnidus elaborated on further theories, tying Deddalo's plan into some vast conspiracy of chaos that included the Knights of Takhisis, a band of smugglers off the coast of Ergoth, and a gully dwarf accountant somewhere on the Seventeenth Level.

Surely it was all nonsense, all Scymnidus's strange and far-reaching anxiety. But something had set Innova's thoughts in motion, and they moved back and forth, up and down like the dipping bird on Scymnidus's desk. . . .

Whose continual, perpetual motion suddenly drew the young gnome's interest, as he began a plan of his own.

It wouldn't hurt to keep Deddalo off that council, after all. And what was more . . .

A glamorous invention and a high position would make folks think well of Innovafertanimus. He would be, as he always wanted to be, the hero of news and of rumor.

It was as though a Life Quest had fallen, from some great and unimaginable height, squarely into his lap.

85

Chapter 11

They had come ashore on the western beaches of Sancrist, a few miles north of Heaven's Claws. Before them the foothills rose steeply into mountains, and even from their scattered encampments they could see the summits of Mount Nevermind cresting the surrounding peaks.

It was country the Commander dimly remembered. But he did not know how to feel: whether at home or ill at ease.

The death of Stormont had already paid dividends, or so Halion Khargos reckoned. The surviving subcommanders and the Acolyte Oliver appeared more submissive and subdued without the old Knight dividing their allegiances. Harmony had returned to Khargos's company, and if it was a harmony born of fear and uncertainty, so be it.

If the Knights of Takhisis were to lay siege to Mount Nevermind, there could be no dissent in the ranks.

On the first day after the landing, they sent forth reconnaissance—a dozen ravens, whose wings and sharp eyes could negotiate the treacherous mountains. Oliver assured the commander that this strategy would work: The birds would return, having scouted the gnome stronghold, and a simple spell would enable the Bone Acolyte to talk to them.

Halion Khargos waited in the gray billows of his spreading commander's tent Beside him, on the beach, a dozen campfires smoked and crackled, hissed as the soft ocean rains swept over them on humid afternoons. The Knights grew testy as the hours passed, the clerics among them auguring and chanting, while the Knights of the Lily, in charge of maintaining order among the brutes, shouted and menaced and finally brought forth the lash.

Again, almost as soon as it had subsided, Khargos began to hear mutterings from the subcommanders. Fleetwood and Hanna came to his tent on the second night, and their bickering lasted until the small hours of the morning.

The task was overwhelming, they claimed. Narrow passes through the mountains, sheer drops and sliding stones would take their toll among the Knights and brutes. Khargos could lose fifty, a hundred fighters before even reaching the slopes of Mount Nevermind.

Once there, the struggle was hardly over. The city defenses would be complicated, would probably backfire on the defenders, but the Knights would lose men due to sheer accident and gnomish incompetence.

The subcommanders cited Sester's Law: "If you want something broken, give it to a gnome."

Moreover, provisions were low. If it took more than a week to solve the puzzle of Mount Nevermind's fortifications, even the Knights would go hungry. And a hungry army is weak and restive.

To the objections of his subordinates, Halion Khargos had few solid answers. He could debate tactics for hours, haggle over morale and transport and supply lines, but in the end his argument was quite simple.

The Goddess and her Vision had brought him here.

A dark faith had set him on these shores. And now, at the mention of the name of Takhisis, Hanna and Fleetwood only nodded and looked away. As Knights of Takhisis, they had their own fragments of the Vision, received long ago at the Test. Who knew what the Goddess had told them in their most private communions?

Their faith was entangling with his own, and their war was a war of words.

Faith was hard. Especially since Halion Khargos's dreams were discordant, peopled with dark undefinable shapes that his waking thoughts could neither understand nor interpret.

*   *   *   *   *

Up the beach, in a cramped black tent removed from the encamped army, the Bone Acolyte Oliver, the solitary Knight of the Skull in Khargos's ranks, dreamed discordantly as well.

He did not know what the ravens would bring him, nor how the commander would interpret their bodings.

Too much chaos . A spell sent out . . .

Returned in a form that only the gods could guess.

It was this uncertainty that plagued the Bone Acolyte in his service to Halion Khargos. Like the Orders of Thorn and Lily, the Knights of the Skull, too, had sworn an allegiance to the chain of command and to the officers who governed them.

"One World Order," they said and believed. Those among them who had matured past slogans, who had undergone the Test of Takhisis, had their beliefs confirmed with a part of the Vision—a glimpse into the vast design of the Goddess.

It was a glimpse upon which Oliver had dwelt for years.

Older than Khargos by a decade, he had lived with his part of the Vision for three years before the Commander passed so readily, so easily through the forbidding Test. He had mulled over the knowledge with reverence, with the plodding scholarship of one who possessed only average wisdom and gifts.

It had been hard for Oliver, this passage through the ranks.

Harder still, when Khargos had dismissed the rest of his Order from this western raid, with the explanation that clerics "were not essential when the Commander is the Arm of the Dark Queen."

Not essential. The words still stung in remembrance.

At night Oliver would remember fragments of his own Deep Vision—how Takhisis had come to him promising that his role would be an important one, his service one of obedience and sacrifice. It had all seemed glamorous: He had fancied a monkish isolation, priestly fasts and long nights of prayer and vigil.

But the goddess had never returned to him. They said she never *did* return, that the quest of your life was to make sense of what revelation she had given you, to mull it in memory and in imagination.

It had left Oliver lonely.

Still, he might have lived with that loneliness, had he not found that his obedience was submission to an upstart boy, his sacrifice the knowledge that, despite all he had been told, this Halion Khargos was somehow chosen. Chosen to receive the Vision again and again. Chosen to rise into high command.

Chosen above all his fellows, including the cleric Oliver.

There is some part I shall play, Oliver told himself. It will not be the birds—I will be no boy's translator. The Goddess has chosen me for something as well, something precious and unique. Only time will show me the hem of that design. Time and waiting and unwavering belief.

He cast the bones and augured.

In the last few days he had become convinced that the Goddess Herself spoke to him through oracles.

At first he had questioned his own sanity: Takhisis had always spoken through the Vision. What need would the Dark Queen have for bones and needles?

Unless she was testing him, forcing him to find direction by indirection, as his old master had once put it. Here in the underground, where he could no longer augur with stars and winds, and where the water was stagnant and misdirected, the Goddess would naturally come to her priest in other signs, other omens.

Especially if, as he suspected, Halion Khargos's Vision had failed.

Oliver sat back on his heels and surveyed the random cast of the bones. Nothing. Disjointed symbols at best, which contradicted one another.

Nothing, and nothing to do but wait.

That night, in his lonely tent down the shingled beach, time and waiting seemed long, and belief seemed thin and short.

*   *   *   *   *

On the second day, half of the ravens returned. They were bedraggled, their feathers matted with dust and foul-smelling oils. They circled the camp and dropped in near-exhaustion to a perch upon a tent post.

Oliver wakened the commander from a fitful sleep in which dark, reptilian shapes had danced at the edge of his dreams and a steamboat rocked and whistled out on a distant sea. At the sound of the cleric's voice, Khargos lurched toward wakefulness; like climbing out of deep water, the mere act of waking left him dizzy and drained.

The messengers atop his tent croaked and boded, but Khargos felt his hope rising. He fought down impatience and eagerness, waited as Oliver craned his ear toward the sound, murmured some soft incantation, and began to translate.

"The air is thick and hot, they say. They say the city is breathing, that many boats on wheels encircle it."

Khargos sighed. Leave it to a cleric to draw a curtain of poetry between him and what he wanted to know. It was like some damned elven oracle, consorting with wildlife.

But at least the account was easy so far: Mount Nevermind was famous for the machinery that encircled it, for the steam-powered carts that darted in and out of its tunnels.

A breathing city. Boats on wheels. Clear enough.

"What else did they see, Oliver?"

The cleric frowned. "Something about high wind, about circles in the air and weight on their wings."

"And what do you make of this . . . lyricism, Oliver? What happened to the rest of their number?"

The oldest of the ravens cocked his head at Khargos's questions, regarded the commander with bright and brittle eyes.

Began to mutter and bode.

"Three of them, he says, were caught in a whirlpool of wind. And the wind drew them down into shiny tunnels. Made feathers of them—feathers and death cries."

"What does that mean, Oliver?"

The cleric frowned. "Some engine, I suppose. Some sort of wind tunnel or turbine."

It made sense to Khargos. No doubt the whole complex of Mount Nevermind was riddled with engines, with fans and air vents. Treacherous country for a winged scout.

The old bird coughed again, its murmurings so close to a recognizable language that Khargos found himself straining to understand, to translate. But in the end it was all bird cries. He turned to Oliver, who shook his head.

"And the other three," the cleric announced, "were felled by crossbows and baked into pies."

"Which means . . . ?"

"Which means exactly what I said," Oliver replied. "Or more precisely, what the old bird said. Somewhere up in that mountain, three families of gnomes are dining upon our reconnaissance."

*   *   *   *   *

It could not have been worse, Khargos supposed. An army stranded by the shoreline, awaiting information it could not gather.

Then the sea struck with surprising guile and cruelty.

Scarcely an hour after the ravens returned, the western horizon darkened with scudding clouds. A hard, warm rain bathed the beaches, and the tents pocked and buckled.

At an order from the commander, the Knights of Takhisis moved their encampments inland, into the spare woods that bordered the foothills. Now they had passed into country more dangerous, where the view of the sentinels was blocked by formations of worn rock, by scraggly evergreen. At once their morale, already low, seemed to sink further, bottoming in quarrels and threats.

Subcommander Fleetwood ordered his Knights to beat a squadron of the brutes, who had taken the opportunity to scavenge further inland. Scattering into the foothills, the barbarians returned to their punishment with the carcass of a drowned rabbit and a handful of inedible plants, the blue of their skins mottled now with rain and ill health.

One of them struck back at a Knight and was put to swordpoint before the glaring eyes of his companions.

As the Knights raised his tent amid a tangle of storm-downed limbs and branches, Halion Khargos took to the woods, seeking a quiet place to consult the Vision. A hundred yards from the new campsite, he found a level outcropping of rock in the shadow of a vine-covered cliff.

There he knelt, closed his eyes, and awaited the Goddess.

The green afterimages of sunlight on his eyelids gave way to a grayness. That grayness gave way in turn, to a cavernous darkness in which the rush and retreat of the sea faded into silence.

He shivered. Takhisis was approaching. At last, after a long absence of weeks, she was returning to her acolyte.

There among shadowy rocks, he watched the darkness in his soul take a darker shape, as the form of a woman began to materialize in the heart of the blackness. In a moment there would be words, gestures, a clear sight. Something to drive away confusion.

He could see her face now, pale in the midst of eternal night, extraordinarily and poisonously beautiful . . .

A shout from the shoreline dispelled the Vision.

* * * * * *

Out of the sea the creatures came—if you could call them creatures.

Shapeless eddies at the tide's edge, they rose to a man's height and drifted among the beached ships. The rain seemed to enter them and vanish, and a faint, silver steam swirled around them as they took on remotely human outlines.

Up the shore they came, the sand behind them vanishing as though they plowed deep furrows in the beach. The waters followed in their wake, filling the trenches and beginning to boil.

Helpless, too far away to order or command, Halion Khargos watched in horror.

The first sentries to reach the creatures were Ian and Davit, gallant Knights of the Thorn. Davit stepped forward with his sword drawn while Ian held back, his voice rising in an incantation above the crash and rustle of the breakers.

Stand back! prompted a voice from somewhere within the Commander. *You can do nothing.*

Let this take its course.

Dumbstruck, Khargos watched as one of the creatures extended a swirling, disjointed limb. For a moment the arm or tendril seemed to hover by itself in the rain. Then, wrapping around Davit's sword arm like a constricting serpent, it drew the young Knight into the whirlpool of rain and light and buckling air.

Davit cried out, but the cry was cut short. He vanished into the bowels of the thing—sword, armor, and all.

The creature continued up the shore toward Ian, trailing steam and ash and ignited sand.

For a moment, Ian stood his ground, his hands raised in supplication to the Goddess, a dark spell of warding half-chanted. Then he stopped.

He was listening to something in the sound of the waves. Something that drowned out his words and thoughts.

With a faint, despairing cry, somewhere between a sigh and a scream, he turned and ran toward the foothills. The thing behind him followed, then slowed, then spun into nothingness at the rocky margins of the beach.

By now a number of the Knights had armed themselves and come running, but the scene before them shook their considerable courage. Hesitant, they circled the churned and burning sand, the fires that not even the rain seemed capable of quenching.

Nothing happened. The creatures had vanished.

From his perch high among the rocks, Halion Khargos watched as steam wreathed the burning beach, as his company circled, broke ranks, and backed uncertainly toward the encampment.

Shadow wights, prompted the voice in his ear. *First wave of the oldest enemy*.

It was the voice of the Goddess. He cursed himself for thickheadedness, for stupidity.

Yet the Dark Queen sounded different, faint, as though she spoke at a mile's remove.

And . . . *tentative*?

The old seduction had faded from her voice, replaced by a thinness, an almost plaintive whining.

Perhaps I am imagining this, Khargos thought, as he hastened through the thin woods toward the camp, toward the fractured beach.

After all, it has been weeks since I heard her voice.

Perhaps this uncertainty is nothing more than my own doubt and fear.

He stopped at the edge of the smoldering sand. The rain had picked up, and the winds from the sea rushed across the breakers. Now the fires were flickering, guttering.

My own doubt and fear, Khargos thought.

That offers me no solace.

* * * * *

On the next morning, a cry from the beach awakened the Commander.

Blearily, with a feeling of unfocused dread, Khargos burst from his tent and stood on the rocks. Sunlight spangled the black ocean and, knee-deep in the receding tide, several of the Knights shouted and gestured, pointing out to sea.

Far beyond the Knights a solitary form in full armor, waded away from the shore, toward deeper and darker waters.

Not bothering to arm himself, dressed only in a black tunic, the Commander hastened toward the shoreline. As he ran the cries rose up to meet him.

Ian, they were saying. *Too deep . . .*

Crashing through branches and down an incline of rocks, catching his balance again and again, Khargos burst out of the tangle of trees and onto warm sand. Now the gesturing Knights were a stone's throw away. . . .

But the form in the far water had vanished, gone under.

"He spent the night alone," Subcommander Hanna explained quietly, as Khargos, dizzy and panting, reached her at the edge of the tide. "Lost in some kind of meditation. This morning he rose and armed himself. Walked between the sentries out toward the water. One of them said he was talking about *spent courage and failed spells*, about the *slow transformation of bone to coral*.

"They said he looked eager. Like he was going to pay court to some beautiful woman."

Khargos blinked. It was all too confusing.

"Whatever it was," Hanna said, "he was called out there. The sentries said he stopped and cupped his ear like he was

94

listening to something in the waves. Before they realized it, he was out beyond recall."

Together Khargos and Hanna stood on the beach, staring out over the shuddering water. Behind them, Subcommander Fleetwood called for a lifeboat, for strong backs at the oars, for divers. Everyone knew it was too late. Whatever new darkness the shadow wights had brought ashore had somehow entered young Ian, and summoned a darkness in him.

He had walked out to meet them, speaking desperate things to the air . . . with something like love in his eyes.

Chapter 12

There was a story Halion Khargos remembered from a childhood he would not mention. It had made him laugh because of its cruel absurdity, and now, beleaguered by powerful enemies on the beaches of Sancrist, he thought of it again.

He thought that it was no longer as funny.

A old gully dwarf, it seems, recently wedded to a young bride, had sought a way to renew his youth. The story of his quest was a long and rambling one, but at each stage of the journey the dwarf had lost an appendage—a finger bitten off by a bird, two toes crushed in a rockslide, his nose fallen off from frostbite when his quest took him to the edge of the Icewall.

Finally he achieved his goal. He found the potion in question and persuaded a dimwitted young countryman to lift the vial for him (after all, he was fingerless and could lift nothing himself). After drinking his fill, he offered his stupid companion a great reward if the lad would push him back home in a wheelbarrow.

Together, the two had weathered other adventures in which the old gully dwarf had lost one of his ears and what remained of his toes. At last he arrived home, lusting for his bride and gloating over having duped his thick assistant into carting him all over Ansalon.

The girl took one look at the pruned creature in the wheelbarrow and screamed with fright. It was less than an hour before she ran away with the dimwitted assistant.

Left on his own, abandoned by wife and fingers and toes, the old dwarf learned a hard lesson about appendages: Sometimes the last thing you keep is what you should have given up in the first place.

Halion Khargos felt like that hapless dwarf, there in the mountain foothills. It was as though all kinds of disorder had converged upon him, gradually paring away his strength and resources.

On the evening after Ian walked into the ocean, the commander decided that any action was better than no action at all. Calling together his captains, he announced his intentions to lead a party of Knights to the brim of Mount Nevermind. There, in full view of the strange gnome city, he would scout and reconnoiter and would plan the inevitable siege.

Subcommander Hanna and sixty-five Knights—three score chosen from the Order of the Lily, along with the four remaining Thorn Knights and the Bone Acolyte Oliver— would accompany him, along with a hundred of the brutes for transport and protection. They would climb through the foothills and find a path, for Khargos was reasonably sure that all roads in this part of Sancrist were of gnomish fashioning and would therefore lead to Mount Nevermind.

Fleetwood would remain on the shoreline in command of the rest of the company, still numbering nearly two hundred Knights and at least as many of the brutes. If two weeks were to pass with no report from reconnaissance, his orders were to give up the scouts as lost and set sail back to Ergoth.

It was not a plan with which the Subcommanders agreed. Hanna objected that a gnome road would be filled with false turns and pitfalls, that a scouting party would run a rocky gauntlet from which no survivors would return. Or if, by some incredible luck, they were to complete the journey, it would take far longer than a fortnight, and they would reach the shore to find that their ships had departed.

Very well, Khargos conceded. Let them wait for a month. Otherwise he held firm.

Fleetwood raised his voice in protest. He would be alone in command, at the head of demoralized Knights and increasingly unruly brutes. The main force on the beach would be subject to all kinds of upheaval—from a possible Solamnic attack to whatever new creatures the sea would offer. His part of the Vision spoke against it, he emphasized. The strategy edged on disaster.

At mention of the Vision, Khargos stared long and hard into his Subcommander's eyes. He could not tell whether

Fleetwood's thoughts were in communion with the Goddess or with his own doubts and misgivings.

After all, the Goddess was silent to him on this matter, as well.

There was a time, he thought, when I trusted these captains implicitly. He struggled to remember that time, to recover the trust that he once held for his subordinates.

That time was passed. The sea and the long silence of Takhisis had taken away much of the loyalty, and there in his rocky encampment, he imagined that he felt much as the dragon lords had in the long and disastrous War of the Lance.

Without the Dark Queen's guidance, evil was turning on evil again.

So he lied to Fleetwood and Hanna. He told them that the Goddess had visited him in his afternoon meditation, had set this very plan before him. Now there was nothing to do but follow her command, whether it led to victory or defeat.

For a moment he expected the ground to open and a dark cloud to cover him, usher him off to that part of the Abyss eternally reserved for liars and oathbreakers.

Instead he was surprised when the Subcommanders lowered their eyes, nodded in agreement. Something in the success of that lie shook him deeply—more deeply than any imagined vengeance.

* * * * *

They departed at dawn, choosing the most gradual incline into the foothills, and walking until the sun was clear of the mountains ahead of them.

At the head of the column were two of the Thorn Knights, distinguished for their sharpness of vision and intelligence. Following them were the brutes, tended by four ruthless Knights of the Lily, known for their strict devotion to discipline and the Commander.

Halion Khargos walked with Oliver and Subcommander Hanna in the midst of the remaining Knights of the Lily, and bringing up the rear were the remaining two Thorn Knights, who watched for pursuit and ambush and magic in the stark country through which the column passed.

Looking back from the heights onto the encampment, Khargos saw the shadows of tents and lean-tos begin to narrow as the morning pressed midway to noon. From this vantage the figures of Knight and brute were dwarfed, insectlike, mere markings on the long western coast of Sancrist.

He remembered looking back on a coast not far from here, years ago, in a fitful moonlight.

The memory made him shudder.

For the first time since childhood, Halion Khargos felt uncertain, unbearably small. But there was no retreat from this mission, unguided though it was by the judgments of Takhisis.

Only in the service of the Vision was a Knight of Takhisis allowed to lie. He had lied in what he believed to be the service of the Dark Queen's power, but no voice had confirmed or sustained his decision.

Would there be retreat from the lies he had told Hanna and Fleetwood? He was not certain, but he knew he was bound on a sharply different path and what lay before him was something out of his control.

A shout from ahead disrupted his thoughts, brought him back to the here and now. Torbern, a young Knight of the Thorn, had located a footpath and was calling him now.

"It winds through that notch in the hills and up the side of that mountain," Torbern proclaimed. "Heads roundabout, but eventually east, sir. I believe we can camp well within range by nightfall."

It would do for a good day's journey. Already the winds were picking up, and the company had cleared the line of forest in the foothills. Though the day was warm, several of the Knights drew forth their winter cloaks as protection against the gusts. Onward they traveled, their garments fluttering like gray wings, as the sky to the east grew cloudy and dark.

Two miles into the mountains as the scouts reckoned distance, the path curved upward along the side of a steep cliff. On the left hand the rock face jutted up hundreds of feet into low-hanging cloud. To the right, the edge of the path dropped away into a sheer canyon, littered with jagged rubble and parted by a shallow, slow-moving stream.

Khargos looked down over the precipice. The streambed some hundred feet below was tangled by stunted, scraggly plants—leafless, woody undergrowth that snaked over the rocks like dry, arthritic fingers. It was a menacing landscape, and immediately his instincts shouted *ambush*.

Hanna paused beside her Commander, looked down into the bleak gorge.

"It won't come from that direction," she advised softly, reading Khargos's thoughts. "My fears lie above us. That canopy of cloud could hide an army, not to mention a well-trained band of partisans, who could rain rocks and arrows on us for days."

Khargos shook his head. "If we can't see up, they can't see down," he concluded. "But something tells me this place is dangerous not for the drop alone."

So they stood, contemplated, and at last sent the sure-footed Torbern, escorted by three brutes, up the path before them.

The capable Thorn Knight climbed up the trail, sometimes dropping on all fours to clamber up shifting rubble, then standing upright again, his back against the cliff face, to slip around a boulder that had apparently dropped upon the path in some long-ago time. Always, the gnarled plants were a hazard, for some of them had sprouted between fissures in the stone, surprisingly far away from a constant source of water.

Behind him, the brutes followed slowly, muttering and whining, sometimes crouching in a posture of fear.

It unsettled Khargos, who had come to believe that the barbarians were afraid of nothing. There was something amid the rocks and thin air that had cast a pall over the whole party, and behind him Khargos heard the sounds of muttered prayer—to Takhisis, to Zeboim the protectress of sea journeys, to whatever unnameable gods the crude religions of the brutes held holy.

Finally, at the edge of the officers' sight, Torbern paused. The path had crested where he stood and seemed to bend around the mountainside, where it vanished from view.

Torbern signaled, beckoned the company up the trail.

Suddenly, the path dissolved beneath him. One minute the rocky trail supported the Thorn Knight, as solid and substantial as accustomed ground. Then, in an instant, the stones at Torbern's feet clouded in a gray and whirling mist, and the Knight fell through them as if he was falling through smoke or vapor.

He was gone, and the far-off sound of a cry and something slapping the side of the cliff face echoed down the path until it reached the shocked ears of the commanders.

Instantly, the company sprang into confused action. Swords were drawn, Knights fumbled at helmets and shields. The brutes huddled and roared in fear and anger, their unnatural outcry drowning Khargos's commands.

The Commander stalked up the column, restoring order. He seized a yammering brute and shook the thing to silence, as its blue-coated companions, scrambling up the cliff face in outrage and chaos, fell silent as well, their haunted eyes fixed on the young Knight before them.

Khargos raced up the trail, wrestling down the fear that the rocks at his feet would dissolve as well. Sheer recklessness goaded him on—sheer recklessness and an instinct that told him disorder would be worse than this unstable trail, more disastrous than a vanishing foothold.

Finally, breathing raggedly, he stood at the spot where Torbern had fallen. Instead of a crest to the path, there was nothing. The trail along the side of the mountain had sheared off, resuming ten feet ahead after a sudden bend.

He looked down the face of the cliff. The dry plants were churning like swarming flies over the shattered body of Torbern. From a distance, Khargos caught the dark glitter of blood, the white of bone amid the thrashing branches.

The plants were devouring the Knight. There in the gorge, some terrible thing was feeding.

"I have heard of such things, Commander," a soft voice whispered at Khargos's shoulder, "but until now, I had never seen them."

101

Khargos startled. For a second swifter than thought, he imagined that the Goddess had returned to him.

But it was the Bone Acolyte Oliver, standing beside his Commander, his gray robe rent with the rocks and running.

"What . . . what *is* it?" Khargos asked, when he had recovered his breath.

"Mirago," Oliver replied. "Yet another of the monsters of Chaos, a cousin to those things that rose from the water back at the encampment. This mirago is an illusion with some kind of crude will and intelligence. I have heard that they could mask themselves as rocks, as pools of standing water, as a fork in the road, all the better to waylay whoever believes they are what they appear to be."

The cleric drew in a deep breath. "Never did I imagine how large they were."

Khargos followed his gaze down into the mindless flailing of branches.

They were still far away from Mount Nevermind. There was still time to return to the encampment on the shore. But to all the Knights under his command, retreat would mean that the Vision had somehow failed.

Or, worse still, that he had not followed the Vision at all.

"Gather the brutes," he ordered quietly, his right hand slipping to his sword by reflex. "Build a bridge of rope across the break in the pathway. I will bring this island to order or die in the will of the Goddess."

*   *   *   *   *

The path broke again and again in the journey to Mount Nevermind. Once a tangle of brush at the trailside sprang to a nervous life as the company passed, whipping its dry tendrils about the ankles of a straggling brute and flogging the roaring creature to death against a mottled rock face.

Once the path stopped altogether at a wall of stone, and it was an hour before a desperate Khargos ordered a brute at sword point to walk straight into that wall, which opened to swallow him, then vanished, leaving a rubble of charred flesh and ash scattered over the now-unobstructed trail.

It was a ruinous journey. By the time Khargos saw the smoke from the crest of Mount Nevermind, he had lost five Knights and twenty brutes. Now the company balked at the whistle of winds, at the distant cry of a mountain eagle, fearing that their numbers could no longer withstand an assembled army.

The mountain lay at the end of this rocky gauntlet, and from a steep overlook, Halion Khargos looked across a wide canyon at the fabled, extinct volcano, the maze of tunnels and cart tracks.

For a long time, the Commander crouched amid rubble and brambles, inspecting the city complex. His siege-trained eye looked for gaps in defense, for weaknesses in the fissures and shafts.

Most of the mountain was veiled in steam, its entrances guarded not so much by a garrison as by incomprehensible machines. Bells rang, whistles shrieked into the thin air, and from somewhere in the midst of the vapors a pair of roman candles spurted out blue fire that fell harmlessly over a faraway southern valley.

"A defense of absurdity," Khargos said to Hanna, who had taken a position beside him. "There is no logic in these defenses, but they make an illogical sense."

The unpredictability and sheer incompetence of the gnomes is their strength, was the reply. It came from Hanna's direction, but not in her voice.

Startled, Khargos glanced toward his subcommander, who crouched in deep thought, her eyes on the ragged floor of the canyon.

She had not spoken. The voice was from elsewhere.

Khargos closed his eyes. The afterimage of sunlight cast a green, hulking mountain shape on the back of his eyelids, but soon that image faded into a welcome darkness . . .

At the edge of which a pale woman sat enthroned, black stones glittering from a pendant at her throat.

There is something different now, the Goddess whispered. *Look again at Mount Nevermind. No, with your eyes closed. I will allow you sight in darkness.*

As though it, too, was an afterimage of light, the city appeared on the back of his eyelids, the confusion of gadgetry and noise somehow less confusing.

As though somehow, all the machinery was becoming synchronized, running together in some new order, too complicated and large for him to understand.

The Vision faded, its largeness eluding his thoughts. Now the Goddess stood before him again, and he was ashamed.

Yes, it is there, he confessed in silence. The order. The intricate binding of machine to machine.

Something I had not figured.

It is not completed yet, the Dark Queen replied. *This order that you sense is . . . in process. It will bear fruit, but not now.*

And not for the gnomes. You will reap its advantages in a fast approaching time.

But I have failed, Khargos thought. Failed the Vision. Failed you.

You have not failed me, she said. *Not yet.*

For your promptings are my promptings, Halion Khargos. Your instincts are so aligned with my will that your thoughts are a perpetual Vision, your actions the flesh of my desire.

Darkness stirred in him, and the familiar wild passion.

He waited for her command, and her words, though they were obscure and strange, seemed to interpret his waiting.

Stay here, she said. *Oh, that is right and true, stay here.*

Your entrance to the mountain is approaching. Not by strategy, not by siegecraft, but in the disenchanted journey of one who dwells in the city.

Betrayal has always been a favorite pastime of mine.

And treason will hand you this city.

Chapter 13

Khargos had noticed with his siegemaster's eye, the machinery on the surface of Mount Nevermind had begun to change.

But it was changing in a way that no observer of gnomish life could predict or understand.

The same gadgetry had encircled the mountain for years: innumerable devices designed for communication, transport, and defense. Steam cart rails snaked over mazes of spring snares and pulley lures, cogwheel winnowers and hydraulic trapdoors.

Only a few of the devices worked; the rest misfired or lay idle. Instead of repairing them, which was not as interesting as inventing something new, each generation of engineers simply layered them over with different, new, and equally worthless contraptions.

The catch was that any one of the machines *might* work at any one time. Any intruder or invader (and even visitors, for that matter) stood a fairly good chance of being waylaid, mauled, or entangled before reaching the tunnel systems of the mountain.

But in the last few days, the machinery had adjusted.

Perhaps it was mysterious repairmen. After all, an old gnome folktale claimed that elves would come at night and fix broken things. But philosophers maintained it was simply the law of averages, that sooner or later a machine will work, if only by chance. This was a unique period in gnome history when almost everything was working, exceptionally well and all at once.

Pulley systems were lifting and lowering better than usual, but it was more than that: All of a sudden, folks were discovering that the pulleys were unaccountably connected to other systems deeper in Mount Nevermind.

There were also the cart tracks along the western face of

the mountain. Once the source of hundreds of minor accidents and the butt of hundreds of jokes, they had degenerated into a sort of amusement park ride for the most reckless of gnome adolescents. Imagine the surprise when these tracks were suddenly and safely linked to one another, and when the carts ended up at real destinations!

Smaller, more particular things began to work as well. The system of spike traps on the southern crest, set hundreds of years ago by a military engineer, sprang suddenly to life, nearly impaling a family of gulley dwarves who had nested in its workings.

Even the metavox was working—that system of pipes and tubing that netted the mountain surface like tracery. It was designed two centuries ago to provide a means of communication between sentries throughout the citadel. Over two hundred years, voices and sounds had raced through the tubes and blended into complete confusion, inventing three new dialects (Tubish, Shout, and Metaphonics) as listeners sought to understand the chaos they were hearing. Now, for some reason, everything raced down the pipes in perfect gnomish—perfect because grammar was corrected, lisps healed, and even tone-deafness was becoming a thing of the past.

Whatever was happening, it was untraveled country for the gnome society.

Some were saying that it all had begun a week ago, at the Philosophers' Test.

* * * * *

The Test was convened as competition. A seat had opened on the Guild Council, and though most of the peoples of Krynn would have filled that seat with an experienced and qualified guild member, the gnomes had long ago discovered the excitement of untrained or unstable governors.

Hence the contest, set by the High Justice Gordusmajor, to design a Philosophical Machine. This machine, according to the rules, was to perform an action most representative of the gnome people, outlook, and civilization.

The essence of gnomitude.

The fact that the purpose of a Philosophical Machine was so lofty was perhaps part of the reason there were so few competitors. Only six had announced their intentions to compete. Three of them—Talos, Deddalo, and Dioptra, a big-eared fellow from the Twenty-Fourth Level—had managed to survive the testing of their respective inventions.

The finalists stood before the Philosophers' Tribunal, in the same onyx-floored hall where two of them had been tried only five months before. As circumstance would have it, only three justices were present. Julius had fallen from some height during the previous week's cross-examination of a character witness, and his place in the scales had been assumed by an iron anvil.

There was a joke going around Mount Nevermind that the intellectual weight of the bench had increased.

To the three remaining judges—Harpos, Ballista, and of course the redoubtable Gordusmajor—the contestants presented their inventions. It was obvious that each had differing thoughts as to what constituted "gnomitude."

Gnomitude was an elusive quality, Dioptra explained, the bronze, onion-shaped device in his hand beginning to whir and whistle. It was his conclusion that a principal ingredient was curiosity. That was why—

Before he could go any further, Gordusmajor interrupted his little speech.

"Go away," the High Justice ordered. "I don't want to know about your invention."

"But Lord High Justice! Your Eminent Part and Parcel!" Dioptra exclaimed. "Why, by the omnipotent tools of Immortal Reorx, would you—"

"I am just not interested," Gordusmajor interrupted again. "Go away."

Having pronounced, the High Justice glared down any objection from his colleagues on the bench. Harpos looked away, while Ballista buried his sizeable nose in a scroll of domestic disputes.

The anvil, predictably, was silent.

"Generosity," Talos began, "is the defining characteristic of our people. Which is why this machine reflects the essence of gnomitude."

He produced a machine that looked, for all intents and purposes, like a double boiler on wheels.

"And what is this?" Gordusmajor asked eagerly. The prospect of wealthy young Talos speaking of *generosity* was encouraging, even exciting.

"What is, High Justice, the philosopher's stone?" Talos began.

Those in the gallery could see that the youngster was quite pleased with himself.

"Old wives' tale," Gordusmajor replied. "It was supposed to turn lead to gold."

Then the enormity of his answer hit him.

"Talos! Do you mean . . . "

Talos nodded triumphantly.

The old justice's eyes narrowed. "Then give it to me," he commanded. "Of all machines it is this one I want for my own."

"Remember, Justice Gordusmajor," Justice Harpos chided, "according to Master Talos, the essence of gnomitude is *generosity*."

"Which is why he should give the machine to *me*!" Gordusmajor cried, reaching for the device in question.

"I am fully prepared to do so, Lord High Justice," Talos offered. "But first, perhaps you would want to see how the machine operates."

It was then that Deddalo entered the chamber, accompanied by two veiled females. He was always one for a dramatic entrance, and the justices, remembering his speech in this very room a few months before, turned their attention to him and to his mysterious companions.

When all eyes but his own shifted to Deddalo, High Justice Gordusmajor leaned forward dangerously over the lip of the scale pan, wrapped his thick fingers around Talos's invention, and confiscated the contraption as Guild Exhibit Number One.

Meanwhile, Deddalo had begun to speak. "I place before you, gentlemen of the Philosophers' Tribunal, the Barium twins, Beryl and Meryl."

The two figures in his company lifted their veils.

"And I challenge you," Deddalo continued, "to tell me which of these is flesh and bone, and which an apparatus of my own contriving, made of wire and metal."

"The one on the left is the real one," High Justice Gordusmajor said at once.

The other justices agreed.

When all was considered, it was an easy decision. The gnome-fashioned Barium twin was distinguished by the rivets in her neck, the bronze hinges on her jaw, and the lazing right eye, which creaked softly as it turned in the socket.

A faint, cracked chiming from somewhere in the interiors of the creature marked a feeble attempt at a heartbeat.

For a moment, the Tribunal was shocked into silence. From his place at the center of the hall, Talos cried out and stepped toward the living female, crying "Meryl!" until the strong hands of the bailiff restrained him.

His Meryl, standing by Deddalo and the ornamental pool, did not seem nearly as glad to see *him*.

At last, Gordusmajor, having hidden Talos's profitable machine in the rubble that littered his scale pan, spoke up in disbelief and outrage.

"Why, Master Deddalo, in the great metallic and laboring name of Reorx, did you think we would be deceived by this . . . this . . . *contrivance*?"

"Not for a moment," Deddalo replied. A strange, conniving smile spread over his face. "To deceive you was never my plan, High Justice Gordusmajor. Instead, I followed the rules of the contest, to express the *essence of gnomitude*, which is neither deceit nor duplicity, but ambition alone."

Gordusmajor leaned back on his bench. "Then explain."

"Why, it's simple. What, I ask you, is more ambitious than to attempt the creation of life? And what if I have fallen short, Your Excellency, when it is ambition alone that defines the essence of our people, and in the attempt I have shown the greatest ambition, the reach that exceeds my grasp?"

Gordusmajor's eyes narrowed. The cogs and sprockets that animated the false Barium twin were no longer the only wheels turning in the chamber, as the outsized Justice schemed and reckoned.

It was clever. The idea overshadowed the invention, but all in all it was ingenious.

When all was said and done, wasn't it Deddalo whom Gordusmajor wanted on the council?

"Admirable effort, my boy! Your invention is *philosophically* the best by far, and if there are no further challengers . . . "

It was then that Innova stepped into the Tribunal Chamber.

*   *   *   *   *

Something about the young gnome seemed hardened, weathered, as though he had passed through a fierce and remarkable storm. His clothes were ill-fitting, as though travel had made him lean, and in his eyes was a look of terrible determination.

In confidence he stepped to the bench and handed a note to the High Justice.

Gordusmajor read and gaped. His plump cheeks billowed and flushed, and he cast a sidelong glance at the other justices, at Dioptra and Talos and Deddalo.

"I have before me a motion from the Counselor Scymnidus," he said. "In this note our esteemed colleague points out that the laws of Mount Nevermind—especially those laws set forth in Codex Seven Hundred and Two, Subsections Twenty-One, Twenty-Seven, and Seventy-Four—maintain that a contest is not over until the winner has been announced. The Counselor adds other contributing evidence, which, since it relates to the activities of *one* of our Justices regarding the wife of the absent Justice Julius, will go unheard in these chambers."

Gordusmajor cast an accusing eye toward Justice Ballista, who stared back with a look of blank consternation.

Everyone in the chamber knew that Diamant Julius was free with her affections. Everyone also knew that Gordusmajor himself crept through the Twenty-Eighth Level at night, and that the back door of Justice Julius' house was opened to a particularly heavy knock, wide enough to permit a particularly girthsome entrance.

"Given this . . . *legal precedence*," Gordusmajor continued uncomfortably, "it is only right that we hear out the motion of Innovafertanimusmutatasdicereformas."

It was then that Innova wheeled in the Paradise Machine.

* * * * *

Of all the machines in the Guild Contest, it was the most simple.

As far as the Justices could tell, it was a lever made to resemble a goose or an ostrich, oversized and painted in gaudy oranges and yellows. Innova set it by the ornamental pool in the corner of the chamber. Producing a vial from his pocket, he oiled the fulcrum with a viscous, silvery substance, then dipped the beak of the fanciful creature into the still water.

Back and forth the lever went, as though the creature had taken on life, as though it was rocking and drinking. Its small jewelled eyes stared flatly into the pool, and there were some in the audience that day who would swear later that they saw the glitter of thirst arise from the creature's face.

It continued, rocking and drinking, drinking and rocking. Innova stepped away from the device and faced the bench.

"Most eminent Justices, colleagues, and witnesses. I give you eternity—technical and mechanical and no doubt actual—in the form of a wooden goose!"

And sure enough, the thing kept going. For an hour, the justices watched skeptically, and then with increasing awe, as the absurd mechanical bird swivelled and dipped. Soon the interest of those in the gallery began to flag, and snores and coughs rumbled through the chamber.

Deddalo's mechanical Barium twin, left unattended, chugged merrily across the floor until she bumped into a corner, then whirred and whistled, her wheels turning uselessly, sending up sparks into the smoky air.

All the while, the perpetual goose held Gordusmajor's attentions.

By the third hour, even Harpos and Ballista were restless. They called out from their perch in the scale pan, letting it be known that they had reached a decision. Innova's remarkable machine had won the contest.

Still High Justice Gordusmajor watched, as the long afternoon passed into night, and the gallery emptied. Nor had the old gnome reached a verdict by morning, watching attentively as the machine still bobbed and tilted, unflagging in its mindless energy.

It was then that Innova attached the butter churn to the back of the bird and declared that his invention had conquered the Second Law of Speculative Dynamics.

"For if this machine will churn butter until the end of time," he explained proudly, "think of what it might do with a piston attached to its tail!"

At once, there was a commotion in the upper gallery. The loftiness of the idea, Innova told himself, had caught on and floated to the rafters, where a pair of enterprising gnomes understood its implications. The two leapt heroically from the balcony—one equipped with springs on the soles of his boots, the other clutching a tattered umbrella.

In violation of expected physics (or perhaps because the umbrella turned inside out in mid-flight), these foresighted fellows struck the floor at the same time, one recovering from his daze at about the same moment the other left off bouncing. Together they scurried toward the machine and, producing an auger and mallet from a bulging sack, began hammering a hole at the base of the churn.

"Perpetual motion, High Justice Gordusmajor!" Innova continued. "An eternity of power to spark any and every machine in the city! To light every level and power each drill and handcart!"

By this time, the hole in the churn was wide enough to insert powder and percussion caps. Now another device was attached to the slowly moving shaft of the machine: a sharply curved metal rod, to which the smaller of the gnomes—whom Innova now recognized as a rather ambitious young scamp named Trevantine—began tying a spoon, clumsily because of the great difficulty in tying anything to a moving object.

"The young fellow has a notion, Most Discerning Justice Gordusmajor," Innova announced, his speech becoming more involved, more legal. "Oh, this bird alone is probably not enough for my vast and airy design. There's no space on one particular machine to attach *everything*, and even attachments upon attachments might not be enough to mobilize the whole city. . . . "

Trevantine set a bucket of black powder so that the pivoting spoon brushed through it on its way into the cavity of the churn. And Innova continued.

"But the basic machine is easily made, and with five of them—ten at the most—all of Mount Nevermind would run like a dwarven clock. And it would run for as long as the underground water lasts. Which, given the constant rain over Sancrist . . . "

The powder scattered over the plunging churn shaft and the percussion cap, and the first of a series of rapid-fire explosions echoed in the Tribunal Hall.

"All machines would run forever!" Gordusmajor shouted over the noise. "Or as close to forever as we can imagine!"

It was a dizzying concept. The chamber fell silent except for the powder explosions, and after a while, the continual bangings and sparks became part of the background, almost indistinguishable from the faint explosions from distant, unconnected machines on the Thirtieth Level and in the levels below.

The enormous High Justice fell silent at the thought of eternity. Those who remained in the chamber, when their attentions turned from the rattle and backfire, could only guess at what was passing through his mind.

Was his personal ambition warring with his philosopher's instinct? Or was it something far more simple: Was he figuring the angles and benefits of Innova's amazing machine for his own brimming pockets?

It was probably a little of both, Innova guessed later. But there was *room* for both. And with the Paradise Machine, there would be *time* for both, as well.

"Innova will sit on the Philosopher's Council," Gordusmajor decreed at last. "He has won the contest and won it ably."

The Paradise Machine tilted and pumped serenely. The spoon slipped ineffectually over the lowered powder in the bucket.

The explosions stopped. Trevantine and his companion were already examining the Paradise Machine, searching for a way that its constant motion could be used to replenish the powder.

The remaining spectators burst into applause.

"But the contest has been won *illegally*!" Deddalo protested over the noise. "Innova has yet to serve the remainder of his sentence for undue cause and effect!"

"A sentence he has fulfilled," Gordusmajor replied quickly, with a glance at the note from Scymnidus. "For Miss Meryl Barium serves as evidence that *both* of the twins were not vaporized, and therefore, by simple arithmetic, the sentence is halved."

It was pure, self-serving mathematics, Innova thought, but by Reorx, it would work! Now whatever outrage Deddalo was planning—to Talos, to the Barium inheritance, to anything and everything in Mount Nevermind—he could no longer do it from the powerful seat on the Philosophers' Council.

Innova could use that same, far-reaching power to stop whatever crimes Deddalo had brewing. What was more, as a new council member, he would be a celebrity of sorts, the talk of the upper levels, the inventor of a perpetual machine.

And he would get to wear those ornate council robes.

Deddalo muttered an angry *congratulations* to his old friend and stalked from the room with the living Barium girl, leaving his automaton chugging aimlessly in the chamber corner.

Talos rushed after them, calling out for Meryl, but Deddalo's companion did not look back. Guardsmen restrained Talos, and finally he ceased struggling, watching the departing girl as a look of profound sadness passed over his face.

As he watched Deddalo leave, Innova remembered the last time they had stood in the court. He recalled how his capable, eloquent friend had transformed the facts into a glorious lie with the skill and invention of a master alchemist.

Yes, Deddalo was a capable friend, with talents that did not lend themselves to honesty. He would continue to use those talents.

Innova would have to be on guard.

Chapter 14

Halion Khargos was on guard as well, from his vantage near Mount Nevermind.

The Goddess had told him to wait, and he waited mindfully, his days spent in the high rocks, his nights in meditation.

Those nights were disappointing. Time and again over the course of a week, he awaited the Dark Queen, who chose not to reveal herself.

When each morning came, Khargos would look across the yawning canyon at the gnome capital, where it seemed that the defenses were changing daily. In the midst of the chaos of gates and rotating bronze battlements, encircling tracks and a strange new series of warning bells that seemed to be powered by levers, he began to glimpse a larger order he had not seen before.

Each day some of the defenses would vanish. Most were replaced by new engines and devices, but in some places the groma and hodometers and double-action pumps gave way to what seemed to be solid rock face but was probably a new and effective form of camouflage.

Mount Nevermind's defenses were being linked together by resourceful engineers, Khargos thought at first. He saw some gnomes on the outer slopes of the mountain, staggering behind huge wheelbarrows containing levers and wires. However, he had little confidence in their constant tinkering and their connection of machine to machine: After all, resourceful engineers were virtually unknown among the gnome people.

It was a contradiction he could not understand, until the third day of his vigil, when he drew a conclusion so wild that he believed the Goddess herself had bestowed the knowledge.

The defenses were linking to each other on their own, in an almost magical series of reactions, beyond even the fiddlings of the engineers. It defied all physics that Khargos understood, and yet his instincts told him he had been given some kind of answer.

Meanwhile, his escort of Knights had settled into lonely vigil as well. Braving the cold mountain nights without benefit of warming fires, they crouched miserably in hidden caves and alcoves, their food running out and the brutes under their command increasingly surly and restless.

All of them waited, with little or nothing to do.

Except the messenger.

From his ranks, the Commander had chosen one of the remaining Thorn Knights—a young man named Butler, younger even than Khargos himself. This lad was distinguished for his wits and resourcefulness, for his sense of high country and mountainous passages.

It was Butler whom the Commander sent back to the encampment, with orders that he guide Fleetwood and the rest of the company east through the mountains of Sancrist.

For the siege of Mount Nevermind was approaching. Khargos trusted his fragmentary Vision, dwelt in the faith that the Goddess was about to reveal her strategies. Whatever she had promised, she would deliver in due time.

*   *   *   *   *

It did not surprise him when, after a week of waiting, Hanna reported that the sentries had captured a gnome scaling the near side of the canyon.

Khargos had been sitting alone in an outcropping of limestone, his thoughts preoccupied with the elusive Vision. Though he considered himself the most loyal of the Dark Queen's followers, this kind of waiting troubled him all the more.

It was a kind of absurdity. Here he was, in the midst of the mountains, laying siege to a city which did not yet know he was there, whose defenders sat by as the machinery of defense repaired and extended itself.

Halion Khargos felt things slipping out of his grasp. And it unnerved him. So he was grateful when Hanna burst in on his solitude, informed him that, at last, something had *happened*.

"The creature is dressed in black," she explained in answer to his questions. "Head to toe, like some bantam assassin. Hard to spot in the darkness as he slipped out of the city, and he might well have passed through our lines, except that the fool had attached a miner's lamp to his helmet. Even so, we might not have noticed, had he not lost his footing in the rocks above and fallen twenty feet onto one of the brutes.

"That is, if he was traveling farther. If his destination was not this encampment. If he wasn't spying . . . or worse."

Khargos smiled wearily. The Subcommander had already tried and sentenced the intruder. The whole camp was twitching for something to do, and torture or execution— though frowned on in general by the Blood Oath—would probably be urged by one of the Knights, who would suddenly reinterpret his Deep Vision to include these forms of entertainment.

"Bring the gnome to me," the Commander ordered. "I shall question him, then let the Vision decide his guilt or innocence. You may be right. He may have been sent by forces stronger than chance. But I shall determine that—"

He caught himself.

"Or rather the Goddess will determine that. Through my agency."

*   *   *   *   *

Yes, the gnome was frightened.

Khargos had seen to that. He had received the trembling captive dressed in full battle armor, his plumed helmet nodding and menacing.

Faced with such intimidation, the poor thing could only wobble and stammer, pushing back his glowing helmet to reveal a crown of ruddy hair, a patchy beard, and brown eyes—one of which was half-veiled by a drooping eyelid.

Despite himself, Khargos enjoyed the gnome's discomfort.

"I . . . I was coming to you across the mountains," the prisoner began, "braving journey parlous and intricate, past assembling defenses and profusions of wires and inclines.

117

Coming for one purpose alone: to ask your aid. For things have changed in Mount Nevermind, O judicious Knight of our mutual Dark Queen, and they are not for the better, but certainly, inevitably . . . "

"Enough prelude and jabber!" Khargos interrupted. "What is your name?"

"Does it matter?"

"If I *say* it matters, it matters," Khargos declared, his voice soft and level. No shouting, he thought.

Greater fear arises from understatement and quiet.

"Innova," the gnome murmured. "By all the gods of the gnomes that watch over my enterprise, my name . . . is Innova."

The creature met the Commander's gaze. His drooping eyelid fluttered open, until to Khargos he looked like all other gnomes, a shivering, pathetic little figure crouched between two Knights of the Lily.

"I fear that the changes are partly my fault," this Innova said, searching Khargos's face for any response, any reaction. "For you see, I have invented . . . a machine to set all machines in order. A device that transforms the disorder of our infrastructure into something rich and strange, as complicated and efficient as the physics of a small universe."

Khargos sighed. He had heard such foolishness before, usually from the mouths of traitors. A boast, a promise, a prophecy, that would serve as a prelude to some vile treachery.

This creature would ask for favors in return—for money, for a position of power in a puppet government, sometimes for a female or for obscure knowledge.

For something to soften his betrayal of family and friends.

Halion Khargos already knew this Innova. The smell of his kind, whether human or dwarf or elf, had clouded the air of Krynn for generations. Eventually this creature would receive nothing short of justice. The Commander would see to that.

In the meantime, the gnome could be used. If there were anything to its boasts—anything at all—Mount Nevermind might be a place where the Knights of Takhisis could stand against Chaos. At the least, with the gnome city conquered, Halion Khargos would have fulfilled the will of the Goddess.

After all, she had told him to wait for something. For *the disenchanted journey of one who dwells in the city*.

"Tell me, Innova," Khargos said, his voice soft and with a hint of an actual kindness, because despite himself, something in him pitied the wretch, pitied a falseness he would never forgive in himself. "Tell me your offer, and tell me what you hope to receive in return from Takhisis."

The gnome cleared his throat. "The process of aligning our machineries," he began, "seems to be—shall I say *is*? an intricate one. It will take days at best, for all reactions and circuitry must be tested for its causal proclivities, its ... interrelatedness."

Khargos sighed. "Go on."

"Passages into the city remain unguarded," the gnome explained. "Some near the highest levels of the mountain, where the mirrors have been trained on a single point in an experiment to see whether reflected light can ignite stone. I know the city up and down, like the rooms of my own chambers."

"And ... "

"And can serve as your guide. Providing, of course, that one such as I could enable your ... higher purpose."

Khargos removed his helmet, set it gently on the ground. "And you will do this for ... what compensation? What reward?"

"No money," the gnome began. "I am beyond the limiting demands of coinage. And no position of power in your government, for I assume that you *will* govern Mount Nevermind once you have—settled there."

"Most generous of you," Khargos observed ironically.

"I am the soul of generosity," the gnome replied, "and of honor itself. For though the betrayal of one's own city may seem abject and dishonorable, it is my allegiance to a higher principle that motivates me."

"No doubt." Khargos could barely mask a smile.

The gnome nodded enthusiastically. "And it is honor— *your* honor—that I would ask in return. I would ask your

119

promise, on your Blood Oath and on your Code, on whatever else accrues to your splendid and knightly dominance, that you would leave untouched only the workings of the Philosophers' Guild and the procedures of gnomish inheritance laws. For our people must know a sense of continuity, and must retain their powers of free thought and of speculation."

Continuity. Free thought. Khargos stared at the wide-eyed gnome.

He had underestimated his captive. The creature had an obscure agenda—some gnomish dispute, no doubt. Some small prospect of riches or prosperity.

No money, no power, indeed!

Khargos considered his own situation. His troops beset by fierce, unpredictable enemies. He did not have much time.

Mount Nevermind seemed even more important if there was anything to this gnome's report that the defenses of the city were shifting, evolving, becoming something almost magically formidable.

"Is that all you ask? It will be dangerous country for you, Master Innova. The betrayer, the invader's gnome."

"There are plenty of places to hide in Mount Nevermind," the gnome replied, "caverns and abandoned tunnels. Chambers unoccupied for centuries. High-rise housing that was interesting to plan and boring to build and was therefore abandoned."

The miner's candle in the gnome's helmet sputtered and went out, but the creature was caught up in his own descriptions, and scarcely seemed to notice.

"The city is a maze," he concluded, "and no Paradise Machine will change that fact—at least not for years, until old wrongs are forgotten and Mount Nevermind has settled into your wise and honorable governance."

Khargos stood beside the gnome, towering over him. "So in return, all you want is this: noninterference in the workings of a solitary guild and a solitary series of laws? My honor would be bound to nothing else?"

The gnome smiled. "You are the right hand of Takhisis in Sancrist. I know that you will rule my people with wisdom and justice."

You know nothing of the sort, you despicable schemer, Khargos thought bitterly. Nor do you care what I do, as long as my hands are off your little bailiwick. But this agreement gives me room to maneuver. And justice will find you, Master Innova.

There will be no tunnel in which you can hide.

"Very well, then," Khargos agreed coldly, putting on his helmet and signaling to Subcommander Hanna to muster the troops. "We are agreed, and there is no better time to set forth than the moment at hand. I shall consult with Oliver for augury and prayer, and we shall depart within the hour."

Chapter 15

When the anvil fell on old Incline Barium, Talos was the first who was blamed.

After all, the mishap took place in the narrow courtyard off Talos's chambers, and the rumor swept quickly through the Thirtieth Level that the old gnome had been invited there. Paying one of his many social calls, Incline had not noticed the springboard beneath his feet—the very board that sent the anvil swinging over the courtyard like a hell-bent pendulum.

Hurtling through space, its heavy iron weight picking up speed in the downswing of the arc, it had slipped from the rope that held it—all agreed that the slipping was carefully engineered—and sailed fifty yards in the air toward the secluded open space where Incline Barium stood, his view blocked by high trellises of rose quartz.

The old miser never saw it coming. They heard the crash two levels below.

Needless to say, the Barium girl was outraged. Weeping before the sympathetic gnome constables, she mapped out a sinister plan of vengeance.

Crazed by sorrow at the loss of his prospective bride—even more crazed at the loss of her considerable dowry—Talos had approached the old fellow in private. He had asked for that dowry as compensation for his pain and suffering. Incline had justly refused, on the grounds that Talos had been involved in the bride's demise.

A last meeting had been arranged—to "iron over" all hard feelings, Talos had supposedly said. Then the anvil, hurtling into the courtyard, had found its ingenious target.

Even the dimmest of constables wondered at the story. How someone from a family as rich as Talos's could murder for a simple dowry, and why he would arrange that murder so close to his own dwelling, where suspicion would fall like an anvil on his own head.

But the girl was weeping, was inconsolable. "First my sister," she claimed, "my intimate soul- and womb-mate, for whom I have mourned these long and sisterless months! And now my father! What kind of monster could plan such a thing? That is, without substantial money, family prominence, and a metaphorical axe to grind?"

* * * * *

"I smell a two-headed monster," Scymnidus said, "Deddalo and this conniving hydra of a girl."

The barrister sat with his cousin in the unkempt offices. Innova had come to visit him shortly after news of the murder had spread through the upper levels, and together the two of them pondered the details.

"I can figure the *how* but not the *why*," Scymnidus continued. "The trap set near Talos's chambers. The blubbering girl drawing all sympathy to her orphaning. To top it off, there's her whole sensational story of wronged love and bloody family intrigue—just the kind of thing we love around here, a story that would convict Talos by sheer entertainment alone."

Innova paced the study, his eyes drawn to his cousin's collection of onyx figurines—black statues of scantily clad elf maidens, some in the most compromising and embarrassing of postures. He was thinking of his return to Deddalo's chambers, of what was revealed by his old friend's infamous eyelid.

He was almost certain. But was "almost certain" enough?

"Have you seen Deddalo since the contest?" Scymnidus asked.

"He's been hard to find," Innova admitted. "I've called on him at home, searched for him afternoons at the Hair of the Dog. The Barium girl says she's seen him on occasion, that he's come by to offer condolences and beer, but that's all I know. All I know for certain, that is."

"Such are the facts," Scymnidus said quietly. "Now for the suspicions behind the facts."

123

Innova picked up one of the tamer figurines—an onyx elf maid running through an onyx field, her tunic slipped appealingly free of her left shoulder, her little onyx breast even more appealingly free, exposed to a wanton sculptor's imagined breezes.

"I'm stuck on the *why*," he said, turning the statue in his hand. "I suspect that love has something to do with it, and the philosophers tell us that's a form of chaos, don't they? Who's to tell what love will make the best of us do? And Deddalo isn't the best of us."

"You're very young, Innova," Scymnidus said. "Suppose you tell me what you suspect, and leave the *why* to my older and colder imagination?"

Innova set the figurine back on the shelf, in the same clear circle where the dust had once settled around its base. He didn't want to betray Deddalo, but it seemed like the time had passed for his more tenderhearted feelings.

Reluctantly, he told Scymnidus about Deddalo's infamous eye. The barrister's own eyes widened as he heard the story about Innova's return.

"It's clear to me now," he said. "If your suspicion is correct—"

"*If*, Scymnidus," Innova emphasized.

The barrister nodded. "If it's correct, then the *why* is money and power. The old grease and tickle of policy public and private. The heart's blood of betrayal."

Innova flushed. Wasn't he guilty of betrayal himself?

He looked around his cousin's office, at the stacks of paper, the dipping goose that had inspired his invention. The portrait of Gordusmajor with the hollow eyes, and this naughty collection of figurines, which somehow seemed more fragile now, as though anything he had touched with his hands was inclined to break.

No matter what the Paradise Machine was doing throughout the levels of Mount Nevermind, the first corollary of the old Second Law still applied in the physics of friendship.

All things run down eventually.

"There'll be no moping," Scymnidus ordered, settling into his scroll-covered chair and writing something on a folded piece of parchment as the scrolls dropped to the floor. "You're a member of the Council now, by judicial appointment one of the most respected philosophers in Mount Nevermind."

It was obvious from the look on his face that Innova's newfound importance was a source of mystery to him, like a donkey being crowned King of Ansalon.

"And as a prominent citizen, you have direct audience with High Justice Gordusmajor, an audience that can be used for subtle and less subtle leverage. Take this note to him; in it I tell him that I shall defend Talos against these capital charges. But I also tell him that there are things he should know before this whole nasty business goes to trial."

"You're . . . influencing a justice, then?"

Scymnidus laughed quietly. "Bias and influence are my best friends," he said, "my companions for years in the trenches of jurisprudence. When all is said and done, these companions have stood me well. What of *your* friends, Cousin Innova? How well have they treated *you*?"

*   *   *   *   *

Innova was surprised to find a similar set of figurines lining the shelves of Gordusmajor's chambers—a collection that, if anything, was even more extensive and indecent than that of Scymnidus.

The onyx statuary told him nothing but the Justice's appetites and weaknesses. Nor did the scattered pages torn from law books and smeared with mustard and icing, except that Gordusmajor's regard for law was no greater than his attention to table manners. The tubes of the metavox reared from the wall like striking cobras, but it was obvious from the cloaks, hats, and underwear draped over them that Gordusmajor was listening to no one.

Finally, there was the portrait of the Tribunal painted decades ago. Gordusmajor stood between Harpos and Julius, his huge, meaty hands on their shoulders in a gesture of either friendship or aggression—it was hard to tell. Like the portrait in Scymnidus's office, the eyes were missing, but they were missing from each of the faces, and all of Ballista's figure from the waist down had been sliced neatly out of the painting, revealing a narrow passage in the wall behind the frame.

Innova looked into that shallow darkness as the High Justice looked at Scymnidus's note. Then they looked at each other.

Both faces registered astonishment and disbelief.

"Do you know the contents of this letter, notable colleague?" Gordusmajor asked. "It's ... why it's downright *illogical*! Philosophically and ideologically *inconsistent*, like a gully dwarf in charge of protocol! I've been the counselor's friend almost as long as I've been his enemy, and this whole idea he writes about is laced with contradictions!"

Innova only nodded. As usual, he doubted that it was logic and evidence that influenced the old bounder's opinion.

Skeptically, Gordusmajor spelled out the argument of his old friend and enemy. Scymnidus, it seemed, believed that the whole untimely death of Incline Barium was the fruit of an inheritance conspiracy. The demise of one of the twins months ago was no accident of wounded love at all, but a cold, cash-inspired murder, engineered by Deddalo himself. The so-called Meryl Barium, the older of the twins by minutes and consequently the heir of the major part of Incline Barium's fortune, was in reality *Beryl* Barium, the younger and less economically promising of the two.

It was a case of probate overkill. According to Scymnidus, Beryl and Deddalo had plotted the murder of Meryl Barium, thereby assuring that Beryl would not only be the principal heiress but the *only* one. Of course, to calm all suspicion, Beryl would masquerade as Meryl, would be discovered lost and wandering in the depths of the mountains. On returning home, she would "have a change of heart," "fall for" and marry Deddalo, thereby assuring, they thought, that the primary schemer got his hands on a large portion of Incline Barium's money.

There was still the problem of Talos, the real Meryl's bereaved lover. Deddalo's and Beryl's solution, Scymnidus maintained, would be irresistible to an engineer—a situation where two birds were killed with a single anvil. Framing Talos for the murder of Incline Barium would get him out of the way, and it would also hasten the moment when Beryl Barium's inheritance lay in her fat little hands.

126

It was enough to leave Innova breathless. It all made sense to him—all the evidence led toward a conspiracy worthy of Scymnidus's paranoid imagining.

Though Gordusmajor claimed not to believe a word of it, you could tell that he was fascinated by the story, that the inner workings and the plots layered over plots gratified his gnomish heart.

Then why did he not believe it?

Probably, Innova thought, because the High Justice stood to make more money by believing something else. His thoughts confused and muddled, he inspected Gordusmajor's figurine collection once again.

One of the figures, her sculptured clothes shed in an onyx pool at the base of the statue, performed an action that was not only lurid but, as far as Innova could guess, anatomically impossible.

"But here is the funny thing," Gordusmajor said, interrupting the young gnome's thoughts. He wheezed and coughed, a smile spreading over his oatcake-encrusted lips. "Even if Scymnidus's whole fantasy harbored only a *grain* of truth. The whole matter of Incline Barium's legacy. Whichever of the daughters expected to take the lion's share would have been disappointed at any rate. For years ago, when the old miser drew up his will, I was the lawyer who helped him to draft it, to seal his money away from the grubbing hands of family and friend and charity. All of his considerable money is bequeathed to a monument foundation, which has been instructed to buy out all residences and businesses on the Twenty-Sixth Level of Mount Nevermind and turn that level into a tomb and memorial. A whole level of the city will honor the generosity and civic-mindedness of Incline Barium as long as this city stands. As you can see, Innova, though the proverb says that 'you can't take it with you,' that old bastard Incline Barium has found a corollary: 'but if you can't take it with you, you can spend it all on the funeral.'"

*   *   *   *   *

There was still the matter of Talos's guilt or innocence. Innova could tell that it was fruitless to argue evidence or logic, when the thoughts of the High Justice circled around profit and kickback.

"It seems to me," Innova began, knowing he was on slippery ground but determined to save his friend nonetheless, "that Talos might . . . more effectively serve justice in Mount Nevermind through freedom rather than imprisonment. After all, he would be able to use his money to search for Incline Barium's *real* killer rather than letting it lie wasting in the safes and coffers of his ancestral vaults."

"Wouldn't lie wasting there anyway," Gordusmajor mumbled. He had filled his mouth with sweet rolls as he looked again at Scymnidus's letter. Raisins and pine nuts tangled in the white hair of his beard, and he licked his fingers absently, as though he was lost somewhere in thought.

"Wouldn't lie wasting there. According to Statute Twenty-Four, Subclauses One Hundred Seven and Eight of the criminal codes, his ancestral fortune is confiscate in the case of murder."

Confiscate? Innova didn't like the sound of it.

But he could see that Gordusmajor did.

"In cases of confiscation," the old justice declared, a joint session of guild tribunal and guild council determines the allocation of seized funds. In rough translation, that means we'll decide what becomes of his money."

A rough translation of *that* was that the High Justice himself, who sat at the head of both Council and Tribunal, would have the last word as to Talos's guilt, innocence, and riches. When all was said and done, Gordusmajor stood to be more wealthy than bribes could reckon by simply believing that Talos's hand was on the fatal anvil.

"High Justice Gordusmajor," Innova began, intent on defending his old friend but uncertain where his argument would take him, and doubtful that he could succeed where the able Scymnidus had failed.

He was almost relieved when, in a flutter of clothing and a long, crackling *honk* from somewhere on another level, the metavox sprang to life.

It seemed to startle the High Justice as well. Gordusmajor pivoted in his chair, rocked dangerously over the floor, then recovered his balance amid a spill of sweet rolls.

"How . . . how do you *answer* the thing, Innova?" he asked.

The younger gnome shrugged. "As though you were talking to the speaker face to face, I imagine."

The metavox blasted again—a rude and discordant sound like something from the wrong end of a goose.

"As though the speaker were before you? Standing face to face? In full glory?"

Innova nodded.

"In your veritable presence?" the High Justice continued. "In the tangible? More than virtual?"

Innova nodded. "All of those."

"Then go away!" Gordusmajor shouted at the tubing as he slipped from behind his desk and headed toward the passage behind the portrait. "I'm . . . leaving this moment on philosophical business. Please call tomorrow!"

Again the metavox trumpeted, and this time, after the loud, tuneless call, a voice from somewhere along the network of tube and piping called out nervously, in a voice intended for whoever was listening.

"Alert! Alert! Invading forces on Level Twenty-Four!"

Chapter 16

However despicable the creature who conducted the Knights through this maze of defenses, one thing had to be said for him: he knew the terrain and the traps.

Even with the gnome's help, it had been an uncertain journey.

In the first moment that the Knights had begun their climb out of the high rocks overlooking Mount Nevermind, bright Solinari had slipped from behind a cover of clouds and bathed the canyon with light. Khargos had looked up among the fortifications, expecting shouts and challenges, a rain of arrows.

He breathed a prayer to Takhisis, and no resistance came.

Quickly, Khargos sent a party of Knights to the crater above the city complex. Their job was simple and direct: to cut off the upper water supply. His informant had told him that the city had another source of water—bubbling up under its own pressure from the depths of the mountain. This, apparently, had ornamental uses only—in fountains and pools and decorative geysers spread over the upper levels, apparently feeding this new machine that so concerned the traitorous gnome.

That could be dealt with later. For the time being, Halion Khargos wanted the so-called Paradise Machine in working order. The prospects of what might be done with it were dazzling.

As the Knights made their way into the labyrinth of Mount Nevermind, the quiet became almost eerie. Guided by the gnome, they slipped easily past the guard posts, the spike pits, the smoldering pots of oil and the moveable trip wires.

As they ascended a circular stairwell somewhere roughly in the middle of a level, Khargos's keen hearing caught a faint sound of rumbling from somewhere far below.

He asked his gnomish guide who, for the first time, had no idea what something was.

Finally, somewhere in a torch-lit chamber that he identified as the Twenty-Sixth Level, the gnome took leave of them.

"From this point on," he whispered, "your task is easy. Easy, that is, by invaders' standards, where unfamiliar terrain and concealed enemies are a given, but where your tactical gifts and the favor of your Goddess will no doubt surpass all defenses. You're past the far reach of the Paradise Machine—the bristling, dangerous part. From this point on, one might say that the machine works *for* you. The lamps are restored, adit and tunnel clearly marked. Why, even the handcarts run on time, like a clockwork toy. But I can't be seen among you, for obvious reasons."

As abruptly as that, without the complicated and silly salutations that usually go with gnomish arrivals and departures, the creature was gone. He stepped upon one arm of a lever, and a heavy, swiveling hammer painted to look like the head and neck of a goose struck the other arm, and the guide they had come to know as Innova was airborne, propelled toward a vast and cavernous ceiling, vaulting over a dim balcony and vanishing through a door.

It was like something in a strange, visionary dream, and for a moment Khargos looked around him, attentive for signs of the Goddess.

From all the stories he had heard of Mount Nevermind, the Commander had expected a chaos of clashing machineries, a city of litter and lost passages—a place that was, above all, *unkempt*. But here a cart track led, smooth and unbroken, around a huge but simply designed marble building. Having circled the structure, the track forked, each branch headed off toward some sure destination under steady, soft light.

It was like a gnomish afterlife, Khargos thought. A time and a place where everything worked as it was intended to work. But there was certain disinfected coldness to the whole level, as though all this competence had taken away the juice and vitality of the place. He remembered the

131

energy of the gnome steamboats—up by the reef and also much earlier, in a time that seemed like a dream.

Something in this city had deadened, had fallen asleep.

Despite himself, Khargos was disappointed that what lay before him was so crisp and efficient—so ungnomish. Disappointed, and a little uneasy, for if the machinery of axle and wire had been brought into order by the Paradise Machine, who could tell how the tactics of a defending army might be transformed, streamlined made utterly lethal in a maze where the gnomes knew the country.

Khargos looked up into the dark vault for a sign of the departed guide. Unbroken shadow lay over the dome of the chamber, and far away the shriek of a steam whistle echoed on a higher level.

A lesser man, perhaps a wiser man, would have been afraid. But Khargos's senses, sharpened by years of awaiting the Goddess, were tuned to the sounds and sights and smells of the cavern. To something beyond the senses—to a strange, intangible unease amid all this efficiency, as though Mount Nevermind itself could not bear proper working.

Now the invaders followed the cart tracks out of the chamber, and a steep incline up the corridor told Khargos that they were approaching another level. Here the sounds were more discordant, more tuneless, and a sputtering light told the Commander that it was country not yet thoroughly linked and governed by the so-called Paradise Machine.

"It was a tomb below us," Oliver insisted. He had snaked up the column toward Khargos and now stood at the left hand of the Commander, his glittering eyes focused on the things of this place—on the steam and the overhanging buildings, the cracked pavement and the sputtering sound of misfiring machinery. "A fresh tomb, to judge by the tremor in the marble."

"The tremor?" For once Khargos was interested in the heavy-handed theology of his chaplain.

"The tremor," Oliver repeated. "Whoever was buried there, gnome or possibly dwarf, he had not yet given the world away, his thoughts and soul lingering amid *things* and the *evidence* of things like flies around a carcass."

"An attractive comparison, Oliver."

But the cleric was in full lecture and full assurance, belaboring Khargos with divinity and the latest theories on afterlife.

The Commander was no longer interested. He was as tired of such certainty as he had been of the chaos on the seas and the beaches. Lengthening his strides to outpace the smaller man, he loped to the head of the column where a pair of Lily Knights—Angus and Donald— walked at the point, the eyes and ears of the rank. It was there, in the strategies and surprise of war, that he felt most at home.

"Opening ahead, Commander Khargos," Donald observed, drawing his spear from its sling over his back. Angus, in turn, readied himself, and the three Knights paused at the opening of the tunnel, their battle-sharpened eyes sizing the chamber for possible ambush.

"They're here, sir," Angus whispered. "Feel the air flicker?"

And indeed, he did. Perhaps it was like Oliver's sensation over the marble of tombs, or the Thorn Knight's instinct when a sword or amulet blossoms with light.

Halion Khargos knew tactics. The placement of troops and ambush were an instinct to him, a scent in the air or a bristle along the hairs of his arm.

The short of it was that the three Knights entered the chamber, fully expecting the assault that awaited them.

And the assault came, crossbow bolts and sling stones hurtling from the windows of gutted buildings, from the cover of ramshackle lean-tos. Projectiles skittered over the stone floors, and a cry arose from the loft of the chamber where shadowy forms danced in elusive gaslight.

The rest of the column burst into the chamber. Well trained and harshly disciplined, the Knights raised shields and formed a canopy over the assembling party.

Metal struck metal in a lethal rain. Beneath the cover of the shields, his uncertainties fading into a peculiar battle calm, the Commander shouted orders, and the column began to move, like a lumbering armored animal, through the center of the chamber toward a wide entrance at its other side.

There was no need to join combat here. The gnomes around them were sentries, pickets placed to inflict casualties and then retreat into the hollows and tunnels of the mountain. Greater resistance lay in the levels above, and Khargos would need all of his brutes and Knights to defeat it.

Into the darkness the company stalked, the gnomish shouts, now punctuated by explosions, fading with the light behind them. Alert, almost eager at the head of the column, Khargos guided his troops up a gentle incline.

Once again, a faint light bathed the passage ahead. Bells and hydraulic claxons sounded their approach, and the Commander steadied his soldiers, himself, for the oncoming battle.

What he got instead was past his imagining. For if this was the Twenty-Eighth Level of Mount Nevermind, the edge of the city's heart, the gnomes had abandoned the fortress to the invaders.

Khargos entered an expanse of chambers, streets built in a subterranean maze of city blocks and squares. Smoke still curled from the chimneys, pooling on the chamber vaults and slipping into vents and fissures. On the street in front of him, a unicycle lay capsized, its wheel still spinning slowly as though its rider had left it in mid-ride.

They had to be near. Nobody could have retreated so quickly.

Slipping from the canopy of shields, Khargos stood in the middle of the street. Unprotected, offering target to assassin or hidden bowman, he strode recklessly toward the closest of the buildings and, placing his foot against the door, opened it with a powerful kick.

A carillon of small bells, like a wind chime, sounded alarm at his entry. Somewhere, in the darkened depths of the little dwelling, a strange metallic squawking rose above the chimes.

A shrill chorus of voices, sounding a warning.

Something about *battlements* and *Thirtieth Level*.

Instantly he knew that above them, Subcommander Fleetwood and his forces had marched through the North Pass—that level gap which the gnomes called Getinandgetoutherebecauseitistheonlypasswehaveclearedin thelastcentury.

The full force of the Knights of Takhisis had joined the attack.

*   *   *   *   *

Sandwiched between the invading forces, the gnomes surrendered after a brief, fiery fight.

Casualties among Fleetwood's forces were heavy. On the topmost level, it seemed that the Paradise Machine had rendered the defenses coldly efficient. Trapdoors sprang on once-rusty hair triggers, a series of elaborate nooses hoisted a dozen brutes to an executioner's death, and brave young Butler, who had survived the Goddess-knew-what in a perilous journey through the mountains, fell victim ignobly to some sort of ceremonial decapitator, designed to remove the tops of barrels, but transformed by the Paradise Machine into something deadly and ruthless.

Halion Khargos would not know these things for another hour. There, on the Twenty-Ninth Level of Mount Nevermind, he could hear the faint clash of battle through the stones above, the frenzied reports down the pipes of the metavox.

It was like the edge of the Vision, all darkness and rumor.

In his new headquarters—the ransacked Geometers' Guild Hall—the Commander waited amid bottled theorems, outsized compasses, and a curious protractor marked with the names of stars and constellations instead of numbers and degrees. Coordinating his troops with Fleetwood's attack above—or at least the attack he *thought* the Subcommander was planning—he set barricades at each of the entrances, at the nets and platforms of the gnomeflingers, until his troops and their brute foot soldiers were spread dangerously thin throughout the level.

He did not like this courting of chaos. Circling himself with Knights, Khargos waited uneasily as his part of the battle slipped into rumor and guesswork. He closed his eyes, tried to touch the hem of the Goddess's robe, but Takhisis was silent, waiting.

She is letting me taste abandonment, he thought.

She sends me to a hard school.

All around him the metavox pipes whined and choired, a hundred voices mingling and drowning out the voice he listened for, if that voice was even still present.

Oliver regarded him with intent, probing eyes.

* * * * *

Though it *did* lie in the power of the Paradise Machine to link together all the gadgetry of Mount Nevermind, from the simplest pulley to the complicated system of gears and cogs that counted the money in the treasuries, some adjustments lay beyond its power.

There was chaos in the very nature of what Gordusmajor called "gnomitude," and any transaction between gnome and gnome, from marriage to inheritance to the simple planning of a picnic, was subject to all kinds of misunderstandings and disruptions.

The gnomes lost the battle of Mount Nevermind because one of their generals stopped for a drink.

It was as simple as that. Marching his reinforcements from the Nineteenth Level all the way up to the pitch battle on the Thirtieth and Twenty-Ninth, the Most August Generalissimo Glorius Peterloo, commander of the gnomish militia and suppressor of gully dwarf labor unrest throughout the middle and lower levels of the city, looked forward to testing his tactics and resolve on a real army.

An army, the metavox warned, composed of humans, and trained humans at that.

Oh, it was what he had waited for! The August Generalissimo had dreamed of this chance in the long halls of the Law Enforcement Colleges, and he had made a quick stop in the Twentieth Level barracks to retrieve his gold braid and the white cap with the billowing purple plume.

He would look the part this day. He would add new honorifics to his rapidly growing name.

August Generalissimo GloriusPeterlooVolcanoMouth-VanquisherofThornBoneandLily . . .

It was already sounding more noble, more historical.

But as the troops stalked through the streets surrounding Deddalo's old quarters, on their way to the new service elevators provided by the Paradise Machine, the Generalissimo noticed the solitary light in the window of the Hell With Dinner.

After all, there *was* time, wasn't there? From the sounds of explosion and outcry on the levels above them and the sputtering reports from the network of the metavox, his troops were holding their own against intruders.

There was time for a short ale before he marched into immortality.

Leaving his three generals jittery at the head of an army of six hundred, the Generalissimo stepped into the pub, where a barman, remotely familiar, regarded him nervously.

Ruddy hair, a patchy beard, and brown eyes—one of which was half-veiled by a drooping eyelid.

Where had he seen this fellow before?

"Ale!" the Generalissimo called out, in his heartiest and bravest voice. "Light and sunny, bolster of tactic and stratagem!"

But the barman, with widening eyes, suggested something more bolstering—a dwarf spirit distilled among the darker and more romantic of the dwarven numbers.

"TullaMorgion, they call it. Bearer of a deeper wisdom, of subterranean and volcanic truth. The true and utter Hammer of Kharas."

Hammer it did, through the first glass and the inevitable second, while a rescuing army gaped in frustration at the boarded windows along the pub row, wondering why, on this auspicious and dangerous day, the Hell With Dinner had remained open.

And why, out of all his duties and ambitions, the August Generalissimo, bleary-eyed and tottering at the edge of the bar, was raising his third and razing glass.

*　*　*　*　*

Without the expected reinforcements, the gnome army at the height of the city was forced toward a swift and bloody retreat. In the memories of most of the militia, their battles had been bluster and bravado—one soldier daring another, the dare taken up in a reckless charge that stunned and bruised all combatants.

For years it had not been serious. Not like this.

In haggard waves the defending legion, now numbering less than a hundred, pressed toward the central stairwell leading down into the mountain. Borne on litters and bearing scars, their short spears turned to makeshift crutches, they huddled at the mouths of the tunnels, awaiting the relief that would not come.

The acting superior officer of these beleaguered gnome forces was Full Colonel Grex Pointillo. The colonel was not born of a military family; instead, he was one of those aimless lads whose ancestral guild had been absorbed, forcing him to seek his fortune elsewhere. Twenty years he had spent on the staffs of generals and generalissimos, always a comfortable fourth or fifth in command. Barely consulted in strategic and tactical maneuvers, he was generally no more than a courier when battles began, delivering messages to and from whatever superior officer he assisted.

But in the hot fighting on the Thirtieth Level, Generalissimo Hardly Panoramicus had fallen, and with him four hundred troopers and a pair of gnome generals—Tarsus Metatarsus and Nonne Composmentis. Command had fallen onto the shoulders of the colonel, and now, staring through the jets of steam and the gauntlet of sharp pendulums at a charging, dodging wave of brutes, Grex Pointillo wondered how long his battered forces could stand against a trained, relentless army.

Still, the stairs were behind them. The lower levels. The wounded beginning to be lowered in pulleyed baskets.

If they could stand against this first assault . . .

The brutes struck the gnome lines like fire cutting through a dry thicket. Up and down the hurried defenses, Pointillo heard the sounds of screams, muted horns in alarums, and metal on metal as the gnome positions bent, buckled . . .

Then held fantastically.

You could feel the surge in the line, a subtle change of energies as the troops pushed back, pushed forward again, and the close air in the tunnels filled with cries and flickering knives.

Now, from a distance, the Knights of Takhisis mustered their first charge. A wave of black-armored warriors, the standard of the Death Lily aloft in their vanguard, marched toward the stairwell, their march breaking into a trot, a run, a charge as the beleaguered gnome archers began to pour bolt and arrow upon them.

The Knights struck the line at its weakest, where the brutes had softened the defenses. Now the fight was a frenzy near the wide and spiraling stairs, brute and Knight against weary gnome, sometimes brute against Knight as the chaos of the battle overwhelmed all who fought in it.

Halfway down the stairs to the Twenty-Ninth Level, racing up and down the bedraggled line of descending wounded, Pointillo urged his soldiers on, encouraging them, bolstering them. Faces came out of the lofty darkness into the light of flickering lanterns, out of his memory into the horrible here and now.

Lozenge, Triquet, Roundell, and Pillaster—solid lads from the Architects' and Geometers' Guilds, volunteers in General Composmentis's Legion. All of them bloodied and bruised, their eyes staring blankly under singed and ravaged brows.

There had been others—four or five more—who had enlisted when these did. Now, Pointillo thought, his spirits drooping, he could not remember the names of the missing.

Yet he encouraged the survivors, consoled them and championed them.

In later years, when they recalled the battle, some maintained that his words, his very touch, renewed their strength and resolve.

At the centermost edge of the Thirtieth Level—near the dome and the crater lake—the bells and whistles were now fallen silent. The silence followed in a third wave after brute and Knight, and soon all sound had collapsed around the stairwell, where irregular, desperate clatter and shouts and screams had continued for almost an hour now.

Scrambling down the steps toward the head of the retreating column, the Colonel sighed with relief to see the gnomes emptying into the Twenty-Ninth Level, seeking shelter in the sturdy, abandoned buildings that surrounded the stairwell. They would be safe for a while.

He had heard in the pipes of the metavox that reinforcements were on their way, August Generalissimo Glorius Peterloo at the head of six hundred troops . . .

And mingled with the military orders and battle intelligence, the faint sound of the Anthem—the old gnomish hymn to Mount Nevermind:

> Hail to Mount Nevermind, beautiful mountain,
> Storehouse to wonderful things past accountin'!
> Long may you stand, neither crumbled nor rotten
> (There was another verse here we've forgotten)
> But nevermind, Nevermind
> Where the passage of days is both noble and kind!

Now healthier troops—veterans who had guarded the withdrawal of the wounded—were descending to the Twenty-Ninth Level, helping the stragglers into the nearby buildings, setting the defenses for a smaller siege within the siege.

Despite himself, Pointillo was heartened. Already, at the edge of his hearing, a trumpet sounded at the farthest reach of the level. There, among the numerous gnomeflinger receiving nets, Peterloo's army was no doubt disembarking, assembling, beginning to march toward a joining of forces at the large spiraling stair.

Give me an hour, the Colonel thought, his hand resting lightly but with great assurance on the haft of his mace.

Give me an hour, and I shall save history.

The trumpet sounded again, somewhere off in the central darkness. It was an unfamiliar tune, somber and exultant, but the Colonel guessed that it was distorted by distance, made minor by a labyrinth of echoes.

He smiled, his confidence soaring.

Give me half an hour.

Now the last of Pointillo's forces had gathered at the foot of the stairwell. Seventy, perhaps eighty of them remained in all, and the Colonel decided to gather them into one building—the sprawling, three-story post office, where the heavy doors and barred windows made the first floor virtually impregnable.

At once, the scouts were dispatched up the wide marble stairs, carrying with them the stilts that would give them the vantage of sight over all the Twenty-Ninth Level.

The trumpets sounded nearer now, the song unchanging. Perhaps it is a call for the lifting of siege, the Colonel thought uneasily. A call the Generalissimo remembers from the old War of the Lance.

For the first time since the retreat began, a true uncertainty had burrowed into his thoughts. Quiet, almost silent at first, but increasing in volume, in urgency.

Until one of the scouts, posted on stilts atop the half-dome of the post office, called out a desperate alarm.

"Enemy approaching . . . or advancing . . . or you might say *charging* from The Inner Hall! Suspected Knight and ostensible brute!"

Colonel Grex Pointillo climbed to the roof of the post office. Lifted into the stilts by two of his soldiers, he peered through a spyglass at the juncture of light and darkness.

A young man, a pale lily blazoned on his black breastplate, walked at the head of blue-painted brutes and Knights as bloodless as their ashen standards.

A young man with death and yearning deep in his dark eyes.

Great Reorx defend us from this one! Colonel Grex Pointillo thought, as he mingled with his handful of soldiers among the elaborate corridors, cubicles and pigeonholes of Mount Nevermind's heart of written communication.

Great Reorx preserve us until the arrival of Glorius Peterloo's army.

Chapter 17

The two wings of the Knights of Takhisis—Khargos's and Fleetwood's—converged on the Twenty-Ninth Level. There they encircled the Post Office, where the courageous Colonel Grex Pointillo had gathered his shaken forces.

It would be a battle for gnomish history, if gnomish history recorded defeats as well as victories.

For the siege lasted only a matter of hours, the gnomes on the third and highest floor of the post office secreted away in chambers, in dispatch bags, in the dead letter office among mountains of undelivered packages and letters. In the last few minutes before they were seized by the Knights, some of the more enterprising gnomes posted packages of explosives to several of the more prominent guild halls under the wild hope that the Knights would leave the seats of government where they found them and that the gnome postal service would deliver the mail on time and to the right address.

Others hopped into boxes, posting themselves to Ergoth and the continent.

Casualties were light. Most of the gnomes were far too exhausted to mount a resistance. By the evening Grex Pointillo and his hastily assembled staff were all in enemy hands. Rumor had it that Generalissimo Glorius Peterloo, self-styled savior of Mount Nevermind, had been found wrapped in chicken wire in the alley between the Hell With Dinner and the Delirium Tremens, and that most of his army had fled in confusion to the lower levels of the mountain.

By the end of the day, Mount Nevermind belonged to the Dark Queen and to her capable right arm, Commander Halion Khargos.

Khargos, the subject of gnome fear and speculation, sat at headquarters in the Geometers' Guild Hall. The first thing he did as Commander of Occupational Forces was to have the enemy officers brought forth for hearing and execution.

It was a hard, unpleasant duty, but a necessary one. After all, was not the Blood Oath "Submit or die"?

His duty was easier with Glorius Peterloo. The Generalissimo was still cloudy-headed from the TullaMorgion, but he knew what he was up against, and he knew the cost of commanding a losing army.

Very little in his corrupt old life was as admirable as preparing for the end of it.

"Make the axe sharp," he told the Commander, blinking tenderly at the torchlight in the Guild Hall. "Let the day be soon, and let the hand of the headsman be strong and steady. I've enough TullaMorgion awash in my head that the pain will be less when I lose it."

The two chief commanders gazed at one another across the hall. For a moment it did not matter that one of them was brilliant, young, and promising, while the other was none of those things. In that moment, each knew what his honor and allegiances demanded of him, that the events that would follow were like some tragic machinery neither of them could stop.

Khargos felt a strange sympathy stirring in his thoughts. It was too soft. He banished it quickly.

The case of Lieutenant Colonel Grex Pointillo was different, He was a young gnome who, in a moment of crisis, had been saddled with command. In the face of troops better trained and better armed, he had marshalled his troops with some skill and much bravery, and had it not been for the errors and luxuries of Glorius Peterloo, this green colonel might have given the invading forces all that they could handle.

Having displayed this new talent, Grex Pointillo was by far the more dangerous adversary.

Quietly, almost timidly, Halion Khargos asked the young gnome the Impossible Question. For when a conquering Knight of Takhisis recognized bravery in his adversary, it was customary to offer that adversary a place in the ranks of the Dark Queen. Of course, if the captive answered yes, he betrayed his old loyalties and was unworthy of the ranks, while if he answered no, trial and execution would follow in the usual order.

Grex Pointillo was a gnome, unworthy by nature for the Knighthood.

Still, his refusal was a bold one, his gaze unwavering as he told the Commander that neither money nor power nor the sparing of his life would bring him to the service of the Dark Goddess, and that the wheels of enforcement should be set in swift motion.

"I have but one request," he said grimly, as a brace of Knights took up their station on either side of him, and the Acolyte Oliver slipped adamantine manacles on his wrists. "Let my head fall after that of Glorius Peterloo, so that some kind of justice will settle in my dying eyes."

His duties dispatched, his opponents sent away to brief imprisonment and impending execution, Halion Khargos leaned back in his chair, resting his boots on the edge of the rhomboid Guild Council table. Quietly, he produced a quill pen and scratched a hasty note on the back of some vanished guildsman's proof that the edges of time and space were measurable with a good abacus and a collapsible yardstick.

The Paradise Machine haunted the Commander. A simple device that, from the account of this spy Innova, moved perpetually and restored small chaoses to a semblance of order.

Given the misfortunes of his army on the beach and in the mountains—misfortunes at the hands of some large and unnameable chaos—Halion Khargos was taken with the prospects of such an invention.

If it linked defunct and failing machines into some vast network of competence, could it do something against the forces he had met on the shores of Sancrist? The forces that had followed him high into the mountains and would no doubt follow him here, dragging confusion and disorder in their wake?

Perhaps it was why Takhisis in her divine wisdom had brought him to Mount Nevermind.

Riding the crest of another victory, Halion Khargos was suddenly certain again. The Goddess guided his right arm, and the city and its surrounding island bowed to his will and the strength of his army.

For the first time in days, the Commander dozed, his head nodding above sheaves of abandoned papers which claimed to contain logarithmic proof of free will and formulae for determining the perimeter of dream. His own dreams, unmeasured by gnomish mathematics, played lazily over the prospect of the Paradise Machine.

* * * * *

While Halion Khargos dozed, both then and in the days to come, the Thirtieth Level of Mount Nevermind was in an advanced state of a strange chaos.

To the outward eye, it was not chaos at all.

The instruments of science and engineering that had littered the topmost level of Mount Nevermind were *working* now, in ways that their inventors had never dreamed that they would work. The carts ran on time, and to their designed destinations; the elaborate systems of heat and ventilation had made the climate comfortable, from the gnome-flingers stationed near the crater's edge all the way past the spiraling staircases and into the farthest reaches of the level.

Even the unmapped crannies and tunnels were habitable, and here many of the soldiers in the defeated armies of Generalissimo Glorius Peterloo huddled in apprehension, sure that they would be picked up for questioning within the hour.

The GSS—the Glass Surveillance System—was working as well, and the gnomish people felt the eyes of the Knights on their every movement and transaction.

It was a curious, idealistic thing, this series of mirrors and lights. Established a century ago by a civic-minded member of the Optics Guild, it had been intended to reflect images of every street and alley on the Thirtieth Level to a faceted wall of mirrors in the Constabulary Hall. There, the inventor had hoped, the gnome police could sit in a centralized station, monitoring all crime, misdemeanor, and mishap that took place here in the most affluent and influential part of the city.

Of course, it had not worked. By now, some of the mirrors were missing, many of them cracked. But those that worked reflected a satisfactory image of the upper streets to the eyes of whoever sat in the Constabulary Hall.

Sitting there now was Subcommander Fleetwood, the supposed right hand of the Occupying General. From his post, he could see most everything, could know escape and rebellion as soon as it began to ferment.

Most of the guilds had surrendered immediately to the invaders, decking the windows of their halls with white banners of defeat and with the standards of the Lily. Several others—the Mathematicians, the Alchemists, and the Librarians—stood anxious vigil in their halls and neighborhoods, having been informed by the occupying commander that they were to surrender all authority, all papers of establishment and daily business, to his offices in the Geometers' Hall within forty-eight hours.

Only the Philosophers' Guild and the Probate Subguild of Mount Nevermind's vast fraternity of lawyers remained intact among the forces of the invasion.

Soon, as it always did among gnomes, suspicions began to rise. Why, of all organizations, were these untouched?

A number of conspiracy theories, always dear to the hearts of gnomes, arose from the circumstances. The possibility that a corrupt lawyer had betrayed the city was dismissed almost immediately as being too obvious, but it was not long before other theories replaced it.

One was that the Commander a level below them, the mythical Halion Khargos, was betrothed to a gnome female: an idea cast aside as biologically nasty and perhaps illegal.

Other possibilities remained: that a pair of philosophers, digging into anthropology, psychology, sociology, and other occult sciences, had been seized by the power of Takhisis, and enchanted, had handed the city to the enemy.

That something about this new Paradise Machine had created a hole in time and space through which a company of Knights, whose bodies lay dead somewhere upon the continent, had returned to the living and to Mount Nevermind.

There were other speculations as well—conspiracies involving a rumored sighting of the half-elf Tanis, a malfunction of plumbing on the Sixteenth Level, and that the post office had mishandled invitations to the annual Festival of Technologies, sending one by mistake to one of the few remaining Knights of the Thorn.

All of these possibilities ranged through the conversations of Innova and the High Justice Gordusmajor as they hid in judicial chambers.

"All lies," the High Justice proclaimed. "As simple as that. We're without military leaders at the moment, and all politics and most philosophy is helpless in the aftermath of defeat."

Innova was inclined to agree. Still, there was something in the whole idea of the Paradise Machine that troubled him. If the lever in the Tribunal Hall and its larger counterparts that now dipped perpetually throughout the top five levels of the city had something to do with Mount Nevermind's defeat and surrender, then he was in some way responsible.

That was what he told old Gordusmajor, who sat calmly behind his desk, nursing a mug of ale.

"Nonsense, boy!" the Justice scoffed. "You've suffered a relapse into cause and effect. Those who contract that disease get lost in speculation, but they always come out finding something for which to blame themselves. Taken to its end, the sickness makes each of us guilty of everything. And I, for one, am entirely innocent."

It was not consoling. Innova looked up at the tattered painting on the chamber wall, at the missing nether parts of Justice Julius and the tunnel that lay behind the tear.

What had the old doddering Julius done to deserve such mutilation? Someone—probably Gordusmajor—had blamed him for something at some time, and even if the wrong was imagined or forgotten, the painting would always carry the scar of an accusation.

"Then . . . what shall we do, High Justice Gordusmajor?" he asked despairingly. "Guilty or innocent, what shall we do?"

"Wait," Gordusmajor replied simply. "If I've learned anything from years on the bench, it's that no harm comes from delay and inaction. So what if there are mirrors all over the level, and most of our actions return to the eyes of this Subcommander Fleetwood? There are actions he can never see—"

"But not *that* many of the mirrors are broken!" Innova protested.

"This has nothing to do with mirrors and light, stupid boy," the High Justice continued calmly. "Do you think I have grown wealthy through years of *visible* action? There are plans and schemes, desires and hopes that remain invisible until the right time. If your thoughts weren't so filled with cause and effect, you'd have room for something else to think."

"Are we waiting for magic?" Innova asked cynically. "For miracle?"

The Justice rose ponderously from his desk and waddled across the room. Absently, he picked up one of the vulgar little statues and turned it in his hand, inspecting it in the steady, unwavering light that the Paradise Machine was providing now throughout the upper levels.

"We are waiting," he said quietly, "for things to break down. "Things no machine can order or mend.""

Chapter 18

They were still waiting when the news came from the lower levels.

In Gordusmajor's chambers, the metavox squawked to life, startling the two gnomes who sat there brooding over the fate of their city.

"Subcommander Fleetwood requests the presence of the gnome Innova in the Constabulary Guild Hall. There he will assist the Knights of Takhisis in their inquiries."

Gordusmajor lifted an eyebrow, regarded his companion skeptically.

"Innova, Innova," he asked ironically. "What have you done, boy?"

"N—nothing!" Innova stammered. "Or at least nothing that will help them with inquiries, whatever that means."

"It means, quite simply, that you're suspected of something. And when a conquering army suspects, can conviction be far behind?"

"But I'm not in the army. Not in government—well, I *am* a member of the Guild Council. . . . "

"Not exactly the king of Mount Nevermind," Gordusmajor observed dryly. "Perhaps it's to do—with your machine?"

"Perhaps. But I don't see what—"

"Nor do they, I suspect," Gordusmajor said. "They're trying to figure it. Trying to get their thoughts around its implications. You may not know what you've put together—how a simple contest can steamroll into something beyond all our understandings. Let's pray that they know less than we do."

"Should I go?" Innova asked.

"By no means," the High Justice replied. "I suggest that you step through Julius's crotch over there and find your way down the tunnel. It's not mirrored. It's not even mapped. What it is, is long. It'll deposit you somewhere

149

down around the Twelfth Level—disastrous ruined country, no place to live, but beneath their notice for the time being. Meanwhile, I'll do what I do best: connive and survey."

"Will you be safe, sir?"

For the first time in Innova's memory, the High Justice leaned back and laughed aloud. It was a high wheezing sound, almost acrobatic from such a ponderous figure.

"Dear boy," Gordusmajor claimed, in the aftermath of a coughing fit that scattered cake crumbs over the chamber floor. "If there's anyone on the continent whom I haven't the goods on, I can console myself with the knowledge that I have the goods on his closest friend. I have heavy leverage; I know that sooner or later, coronary or apoplexy or gout will undo me, but until that fated time, I have no lethal adversary."

He ushered Innova toward the hole in the painting. The younger gnome looked back once into the well-lit chambers, at the big Justice smiling and waving at him as harmlessly, as innocently as an elf-child.

Gordusmajor had long sleeves, with plenty of room to hide things.

Innova felt assured for the first time in three long, anxious days, as he turned his back on the topmost level and fled into enveloping darkness.

*   *   *   *   *

Alone in a chamber of mirrors, Subcommander Fleetwood scanned what he could see of the conquered city and its environs.

First, as usual, he scanned the outermost parts of the Gnomish Surveillance System.

First the mirrors on the surface of the volcano mouth, all absently trained upon a pile of soggy kindling in some recent experiment of physics.

He would have to send Knights there, have to direct those mirrors so that they revealed more than moldy wood and drowned paper.

Next, he scanned the North Pass—the uppermost level entrance to the region, what the gnomes called the

Getinandgetout. That was one through which his army had marched in the swift invasion of the mountain. He smiled. There the mirrors were working and the pass was clear.

Not that anyone would dare to challenge the fortified Knights of Takhisis.

Content that the borders remained secure, Fleetwood now looked toward the inner mirrors, toward the streets and the buildings of the city itself.

It was not the Mount Nevermind that common knowledge had promised him.

There were machines in every mirror, as he had expected: pulley systems hauling baskets and pans from the lower levels, those inexplicable dipping geese with wires and tubes attached to their pivoting backsides. Lights were flickering on in all the streets and alleys. Handcarts and steam-powered wagons propelled down tracks that were strangely repairing themselves before his eyes.

Oh, there was machinery enough, but it was all *working*. That was what he had *not* expected: a city that disobeyed the one rule he had heard from his youth about this silly and fractious people.

If you want something broken, give it to a gnome.

It was as though the city had banished chaos. And, if Fleetwood understood the hints and intimations of his Commander, Halion Khargos, this gnome Innova had everything to do with the change.

He did not expect Innova to come at his summons. After all, anyone whom the Knights brought in for questioning had reason to be afraid.

He thought of the rain-washed pillories off the coast of Ergoth. The pit at the bottom of which the brutes had laid rows of razored spikes.

Sometimes the Vision was hard on dissenters.

One only had to look at the Twenty Sixth Level, where tombs and monuments scattered over a torchlit landscape, to know that the Vision was hard. Fleetwood could see it all from the curtained mirrors that enabled him to look four levels below.

There, in the place the gnomes had come to call the Necropolis, for reasons more large and dangerous than the postmortem fancies of Incline Barium, the bodies hung in arches, lay buried and struggling in stone sarcophagi.

Dissenters, some of them, perhaps even revolutionaries. But others no doubt innocent of all subversion, though Fleetwood told himself that, in the darkened glass of the mirrors, their true nature was visible.

If these gnomes were not conspiring now, they soon would be.

Hence the Necropolis.

Fleetwood had arranged it all carefully. The mirrors on the Twenty-Ninth Level—those around the Geometers' Guild—would not reflect the punishments and executions in the Necropolis: Halion Khargos was fierce in honor, in the Blood Oath and the Code, and he did not need to see his fanciful notions . . . compromised.

After all, Halion Khargos claimed to see things. Secret, visionary things.

Wasn't it Fleetwood's right to see things of his own?

Secretly, almost pruriently, he fingered aside the curtain that covered the mirrors in which the reflection of the Necropolis glittered with a jaundiced light. He could see them struggling beneath the arches, the torchlight playing over their robes, their desperately kicking feet, as they swung in and out of the darkness.

He could imagine the sound: the choking. The creak of rope against the makeshift scaffolding. A smothered scream from one of the sealed sarcophagi.

Fleetwood prayed to the Goddess, there in a tumult of mirrors.

O Mother Takhisis, he whispered, his thoughts rising through rock and cold magma to the dark, starless sky he imagined above.

O let this be the iron of order. Let the gnomes bend to my . . .

. . . to your . . .

. . . ruling hand.

Let the Commander not know, until it is time for him to know it.

And beneath all, Mother, beneath the gibbet and the tomb, the flaying knives and the boiling pitch . . .

Let me not enjoy this too, too deeply.

And bring me Innova. For your great, incomprehensible sake, bring me the maker of the Paradise Machine.

Fleetwood exhaled, opened his eyes.

Regardless of this Innova's fear and caginess, *someone* would bring him to the Constabulary Hall. If not the Goddess, someone who, consciously or unconsciously, rode the dark tide of her will.

Already Mount Nevermind was peopled with spies and informants—"good gnomes" who saw their welfare mingled with that of the occupying army, and would sing out the whereabouts of any who stood in the way of that welfare.

Confidently, Fleetwood's eyes flickered over the labyrinth of mirrors.

There was a change in demeanor as well. A hectic, dithering people transformed, their movements already slower, more deliberate and heavy.

Heavy with order. With fear.

All of them headed for their jobs in the heart of the level, up and down pulleys and vanishing from his surveillance.

Vanishing for now.

But soon enough he would be able to see all of the city, from the nooks on the lowest level all the way to the threshold of the hall in which he sat now, contemplating the next step in his strategy.

Two things were to remain unharmed, Commander Khargos had decreed: the conduct of the Philosophers' Guild and the procedures of gnomish probate law.

Therefore, this Innova must have connections with both of these institutions. Part of some deal they had cut.

Still, one could . . . interrogate without harming. One could call into account those who knew the gnome in question. So the Bone Acolyte Oliver had suggested.

Oliver was right. Even though Fleetwood had never seen Innova, having been on the coasts of Sancrist when the little traitor came to Khargos in the night, there were those among the Philosophers and those in the courts who were his companions, his friends.

The gnome girl—Meryl Barium, was it?—had already suggested two names to the listening Fleetwood.

So if the search turned up empty and the spies returned without their quarry, he would summon those officials . . .

Those *former* officials . . .

. . . to a little chat in a mirrored room.

Counselor Scymnidus would be persuaded to counsel well. And as for the High Justice Gordusmajor . . . he would learn true justice at the hands of the Goddess.

* * * * *

A level below him, Commander Halion Khargos dozed in a room of compasses and sextants.

For an hour or so She had hovered at the perimeters of his thoughts—a dark shape edged with embodiment, as though a cloud was taking human form. He had tried to direct his imagining toward that form, had tried to focus on her, pick her out in a wavering dreamscape.

But the Goddess eluded him. It was as though she teased him back and forth from sleep to wakefulness, and it was all he could do to hold down his rising irritation.

Unbidden, thoughts of the waking world trickled into his dreams. For a moment he glimpsed, or thought he glimpsed, Subcommander Fleetwood in a darkened room somewhere below him, and Subcommander Hanna on patrol through the same cloistered regions, her hand on her sword and the glitter of lamplight in her suddenly golden eyes.

All of this was false, was a dream's distortion. Even as he waded through sleep he knew that much, knew his commanders were where he had ordered them, about the business he commanded.

Wearily, he pushed away the illusions and sought the Goddess at the twilight edge of his dream.

Why don't you appear? he found himself asking. Why so long an absence, my Queen?

From the gray and cloudy edge of his imagined sight, a voice rose, calm and only mildly chiding.

Who are you to question my presence and absence?

Know this, if you know aught: I have been about business in which you will figure. Been about it for years, since before the days of your testing and even before your birth, my darling.

154

He had no choice but to accept this explanation. But a part of him yearned with hunger and loneliness, and now that She had returned, he wanted answers.

You are on the border of those answers already, the Dark Queen soothed, anticipating his questions. *Arrived by your own ingenuity and intuitions.*

And by my guidance, of course.

Have I not told you, time and again, that my will and intelligence flows through your very instincts, because you are the one I have chosen?

But the choosing is long, My Queen, Khargos protested in his thoughts. Long and difficult, and clouded with false images.

Do not despair, soothed the Goddess. *You are in a nest of old chaos. The fabric of dreams is seldom transparent, and the images placed before you are deceptive but never entirely false.*

Khargos started to ask yet another question, but the voice of the Goddess stilled his thoughts.

I am concerned with a more constant, less dramatic chaos , she explained. *Perhaps you might call it a natural disruption, particular to this place and this people.*

Though the gnomes may amuse you—and do not think I have failed to notice that, Halion Khargos—they would eventually have come to annoy you, were it not for this machine in their midst.

The Paradise Machine?

It will bring a kind of order to them, though it will never still the confusion in their hearts. But the importance of this machine is far greater than controlling an undisciplined people.

The shadow wights. The miragos . . .

My prophetic soul! Khargos exclaimed to himself.

My prophecy coursing through your soul, the Goddess corrected. *But ultimately, it is all the same.*

And ultimately, the wights and miragos cannot stand against this . . . chain reaction of order. Your intuitions were right on this.

As I knew they were, because I am the mother of your intuitions.

Keep this in mind in the days to come. Your task will be to let the Machine . . . complete itself. Soon, Mount Nevermind will be a network of efficiency. But for this to happen, you must hold fast for a time.

Against all chaos—the chaos spreading through the Isle of Sancrist, and the chaos lodged forever in the hearts of its inhabitants.

But why this wait, Mother? Halion Khargos asked. Why so long between our communions?

A long pause followed the questions.

What I shall tell you instead, the Goddess answered at last, *is why I have chosen to commune with you now.*

Something new has arisen. You must hasten to find this gnome Innova.

So I intend, my Queen. When we agreed to employ his treason, I bound myself in honor only to the preservation of a single guild, a single set of laws.

I did not agree to Innova's protection.

Nor did you agree with the true Innova. The gnome who came to you that night in the rocks overlooking Mount Nevermind was not the inventor of the Paradise Machine, but an impostor, intent on having another suffer for his treason.

His treason is immaterial to me. It is the real Innova I seek.

So I shall seek the true Innova, Khargos replied.

That process has begun. Above you, the Subcommander Fleetwood has begun the search.

Very good.

He has begun . . . by making inquiry amid the courts of law and the Philosophers' Guild.

Khargos was outraged. "Insubordinate!" he said aloud, his waking voice jostling the flow of his dreams. For a moment he seemed to rise toward light.

But then, with a soft tug from the Goddess's voice, he settled again into visionary sleep.

Insubordinate, yes. But immaterial as well. For your honor is not compromised when you break a pact with someone who has represented himself as someone else, now is it?

I'm . . . I'm . . .

You're uncertain. Sometimes this affinity with honor is rigid. You did not treat with Innova: Let that be your guide.

And the insubordination was not Fleetwood's. At least not his alone.

Oliver suggested this strategy to the Subcommander. Oliver's hand guided the plan and direction.

You should watch the hand of Oliver, my darling. He has vast and visionary designs.

Now the Goddess began to fade. The solidified edge of the dream, in outline vaguely female, seemed to dissolve into an enveloping mist, and Halion Khargos felt the presence leaving him. Faint sounds from the rooms of the Geometers' Guild trickled into his consciousness, and he felt himself moving, slowly and inevitably, toward the threshold of waking.

Wait! his soul cried out. By your own holy and limitless name, wait!

At the edge of light, his dreaming hovered.

I know what you want, the Goddess declared.

The touch, Khargos said. Let your communion fill me entirely.

Chapter 19

The grand process of reforming Mount Nevermind was like the movement of the machines that reformed it. It was constant, quick, and dramatic, and for a while, even given the horrible rumors of what was afoot in Incline Barium's Necropolis below, the gnomes appreciated its efficiency.

For after all, who would not enjoy a walk on the Thirtieth Level, free from fear that an improvised building would collapse on your head or that a gnomeflinger would rocket you seven levels down to an untimely end somewhere in the depths of the crater?

The carts ran on time, most of the lighting worked, and the complex and often-malfunctioning plumbing system bubbled and drained and flushed like a pipefitter's dream.

Even the little-known Publishers' Guild was back to work, its bookmills running for the first and only time. Now, all you had to do was push the log into one side of the long, grinding tube, insert the leather for the cover, and breathe the spoken words over the megaphone in mid-process, and the fully bound copy of *Song of Huma* would emerge from the other side, free of misprint and typographical error.

It was all competent. It was all reliable.

It was all boring.

For something paled in the act of invention, in design and in engineering, when there was no prospect of failure. It diminished the joy of hurtling by gnomeflinger into the receiving nets when you knew that there was no prospect of hitting the wall or of missing everything altogether.

The excitement of receiving mail diminished when it came reliably and on time, and getting from one place to another by steam cart was no longer an adventure.

More idealistic souls saw the trouble early. Within two days after the Knights had seized the Thirtieth Level, the perfectly functioning metavox echoed with the news of an attempted sabotage. A handful of gnomes—stragglers, it was said, from Glorius Peterloo's dismantled army, took axes and light explosives to one of the dipping devices.

They were amazed when, in a matter of moments, the thing began to reassemble. The Paradise Machine, it seemed, housed the secret not only of perpetual motion but of perpetual renewal.

The saboteurs, on their way under guard to the notorious Twenty-Sixth Level, set aside most of their fears in typical gnomish speculation.

What *is* this machine? they asked themselves, as the Knights of Takhisis tightened the shackles.

And how, in the name of great hammering Reorx, does the blasted thing work?

It was enough distraction. Gradually, the more rebellious citizens of Mount Nevermind were brought to the place of torture, while the whole city brooded on speculative mechanics. Faced with the new technology, the astonishment of a dozen guilds changed quickly into acceptance.

And acceptance changed back to boredom.

So, that part of the gnomish character that delights in surprise and intrigue flared into new, uneasy life when a message from the Geometers' Guild was blazoned over the metavox into all awaiting gnome ears.

Halion Khargos, Commander in the Knights of Takhisis, Occupying General, and Sovereign of the Provisional Government of Mount Nevermind, requested the presence of the High Justice Gordusmajor and Public Counselor Scymnidus Carcharias, for a council on the Twenty-Ninth Level.

They will not show, maintained the gossipmongers.

It was an opinion based on more than logic. After all, Counselor Scymnidus was Mount Nevermind's most notorious paranoid, and the High Justice was . . .

Well, he was Gordusmajor, the Mediator of Surprises, who answered no human summons.

If he had sprouted wings and circled the mouth of Mount Nevermind's volcano in robes of pink velvet, he could not have surprised the city more than he did when, carried on a litter above six puffing law clerks, he rode to Khargos's headquarters in the Geometers' Guild Hall.

He made an emperor's entrance. The law clerks, flushed and sweating, carried the litter up the long steps to the hall entrance. Tilting it ever so slightly to negotiate the wide doors that were just not wide enough, they staggered into the anteroom and set their burden down before the wide-eyed Commander.

This creature was unlike anything Khargos had ever seen. Clad in wooden ceremonial armor, topped with a wide-brimmed hat that was heavy with bells and plumes and silk flowers, Gordusmajor looked more like a courtesan's barge than a High Justice.

Dismissing his litter-bearers, the enormous gnome produced a bag of walnuts and began to crack them between his heavily ringed fingers. Lazily, his gaze sought Halion Khargos's.

"So at last we meet, Halion Khargos," Gordusmajor rumbled.

"I had no idea you were eager to see me," the Commander replied ironically.

"Oh, eagerness has nothing to do with it, Commander. I simply thought that 'so at last we meet' had a ring of drama about it. Something out of a high-flying romance, worthy of a convergence of two . . . noted figures."

So *that* was how the old bounder meant to play it, Khargos thought. Trying to brave his way by me.

Very well. I have faced down more formidable enemies.

"If it's drama, you're after, High Justice Gordusmajor, I regret to disappoint you. I have summoned you here—"

"*Asked* me here," the Justice corrected.

"Very well. *Asked* you here but to answer a series of questions. Where is your colleague Scymnidus Carcharias? For I requested his presence as well."

"Where is Lord Ariakan?"

"On the continent, I suppose," Khargos replied.

"You aren't *sure*?" the High Justice asked, his tiny, glittering eyes narrowing further.

Khargos sighed in annoyance. "You are not party to our strategies, sir."

"So you know where he is, but won't tell me."

Khargos frowned. "It would be a lie to say I am certain of his whereabouts."

The High Justice Gordusmajor smiled. "And you and the Lord Ariakan are close in alliance. Judge and barrister are restrained by legal ethics from too intimate a friendship."

Khargos smiled despite himself. It was the first time, he guessed, that this old bastard had considered legal ethics. Why, the very words seemed difficult for Gordusmajor to say!

"Then we shall talk of what you know alone, High Justice. Of the whereabouts of a gnome named Innova."

Gordusmajor waved away the question with stubby, sparkling fingers.

"I know nobody by that name."

"My intelligence tells me otherwise," Khargos said. "I have heard that he sits on the Guild Council with you. That, indeed, he was your appointment."

Gordusmajor cracked another pair of walnuts. "Oh, *that* Innova. He vanished not long after the appointment. 'Into thin air,' as the poets have it. Things around here have been a bit confusing and dramaturgical since you arrived."

Khargos dismissed the dismissal. "You have heard nothing of him since?" he asked, scouting the old Justice's face for revelation.

Gordusmajor gazed into his palm, picking walnut meat from the fractured shells. "It seems so long since I spoke to the lad. I suppose that what I could tell you would be quite irrelevant by now."

Halion Khargos stood and began to pace the room. "Enough of this dodging and doubletalk!" he snapped. "This is no conclave of philosophers! I have asked you a simple question—"

"And you have not learned that, among the gnomes, there are no simple answers?"

The Justice's face was serene.

Khargos wrestled down his rising fury. "Then perhaps you should stay with us," he suggested in a voice that was stripped of all suggestion, all protocol, "until you can devise a simple answer."

161

"Oh, I must decline that invitation," Gordusmajor replied merrily. "I have work to do at the guild. Dues to collect and questions to hear and consider, followed by more dues, if my answers are the answers I foresee them to be."

"Perhaps I have been unclear," Khargos said. "This is no invitation. It is a command."

"I should hesitate to command a justice if I were you, Halion Khargos," Gordusmajor replied, a subtle note of steel lacing like a needle through his booming voice. "I know of your talents, of your fabled brilliance and continual communion with the Goddess. I know how early those talents were recognized. . . . "

He paused, cracked another walnut, and gazed slyly at the young Commander.

"In fact, it amazes me that those talents were not recognized earlier. If not by the Knights of Takhisis, by the powers that be in . . . oh, perhaps another Order?"

Halion Khargos stopped short in his pacing. "Just what is *that* supposed to mean?"

Gordusmajor laughed coldly. "Oh, we both know what it means, boy! *You* know, *I* know, and a dozen of my clerks know as well. A dozen well-placed young guildmembers, sworn and bribed to silence, unless I am detained or otherwise dispensed with. If, however, I do encounter obstruction or misfortune, you and your followers will hear what we *all* know, trumpeted from the newly efficient and highly widespread metavox network that is only one sign of your glorious efforts in renewing Mount Nevermind."

Khargos stood over the old gnome now, rising to his full height. His hand, resting lightly on his sword, shook slightly and for only an instant.

Gordusmajor saw it. Nothing escaped Gordusmajor.

"And there is something I should ask of you in turn," the old gnome said slyly. "The presence of Subcommander Fleetwood at the continuing hearings of the Philosopher's Tribunal."

Khargos was stunned. The old bastard was trying to dictate policy—the conquered calling the shots, while the conqueror jumped to attention!

"Don't trifle with me, old fellow," Khargos muttered, softly and venomously. "Divinity runs in my veins."

"And ale in mine," Gordusmajor replied. "We'll see which is the stronger. But I think that the Subcommander's presence would do much to allay . . . *loose talk in high circles*, if you understand."

"I understand more thoroughly than you might imagine, High Justice," Khargos replied, doing his best to muster his shaken authority.

"Then, if we understand each other," Gordusmajor continued calmly, "I suppose we have an understanding. I shall expect the Subcommander's attendance within the fortnight."

"How dare you!" Khargos muttered, but the keen ears of the Justice heard him clearly.

"The question, Commander," Gordusmajor replied coldly, slowly, "is how you can dare otherwise."

* * * * *

The old gnome knew. Khargos was certain of it.

At least part of the story.

It was a history he had struggled to keep secret—his early days on this very island.

Now, left alone amid geometers' tools, in the littered and crumbling anteroom of the guild hall, Halion Khargos remembered his early call into the Knights of Takhisis.

His beginning in a village of beachcombers was humble enough. The mornings of unseasonable cold and of salt spray, when his father and mother had risen before sunrise to scavenge the shorelines for driftwood, for flotsam they could peddle in the neighboring communities scattered along the coast of Sancrist—monotonous little towns impoverished by the War of the Lance.

Mant and Lyra Kannay.

His name had been Hylon then. A Knight's name, chosen instead of Nob or Kettle in a peasant's feeble attempt to give an only son some kind of grandeur at his beginnings.

Never mind the disappointments and failures that would follow of necessity, the growing years in which a boy's achievement and sputtering glory would be restrained by the fact that he was a beachcomber's son, and the name would mock him.

That is Hylon, selling dried seaweed and sand crabs.

That is Hylon. Give him a coin for his troubles.

All the time the boy dreamed of the War of the Lance. His father had served under Solamnic banners—no Knight, no officer, but a foot soldier whose tour of duty was a watch on the edge of the island.

And yet Mant Kallay was a kind of hero to his son, his flesh and blood connection to the high romance of lances and dragons, of elves and fabulous armies. Of Sturm Brightblade and Tanis Half-Elven, true heroes who peopled his dreams when Hylon stalked the beaches, swinging a driftwood sword at imagined draconians.

The Solamnic Order was beyond his grasp. He had been weaned on that knowledge by parents who tried to spare him the greatest of injuries.

If he did not hope, he would not suffer. That was their philosophy, and though his childhood was bleak because of their discouragements, it was not horrible, no matter how hard he tried to imagine it so.

For there was always time to dream, and in his dream a dark woman came to him, enticing and nurturing him, leaving him confused but somehow sustained.

Hylon's waking thoughts were filled with the Order, with nobility and glittering armor and high honor on the fields of the distant continent.

He watched the shorelines, expecting wonders.

On many occasions he saw the gnome steamboats chugging through the tides, raising and lowering banners in a frenzy of indecision. They made him laugh with their machineries, and in later, darker times, the laughter sustained him.

It was why, in later years and as Halion Khargos, the lad had more sympathy with gnomes than a Wing Commander should allow himself.

More importantly, he saw the Solamnic Knights on maneuvers three times during the drudgery of his youth. Rose, Sword, and Crown on their bright banners, the glitter of armor, the battle cries as pure and clear as the evening bells from the chapel at Castle Uth Wistan. Twice he watched them from a distance, gaped at the beauty and precision of their ranks.

The third time, like in the old stories, was lucky.

They were farther north than he had imagined they would come. Five riders coursing the beach just south of Xenos, where the boy was drawing in the tidal nets, heavy with the ocean's leavings.

One of them reined in his horse, regarded young Hylon with a look that was distant, but not unkind. Encouraged by the attention, by a strange wild prompting in his blood, Hylon drew a heavy piece of driftwood from the tendrils of the net and, wielding it like a sword, began maneuvers of his own.

Up the beach he danced, pivoting and whirling like a cyclone, like a high wind off the straits. He imagined himself in this august and mounted company, and for a moment the nets and the clinging sand seemed to vanish, the smell of seaweed and rotting mollusks faded into a surpassing sweetness, and the sodden wood in his hand took on lightness and leverage.

Spinning and dancing, he finally knelt on the beach, his lungs burning from the long exertion. Like a vassal or, better yet, like a squire, he offered his weed-covered weapon to the young knight seated above him.

Who smiled, and asked his name.

The young Knight, it seemed, was Mallon uth Gargas, new to the Order, in search of a squire of his own. Something in Hylon's boldness and skill had touched him, and as he rode away, he looked over his shoulder at the weary boy, waving as the sunstruck horizon opened to receive him.

He returned to the beach that evening, to the campfire of Mant Kallay, with an offer that stunned the father and delighted the boy.

Despite Hylon's origins, the young Knight told them, the Order was open to a resourceful boy. No, it had not always been like that; there was a time when the Solamnics had chosen their number from old, aristocratic families. But it was a new age—the War of the Lance had seen to that.

165

Mallon uth Gargas was part of that new age.

Dumbstruck, coaxed and begged by his son, the beach-comber consented. For two months, Hylon Kallay stood on the threshold of a miracle.

He kept his belongings packed, there on the beach in his father's tent. At night, before he slept, his eyes would rest on his only decent clothing—a red tunic, embroidered by Lyra with silver thread toward the day when he *went off to seek his fortune*.

For the first time in his memory, his nights were calm and dreamless.

But the summons never came. Mallon uth Gargas never returned, and eagerness turned to impatience and then to despair. And at last, as if to console him, the dark woman came back to the edge of his dreams.

Perhaps he has been injured, Hylon told the dream-figure. Perhaps he has been called away, delayed in his returning.

Perhaps he has forgotten, was the reply. *Or perhaps the rules of the Order were more . . . severe than he realized.*

You are a beachcomber's son, Hylon Kallay. Despite their high-sounding words, none who follow the Rose, the Sword, or the Crown will forget that or let you forget it.

Six months passed. Despair turned to anger. In his dreams he saw Mallon uth Gargas fall on the field of battle, a dark lance piercing his side. Hylon awoke from the dreams uncertain whether to mourn or to exult in grim resentment.

Shadowjoy, they called it, delight in the misfortune of others. It was dishonorable. He told it to go away.

But it came in his dreams with the woman, and eventually he listened.

No Knight of Solamnia, the dark lady said, *will forgive you your origins.*

But an Order is forming in which you will be welcome. An Order that recognizes courage and resolve as the true signs of aristocracy.

He was heartened at the news. Heartened, even when She told him that courage and resolve would mean one thing first: He must erase his past, his origins and must enter this Order as a blank slate, all present and future.

He consented. By his honor, he consented. And though his thoughts wavered when She directed him to his father's side of the tent in the dead of night, when She guided his hand on the dagger . . .

After all, Mant Kallay had been his son's prison. The mire of a beachcomber's line had kept him from true service and sacrifice.

When it was explained to you, it no longer seemed like murder.

He fled the still tent at sunrise, leaving behind him the torn red robe, its silver stitchery dabbed with blood where he had wiped the dagger. Climbing into the foothills, looking back only once, he had seen a horseman approaching the tent of his father.

A man in armor, whose shield bore the sign of the Sword.

And Hylon Kallay, renamed Halion Khargos by the Goddess he had chosen to serve, fled into the forest and the high rocky ground of northern Sancrist. He had nothing left to say to Mallon uth Gargas, and the Goddess told him later that the Knight had returned out of a counterfeit honor, to soothe his own soul by telling a peasant boy, face to face, that the boy was unworthy.

It was the story She had told him for years. He told himself through the time of his calling, through his swift and grueling training, and even at the moment of the Vision, when, in accordance with the dictates of the Order, his soul had meshed with Takhisis herself, and he had received his future in Her black and glittering eyes.

He had not been surprised that the Dark Queen was the lady of his dreaming. Nor was he surprised when his version of what happened on the beach south of Xenos was confirmed by her every word.

After all, could he have returned to face Mallon uth Gargas, who could not have understood the ghastly scene amid the tents on the beach? Who could not have understood that it was a form of erasure?

Of cleansing?

Yet, in the darkest hours of the Goddess's absence, he would sometimes forget Her explanation. Sometimes the horror of what he had done would rise to meet him in that swimming country between dream and waking, and he would be afraid—afraid for himself, and for the honor he grasped desperately as his armies spread across the western frontiers.

Do not think of Mant Kallay, he told himself.

But he was sure that Gordusmajor knew. Somehow, the assurances of the Goddess—*no one knows, none will ever know*—had become, in their recent infrequency, thin and strained.

Cursing himself for his doubt, he cleared his throat and stepped toward the metavox called the name of Subcommander Fleetwood.

* * * * *

He had finished his orders when the guard announced the visit of Subcommander Hanna.

She came with mixed news. The sought-after Counselor Scymnidus seemed to have vanished from the city, leaving behind a series of taunting notes that had the Knights scattering in all directions through the upper levels, nosing out clues that led them to sheer walls, to caved-in tunnels, and (in one especially unfortunate situation) a spring trap that had launched the searcher into the rafters of the Carpenters' Hall, where, lodged among the beams, he was proving a rough customer for the guild members to free.

Innova was missing as well. Both Innovas—the impostor and the true designer of the Paradise Machine. The search continued for both of them, but the false Innova had covered his tracks and the true Innova had no tracks to cover.

Oliver was missing. The Subcommander feared that the Skull Knight had been ambushed. After all, it was well known that the gnomes mistrusted clerical magic.

Halion Khargos feared something else. But he kept silent, in accord with the Goddess's promptings.

There was good news, Hanna reported. Good news from the battlements surrounding the city.

It seemed that a pair of shadow wights—the swirling, undoing creatures the Knights had encountered on the beaches of Sancrist—had followed Fleetwood's forces to the lip of Mount Nevermind but no farther.

One of them, it seemed, had attempted to gain entry by one of the adits along the upper west side of the mountain. Caught up in a pulley system, it was rent apart with a series of unearthly shrieks.

"It was odd, though," Hanna explained. "For when there was nothing left of the creature, when it was . . . *absorbed* into the machine, the screams did not really stop. The guards said that they *faded*, became a part of the creaking of the ropes through the pulleys. It was like they blended in, the guard said."

Khargos leaned forward in his chair intently. This was news, but already it stood on the brink of making sense.

"And the other one?" he asked Hanna.

"Still hovering outside the city. You can see it wavering there in the high rocks, absorbing the light, sucking in the air."

"But not approaching?" Khargos asked.

The Subcommander nodded. "It's as though the thing is . . . confused, has met up with something past its knowing."

Khargos knew the feeling. Though he was somewhat sure that the Paradise Machine was holding off the advances of the Chaos creatures, he was sure of little else.

Why was it working? Was it the machine itself or something about the mountain?

Chapter 20

"But they will know *something* if I wear the eye patch!" Deddalo protested.

Beryl Barium faced him in the shadowy common room of the Hell With Dinner. At a far table, two gully dwarves peered despondently into the bottoms of their mugs, ignoring the arguing gnome couple at the bar.

Deddalo stared at his estranged fiancée. The patch she held before him was a monstrosity—gold cloth embroidered with the Barium coat of arms, as though she was laying claim to his drooping eye.

He had come to dread Beryl in the last week. Her voice, once soothing and oiled with the prospect of money, grated on him now. Everything he did, from sweeping the pub floors to hiding from the Knights, was a source of criticism and complaint.

We'll wait, she commanded him. Wait till this all blows over.

And even the way he waited was not good enough for her.

In fact, he had been relieved when she vanished two days before. Had spent the time in serene quiet, waxing the bar and imagining trapdoors in her path, her feet stepping out in darkness and descending on nothing but a sheer drop—

"I don't know why you won't wear it," Beryl protested. "You're safe down here, after all. You'll be safer still when the *real* Innova is brought into custody, and the machinery of our little plan will grind to its fitting and proper conclusion."

"But until then I'm fair game for every Knight and brute who saw me in the hills around Mount Nevermind," Deddalo whined. "*I'm* the one they'll arrest, the one who brought them here and showed them the avenues, who brought them to power and thereby became liable. They won't touch the *real* Innova. And the gods—from great Reorx himself through their own visionary—have no idea where he is, anyway."

Beryl sighed, leaned against the bar, propping her elbows in the center of two spiraling mug stains. "It's been confining, you know. Downright frustrating, to be an exile in my own city. All because I saddled myself with you, the fanciest talker among dozens of capable suitors. You entangled me with poetry and speeches, bent my innocence to your will, and it turns out you haven't the sense—"

"Sense to do what?" Deddalo growled, tightening a propeller on the back of the mechanical Barium girl and making a note that he would figure out a good use for it later. "This plan has spun out of my hands, like that damnable machine upside—half goose, half derrick, my speculative ass! I don't know what to do next—whether to come out of hiding or draw deeper in, vanishing like a hero into the darkness and the rock. I don't know whether Khargos is after the *real* Innova or whether he has designs on *my* barely protected skin. Whether the Twenty-Fifth Level is safe to walk, or whether that Fleetwood up top has the whole neighborhood mirrored up, just waiting for a chance to pounce—"

"Which explains my quick-witted absence over the last several days," Beryl interrupted. "Or hadn't you noticed?"

Deddalo slipped on the eye patch, regarded his intended with a serious gaze. "I counted the moments until you returned, my dearest."

Behind the embroidered cloth, he could feel his eyelid tightening.

One of the gully dwarves coughed in the far corner.

"I don't know whether to believe you or not," Beryl said coldly. "But I suppose even *that* is better than being *completely* sure you're a liar."

Deddalo shrugged. He would have supposed otherwise.

"But I shall be boiled," Beryl continued, "before I let your cowardice stand in the way of our increasing power in the halls of Mount Nevermind!"

"Power?" Deddalo looked nervously into the bottom of a mug. "What power is there hiding in a pub, five levels away from the movers and shakers, a barkeep to oblivion?"

One of the dwarves coughed even more loudly.

"Shurrup!" Deddalo snapped to the too-insistent customer. "As though you're aware of what 'oblivion' means, all of a sudden!" He fell silent then, tightened the wing nuts on the automaton's temples until her ball-bearing eyes bulged with discomfort.

"I thought that Khargos was as good as his word," Deddalo murmured. "I thought they held with that business of Code and Oath like some kind of sour Solamnics. Now I hear that he's sending Fleetwood to supervise the hearings at the Philosopher's Tribunal, and I'll wager *that* villain will be questioning the judges and lawyers regarding my whereabouts."

"Regarding *Innova*'s whereabouts, my darling, my sweet," Beryl replied acidly. "Remember, yours is *not* the name in question."

It was all too confusing.

"Get out!" Deddalo shouted at the gully dwarves, who gathered their mugs and made for the door.

"And leave those tankards behind you!" Deddalo called after them, but they were out of the pub and onto the street, the faint ringing of shattered crockery telling him that they had dropped their trophies in their panic.

"It's 'Innova this' and 'Innova that,' whichever way I turn!" Deddalo complained to Beryl, trying to mask the rising whine in his voice. "And *I'm* the Innova that Khargos wants!"

Calmly, Beryl traced her stubby forefinger over the waxed surface of the bar. "The one he wants. But not the one he'll get. We'll get him the *real* Innova."

"But he'll *know*, Beryl!" Deddalo whined, his voice rising. "He'll know the difference! They *say* we all look alike, but they never *mean* it!"

"He'll never see the Innova we bring in," Beryl replied. "After all, the fate of a low-priced traitor is no concern of the Occupying General, of the Big Man on the Twenty-Ninth Level. Khargos is wrapped up in romancing the Dark Queen, in some kind of fascination with the Paradise Machine."

"That's part of the problem as well," Deddalo moaned.

"Khargos thinks *I* am the inventor! If he questions me, what'll I do? Show him your artificial sister?"

Beryl laughed bitterly. "I should have hitched my wagon to the *real* Innova's comet. I'd be on the Thirtieth Level now, dining on goose livers and Qualinesti wine. Still, we've a chance to rise in power . . . if the right ones rise among the powerful. Some of Khargos's officers, whom I've asked around—asked that they come and attend us here. 'Sample the wares,' I said, in my voice of superlative espionage."

She batted her eyelids flirtatiously. "Of course, they might be drawn to my . . . countenance. They're young and impressionable, and a pretty face can sometimes persuade when rhetoric and machinery fail. But even if they're thick-blooded and distant—and I wouldn't rely on that, Deddalo—there's enough interest in this Paradise Machine that the Knights are asking all kinds of questions."

"To which I have none of the answers," Deddalo said, glancing furtively at the open door to the pub. "I don't know how the damned thing works—a *toy* that keeps grinding on forever, regardless of the laws of physics. There's no telling what the Knights might do to get information from me—information I don't have in the first place. And if Khargos knows I'm *not* Innova, I'll be punished for lying, I'm certain. The long and the short of it is, if I have to answer to Khargos, I'm cooked either way."

Beryl regarded him slyly. "But what if . . . it's someone else you answer to?"

"I . . . don't understand."

A shadow fell over the open door. Standing at the threshold was a tall, gray-robed figure. Beneath his heavy cape, Deddalo caught a glimpse of a familiar insignia.

Order of the Bone. The darkest of the dark clerics.

"Deddalo," Beryl announced. "I present to you Oliver uth Umbros, Bone Acolyte."

* * * * *

Meanwhile, the real Innova fled into the bowels of Mount Nevermind.

Once he passed through the High Justice's painting, he had not looked back. His sense of depth and distance—a sense that comes second nature to gnomes and dwarves and others who dwell underground—soon told him that he was traveling deeply, that the tunnel from Gordusmajor's chambers wound down at least a dozen levels.

At times the tunnel vibrated with echoing sounds: guild whistles, the trailing shriek of a steam cart. Once a carillon of bells that told Innova he was passing the mousetrap factory, hard against the walls of the Twenty-Second Level.

There was something different in all these sounds. Whether it was something present or absent, he could not tell. Perhaps it was only that the noises of Mount Nevermind came to him strangely, muffled by layers of rock.

"Think!" he told himself. "What is it that you're missing, anyway?"

To aid his thoughts, he sang a song that his father—granulated long ago in that terrible accident—had taught him. A song to use when invention slowed down or failed.

> If thought is the mother
> > of all good action,
> Then what is the child
> > of plain distraction?
> Think! pay attention!
> > Let your mind change!
> Make everyday things
> > complicated and strange!
> There are fish to be fried,
> > but first to be caught:
> So spread wide the nets
> > and get tangled in thought!

The song worked like a spell. It dawned on him slowly. The sounds were orderly, synchronous.

The Paradise Machine.

"My damned dipping goose is setting a schedule," he muttered into the dimly lit tunnel. Something about the idea scared him, and he startled when the torches ahead sputtered suddenly to life, a whiff of natural gas rifling the air, then retreating.

Now the corridor was as well lit as a Thirtieth Level boulevard.

"I don't like this," Innova whispered.

He was still not sure why.

At last the tunnel widened. Innova stepped out onto a crumbling ledge on one of the middle levels—Thirteenth or Fourteenth, he guessed. Two generations of furniture had been stacked there, like an offering to a god of discord or of broken couches. It was strangely heartening, this mess at the mouth of the corridor.

Strangely good to know that *some* things in Mount Nevermind were still in need of arrangement.

With a renewed courage Innova waded through a jungle of chairs and climbed over a capsized table, all the while following a faint light at the far end of the ledge. Spring chairs and a bladed flying sofa littered his path, and he took care to avoid all movable parts.

At last he had walked as far as he could. The ledge broke away over a drop—two levels, he guessed, maybe three.

A fatal fall, by any account, and it was a good twenty yards to the other side, to safe purchase and the far lit tunnel.

"Now where do I go, Gordusmajor?" Innova muttered. He retraced his steps, examined the more kinetic furniture in an attempt to salvage a spring or lever that might propel him across the gap in the ledge.

"Nothing!" he grumbled, turning despairingly back to the gap he had to negotiate.

There was a footbridge spanning it. Misty stone, a low arch from one side to the other.

How had he missed it before?

Perhaps the Paradise Machine had restored it only now. But no, the machine didn't work like that. Or did it?

Innova stepped toward the footbridge, debating on whether to trust his weight to its narrow, cloudy span. Below it, the chasm plunged into unlit depths.

He took a deep breath and set his foot on the stretch of stone. For an instant it seemed that his foot pushed through a hazy substance, as soft and pervious as snow.

He gasped, drew back . . .

175

But suddenly, the stone was solid beneath his feet. He tested his weight, gathered courage, and sprinted across the little bridge, all the while marveling at what had just occurred. Safe on the other side, he turned around. The bridge lay behind him, as steady and unremarkable as the ledges it spanned.

High in the air, echoing at the edge of his hearing, something shrieked in torment, its shrill cry lost in an uncanny crackling, as though the screamer and the scream were glazed over by a swiftly moving, lethal ice.

* * * * *

The first gnomeflinger Innova found was long broken. It told him several things regarding his whereabouts.

Unfrequented country. Somewhere lower than he had imagined—below the levels that the High Justice had sentenced him to inspect and repair.

He sat down, regarded his surroundings. Odds were he could go for days down here without seeing the face of another.

It sounded like a good prospect. Here he could lie low, escape the scrutiny of spies and the patrols of Knights and brutes, until . . .

Until what?

For the first time, the urgency of the situation struck him. The Knights of Takhisis had actually seized Mount Nevermind. Their banners—Thorn and Lily, and even a Bone banner or two to cover all bets—draped from the balconies of the Thirtieth Level. The Guild Halls were back in a limited business—limited because the Paradise Machine had virtually abolished the need for repairs—and sixty per cent of their profits filled the coffers of the Knights of Takhisis.

All the while, armed patrols guarded each of the dipping geese that made up the city's ever-expanding Paradise Machine.

Hiding out would solve nothing. Innova could duck Khargos and the Knights for a goodly time, but all the while their power would establish and grow, and their grasp would tighten on the gnome city.

Eventually, they would seize him as well.

The lowest levels of the mountain beckoned to Innova. Down there, where no one trespassed or patrolled, he would be safest of all. He would barter for time, and he would search for Lucretius. The old gnome, filled with wisdom and plans, would surely have a strategy.

As a last resort, Lucretius could simply stop doing his lifelong task. Let the magma gather, press against rock and makeshift dams, and burst forth finally through the throat of the mountain.

If all else failed, the Life Quest Innova had waited for could be a simple one: to help old Lucretius vulcanize Mount Nevermind.

* * * * *

Dire thoughts soon faded as Innova made his way into the heart of the lower levels.

Down here was more familiar country. The arrangements of the upper levels gave way to a comfortable clutter. Cart tracks broke off into stone floors and crevasses, ending at sheer walls. Frayed ropes dangled like stalactites from the vaulted chambers, and windsocks, placed at the juncture of tunnels to catch long-vanished drafts, hung limp and molded.

Plenty of dangers here, Innova thought. But familiar dangers.

Oh, some things had changed. There was that . . . *evolving* bridge, or whatever it was. There was also that strange, regular rumbling from below, as if the mountain itself had begun to breathe.

But for the most part, things in the lower levels were much as he had left them. Innova was used to watching for pits and rockslides, for roving bands of desperate gully dwarves or for the occasional berserk machine, wrenched free of its moorings and cartwheeling between houses on a path toward eventual inertia.

You could breathe more easily when your only fear was that physical reality would collapse around you.

Because most of the time, it didn't.

Thus assured, Innova found the level's central stairwell, read the runic signs that encircled it, and discovered he was on the Ninth Level. Already he could feel the slight rise in temperature, could smell the burnt, powdery aroma of slowly cooling pumice.

Low enough, Innova told himself. Time to look and listen for old Lucretius.

What he heard instead, rising from the foot of the stairwell a level below, were younger voices. Several of them.

A party ascending the stairs.

Instantly alarmed, Innova ducked into the shadows.

"Slipped clean away!" one of the approaching voices exclaimed. "Right under their perfect aquiline noses. Good thing for him—*great* thing, for us!—that the Occupying General's Reconstruction warn't in full stride yet, and the Thirtieth Level's still filled with holes where a lad could just stomp the floor in and travel for days."

Innova smiled. Gnomes. Working-class fellows, their words surprisingly short and direct.

Probably part of Generalissimo Glorius Peterloo's scattered army.

"Well, *I* for one will be right glad to see him!" another replied. It was a young gnome, heavy-set, umbrellas affixed to his shoulders in what was most likely a simple device to break a fall in dark corridors. The fellow clambered to the top of the stairwell and turned in full view, talking to someone behind him. "They say he's the one last chance against the Knights of Takhisis."

"Just plain folk at the end of the day," an older gnome agreed, puffing on the last pair of steps as he climbed to join his younger companion. Lanterns swiveled atop his helmet— a more practical device, Innova thought.

"He's always been a good sort," the older fellow said. "A good sort if I ever seen one."

Innova smiled. These soldiers had heard of his escape, evidently. For after all, who else could be the subject of *that* conversation?

Here in the lower regions of Mount Nevermind, he would find support and sympathy.

It was enough for Innova. Imagining himself in full hero-ism, swashbuckling at the head of the forces of resistance, Innova stepped confidently from the shadows, lifted his open hands in salute, and called out merrily to the gnome soldiers.

"May the dozen-and-a-half gods, the whole deific pan-theon—bless all here!"

The two gnomes at the top of the stairwell leapt and col-lided in astonishment. One of them—the younger one—slid three steps down before one of his umbrellas hooked the railing and steadied him. Together, they regarded Innova with wide-eyed gazes.

Suddenly, those gazes narrowed.

In an instant they were on him, joined by two others. A flurry of limbs and robes and beards closed over Innova. An avalanche of punches rained on his head, his shoulders, his chest, and his stomach.

Innova gasped as his breath fled, and then, like a drown-ing bather, began to wrestle desperately for consciousness, perhaps for life. He pushed one assailant away, heard the fellow hit the wall with a thud. He kicked yet another, his foot rising in the fork of the trooper's legs, and with a sound like a strangled frog, the booted soldier somersaulted back-ward and out of view.

Finally, someone struck Innova a blow that scuttled his senses, a firm whack on the right ear. Reeling, his vision spangled like a geode, he wrenched himself from the grip of the gnome who straddled him and scrambled for the stair-well . . .

Which was the stupidest attempted escape in recent gnomish history.

Five others, veterans of skirmish and battle since Gener-alissimo Peterloo's youthful heyday, came up the steps to grab him.

"Hold him down!" a voice behind him called. "Magne-tize him to the pyrite on the corridor ceiling! It's Innovafer-tanimus, inventor and traitor!"

A heavy boot lodged on the back of Innova's neck, and he felt himself hoisted, wrapped in straps studded with magnets.

Fergus Ryan

He heard the imprisoning *click* as the straps locked into the low corridor ceiling.

"Let's see yer Paradise Machine get ye out o' this one, muckflipper!" a gravelly voice rumbled, and Innova, the back of his head pressed against cold stone, rolled his eyes to meet the gaze of a gnarled old sergeant, scotched with dueling scars and missing two fingers on the hand that was raising a spiked and formidable club.

Chapter 21

It was a wonder that the sergeant stayed his hand.

As a matter of fact, Innova thought, as the gnomes dragged him down the stairwell toward an unknown destination, it was pretty near a miracle. For the club-wielding sergeant, digits short of a full number, was none other than Flurious Akimbo, Hero of the Suppression and a favorite of the imprisoned Generalissimo.

This was the gnome who had quelled the gully dwarf uprising at Peterloo almost single-handed. When the rebels had walled themselves into a corner of the Fifteenth Level, it had been the Generalissimo's intention to starve them out.

After all, the gully dwarves had walled their provisions outside.

But Sergeant Akimbo, to whom patience was unknown, had ordered a battering ram set against the ramshackle gates of the rebel fortress, and as if that weren't enough, had lashed himself to the head of the ram, riding it as it broke through the rusty bolts and rotten wood.

He had wanted to be the first to breach the walls.

Instead, he had been the last to regain consciousness, a week later in the hospitals on the Twenty-Seventh Level.

It had been the gesture that mattered, the bold placing of himself in immediate danger, that had made Flurious Akimbo the hero of the hour in Mount Nevermind.

The old sergeant growled and lowered his club, as rough hands seized Innova and wrestled him to his feet.

Silently, the gnomes dragged Innova by the ankles to the spiraling staircase, then down one level, and another.

Innova tried to cry out, to beg for mercy, but his head smacked against each metal step, and soon the dark of the stairwell was overwhelmed by another dark, and he thought and remembered nothing.

*   *   *   *   *

Innova awoke in a shabby encampment—an old, unsettled chamber draped with stalactites, where stale water dripped steadily somewhere in the narrowing shadows.

An officer stood above him, regarding him skeptically, but with no real malice.

"Who . . . " Innova began, but the officer shook his head.

"If half of what is said is true," he said, "you're in a dungheap of trouble, Master Innova."

"Half of what is said is rarely true," Innova replied, masking the tremor in his voice.

"I know," the officer replied. "That's why you're still alive."

It hurt to breathe. It hurt to even blink. His eyes adjusting to the play of firelight and shadow, Innova caught a glimpse of the sentries stationed at the mouth of the chamber.

A famous insignia. A red gate broken by a dragon-headed ram.

Generalissimo Glorius Peterloo's army. Or what was left of it.

All around him lay wounded soldiers. Bandaged heads, arms in slings, or sleeves pinned where an arm was once. A jungle of limbs and broken bodies, the only sound a long chorus of moans.

Moans and the rumbling cough of the pneumalaise—what the physicians called the disease that had come with the Knights into the city. Where the lungs filled with dark fluid and drowned the desperate breathers.

Some desperate medical technician had set up an enormous bellows, and two of the younger soldiers pumped at it heroically, stirring the stagnant air into warm, moist winds that circled the field hospital.

Moving air breeds less infection, some philosopher had told them.

The soldiers didn't believe it. They had come here to die. From all corners of Mount Nevermind they had assembled, less than a week ago, their glorious duty to repel an invading army. But someone had betrayed them: Deep in the hollows of the mountain, someone had shown entry to the Knights of Takhisis, and these courageous gnomes had been caught in a withering vise of steel and magic.

Someone had betrayed them. It had not taken long for that rumor to reach every gnome within the sound of the metavox.

And the Paradise Machine, up and running in the topmost levels, was sealing the Knights behind a web of defenses. The Paradise Machine that was Innova's own invention.

Cause and effect, he thought. That old madness.

"You *are* Innovafertanimusmutatas . . . " the officer began.

It took no genius to realize what would follow.

Innova stared into the eyes of the gnome Commander—two gray pools that he hoped were not without a small eddy of tenderness and compassion.

"I am that notorious Innova, sir," he began. "But before I go further, I believe you are honor bound to tell me your name. I am entitled to know my interrogator. My . . . my confessor, if you will."

The officer nodded. "Only fair. I am Lieutenant Colonel Grex Pointillo, late of the staff of Generalissimo Glorius Peterloo and provisional Commander of the gnome army of resistance."

"Pointillo? But I had heard you were—"

And suddenly, the conversation he had overheard on the stairwell became clear to Innova.

Slipped clean away. The one last chance against the Knights of Takhisis.

Just plain folk at the end of the day.

Pointillo was the one whom the soldiers were talking about on the stairwell.

Innova laughed bitterly.

"I am turned in by my own vanity," he muttered.

The colonel's eyes widened. "Tell me *that* story," he urged his captive.

He was blunt. To the point. Immediately, despite the awkward situation, Innova struck a liking for his captor.

They talked alike. Perhaps they listened alike as well.

So he began. As Pointillo helped him to his feet, Innova recounted the events surrounding the philosophers' contest, the competitive inventions, and his own appointment to the guild. He spoke as well of his own sorrow that the Paradise Machine, devised with mostly good intentions, had come to haunt Mount Nevermind, as the machines of defense and control had begun to function at last.

It felt almost like a last confession.

Of course, Innova sincerely hoped it was not.

All the same, there were some things he held back. He carefully avoided too much mention of Deddalo. Something within Innova balked at blaming his friend for the death of old Incline Barium, the false accusations surrounding Talos, and the betrayal of the city.

Perhaps his old companion was guilty of all these things. He would leave that decision to the barristers and judges.

At the end of his account, Lieutenant Colonel Grex Pointillo regarded him skeptically. With a gentle gesture, he guided him through the litter of bodies toward an open space in an adjoining chamber.

"You don't believe me, do you, Colonel?"

Pointillo seated himself on a low stool in the center of the room. Scrawled on the floor were elaborate lines of chalk and charcoal—something runic, perhaps, or perhaps a battle plan. From his prospect at the threshold of the chamber, Innova could not tell.

"I believe you in part," the colonel replied, "which is as much as I believe anyone these days."

"So you said."

"There's more, isn't there?" the colonel asked, lowering his eyes to the scribblings at his feet. "Some things you aren't telling."

"I confess it, sir. But as a prisoner in time of conflict, I reserve the right not to betray my comrades."

Pointillo's eyes met his. In the shadowy room, it was difficult to read the colonel's face.

"It would be odd," he said, "if Mount Nevermind's most abject traitor refused to betray his friends. Especially to save his own neck."

"But I never betrayed the city!" Innova protested.

184

"I said it would be odd," Pointillo replied. "Not that you were that traitor. Now tell me about the Paradise Machine."

So Innova told him.

About his inspiration in the offices of Scymnidus Carcharias—the continual motion toy at the heart of the device. He explained how locating the devices above the self-refreshing pools of water in the upper levels of the city had assured that the motion was not only continual, but pretty near perpetual.

All of this was taken in by the colonel. Even though his eyes were cast upon the drawings at his feet, Grex Pointillo was listening—alertly, intuitively. After a while, he interrupted Innova's account.

"It may not work," he declared. "Something tells me it is basically, deeply flawed."

The machine? Innova was surprised at the strange and sudden hope that rose in him when the colonel spoke.

Was there a flaw somewhere in the making of the machine? A flaw that could be exploited—could set the defenses of Halion Khargos into chaos ?

"A flaw?" he asked aloud. "But where—"

"Oh, I was speaking of this battle plan," Pointillo said, leaning forward to trace a stubby finger along a black line at the edge of the drawing. "But I'll be bothered if I can figure it myself. What about the friction, Innova?"

Innova frowned. "I beg your pardon?"

"The friction. The Paradise Machine. I'm no engineer, but I do recall something about a Second Law in school. That all machines run down—"

"Except when they don't," Innova said, and told the colonel about the Graygem oil.

"Fascinating," Pointillo said, when Innova's story was ended. "And you say that this . . . *Lucretius* maintains no other earthly use for the substance?"

Innova nodded. "He should know. He's been down there his whole life."

Pointillo's gaze was steady on him now. The gnome officer arose from the short stool and approached him.

"Who is this Lucretius, Innovafertanimus?"

"Lucretius Climenole. Of the vanished clerical family."

Something in the colonel's countenance stirred. His gray eyes widened, and he laid a hand on Innova's shoulder.

"I'd like to meet this Lucretius Climenole," he murmured. "I have things to say to him, things to ask."

* * * * *

"This pneumalaise," Innova asked the colonel. "It's a product of Bone Order magic, is it not?"

"That's what they tell me," Grex Pointillo replied. "Though I also hear there's but one Bone Acolyte among 'em."

The two of them were bound down a long corridor, flanked with gnome guards. At the end of the tunnel a bright light fluttered—a bonfire, perhaps, or a vast assemblage of lamps.

Whatever it was, Innova reckoned, it was there he would see the heart of the army.

"And how," he asked the colonel, "do the Knights square the spreading of deadly disease with their vaunted honor?"

"Either their cleric is a man of great wretchedness," Pointillo replied bitterly, "or the rest of them have partaken of his poison. Whatever the case, there's a lot they need to square."

"I suppose it's to do with that Vision of theirs," Innova offered, and was surprised by the anger of the colonel's response.

"Convenient mysticism!" he snapped. "I heard it up and down in the prison topside, the Lily Knights rattling about 'Vision this' and 'Vision that.' But when it came down to it, they were doing exactly what they wanted, using a faint glimpse of some long-ago ritualized dream to justify whatever desire they had at the moment!"

"I see. But this Khargos, they say, moves in and out of the Vision at will."

"Even more convenient," Pointillo muttered. "The whole thing is like a manuscript in a foreign tongue or a dwarf-spirit delirium: You can't recall half of it once you're through it, so if you're weak enough . . . or desirous enough . . . you make what you remember fit what you want."

Pointillo suddenly stopped in mid-tunnel. Innova brushed against him, felt a tension passing through his captor.

"Sounds as though you're speaking from experience, Colonel," he observed.

Then cursed himself for the observing.

"More than you know, Innova," Grex Pointillo replied quietly. "We'd best hasten. I've a sergeant to disappoint."

*   *   *   *   *

The army of Generalissimo Glorius Peterloo, or what was left of it, had gathered in a vast rotunda that seemed to lie somewhere between levels, as though at one time excavators and engineers had decided there was room for further digging and then, confronted by impermeable rock, had changed their minds altogether.

It was this makeshift arena that Grex Pointillo and his confused captive and companion entered, walking straight into the midst of a tattered company.

A legion of gnome soldiers, three hundred strong, encircled a basket suspended from a huge crane. In the basket stood Sergeant Flurious Akimbo, his stubby arms waving passionately, afloat in waving wicker. All eyes were on the sergeant: some devoted, others horrified, for there seemed no middle ground in dealing with this prodigy.

Innova looked around. The army was considerably the worse for wear. The helmets issued by the militia were mostly missing, replaced by felt caps and kettles and, in one odd circumstance, a wicker basket. Some of the troops carried shields, but for the most part the seats of chairs, lids of barrels, and window shutters had been drafted to do new duty in an army ill-equipped and ill-tempered, banished to the outskirts of what was once their home.

In those outskirts, their imaginations, it seemed, had been unleashed. Bizarre inventions lay scattered on the floor of the chamber: an aquarium filled with brackish water, from which emanated two pulsing coils. A pair of pedal-operated vehicles, resembling velocipedes except for the fan blades set at a strange horizontal angle above the rider's seat. Mounds of disassembled metal parts, stacked haphazardly on the steam-powered handcarts that stood on the tracks that laced the chamber and the adjoining levels. Other gadgets seemed invented in desperation, bizarre things with tendrils, cogs, and levers the function of which Innova could not even imagine. Some of the devices throbbed with glistening membranes; in others, bone-colored, gelid ball bearings rolled in recessed sockets like blind eyes. They were probably weapons or vehicles, but in each of them was something uncannily evolved, like the deep-sea fish that retreat to the darkest depths of the ocean, transformed over generations into grotesques and monsters.

Sergeant Akimbo, it seemed, was concluding an emotional, fiery rallying speech. "Strike now!" he cried. "Strike as we have struck in the annals and levels of history, from this point at the nadir all the way to the uppermost level! Strike quickly, I urge you, before this traitor's damnable machine . . . "

The gesture toward the approaching Innova was menacing.

" . . . seals the city forever from our hands, and Mount Nevermind becomes but another Knight's encampment, but a bead on the necklace of the Dark Queen, a toothless cog in her vast, infernal machinery!"

Two hundred gnomes battered their makeshift shields in approval of the metaphor, spears and clubs and hydraulic wrenches rattling against cured leather, wood, and wicker in an angry drumming that echoed throughout the half-finished chamber.

Grex Pointillo raised his hand. The noise swept over him like an underground rumbling, and it was a long minute before he drew the eyes and ears of the troops he was supposed to command.

Innova swallowed hard. It did not look good. As the room fell into a grumbling quiet, it was apparent that power had slipped from the colonel's grasp and into the grasp of Flurious Akimbo.

"You'd best stand back, Colonel," the sergeant said gruffly. "I got no quarrel with officers, but the time has come when our thoughts must be bloody instead of . . . dainty and roundabout."

"So soon an ultimatum?" the colonel asked wearily.

Sergeant Akimbo frowned, replied bluntly. "We have waited in defeat and in darkness and in the lower levels far too long."

Silence fell on the vaulted room. Innova watched as Colonel Pointillo closed his eyes, seeming to travel to a space deep within his own being.

"Very well," he said at last. "If such is your intention, take your soldiers—those who *choose* to follow you, and none other—and mount your assault in any way you see fit. I shall not stand against you. If, on the other hand, you attempt to take my army, the bloody prospect will become blood in fact, and while I am standing, you will not seize command."

It made no sense. An abdication in the city's great time of need. Innova gaped at the colonel, who was lost somewhere in unfathomable thought.

All rules of strategy and command shouted that Colonel Grex Pointillo had shown an unforgivable weakness here, giving over his authority to a headstrong sergeant. Yet there was still strength in his bearing, as though a deeper force—perhaps the will of the mountain itself—sustained his deciding.

Not that I can choose, Innova thought. But if I could, despite all that I have been told . . .

My choice would lie with the Colonel.

So as Flurious Akimbo gathered his soldiers and a heavy gloom settled upon the gnome encampment, Innova did what he could to stay by the Commander of his choosing. Pointillo was quiet, almost meditative, as nearly ten score of his troopers prepared to embark.

"What . . . what do you plan to *do*, Colonel?" Innova asked.

But he received no answer.

Not until the ranks gathered about the spiraling stairwell at the center of the level, and under crisp orders from the rebellious sergeant, what remained of the Generalissimo's army was divided almost in half—some to a dangerous destination in the upper levels, the others to . . . to where?

Again Innova asked, and this time received a response.

"We are bound, you and I," Grex Pointillo said, "to the lowest levels. I can do nothing else but trust you, since all other trust is shearing away. This Lucretius Climenole is someone I have sought for years. He may know more about undoing this Paradise Machine than even *he* knows."

Chapter 22

Years later, when someone spoke of the Siege of Mount Nevermind, people would ask him which siege he meant.

Was it the first one, the siege of a day, in which the Knights of Takhisis gained secret entry to the lower levels of the city and then, by betrayals and magic and force, seized the government in a matter of hours?

Was it that darker moment in gnome history—the vain assault of Flurious Akimbo's company upon the Twenty-Fifth Level of Mount Nevermind?

Was it instead the siege of the Philosophers' Tribunal, high in the Thirtieth Level, where capital hearings degenerated into the taking of hostages and the issuing of proclamations?

Or was it the hidden siege, known only to the Knights of Takhisis until a far-off time when the histories of the Chaos War were written—the siege in which one Knight, sole representative of the Order of the Skull in Mount Nevermind, plotted against the very Commander who had brought him here?

*   *   *   *   *

The patrols that guarded the upper levels of Mount Nevermind were a mixed group at best.

The few hundred Knights under the command of Halion Khargos were scarcely enough to serve as Commanders in the labyrinth of passages, tunnels, and caverns that riddled the city. So the guard was a hodgepodge of brutes, gully dwarves, and opportunistic gnomes who had sided with the occupying forces.

They were lulled with the prospect of nothing to do— lulled as well by a strange drowsiness that came over them early in the afternoon, minutes before the gnome assault on their outposts, mounted by Sergeant Flurious Akimbo.

Sentries, nodding and dozing by the stairwells and receiving nets of the Twenty-Fifth Level, first heard the fluttering sounds of machinery in the depths.

Some malfunction in the belly of the mountain, they told themselves. It would be mended in days, perhaps hours, when the power of the Paradise Machine descended to the lower levels.

It was then that they saw the aerocycles.

Rising above the receiving nets like a flock of baffled birds, the contraptions sailed above the dismayed guards and scattered into the tunnels.

At the same time, along the various tracks that ran up inclines onto the level, handcarts chugged into view, hooded with outlandish shells of metal and wood. The sentries posted by these entrances—brutes for the most part, and gnomes—fired bow and sling, hurled spears uselessly at the contraptions, which surged by them and over them, bound for the center of the level.

Inside one of these armored carts, Sergeant Flurious Akimbo clenched his fists in anticipation. It was all going as planned, as he had mapped it out for that reluctant colonel— in detail over seven maps and twenty-three diagrams.

Simple stuff, really, by gnomish standards. Then again, he was known for his direct and forceful manner.

Through the narrow slats of the armor, his view obstructed by the other soldiers, the sergeant glimpsed flashing forms, light and shadow, gray upon red and a deeper blackness as the carts passed through tunnel and chamber. Outside it was chaos : the outcry of men at arms mixed with the feral cry of the brutes.

The carts had passed the first outposts, their wheels clattering on the tracks and the steam valves gasping and whistling. Soon they would find the heart of the level.

Then came the appointed moment. The armor sheared away, and for a moment, bedazzled by torchlight, the gnomes stood rapt in the center of an enormous hall.

The Great Amphitheatre. Site of play and pageant in the older days of the city.

A new form of pageantry would be staged there today— a procession of steel and blood. . . .

And redemption, the sergeant thought, his imagination flying into realms of heroism and melodrama.

Amid grandstands of tiered and crumbling stone he set his banner, the silver crossed sword and hammer of the Military Guild on a dark red field. From this point, the cart tracks fanned out through the entire level—a perfect place to reinforce and defend.

Overhead, the aerocycles fluttered near the domed ceiling of the vast underground chamber, the legs of their gnome pilots pumping hysterically at the pedals, keeping the aircraft hovering aloft. The chatter of their rotating blades mixed with an odd clanging sound when blade grazed against the lofty dome of the chamber.

Had the sergeant been blessed with forethought, this ringing would have given him pause, but his thoughts were elsewhere, in the past and in the here and now.

Nerve center, Akimbo told himself. This place is a nerve center of the upper levels.

He remembered the phrase from military school, wished that he remembered more, because the time for tactics was approaching. Already the aerocyclists were shouting, signaling, at a movement in the far interiors of the level, in the alleys that ran between the strip of pubs and gambling houses the gnomes called The Crawl.

A teetotaler out of military duty, Sergeant Akimbo knew the area only by name. The pubs that lined the notorious block were like figures from a soldier's myth—Abstract Yearnings, Hell with Dinner, Delirium Tremens, and Hair of the Dog.

He had seen them twice, maybe three times in passing.

Now, scarcely a level mile away, the sergeant tried to reconstruct the streets in his memory. But memory failed, and it was only the sound of the conch shell, blown by the Knights' trumpeter in Lord Ariakan's mandatory call to Zeboim, that interrupted his revery.

The Knights of Takhisis were in earshot.

*   *   *   *   *

At the head of his own troops, the banner of the Death Lily waved arrogantly by the standard bearer at his side,

Halion Khargos had descended four levels to suppress the gnome revolt.

Behind him, marching in almost ceremonial order, were threescore Knights, handpicked from the ranks of his Wing in softer times, ready for pitched battle in the service of the Commander.

The Bone Acolyte had not shown in the field. Khargos would attend to that later.

For now, he breathed in the smell of this new battle. Oil and steam, the verdigris of brass shield and armor. The faint hint of blood already lacing the air.

It was the best he knew of freedom. He could almost thank the rebellious gnomes for drawing him from the Geometers' Guild, from the paperwork and intrigue and waiting of this vexed and damnable city.

Out here in the field of battle, he was alone with the Goddess, his sword hand communing with the arc of her will.

It was clean: force against force. Neither victim nor oppressor, but simply victor and defeated.

Again the conch shell blew, and ahead Khargos saw the fires surrounding the amphitheatre, heard the whip and whicker of blades above him as those absurd flying craft caught sight of his forces and turned, their pilots peddling toward the gathering smoke.

*   *   *   *   *

In accounts of a battle, almost nothing is ever clear.

It is the historian's task to piece together fragments and shards, to gather chaos into a version of order.

Yet the accounts of the Battle of the Amphitheatre were surprisingly consistent in one thing. Flurious Akimbo, in all of his forthrightness and courage, had not reckoned on the Paradise Machine.

Akimbo's gnomes, so the history goes, were stationed at the circular lip of the stone tiers, guarding level ground against assault on all sides. For all his imagining of the approaching Knights of Takhisis, the sergeant had not considered that the mirrored surveillance system was now working again.

And that Halion Khargos had observed his defenses, from a distance through a polished glass.

Waves of brutes and gully dwarves struck the amphitheatre from almost all sides, falling in droves to the arrows and slings. Khargos's cold tactics with these expendable troops thinned the gnome ranks: besieged from every quarter, each soldier had to rely on the comrade beside him, and breaches in the defenses remained breaches in the first perilous minutes of the battle.

Overhead, the militia in the aerocycles provided the most deadly of Akimbo's weapons. Hovering above the advancing Knights, they rained stones and projectiles into bewildered ranks, and soon Khargos's initial assault faltered.

Battered, the shock troops and their armored Commanders retreated and regrouped.

At the threshold of a far tunnel, Khargos and Subcommander Hanna watched the first charge fail. The Commander counseled his grim lieutenant against despair, with words that would return and haunt the days to come.

They have come to rely, he reportedly said, *on disorder.*
But their own machinery has abolished all chaos.

It would soon be apparent that Halion Khargos's time in the Geometers' Hall had been anything but wasted. The Commander had pored over blueprints and diagrams of gnome engineering, over failed and half-completed plans for ventilation, irrigation, and light. From these studies, he knew that the Great Amphitheatre had been the site a century ago of a most ingenious artifice.

Someone, it seemed, had desired the effects of an open air theatre, there in the heart of Mount Nevermind. The vault above the stage was, in fact, moveable: The metal ceiling, fashioned to resemble limestone, could be drawn away by huge, long-dormant cranks anchored in bedrock on the Twenty-Sixth Level, directly above.

And there was more: His turncoat gnome engineers had told him about the ventilation system, designed to give the theatre the feel of outside breezes and changes in weather. Installed at the foundation of the tiered grandstands, it had failed from the start. Despite good intentions and engineers'

constant tinkering, it had provided no breeze strong enough
to snuff a candle.

But now, with the Paradise Machine galvanizing all
devices in the upper levels, these contraptions, like all the
others, were ready and powered and waiting.

The second assault caught the gnomes in celebration.
The chorus of victorious cheers encircling the amphitheatre
and echoing through the enormous chamber faded into the
roar of the brutes, the clangor of sword, against shields
emblazoned with Lily and Thorn.

Shaken, the gnomes steadied themselves for the next
charge: huge water blasters, hourglasses that spun on axis
to fling sand and rubble on the attacking enemy. The
machines were in order.

Then, just as the brutes and the Knights sprang into view
in the torchlight, a shrieking sound from above drowned
out the rattle of the aerocycles.

The sky was opening. Through the splitting ceiling,
Akimbo's soldiers caught a glimpse of painted stars, of the
three moons, impossibly full.

Then the gusts began.

Five generations of increasing pneumatic power lay
behind the rising wind. Cloaks and banners rippled into the
air. Some of the defenders were borne aloft by the wind,
plummeting onto the stone floor outside the fortifications,
where they were easy prey for the advancing brutes.

Above, just as Khargos had foreseen, the storm swept
away the aerocycles.

In a chorus of screams and curses, the airborne warriors
vaulted toward the painted sky, crashing against the child-
like stars and spiraling into the darkness of the level above.
The rubble would litter the level for months.

Their ranks thinned and their air support vanished, it
was all the gnomes could do to repel this new attack. Fighting was at close quarters, swords and blasters, hourglasses
and wind-powered multifire crossbows virtually useless
against the shields and armor of the Knights . . . who
wreaked mad execution on the crumbling tiers.

Sergeant Flurious Akimbo collected his troops at the
skirts of the stage. There, on the only high ground the heart

of the amphitheatre offered, he staged a ferocious battle for more than an hour. All gnome eyes looked toward the outer regions of the level, toward the tracks that led from the westernmost slopes of Mount Nevermind.

For it was from that direction that help would come, if help came at all.

Fifty veteran gnomes, safe inside approaching armored carts, were already racing along those tracks, bound toward the amphitheatre and the relief of their beleaguered comrades. Khargos's defenders had been drawn toward the battle, and the road ahead of them was clear.

If we can hold them off yet an hour more, Akimbo thought, nursing the first of several wounds as he stood shoulder to shoulder with his tiring troops.

If we can hold them off . . .

* * * * *

All over the level, the Paradise Machine was at work.

The gnomes who rode through the well-lit tunnels, speeding toward the rescue of their comrades, had no way of knowing that, for the first time in the history of gnome transportation, the switches on the rails were working.

Those switches were manned by gully dwarves. Khargos could spare no reliable troopers. In the shrewdness that marked his Commander's insight, he had ordered the benighted creatures to *assure a smooth flow of rail traffic*.

Sometimes, pure stupidity is as reliable as an oiled machine.

They argued among themselves as the battle began. Scratched plans on the stone cavern floors, disagreed over maps and tunnels. Came to blows, and, at the sound of the approaching carts, panicked and threw the switches according to nothing more than whim.

It was what Khargos had relied upon. Ten armored carts, in their blind rush toward the amphitheatre, collided at a juncture in the tracks old navigators called The Spider.

The Spider claimed them all.

The glow of fire from the wreckage was visible in three of the far tunnels. The escaping steam from the shattered carts soon quenched the flames, and low, billowing smoke swept over the tiered grandstands where the battle raged.

Then, steering through the fumes by magical sight, the Thorn Knights rained new fire upon the defenseless gnomes.

A gray flame, indistinguishable from the smoke until it was too late, rushed over the stage. In its wake it left blackened rock, charred wood and flesh.

At center stage, chief actor in a drama he had commissioned but could not finish, Sergeant Flurious Akimbo felt the blast of dark fire. For a moment his thoughts spun in confusion, in a dozen regrets and options.

I am sorry, he tried to say.

I am sorry, colonel.

But it was too swift, too soon. And almost at once, his thoughts shut down in unearthly heat, his lost regrets rising like smoke among the painted stars.

Chapter 23

News of the gnome defeat spread rapidly through the upper levels. It reached the Philosophers' Tribunal barely an hour before the opening of the most celebrated session since the occupation by the Knights of Takhisis.

The news mixed with the standard flurry of rumor and counter-rumor, with the strata and substrata of leakings from reliable sources that High Justice Gordusmajor had, with some kind of intrigue and doubletalk, preserved his station on the bench of Mount Nevermind.

It was a session long awaited for two principal cases, the more important of which was the trial of Talos Croesissimo for the murder by indirection of old Incline Barium. But before that case was heard, there was the matter of Generalissimo Glorius Peterloo to dispense with.

The General's petition for a stay of execution could not have been less fortunately timed. The other imprisoned gnome officer, Lieutenant Colonel Grex Pointillo, had escaped from the Knights' custody and was rumored to be among the gnome resistance somewhere in the lower levels.

The Generalissimo, it seemed, lacked even the gumption to escape.

Most observers believed that *this* case would be easily and quickly resolved—that a brief appearance in court would end with the judge's simple refusal, and that the Generalissimo would keep his appointment with the headsman, scheduled for early next week.

But the continuing presence on the bench of the august High Justice lent uncertainty to the proceedings. Gordusmajor was completely arbitrary, deciding cases on mood or whim.

Still, when the government of Mount Nevermind changed hands, so had the instruments of prosecution, it seemed. The news was that Subcommander Fleetwood of the Knights of

Takhisis would arraign both Talos and the notorious Generalissimo according to the dictates of the Blood Oath and the Code.

A prospect Fleetwood dreaded as he crossed the threshold of the chamber.

Why had Khargos ordered him here? His dignity rankled at the insult, and he promised himself to be strict, to be stern.

He would evacuate a level, send them all to the Necropolis when this bickering business was done.

If it was *ever* done.

Already irritated, Fleetwood toyed with the hilt of his sword, waiting for the hearings to begin.

Among the Knights, a jest had circulated about "gnomish standard time"—thirty minutes to an hour late for any appointment. But the galleries in the Tribunal Chamber were already full, and three of the justices—Harpos, Julius, and Ballista, the subcommander recalled—were seated in one pan of that absurd and enormous balance that stood for a justices' bench in this city.

Silence greeted the subcommander. Somewhere in the rafters of the chamber, a solitary *blatt!* from a raspberry horn expressed the gnomes' discontent with their conquerors. But whoever blew the horn hid it well: the guards who accompanied Fleetwood searched the balcony to no avail.

Meanwhile, another noise was rising on the chamber floor, a murmur from the crowd—curiosity, perhaps, and anticipation.

The august High Justice Gordusmajor had entered the room.

He was a good forty-five minutes late, full in the range of gnomish standard time. For the occasion, he had worn the red judicial robes of the Philosophers' Guild—huge, tentlike things that swallowed a body even as large as his.

Enough fabric to carpet the chamber, Fleetwood thought in further irritation.

With a grunt, Gordusmajor hoisted his hems and climbed into the other scale pan. With a jerk, Harpos, Julius, and Ballista were aloft over the chamber, straightening judicial caps and recovering dignity.

Once again, noise from the rafters. A scattered applause for the damnable old judge.

Fleetwood frowned, folded his arms.

This task was bound to be unpleasant.

High Justice Gordusmajor cleared his throat. "If you have no objection, Commander Fleetweed—" he began.

"Fleet*wood*," the prosecutor corrected. "*Subcommander* Fleet*wood*."

"Very well," the Justice conceded. "If you have no objections, *Subcommander* Flitwad . . . "

Snickers from the balcony told Fleetwood that this argument was a lost cause. Better to permit the name-calling and stand up to the Justice when it came to more important things.

"As I was saying, if you have no objections, I shall hear first the case of Talos Croesissimo."

"This is most irregular, High Justice Gordusmajor," Fleetwood objected. "It is not customary for—"

"This is still my court," the High Justice declared. "Bought and paid for back in the War of the Lance when your uncles were no doubt hunting kender with tongs and a chain net. And since we shall honor *my* tenure and stand on *my* procedures, and since you have no objections, Subcommander, we will bring forth the defendant Talos Croesissimo."

Talos shuffled into the room, manacled and flanked by a pair of Lily Knights.

It was a shock to many in the chamber to see how imprisonment had altered him. He was gaunt, his beard patchy and matted, and his face unnaturally pale.

Fleetwood himself almost pitied the sorry creature paraded before the bench. But he was a prosecutor—the Dark Queen's instrument of justice.

And in justice lay no mercy. Better to drop the creature four levels and get it over with.

"What do you plead, son?" Gordusmajor asked the prisoner.

Fleetwood noted the softness in the justice's voice.

"Guilty or not guilty?"

Talos took a deep breath, raised himself to his full height. Even at that full height he barely reached the elbows of his

Knightly escort. But there was a certain dignity about this prisoner that Fleetwood noticed despite his own frustration at the games and doubletalk of gnomes.

"Neither, High Justice Gordusmajor," the young gnome replied.

The chamber buzzed with gnome voices. Gordusmajor raised his hand.

"Neither, you say?"

"Neither. I am a newly appointed captain in the Gnomish Army of Resistance and Gnomish Liberation Enclave, and in accordance with my rank and station, I refuse to acknowledge the jurisdiction of this court."

The buzz became a murmur. The old enormity in the scales smiled faintly and shifted in his robes.

"You refuse to acknowledge *my* jurisdiction?"

"Nothing of the kind, sir!" Talos replied. His face was less pale now; he was gathering courage. "For after all, this High Justiceship was duly finagled, duly bought and bribed, and impressively swindled."

"As I was trying to explain to the subcommander!" Gordusmajor agreed.

Talos bowed. "I simply refuse to acknowledge the jurisdiction of this court while it serves as an instrument of an illegally occupying army—"

A shout from the balcony. The Knights beside the defendant drew swords.

"Put your weapons down!" Gordusmajor shouted, leaping to his feet in the balance pan. Harpos, Julius, and Ballista lurched toward the chamber ceiling, fumbling to put on their padded helmets.

Cautiously, the High Justice settled back onto the bench, and the balance pan containing his three colleagues descended slowly, almost elegantly, from the shadowy lofts.

"Who is this Gnomish Liberation . . . whatever?" Fleetwood growled.

"Gnomish Army of Resistance and Gnomish Liberation Enclave," Gordusmajor repeated. "Called GARGLE for short, it is the tentative alliance of two splinter groups from the radical Free All Right Triangle movement in the Geometers' Guild which arose right after our

city and their guild hall were both occupied by Halion
Khargos."

Fleetwood's eyes narrowed. "You seem to know a lot
about these . . . subversives."

"Oh, I seem to," the High Justice agreed serenely, "but
I'm making some of it up."

Chuckling and puffing, reaching into a pouch and producing an oatcake, Gordusmajor now turned to Talos. "And
this," he asked, "this refusal to acknowledge jurisdiction
and rule of occupying law . . . is a position . . . of your own
devising, Master Talos?"

"A position, High Justice Gordusmajor, suggested to me
by my counsel."

"And your counsel is . . . ?"

"Scymnidus Carcharias, Your Honor!" exclaimed a voice
from the balcony. "Public Defender in the True and Unim-
peded Government of Mount Nevermind!"

Pulley ropes fell from the balcony, and slowly a wicker cage
was lowered from the heights, within it a slight gnome figure,
hooded like a conspirator. When the cage reached the floor of
the chamber, its occupant unhooked the ropes, unveiling himself before the gallery who, by now, were only mildly surprised.

"Counselor Scymnidus," Gordusmajor announced dryly.
"For the defense. And what is the purpose of this wicker . . .
enclosure?"

"Stay against assassination, your honor," Scymnidus
replied soberly. "I shall speak from these confines, if it
please the court."

"I must demand, High Justice Gordusmajor," Fleetwood
proclaimed, "in the name of my Commander, Occupying
General Halion Khargos, that the Counselor who has been
so . . . *ceremoniously lowered* be delivered into the custody of
the Knights of Takhisis. The General has desired his presence in an audience of inquiry, and refusal to cooperate with
the Knights of Takhisis is treasonous disloyalty—a violation
of Code and Blood Oath."

The dozen Knights in Fleetwood's presence murmured
agreement.

"*I* was called before the Commander in question, Staff
Container Flywater!" Gordusmajor exclaimed. "And I was

unable to cooperate with the audience of inquiry, owing to an infirmity in my ethical constitution—"

"A *grievous* infirmity," the Public Defender agreed, lacing his fingers through the wicker weaving.

"Under those circumstances," Gordusmajor asked, "would the notable Knights' Counselor regard the High Justice as . . . 'treasonously disloyal'?"

Fleetwood paused. He had drawn himself into the narrows. The orders of Halion Khargos were fresh in his thoughts: that the Philosophers' Tribunal, and this justice in particular, must be treated with honor and deference.

But then there was the rebellion of the prisoner, the mysterious business of the fugitive defender.

Fleetwood wished for Oliver's counsel. Not for the first time, he wondered what had become of the Bone Acolyte.

Confused, doing his best not to display confusion, Fleetwood paced the floor of the chamber.

"I believe . . . " he began, "that it might be discourteous to imply the disloyalty of a prominent High Justice."

"As do I," Gordusmajor agreed. "So the trial will proceed without further delay."

* * * * *

"What evidence do you have, Counselor Scymnidus, that the defendant is not subject to the laws of the Occupying Army?"

Scymnidus gestured toward the scales. "I have three bags of steel coins that speak to the irrelevance of the Knights of Takhisis, sir."

The bags, hoisted by eager law clerks, rang softly as they landed in the scale pan of the High Justice. Under the weight of a century's tradition, the pan containing the three other justices rose ever so slightly, and Subcommander Fleetwood, outraged at the clear and open bribery, paced into its shadow.

"This is most irregular, High Justice Gordusmajor!" Fleetwood objected. "It is a practice that flies against—"

"Overruled."

"But in no system of justice, neither our own nor elven nor human, Solamnic or—"

"Overruled."

"I *must* protest, sir! In all fairness, sir, and on behalf of this occupying army! Else I shall be constrained to overrule *you*, and bring the authority of the Knights of Takhisis to bear—"

For a third time, the High Justice interrupted Fleetwood's swelling outrage.

"You would do that, Stuff Collector Flatwad? You would disavow the authority of this court?"

"If forced to do so . . . " Fleetwood replied tentatively. He could feel the argument shifting, as though a ship's deck were breaking beneath his feet.

"Then you would avow," Scymnidus Carcharias said, swimming like a shark through those dangerous rhetorical waters, "that certain courts apply to certain peoples?"

"Yes . . . but I mean, no!" Fleetwood replied. "I mean . . . "

"You mean," Gordusmajor boomed over the murmuring gallery, "that you hold no regard for the courts of Mount Nevermind!"

"It seems, sadly," Scymnidus echoed, "that this is what he means, High Justice Gordusmajor."

"In which case," Gordusmajor continued, "there is little that separates you from the defendant."

Fleetwood's voice rose from the shadows beneath the other three justices, shaken and uncertain. "Except that . . . the defendant *murdered one of your own*!"

"If neither of you acknowledges the authority of this court," Scymnidus asked, "then who is to say that it has the right to determine any act—even murder—as a punishable offense?"

Fleetwood's head was spinning. He knew he was webbed by language—not philosophy or principle or even law—but he was damned if he could figure his way back to a reasonable argument in the midst of these wild and unruly creatures.

The whole idea began to strike him as absurd. A suspended judge and a co-opted defender, tangling him in a net of semantics. And his was the power in Mount Never-mind, was it not?

"Since neither defendant nor prosecutor," Gordusmajor continued, "owns to the authority of my judgment, I shall consider only the evidence provided by the Public Defender in reaching my verdict. That verdict . . . is still a bit uncertain, however. I shall need to see more persuasive testimony."

Scymnidus nodded. Apparently he had prepared for this. From his robes he produced an object, wrapped tightly in black cloth, and handed it to one of the young law clerks. Ceremoniously, the lad bowed, presented the item to High Justice Gordusmajor, and bowed again.

The justice disrobed the evidence, and to this day the jury is out as to just what it was that passed into his hands. Some say it was jewelry, others a fashionable gemstone.

Those seated nearer the scales maintained that it was an onyx figurine.

Whatever the case, it widened the eyes of High Justice Gordusmajor. He leaned over it as if it were especially savory oatcake, a glass of ale presented to a desert traveller after a long journey. The look on his face sank the hearts of the prosecution.

"Great Reorx!" Gordusmajor exclaimed. "'Tis the very one I have sought for a decade! This evidence is more than conclusive. It . . . is downright *inspiring*, by the gods! Just look at her little . . . "

He gathered himself, was suddenly judicial again.

"The court finds Talos Croesissimo guilty of being in the wrong place at the wrong time, of misplaced trust and dire affections. Let the defendant step forward."

Talos shuffled toward the bench. After all, he had just been found guilty, and Gordusmajor's sentences were notoriously bizarre.

"Master Talos," the High Justice began, leaning over the scale pan, a look on his face that others would describe later as "not unkind." "Do you acknowledge that you were, in fact, in the wrong place at the wrong time?"

"I . . . suppose I do, sir."

"And guilty as well of the charges the bench has set forth: of misplaced trust and dire affections?"

Talos sighed. "Those charges as well, High Justice Gordusmajor."

"And you have virtually rotted in prison for how long?"

"Ten days, sir."

"Would you say that this grievous imprisonment, in which I understand you were deprived of sunlight and breezes and were fed only three or four times a day, was punishment cruel and unusual to your delicate and youthful spirit?"

"Would I, sir?"

"I believe you would," Gordusmajor rumbled, slipping the conclusive evidence into the folds of his robe. "And I believe that the court is in harmony with you."

The three justices high in the dome of the chamber nodded in agreement. Or so it seemed to those on the floor below.

"I believe your stay in custody has been punishment enough," the Justice announced. "You are hereby released to your own recognizance. Sentence commuted to time served."

A cheer rose from the gallery, a ringing of cow bells and a thumping of drums. Gordusmajor stood and bowed in the scale pan, sending a shiver of imbalance through the other three justices high above.

"This is an outrage!" Fleetwood cried. "This verdict is irresponsible! Dishonorable! You are no justice, sir, but rather a piece of fluff on the breath of this gnome-sponsored chaos !"

"And you, sirrah," the Justice replied serenely, "are a piece of fluff on the monstrous and never-ending surface of *this*!"

As to what happened next, almost all sources agree—whether Knight or gnome, justice or barrister or simple thunderstruck bystander. High Justice Gordusmajor turned his back on Subcommander Fleetwood and lifted his robe, baring a moon that rivaled Solinari for size, Lunitari for redness, and the dark Nuitari for the kind of thing that respectable folk would rather not see. The gallery gasped, and then a wave of laughter surged through the room.

Laughter that stilled in the disaster that followed.

jergus Ryan

For what Gordusmajor gained in emphasis and drama, he altogether lost in balance. For a breathtaking second, he teetered at the edge of the scale, his enormous hams blocked by the tilting pan and the ruffle of his robe.

He lost hold then and fell twenty feet to the floor of the chamber.

A fall only half that of his three unbalanced colleagues, who, missing their considerable counterweight, plunged forty feet—bench, pan, and all—to crash heavily upon the hapless Subcommander Fleetwood . . .

Who was instantly crushed and killed by the impact.

Here the accounts part company.

Some say the gallery or the Philosophers' Tribunal began to empty at once. Others that the Knights, or the officers of the court, or even the bystanders barred the doors.

Most agree that High Justice Gordusmajor, protected from serious injury by a long-cultivated layer of fat, regained consciousness almost immediately. He staggered to his feet, blinked, and remembered where he was.

Fumbling in the folds of his robe, he produced the final piece of evidence, which apparently was in its final pieces owing to the considerable fall.

Contemplating the shards of onyx—or of *something*—wrapped in the pitiful black cloth, Gordusmajor lost control.

"Seal the room!" he shouted. "Seize the interlopers!"

Everyone—from Knight to gnome to the solitary gully dwarf whose job it was to skim litter from the perpetual fountain in the chamber—gaped at one another. Nobody was quite sure who the interlopers were.

It was then that Generalissimo Glorius Peterloo, inglorious in manacles far back in the lower tier of the chamber, redeemed himself, recovering most of the glory he had lost five levels below, when he nodded over a bottle of Tulla-Morgion while his army lost a war.

He was sober now, and he rattled to the side of the capsized justices, the old martial spark returned to his shifty eyes.

"I claim this chamber," he announced, "in the name of the Provisional Government of Mount Nevermind!"

The gnomes in the room roared their approval.

"A government," the Generalissimo continued, "who recognizes the authority of *this* court, *these* justices."

The gnomes in the room encircled the handful of Knights.

By this time, the interlopers had been identified.

The struggle was brief, but costly. Five Knights and a dozen gnomes fell before what remained of Fleetwood's guard were subdued. Armed with a hodgepodge of weapons—from genuine knives and bows to hatpins and justices' gavels—the gnomes secured the room. Several of the rebels, sparked by the wildness of possibilities, tried to still or slow the dipping Paradise Machine that still churned merrily in the corner of the chamber. It was to no avail. When stilled, the thing started up again; when turned over, it righted itself, and even a well-placed sword blow against the neck of the damned contraption decapitated it only briefly, its dripping head springing from the water and reattaching itself to the severed neck.

The saboteurs gave up, turned to bullying the captive Knights. Mount Nevermind, always a place where innovation ruled hand in hand with insanity, embarked with great enthusiasm on its first hostage crisis.

Chapter 24

It is the physical nature of short creatures to get in over their heads.

Or so Deddalo told himself bitterly, as he knelt on the tavern floor, tightening a new appendage to the machine that had betrayed his hopes once before.

That was the way he thought of the artificial Barium girl—the primitive automaton that had been his ticket to guild advancement. She stood before him in disarray, her face as ornate but lifeless as a dwarven clock. Yet this thing had to perform unexpected duty, or he was in dire trouble with the Bone Acolyte.

Beryl had arranged it all—had brought them together in the common room of the Hell With Dinner. There Oliver had soothed and cajoled him for hours.

Deddalo was afraid of this army from the mainland—of their dark armor and dramatic symbols and the simple fact that they bore magic and weapons. He had never trusted clerics in the first place, subscribing to the saying of the recently vanished Belisarius, who before his fatal balloon ride had pronounced that science would fill the god-sized hole in all of us.

But something in Deddalo warmed to the words of this cleric. He could not figure the source of that warmth.

Oliver had talked of many things—of money and power, available to the more enterprising of collaborators. He had explained a little of the mystery surrounding Commander Halion Khargos.

A mystery that had become difficult to bear.

Deddalo did not understand this business about the Vision. He supposed that most religions were peculiar enough, and that the Knights of Takhisis were no more unusual than the Solamnics or the elves on that account.

He did, however, understand jealousy. This Oliver, who had seen the Goddess once long ago in some kind of training dream, resented the fact that Khargos could talk to her continually, almost at will.

That is, if Khargos could talk to her at all.

Deddalo stood, circled the artificial creature. There was a time when he had fancied her almost beautiful. She was his own creation, after all, and his mother had often told him that the ugliest child could pass for presentable in a parent's eyes.

Deddalo sighed. Perhaps Mother had been trying to tell him something.

At that moment, Beryl Barium entered the common room.

She, too, was nowhere near as beautiful as he had once imagined. And the last few days had taken a toll on her appearance.

Once, in a moment of romance, he had likened her hair to spun gold. But now copper wire would be more accurate—copper intermingled with steel, because dealing with Oliver's conspiracy had grayed her considerably.

And yet she insisted on being the go-between. She was the one who spoke to Oliver, in quiet conclaves in the upper story of the pub. It was Beryl who brought him the cleric's instruction, who had set the plan before him.

She grew haggard in the process. Something about Oliver was eating her away.

There was the matter of her voice. What kind of music could he compare to it now? No longer an elven harp, that was for sure: more like the gully dwarf bladder-and-pipes, the strange, squawking instrument only a gully dwarf could abide, its sound somewhere between the tearing of metal and the torment of a small, loud animal.

He glanced at Beryl from the corner of his eye. He wished that she would go away.

"Is it ready yet?" she asked.

She already assumed the answer.

"Genius is never swift, my darling," Deddalo replied dryly, his eyes fixed on the automaton.

"But what about *you*, my dear?"

He wished that the explosion at the distilleries had spared her sister instead. He could have courted Meryl

Barium from the beginning—outdone Talos in words and in charm, and avoided all this conspiracy and confusion.

Leave it to a gnome to take a more complicated path, he thought in disgust. For instead of sitting atop the Barium millions, he was perplexed, badgered by a girl he was eager to be rid of and flummoxed with this heap of metal and plaster.

How could it be made to do what Oliver expected?

And here was Beryl, nagging at the edges of his great undertaking.

"I am certain it can be done," he said aloud, adjusting the eye patch. But they both knew he was lying.

"Still, there is still something missing, Beryl. I've tried my best chemistry, my best mechanics, but something—a small thing, I'd wager, but something yet—slips away. Oliver wants her ready within the week to be presented to Halion Khargos as an example of the newfound order in gnome invention. He wants her plausible enough to gain entry to the Geometers' Hall, autonomous enough to locate the Commander, and durable enough to survive the disaster she will cause. I suppose she's plausible and durable, but I can't get my thoughts around the autonomy business."

"So much for your mechanics, your chemistry," Beryl chided. "Second place in a guild contest is not up to the Bone Acolyte's snuff. We could use your more ingenious friends now—Talos's chemistry, or Innova's talent for invention."

"I incriminated them both, Beryl, or have you forgotten?" Deddalo growled. "Those bridges are pretty thoroughly burned."

"Maybe not quite," Beryl said.

Exasperated, Deddalo turned to face her.

"Oh, I don't mean it like you think I do. We're not going to march up to the Tribunal, through those barred gates in the midst of Gordusmajor's and the Generalissimo's siege, and ask Talos to lend us a hand. Instead, we need to think about the things *they've* done—their inventions and strategies. To go about this thing second hand, if you catch my meaning."

212

THE SIEGE OF MT. NEVERMIND

Deddalo had caught. "Go on," he said.

"That Paradise Machine, up in the topmost level. Why doesn't it wear down?"

"Lubricated, I guess. Well oiled with cod liver or vegetable expression or graphite."

"You guess?" Beryl rolled her eyes. "Great Reorx, I should have corrupted Talos when I had the chance!"

"How dare you think of such a thing!" Deddalo shouted righteously. "But . . . do go on. Enlighten me with your superior knowledge of mechanics. What about the Paradise Machine?"

Beryl stepped to the side of her automated sister. "Doesn't it strike you that by this time those machines should be wearing down? And what is it that enables them to self-repair and self-renew, like . . . like a living thing healing itself?"

"Something in the water?" Deddalo ventured.

Beryl snorted disgustedly. "Something in the oil, dolt! Now *where* would Innova have found a substance that would work these kinds of miracles?"

"He . . . was serving a sentence on the lowest levels. Repairing the gnomeflingers . . . "

Dawn was slow coming to Deddalo, but finally the sun had risen.

"I see! I see what you mean, Beryl! While he was downside, Innova discovered some elixir, some element . . . "

Beryl turned from the automaton, shuffled to the bar. "Tighten that bolt in the back of my sister's neck."

Deddalo obliged. The automaton suddenly seemed straighter, more lifelike.

Beryl shrugged. "I know little of these things. But *that*, my dear, was obvious."

Deddalo muttered something foul, set down his wrench.

"Pack your bags, Deddalo," Beryl ordered suddenly. "We're in over our heads, and I expect you're prepared to duck and hide, but there's only one way out of this, and that's to see it through to the end. Which means we're bound for the lower levels, on what we might call a voyage of discovery."

213

*   *   *   *   *

Others were bound to those depths as well. As Deddalo was packing his bags according to the directions of his shrewish companion, a small party of gnomes and gully dwarves was already negotiating the Fourteenth Level, on its way toward parts even lower.

Lieutenant Colonel Grex Pointillo walked at the head of this company. Beside him was a most unlikely companion, a young gnome wanted in the upper regions for betraying the same city the colonel was sworn to defend.

Yet a bond of faith was growing between the two of them. Growing, because both had been betrayed by the weakness of their former comrades and because, quite frankly, neither of them had anyone else to trust.

"This was the topmost level I ranged," Innova whispered, "while I served my time here. Watch out: The rocks are shifty here, and it's possible that magma has slipped through crevasses even this far up. Barring some great disaster, Lucretius is no doubt below. Perhaps far below. He told me once to look for him where I first found him. Something about circles . . . "

Pointillo nodded. It was as though he understood.

Innova cleared his throat. "But you've never answered my question, Colonel. How you know of Lucretius Climenole. And *what* you know."

There was a long silence as Grex Pointillo seemed to test the waters of his own common sense. Innova could see that the colonel had something private to tell him—something perhaps not meant for the ears of even the soldiers who followed them.

He was not surprised then, when Pointillo took his arm and the two of them quickened their pace, outstripping the soldiers and approaching a neglected gnomeflinger, which loomed up at them as their torchlight swept over it.

"Stay back," Pointillo called down the corridor, "while the philosopher and I investigate."

Then, more quietly, "Kneel down!" he whispered to Innova. "Pretend to be repairing this contraption, while I tell you what I can."

Dutifully, Innova knelt, although the next words might have brought him to his knees anyway.

"The Pointillos were my father's people," the colonel whispered. "Agronomists for the most part, more interested in irrigation ditches than military trenches."

"I see," Innova replied. "That explains why you aren't as . . . spit and polish as some of the others in this militia."

"Only in part, Innova. My mother's people were Malonados and Sardonicans—have you heard the names?"

Innova rummaged through his memory. Something about the words chimed with the place he was in—with the gnomeflingers, the rough-hewn tunnels, and the feeling of great depth.

"They're . . . they're . . . "

Pointillo took a deep breath. "Clerical families, Innova. Or, they were once clerical families, now long absorbed into other guilds. The Malonados were theologians, the Sardonicans healers—there were guilds within guilds at that time, for as you know, we never do things simply. All of this would make absolutely no difference if it weren't for . . . the promptings."

Innova stopped what he was doing. The gnomeflinger was in good repair anyway. He searched its undercarriage and found his mark. No doubt he had fixed it in the months before.

" 'Promptings'? What do you mean by 'promptings,' Colonel?"

"I'm not sure what I mean. There were spells, of course. Back before the Cataclysm. But none in the absorbed families remember them. And yet . . . "

He glanced over his shoulder, as if expecting eavesdroppers.

"And yet many of us carry intuitions. 'Promptings,' I call them, in which something in you stretches out toward the people and things around you, toward the time to come. Often when I've failed at undertakings, when I've felt unmoored and alien among my own people, I've thought— I've even hoped—that the promptings were telling me something about a larger purpose, that I couldn't do these things because I was being called to something else."

"I see," Innova replied. Though he really didn't see.

Or maybe he did. After all, he'd failed a few times himself, felt out of touch and even—to use the colonel's word—"unmoored." He'd always hoped it was some kind of destiny, some way that his yet unenvisioned Life Quest was keeping him away from distractions, that he was fated for a larger role in a larger story.

Now, hearing someone else talk about such things, he began to wonder if it was foolishness to think that way—foolishness to begin with.

"We've always heard stories about those who went away," Pointillo said. "The Climenoles among them. This Lucretius you speak of . . . he must be very ancient. And more than that, he is unabsorbed."

"You think he might know something of the old clerical ways?"

Pointillo did not answer. The soldiers were within earshot.

There were things Innova thought he could tell the colonel. Had not Lucretius told him that gnome spellcraft was a thing of the past? That none of his family remembered the chants and prayers that defined the vanished clerical orders?

Perhaps Lucretius had kept the answers back for his own reasons. Perhaps, Innova reckoned, this meeting under the mountain was part of some great story, in which both he and Pointillo would figure as heroes.

It seemed unlikely. Far-fetched at best.

Innova wanted time to mull over this revelation. But a cry from one of the approaching gnomes scattered his thoughts, and he rose slowly, checked by the pain and the memory of pain in his backside, and followed Pointillo to a recess in the little alcove, where the soldiers had gathered around the floor.

They were marveling at a deep indentation. From a great height, something had fallen to this spot, and the stones themselves bore record of its furious impact.

"It's a meteor, is what it is," one of the soldiers asserted. "Or, even more interesting still, perhaps the remains of a *comet!*"

"It's a *supplosion*!" one of the gully dwarves maintained. His comrades nodded in agreement, while the gnomes looked at him in disgust.

Innova crouched before the markings. A sign of searing, of powder at the perimeters. Scorched hair and cloth.

He recalled an epidemic of several years back, in which some of the chemical engineers had spontaneously combusted. It had some of the signs of this, but not all.

Why had he not seen this before when he repaired the gnomeflinger?

His hands ranged over ash and bone in the shadows. They came to rest on something hard, metallic, still warm from an old burning.

A ring. He lifted it to the light.

On its face was carved the runic "B" of the Barium clan. And bisecting the "B," a runic "M."

The signet ring of Meryl Barium, the vanished twin.

*　*　*　*　*

"But it *can't* be!" Innova protested, as he and the Colonel led their party down yet another level, and a rising warmth in the air told them they were approaching the fields of magma, far beneath the city.

"I would have noticed the remains when I fixed the gnomeflinger. Meryl . . . well, she *exploded* before my sentence was handed down. It doesn't make sense!"

"I have a feeling," Pointillo said quietly, "that many things we encounter from this point on will not make sense."

"Is that a feeling or a prompting, Colonel?"

Pointillo took the ring, turned it in his hand. "I'm not certain," he said. "Could it be that everything disorderly and chaotic about Mount Nevermind has not been re-ordered, but just *pushed back*? That we've reached the edges of what the Paradise Machine controls, and that everything beyond is much like it always was, only worse?"

"Worse?"

Pointillo nodded. "Worse, because it has been compressed and cramped into a smaller space. Maybe disorder is more . . . manageable when it rises in pockets of order. When it's all tossed together, there's no telling what might occur."

But Innova was barely listening. His thoughts raced back to the girls on the silo, the plan he had consented to, half in curiosity, half in play. The explosion, and only later how it had dawned on him that what had happened that day among the distilleries had echoed through the days that followed.

Cause and effect is a disease, he remembered.

He mourned the poor creature whose death had ignited it all.

Chapter 25

The party crept lower and lower into the belly of Mount Nevermind. Sometimes they wound around the central, spiraling stairs; on some occasions, they followed abandoned cart tracks down steep inclines where torchlight had failed, and eerie sounds rose up from the darkness ahead.

Once, at Innova's suggestion, they gathered around a gnomeflinger aimed across a steep crevasse to a receiving net at the mouth of a huge, eroding cavern. But the gully dwarves crouched and cowered, maintaining that if gully dwarves were meant to fly, the gods would have given them several lives.

Some of the water at these depths was potable, in pools cleansed and purified by a perpetual boiling from the heat of the magma. Standing over steaming fissures, the gnomes gathered water gingerly in their helmets and set it aside to cool. The gully dwarves in the party took special delight in the process. Small creatures, trapped by the flow of scalding water, floated on the bubbling surface, and steamed crickets and poached spider and soon became gully dwarf delicacies.

All the while, the environs grew stranger and stranger. Often Innova saw runes scratched on the tunnel walls—runes that would dissolve into insects and scramble into cracks under steady light—and drawings that were far older than the gnomes themselves.

"We forget," the colonel whispered to his uneasy companion, "that even in this place, we are only tenants—that someone or something was here in the ages before us, and will probably survive our stay."

But it was no time for history lessons. Strange shapes fluttered at the edges of the torchlight, sometimes only an incoherent ripple in the darkness, but often taking the form of armed men.

It startled Innova at first. He feared that the Knights had followed them into these lower levels. But the creatures, whatever they were, avoided the light, maneuvering at the margins of sight. Not even Grex Pointillo, with all his intuitions and promptings, had a sense of what they were.

And there were noises as well, a deep rumbling from somewhere near the absolute bottom of the mountain—a sound unlike anything Innova had heard in his lengthy stay among the lower levels. It was not a sound of rocks shifting, or of the bubbling magma. He had heard those sounds before.

Instead, it was cold, and almost animate, rising out of the shifting and bubbling, and yet separate from those constant and familiar sounds.

Innova shuddered to think of something that could live amid molten rock, but when he voiced this fear to Grex Pointillo, the colonel merely shrugged.

"Stranger events are happening in the world outside," he told Innova. "The Knights of Takhisis fell prey to such things. I heard tales from my guards in the prison—of creatures who snatch the essence of their enemies. Of rock faces and natural bridges that dissolve into nothingness under the feet of travelers."

The mysterious bridge made sudden sense to Innova. "I saw something like that!" he exclaimed, "not long ago, and in the levels not far above us. I tried to follow a passage along the edge of a chasm. And then . . . it was nothing but a drop before me. Sheer grace of the gods that I didn't fall for days."

The colonel paused. An odd, unreadable look passed over his face.

"Then they are among us," he said. "Whatever they are, they have come to Mount Nevermind."

"If they oppose the Knights," Innova asked, "doesn't that make them our allies?"

Pointillo shook his head. "Perhaps. More likely not. The world is passing out of old alliances, Innova, out of old oppositions. Sharing an enemy no longer makes you friends."

* * * * *

As their journey took them lower into the recesses of the old volcano, Innova began to learn the names of those who traveled with the Colonel. Four gnomes—Lozenge, Triquet, Roundell, and Pillaster—bore faces he recognized as members of other guilds, but perhaps he had met them at the Hair of the Dog in his roustabout days.

He guessed they were of roughly the same age, all born in that time when it was the fashion among gnome parents to name their children after ornamental shrubbery. For the first leg of the journey, the four had seemed more or less alike—as indistinguishable as a line of manicured bushes.

But soon, distinctions became clear. Triquet and Roundell were stockier, more silent—Triquet, it seemed, because of some uncharacteristic distaste for words, and Roundell from a far-reaching simple-mindedness. Lozenge, the most amiable of the four, had actually introduced himself—*Lozengeunderneathwhichwehavehiddenthesilverware . . .* he began, before the surly Pillaster stopped him short with a cold glance.

Pillaster himself was a piece of work. The closest to what Innova would call a veteran, he bore numerous battle scars, among which was a jagged, purple cut on the forehead. His left ear was also missing, though he had bronzed the severed part and wore it as an amulet around his neck. As a result of this injury, his helmet tilted so awkwardly over the left side of his head that he used the thing only as a cooking pot, preferring to remain hooded and glaring—an intimidating figure, especially in the mottled light.

Even more curious were the pair of gully dwarves who accompanied them. Shagg and Ragg Karputt, they were, sons of scullery servants, proclaiming proudly that their parents had named them after some especially admired floor covering in the house of one of Talos's cousins.

The dwarves were the first to warm to Innova, the first besides the colonel to address him as comrade rather than prisoner. It seemed only fitting: To gully dwarves, gnomish complexity, alliances, and feuds were as far from understandable as speculative physics.

Fergus Ryan

The Karputts offered him parboiled crickets.

"Better than bat," Ragg urged. "Even more bitter and salty."

Innova smiled, thanked them, and refused.

When the party circled yet another stairwell, bound for the next lowest level, it seemed that the gnomes' senses heightened. Alien smells rose to them on a warm breeze, and the gnomes sniffed the air, trying to distinguish the hot odor of burning rock from a new, fetid underlacing of rot and rust.

Moving the gully dwarves downwind helped some, but the smell was still confusing.

The temperature was rising as well. Roundell and Pilaster stripped to their flimsy tunics, and the others—still cautious and fearing the shadelike figures at the fringe of their sight—sweated in full leather armor.

Innova urged the colonel to follow the handcart tracks. If Lucretius were still about his business of shoring up the lower levels, they were more likely to find him in or not far from his vehicle.

A faint reddish glow now illumined the tunnels through which the party walked. Still the warriors stalked them. Innova could see only a shimmering, like heat vapors rising on a sunlight road. Yet the shimmering cast substantial shadows, man-shaped and solid as flesh.

The party walked with their weapons drawn.

"What stays their hand?" Innova asked. "Our superior numbers?"

Pointillo laughed softly. "Just look at them, Innova. And look at us. Six gnomes and a brace of gully dwarves. One of them could take us all. It's something else they're waiting for."

The shadows receded as Innova lifted his torch.

"What if . . . they have *no* motive, Colonel?" he asked.

The shapes glided along the tunnel walls like receding smoke, leaving a thin coat of rime on the stones.

*   *   *   *   *

In the same lower levels, unseen by the party of gnomes and gully dwarves that had descended in search of Lucretius

Climenole, a handcart creaked to a stop in a pooling chamber.

Two figures stepped from the dark bed of the vehicle.

As usual, Deddalo and Beryl were bickering about something.

"I tell you, my memory is good!" the girl insisted. "It was around here, if not this very chamber."

"Cavern on cavern, Beryl," Deddalo replied, "and tunnel on tunnel. How can you tell one from another?"

"Trust me, *darling*. I mapped my way down there by instinct and memory. It's on this level . . . see? The tracks make a turn and rise up a steep gradient here. I remember the movement, that fool Innova lecturing me like some kind of engineering student . . . "

Deddalo knelt by one of the pools. "Not this one. This is water only. No telling what's in it."

"But the pool we are looking for *is* around here. I guarantee," Beryl said, drawing out a strange navigational instrument—a compass complete with pendulum and rotating lantern which she had purchased at a recent guild auction.

The lantern spun, sputtered, and narrowed its light toward a rubble-strewn passage that ended in solid wall.

"I was *told* this was functional!" the girl muttered angrily. "A *judge* told me, by the beard of Reorx!"

It turned out, however, that the device had misjudged only by a chamber or so. Within minutes the pair had found the pool of Graygem oil, and Deddalo, marvelling at the stuff he had come to consider a kind of chemical magic, set down his lantern at the pool's edge and stared at his reflection in the shimmering, silver surface.

Beryl stood behind him, compass flickering and rocking in her hand.

"You're sure this is the stuff?" Deddalo asked.

"I wouldn't bring you this far if I weren't."

Quickly, almost as if he were stealing something, Deddalo filled the half dozen bottles the couple had brought with them. Carefully he sealed them, unsure whether the oil was volatile.

Meanwhile, Beryl stood above him and watched. Deddalo caught her reflection on the mirrorlike surface.

He wished he knew what she was thinking.

*   *   *   *   *

It was possible. Beryl knew it was.

There was a story back in the War of the Lance—a story about a gully dwarf who fell in love with a human magic user. Unusual circumstances, yes, and as far as she recalled, the two did not live happily ever after.

But gnomes were not gully dwarves. By the gods, they did not even resemble each other! And the Bone Acolyte Oliver of the Knights of Takhisis was no ordinary human.

He had spoken to her kindly, softly in the upper story of the Hell With Dinner. Told her she was unlike the other gnome girls, all squat rebellion and narrow eyes.

After all, she *was* different, wasn't she?

For all intents and purposes, after her father's fortune ran through the gauntlet of probate hearings, she would be the second- or third- richest gnome in Mount Nevermind.

That had taken long planning, *that* had. Long planning to surmount great obstacles.

Meryl, her senior by only minutes, had stood in her way. Most, if not all of her father's riches would have followed gnome law into the pockets of his eldest child. It had been a double indignity that the scion of the richest family in Mount Nevermind, Talos Croesissimo, had fallen in love with Meryl and plighted his troth.

Meryl would have been a bona fide tycoon had she lived, the wealthiest creature in the city, on Sancrist, amid the spreading islands west of the continent.

Which was why Beryl had courted Deddalo, in whose behavior she had seen prospects of betrayal and ambition. Together they had plotted the mishap on the distillery silo, timed the explosion precisely.

Wait but a moment, Sister, Beryl had said sweetly, having guiding the unwitting Meryl to the top of the appointed silo. *There's a bakery in the adjoining chamber . . .*

And what's a meal without two loaves of bread?

She had heard the explosion through two walls of stone. The floor of the tunnel had shaken beneath her. And then, her task in the whole messy business completed, she had fled toward the designated spot—toward the chamber that awaited her, prepared for her comfort in the lower levels of Mount Nevermind.

Where, after sufficient time and mourning, she would be miraculously discovered.

Or *Meryl* would be discovered. From this point on, after the distillery explosions, she would go by her sister's name.

Here was where it became complicated. Here was where she had needed Deddalo once again.

Being a sole heiress is a tedious pastime. Given old Incline Barium's health and meanness, he might survive well into another century, He might outlive *her*—a prospect that had filled her waking hours with desperation.

Why be a vulture, she had asked herself, when you can be an eagle, swooping down on your prey from a lofty height?

It was a consoling image. It gave her the idea of how next to employ the adoring Deddalo.

He designed the trap on the Thirtieth Level, outside the mansions of Talos Croesissimo. *Two birds with one stone*, Deddalo had insisted. *We need both your father and Talos out of the way.*

Talos will know that you are not Meryl Barium. If anyone knows.

While in the very act of living, your father withholds your inheritance.

Do the math, Beryl. 'Tis simple cause and effect.

She had been inclined to agree.

But Deddalo had not done *all* the math. He had not reckoned that with her father and her sister's sweetheart out of the way only one gnome remained who could clearly expose her masquerade.

*   *   *   *   *

"Have you filled them all?" she asked quietly, introducing one last note of tenderness into her voice.

Deddalo nodded. "And now what remains is to oil the automaton with this stuff, and set it about the task that Oliver has conceived. Beryl?"

Dreamily, the girl lifted her eyelids.

"Doesn't it seem strange and . . . well, *silly* to you? This plot on the life of Halion Khargos? I mean, no matter how well the machinery runs, no matter how sharply I focus its purpose, anything remotely approaching caution on Khargos's part is bound to foil us."

"Is that so?" Beryl's voice was muted, almost a whisper.

"How will an automaton slip by Khargos's guards? And once past them, how will she overcome a skilled Knight, slip the poisoned dagger between his ribs, and escape the room? What if there's some kind of . . . malfunction? We don't know that this substance has anything to do with the success of the Paradise Machine."

Beryl frowned. Her companion had lost his flowery flow of language. Had lost his confidence, for that matter.

"Look in the pool, Deddalo," she muttered.

The gnome shrugged and obliged. "What am I looking for, *dearest*?"

Beryl watched his reflection near the surface of the oil. His big, crooked nose. The ornate eye patch she had finally persuaded him to wear.

They had a history, she and Deddalo, and for a moment Beryl Barium felt something that might have been the stirrings of conscience. She wasn't sure. It might have been indigestion, as well.

She would have to ask Oliver. Clerics, they said, knew the deeper nature of illnesses.

Swiftly, she set her foot on the back of Deddalo's neck, and pushed his face into the pool. Desperately, as though he passed through surprise at once to realize that this was for real, this was for keeps, Deddalo groped at her ankle, but Beryl kept her footing.

Bubbles rose on the surface of the pool, bursting in surprising little sparks. Beryl watched in wonder.

Oliver was right. There was something wondrous in the nature of this oil. Something almost beautiful.

Deddalo thrashed beneath her foot. Beryl was rather large for a gnome female, and her weight alone kept him down. He kicked, flogged the pool into a roiling eddy.

Soon his futile attempts to wrench away her foot became more listless, almost vague.

At the last, when the bubbles ceased to rise to the surface and Deddalo's hands spread limply afloat, Beryl's senses jostled a bit, and she found herself suddenly more wakeful, regarding the splayed body at her feet with a new and impartial clarity.

All the loose ends had been tied together, she thought, gathering the bottles and setting them carefully in the handcart. Of course, she knew enough about the automaton to give it life without Deddalo's help, and surely Oliver would know the rest—know the habits and vulnerabilities of this Halion Khargos.

They would find the time when the Commander slept or communed . . . and the power of Mount Nevermind would change hands.

And she, she and Oliver . . .

It was possible. She knew it was.

She turned, hastening for the handcart which would take her to the upper levels, back to the automaton she could fashion and direct as well as any half-hearted engineer.

In her haste, her ankle brushed against Deddalo's lantern. The lamp tipped, rocked precariously. Just as it was about to right itself, thin tendrils of oil snaked off the surface of the pool and entangled it.

Beryl shouted, stepping away just as the oil closed over the lamp and the pool burst into a flickering green flame. Horrified, she watched the fire dance over Deddalo's floating body, his damp hair kindling like a wick.

Racing toward the handcart, shedding sparks and batting at her smoldering robes, the girl reached her vehicle just as the chamber behind her ignited.

Her compass lay fractured on the stones behind her.

It must have been what Meryl felt, she thought, as the cart raced up the tracks, a burning cloud behind it and hot waves of noxious fumes welling over her shoulder. Beryl reeled, tottering at the edge of unconsciousness . . .

And then, the dank cool air of the next level, the fire receding.

She could breathe again.

For a moment, she thought she would be sick. She

fumbled in her smoking robes, found the bottles safe. It is all for the best, she thought, as the cart raced toward safety.

Not only do I have the Graygem oil, but nobody else can have it.

Chapter 26

Two hundred feet below this sorry scene, Lieutenant Colonel Grex Pointillo guided his little party through a steaming labyrinth.

A long-abandoned system of steam flutes and whistles, set in this region years ago as a sort of alarm against rising volcanic heat, shrilled rustily as the gnomes and gully dwarves passed. The gnomes had stuffed their remaining rations of bread in their ears to muffle the uncanny sound. The gully dwarves moved on without distractions: a lifetime of accumulated dirt and wax was serving its purpose now as earplugs.

Look for me where you first found me, Lucretius had told him when they last parted. Now, in the steam and the noise and the shifting darkness, Innova had lost all sense of direction.

It even seemed as though there were flames *above* him now, though his science told him that was unlikely.

The shadowy warriors had not ceased their mysterious surveillance. It was making them all nervous, especially the gully dwarves.

"Me say we send Shagg to kill 'em!" Ragg Karputt pleaded with the colonel.

"*Me* say we send Ragg!" Shagg urged. "Ragg *expendable*!"

The gnomes looked at the gully dwarves in amazement.

"Nobody's expendable, Shagg," the colonel said quietly.

Ragg frowned, as though in some way he had been insulted. "The generals say we expendable," he said. "They say that make us fight good."

Pointillo and Innova looked at one another in disbelief. Apparently, as part of some brutal gnome joke, the gully dwarves had been taught that *expendable* meant *brave*.

The lower levels might lie in a brutal chaos, but there were things to answer for upstairs.

*   *   *   *   *

Somewhere in the lowest levels—Third or Fourth, to Innova's best guess—they came upon Lucretius's handiwork.

Large stones straddled crevasses at the mouths of both entrances to this chamber, their undersides lit with a red and throbbing glow. The red light played over an opened bag of uncut jewels and broken glass, creating a brilliance of reflection in a dark corner.

An aqueduct arched over the chamber, steam rising from the water that coursed steadily through its open channel. A solitary cart track bisected the chamber, its rails twisted and buckled by the great heat filtering through the cavern floor. A netting of rope dangled from the far end of the aqueduct like a web.

Innova shuddered at the thought of spiders, and the thought brought back the room to his memory. Hanging from that very structure, entangled in a webbing of cords . . .

"It was here!" he cried aloud, startling his comrades. "This is where I first met Lucretius! And didn't he tell me to look for him where I first found him?"

"Look around you," Pillaster grumbled. "Use your binoculars if you need them. Do you see any philosophers anywhere?"

Indeed, there was no sign of Lucretius. Innova's spirits sank, and he leaned against the side of the entryway as though he had lost for good some precious and elusive thing.

A hand rested on his shoulder.

"Courage, Innova," the colonel urged. "Who's ever known a gnome promise to be what it seemed in the first place? We'll simply follow the tracks. You've said Lucretius is never far from his handcart, or from the baubles he loves to collect. It stands to reason that he's not far from the rails as well."

It made sense, but it was more easily followed in thought than in deed. For the chamber ahead of them—once Innova's hospital room or his prison, depending on how you looked at it—was a perilous passage of fire and unsteady footing.

The magma was not far below the surface here, and Lucretius's patchwork repairs had begun to wear considerably. Innova could feel the stones shift under his feet as the party stepped into the room, bound for the archway at the opposite side.

Suddenly, the shadowy warriors who had dogged their steps for most of the journey wafted like smoke to the far walls of the chamber. Lozenge pointed to one of them, called out an alarm.

It was then that the floor burst into flames.

Surrounded by a circle of fire, Pointillo looked first to one exit then the other. Slowly the fissures in the floor were opening, the chamber rocking in a scarlet light. With a rumble, Lucretius's buttress of stones collapsed and hissed in the magma.

For a moment Roundell tottered at the brink of a chasm, his boots igniting in the searing heat. Lozenge whipped around, grabbed his comrade by the wrists, and yanked him clear of the collapsing floor. Roundell landed onto stone almost as imperiled, as the crevasses widened and the fire spread.

Leaning against the charred support of the aqueduct, Innova scanned the chamber. The shadow creatures had vanished into the smoke, and only his beleaguered comrades remained, trapped on a little island in the midst of bubbling magma, in the midst of unquenchable fire.

Unquenchable! The word itself brought hope.

The aqueduct overhead . . .

Innova shouted, gestured toward the aqueduct.

Pointillo understood him at once. He grasped the near abutment of the aqueduct but pulled away his hands at once, shouting in pain as the smoldering wood seared his skin.

"It's no good!" he cried. "I can't . . . "

Then, out of the rising smoke, a dark form scuttled like a spider up the side of the aqueduct. "Ragg can do it!" it called.

"Ragg as expendable as a lion!"

The gnomes gaped as the gully dwarf clambered onto the aqueduct, teetered at the edge of the channel as he straddled the rush of hot water.

"Ragg done it!" he shouted in triumph, then gazed stupidly down at his comrades.

"Now what Ragg do?"

At once, six gnomes began to shout. Ragg pivoted, ran in circles, loyally trying to follow each separate and conflicting set of instructions. Finally, it seemed to sink in. The gully dwarf raised his axe above the wooden arch . . .

And slipped on the wet wood, falling into the middle of the channel.

Ragg shouted, then screamed, then whooped as his fear gave way to enthusiasm. He was afloat in the aqueduct's powerful current, carried across the top of the chamber, laughing and splashing in the foul water.

Laughing and splashing until the current swept him into a hole in the cavern wall, in a rush toward the gods knew where.

"Us gotta save Ragg!" Shagg entreated. "There're crickets in his pocketses!" And the gully dwarf climbed up the smoldering aqueduct, in pursuit of brother and delicacies.

Pointillo seized onto the hem of Shagg's threadbare cloak, hoping to be dragged to the heights himself. But the cloth tore off in his hands, and he tumbled with a shout to the hot floor of the chamber.

Meanwhile, the other gnomes were more ingenious. Lozenge and Pillaster had removed their traveling capes and wrapped them around their hands. Shielded from the heat of the blackening wood, they climbed the structure easily.

The rest followed suit. Hoisted by Roundell, Innova crawled to the top of the aqueduct and rushed toward the hole into which the gnome had vanished. Bracing his hands against the warm rock, he peered into the narrow conduit.

Ten feet in, the light failed: The water surged on into darkness. No sign of Ragg.

Atop the aqueduct, the gnomes were faced with another dilemma.

All the gnomes had solutions to the problem. Roundell, who had not impressed Innova with his intelligence, argued for sticking with the original plan, because the first plan is always the best. Triquet and Lozenge pointed out that breaking down the structure now would send them plummeting onto the glowing floor, to be crushed and roasted among the fiery stones, and that perhaps the first plan, good though it might have been, could stand revising to breaking away only *part* of the aqueduct, thereby keeping their foothold while allowing the water to course down and quench the flames below.

Flames were licking against the abutments now. Smoke billowed up from below, mingling with the clouds of steam and virtually blinding the gnomes as they considered each plan serenely.

Pillaster said that Triquet and Lozenge were fools. Who'd ever heard of pouring water on magma? It would just steam away to nothing, he claimed. Far better to use the water *selectively* by standing in it until their boots were sodden. Soak gloves and clothing as well, he said, and it will all provide protection against the fire when we descend and replace the rocks that covered the fissures.

Innova shifted his feet on the hot surface of the aqueduct. Old courtesies he had learned in childhood— "never interrupt the plan of another" and "an argument isn't finished until everyone has a say"—warred with the fact of fire and tottering architecture.

He guessed they had only minutes left.

Lieutenant Colonel Grex Pointillo cleared his throat, was about to speak.

"Too much talk!" Shagg squealed, barreling toward the conduit through which his brother had floated. "Not enough running!"

"My sentiments exactly!" the colonel exclaimed, grabbing and restraining the hysterical gully dwarf. "But the wrong way. *That* takes us upside. It takes us back. And if we return, we've failed."

The gnomes nodded. They had all failed enough.

Running was the best idea, but their only hope was to follow the course of water upstream.

The current was too powerful. Twice Pointillo tried to crawl through the upstream hole; twice he was swept back onto the aqueduct, and only the strong grasp of Triquet kept him from toppling over its edge or racing down the channel after Ragg like a log in a lethal flume.

But the second time he came up with hope.

"There's a hole in the conduit!" he gasped. "Four or five feet in! We block the flow of water on the upstream side, and we can climb through it to . . . well, to something safer than burning alive."

"I suppose spiders could not nest that close to water," Innova offered apprehensively.

"Oh, spiders will be the *least* of our troubles," Pillaster assured. "There are always gaseous pockets, blind drops down a thousand feet of chasm, creatures reorganized by living too near the waste dumps . . . You'll be able to choose among all of them before this is over, I'll wager. I remember once, while on campaign with Generalissimo Glorius Peterloo . . . "

There was no time for war stories. Scalded to action by the rising steam, the other gnomes moved quickly, and Pillaster, still finishing his story, worked as he droned on about battering rams and triple-pouched gnomeflingers.

Ripping boards from the top of the aqueduct, the gnomes passed them forward to sturdy Triquet, who braced himself against the wall of the conduit and began to wedge it full of wood. Twice the current swept away the makeshift dam, but on the third try a solitary board lodged, bent, and held.

"Reorx be praised!" Triquet gurgled. "We're halfway out of here!"

It's a good thing, Innova thought, glancing behind him at the aqueduct that was now beginning to burn. It looked as though the nick of time would be the thinnest nick imaginable.

Then the cloudy warriors stepped out of the steam and smoke, their weapons murky in their dark hands.

*　　*　　*　　*　　*

Their coldness had withstood the raging fire, the overflowing magma.

Though the gnomes had no way of knowing, they were facing a band of daemon warriors, the second wave in the great assault of Chaos, as cold as the vast, empty darkness between the stars. Two of the creatures straddled the span of the aqueduct, their weapons insubstantial blades of night that whistled through the smoky air. The fire parted for them, and the rising steam congealed in their wake, raining ice upon the sputtering, hissing magma.

Two of the gnomes—Lozenge and Roundell—drew weapons and closed with the warriors. Roundell's sword passed cleanly into his enemy, but the gnome's triumphant cry was stilled when the blade shattered, its shards toppling onto the hot rocks below with the music of broken glass. Then a cold wind gusted over the hapless gnome, lifted him into the air . . . and dropped him in the roiling magma, which opened to swallow him.

Lozenge backed away. The second warrior lurched at him with swift, unnatural movements, and the gnome lost footing in a desperate attempt to dodge the attack. For a moment he teetered on the brim of the aqueduct, cried out, began to tumble . . .

As Lieutenant Colonel Grex Pointillo snatched him away from the edge, pulling him back to safety and standing between him and his attacker.

For a moment the warrior seemed to shimmer over the arch like a fluttering black banner. Then, an arm that was more billowing air than arm flicked out, slipped past the colonel's shield and struck him square on the shoulder. Pointillo fell back with a cry into the channel of the aqueduct. Around him the water thickened to ice.

With a shout Innova and Lozenge drew the colonel from the channel, dragged him toward the upstream conduit, toward Triquet and the only possible escape. Somewhere they heard Shagg screaming, but the scream sheared off into sudden silence.

Blinded by steam and smoke, carrying their wounded colonel, the gnomes staggered toward Triquet, passing through a drift of smoke that funneled upward and vanished into a hole in the ceiling.

The vent! Innova had forgotten all about it. But it was fifty feet above them. How could they . . .

Something brushed against his face. Back in the room of his dangling and nightmares, he thought of spiders, leapt back, lost his footing and clutched vainly for balance.

His fingers closed around a strand of rope.

He shouted again, and in a sudden irrational movement, hoisted himself with one arm, the other clutched firmly around the cold Pointillo. For a moment the two of them swung out over the glowing floor of the chamber. Innova kicked into vaporous air.

His feet found a rung. It was a rope ladder, dangling from the open vent far above.

How? he started to ask, but there was no time to question. Innova began to climb, and a steadying tug below let him know that someone else was on the ladder as well.

He climbed even faster, the smoke pooled near the ceiling of the chamber choking him now, making him dizzy. The colonel stirred, held onto him desperately with cold hands.

It was only when he reached the duct that Innova looked back. There was the colonel, his face uncannily pale, and but a rung below him a stern Pillaster, waving his sword at the buckling air as he climbed the swaying ladder.

No sign of Triquet or Lozenge or the gully dwarf.

It was like emerging from the Abyss.

For a breathless second, Innova wavered on the topmost rungs of the ladder. He felt his grip slacken, heard a crash far below, felt sight and sound slipping away.

Someone or something clutched his loosening fingers, drawing him up.

In the moment before the world vanished, the crashing and screaming, the heat and a faint spangling, Innova thought dreamily of silly things. Of a reflected light somewhere on the upper levels, of fruit pies and a cool, bracing rush of water over his feet. And he heard a high voice whining in the collapsing darkness:

"Things always circle back in an old story,

"Though sometimes circlings are quite dilatory.

"Now help yourself up, boy. I've only the one arm that works."

Lucretius, Innova thought, scrambling onto cold stone as his thoughts left him.

Am I dead or am I dreaming?

Chapter 27

"Neither one!" a voice exclaimed, as Innova was shaken into wakefulness.

The voice sounded familiar. Innova opened his eyes.

Lucretius Climenole stood above him, a ghost from his recent past.

" 'Neither one'? Wh-what . . . "

"You were wondering whether you were dreaming or dead. I was merely establishing the premises."

Innova groaned, his pleasure at seeing Lucretius warring with the smoke sickness that roiled like magma in his stomach and lungs.

He coughed, spat out coal dust, vomited on the smooth stone. Then he brushed off his robes and stood, trying to appear as dignified as one possibly can after voiding himself in the presence of his superiors.

Innova's old companion was the worse for wear as well. Lucretius's left arm was in a sling, and the tip of his prominent nose was the lurid red and black of a checkerboard, as if something had burned it savagely in the not-too-distant past. Long dark flaps extended from his ankles, as though his boots had unraveled.

He had been talking, it seemed, to Grex Pointillo, who stood reverently beside the old man, huddled in blankets and shivering, charcoal and a clutter of vellum pages in hand.

The colonel, it seemed, had been taking notes. Innova peered over his shoulder at the diagrams, the footnotes. The string of silly proverbs. For some reason there was a shaky sketch of the old Graygem.

Whatever had battered Lucretius had evidently not stilled his voice.

"But the original design of the Graygem," Pointillo insisted, a tremor in his voice and his breath misting, even though the chamber seemed quite temperate to Innova, "was to house the magic of neutrality. It was our magic as well—that is, the magic of the gnome clergy."

Pillaster sniffed, polished his sword with a hydraulic grinder the size of a sandwich.

"So the story goes," Lucretius answered above the grating, metal-on-metal sound of Pillaster's contraption. "And I'm convinced that the Graygem has everything and nothing to do with this . . . this . . . what was the name of the machine again?"

"The Paradise Machine, sir," Pointillo said. "Everything works now—defensive engines and invader traps, and those devices set later when the first ones failed. Why, the whole city is bristling with protection. The machine has shored the upper levels against rescue. Innova invented it with the best intentions, but now it defends the Knights."

Lucretius winked at Innova. "I'm most impressed, young fellow. You've come a long way from misfiring gnome-flingers."

Innova could not decide whether to feel proud or guilty. Probably both were in order.

"So our hope lies," Pointillo said, "in finding a magic to destroy the machine."

Lucretius frowned. "And where do you propose to find it? 'Gnome magic is an unsupported rumor, Like dwarven manners or Solamnic humor.' Feel free to write it down, Pointillo."

"Without that magic, the Paradise Machine is indestructible, I fear," Innova said to his old mentor. "You'd think I could understand it—that what first made it work would somehow make it *not* work as well. But we've tried all kinds of destruction, from axes to explosives to tampering with gears and wires. The machine . . . repairs itself! It's like it has a mind of its own."

"It does," Lucretius replied.

Innova gaped at the colonel. "Do you mean . . . "

"Well . . . it does and it doesn't," Lucretius said. "Let me explain.

"After you left for the upper levels, I began to think about the Graygem oil. How it greased your slide for hundreds of yards. How you might well be sliding still were it not for the resistance of your . . . unoiled parts."

Innova winced, remembering the layer of skin he had left on the stone floors of the Fifth Level.

"I'm nothing if not experimental," Lucretius explained. "And I supposed that what was good for backsides might be doubly good for gears. So I took notice of the pool's whereabouts—remember how you bragged about it to that overdressed girl?"

"Meryl," Innova prompted. "I—I mean *Beryl*."

It was embarrassing to recall.

"So I came back to the spot," Lucretius continued. "Collected three vials of the stuff, and used two of them to oil the wheels of my handcart. Someday, I figured, I'd have the damnable contraption in working order, and perhaps all it really needed was a little lapse in friction. Well, metaphysical lubrication worked like a clock, or like they tell me that a clock is supposed to work, since I've never seen a clock that keeps the time, or that really tells you *anything* for that matter, given that a clock, chronophilosophically speaking, is simply another way of saying that you should be busy . . . "

"Yes, yes," the colonel coaxed. "Do go on, Lucretius."

The old gnome blinked, drawn back from his temporal reflections. "For the first time since I began to repair it, the cart ran smoothly. All of the gears turned in their appointed directions, and even the cart bed seemed to hold more stones, as though the metal were elastic, expanding to accommodate more cargo. All of this encouraged me, and I didn't even ponder the first accident because it wasn't an accident, really, but an accident in potential, as it were . . . "

The grinding stopped. Pillaster grumbled from the shadows.

"What happened," Innova asked, "in this potential accident?"

"I was standing at the brink of a crevasse," Lucretius said, "that opened over a pool of magma. It was a healthy drop—twenty feet, I'd guess, though that guess would do with some more precise measuring—down to heat and the bubbling, and I was preparing to cover the crack with stones. When something bumped me from behind, so that for a moment I slipped over the edge and it looked like the magma was rushing up to meet me.

" 'You're gone, Lucretius Climenole,' I told myself. 'Dissolved like spit on a griddle, and even the memory of you will be burnt away.' Can you imagine thinking such a long thought while you were falling?"

None of the listening gnomes could imagine.

"But thank great Reorx for elasticity and ankle bands!" Lucretius exclaimed, pointing to the flaps at his feet. "It worked like I thought it would, my nose just grazing the surface of the magma before the bands jerked me clean of the crevasse and back into the chamber. Oh, I bounced around a bit, flung back and forth by the tension. Knocked unconscious right away, and when I woke up I was still being hurled from wall to wall. I hit my head again and was out once more. Standard mishap. Could have misjudged my footing. That's what I told myself anyway. And I would've believed it, were it not for the chain of accidents that followed. There was a fire among the steam pipes, followed an hour later by the sudden addition of gears in the back of the cart that entangled my robe and threatened to draw me in and grind me to pieces, and then there was the sudden uncoiling of suspension springs in a low-ceilinged tunnel, accompanied by the chemical discovery that when Thorbardin Oeconomy Malt passes through an engine lubricated with Graygem oil, the result is an explosion that the Ballistics Guild would envy."

Lucretius smiled. "It was all fun, but far too frequent. I expect occasions of . . . this magnitude, say, once a month. But four accidents within an hour?"

Grex Pointillo wrote something down.

"Six is a miraculous number, Innova," the old philosopher went on. "Remember how often it recurs in nature. It's also the limit of the number of times a supposedly inanimate object can fool its inventor. They say, 'Fool me once, shame on you, fool me twice, shame on me' . . . "

The old gnome's voice trailed away. He was trying to remember the silly proverb.

Innova grasped his shoulders, shook him back to the story.

" 'Fool me five times, shame on my cousins.' Or something like that. At any rate, it was the sixth time that enlightened me. I was passing through a room on the level below—the room where I rescued you twice. There were crevasses aplenty there, but the tracks wound around them, and I was imagining I was safe from mishap. I *never* imagined, though, that the damned handcart would choose not to abide by the tracks, so to speak, and take off on its own over bare stone."

"It jumped the tracks, then," Innova said. "Surely *that*'s . . . "

"Oh, but you weren't there, boy!" Lucretius's smile had faded. "It was on a straight grade and it . . . simply decided to go elsewhere. Over the stones toward the far wall, picking up speed as it went. No jumping the track. It was trying to cut a tunnel through the stone."

Lucretius paused. The story was great drama, though Innova was not sure he believed it. His schooling and his experience, layered on a millennium of gnome culture, had taught him that his people were the intelligence behind their inventions—were, as the old skeptic Belisarius used to say, the ghosts in their own machines. What Lucretius was asking him to believe was bad theology and worse mechanics.

He would not hear of it. It jostled too many things.

But Lieutenant Colonel Grex Pointillo was listening.

"How did you escape, Father Lucretius?" he asked.

"The machine had not reckoned on my ejector seat," Lucretius announced proudly. "Of course, it operated in conjunction with the suspension springs, and when I'd recoiled them after the aforementioned accident number four, I had not reckoned on the augmented tensile strength. . . . "

"Which means?" Innova asked.

"Which means that the seat worked, but with far too much emphasis. The whole contraption knocked me ass over teakettle, broke my arm and left me the convalescent you see before you. But it saved me from the handcart. From the machine that was plotting to murder me. And surprisingly, the last vial of Graygem oil was left intact."

He produced a small glass bottle, its silvery liquid glittering and tilting. But for the moment, all attention was on other things.

241

"Oil is well and good," the colonel said. "But what about magic? Aren't there spells or wardings, incantations or—"

"I'm sure there are," Lucretius replied. "The trouble is, I know none of them. I speak the solid and dialectical truth, Colonel. For once, the rumors of magic *aren't* true. I'm as dry of conjury as those gully dwarves who were flushed away."

"Then what's left to do?" Pointillo asked in despair.

It was almost as though the colonel had come to the end of a pilgrimage, only to find the shrine he sought was hollow. He was shivering as well, from the mysterious cold.

"We proceed according to what we know," Lucretius said. "By our own lights and our own stars, dim though they may be. There's a solution to this—whether mechanical or physical or even metaphysical, I'm not sure. But I have an idea, and more heads—even when they're *your* heads—are better than mine alone."

* * * * *

Meanwhile, in the upper levels of Mount Nevermind, High Justice Gordusmajor had concluded that more heads made for more arguments. And nothing more.

For two days now, the Philosophers' Tribunal had been barricaded against an assault that had not come. Armed guards, posted at the receiving nets at the entrance of the hall, were growing restless, and the delight of the gallery in teasing the captive Knights of Takhisis was fading fast.

Flagging attention was being replaced by rising, unspoken concerns. Unspoken, that is, until Justice Ballista broke his two-day silence.

"Does anybody have any cake?" he asked plaintively. "Sesame would do, though I am judicially partial to a three-layer lemon zest and dwarf spirit pudding tart."

A murmur rose among the assembled gnomes.

"Is there no sweet tea, and by the great healing prescriptions of Mishakal, are there no goat cheeses?" Ballista asked, his voice louder and more urgent.

"There, there," Gordusmajor boomed. "More philosophical serenity from the scale pan opposite, if you please! If we are to win a victory here, there will be a time of hardship, a time of deprivation and thin rations."

The High Justice shifted uncomfortably on his broken bench, feeling the oatcakes in the pockets of his robe. Perhaps when they all were sleeping . . .

"Any of those little pastry horns with cream in them?" Ballista whined.

The gallery erupted with protest.

"Why didn't you ask *us?*" someone shouted. And many of the other gnomes, from bystander to clerk to the justices themselves, took up the cry.

Assured by his concealed oatcakes, Gordusmajor counseled restraint. He urged the gnomes to stick together, that only in the spirit of unity could they withstand whatever the Knights of Takhisis had in store for them. Secretly, he wished he had studied more in the world of cause and effect he had so loudly scorned: Had he done so, he probably would have considered the value of arms and supplies when you are surrounded by enemies.

Unity seemed to be on a very far horizon. The gallery was clamoring for mushrooms and whiskey, Justices Harpos and Julius had come to blows over a fruit pie found among the litter in their scale pan, and Scymnidus Carcharias, in his true and natural paranoia, had locked himself inside the armored wicker basket.

Gordusmajor found himself wishing for Halion Khargos. A little stiff and goddess-reliant, but basically an honorable sort, not like that flattened blackguard Fleetwood.

He could do with an honorable man in the chamber. All the more easy to trick and bluff.

For after all, it *had* been a bluff, these threats of revealing Khargos's past. A blind, gnomish shot in the dark that hit its target.

Khargos had fallen more quickly than the city he conquered. He was gullible indeed—gullible enough to have sent Fleetwood to a sort of martial jury duty, thereby unknowingly bringing the tortures to a standstill four levels down. But perhaps he would have stopped such an outrage had he known of it in the first place; after all, Khargos was not a bad boy when it came down to it, and surely whatever sins he was hiding were simple ones. Broken dietary laws, or some mistake in ritual bathing—the kinds of things that stick in the craw of honorable Knights.

Yet, at the bottom, this Khargos was sensible as well, unlike everyone in this damned Tribunal Hall.

A hall Gordusmajor had to bring, once again, to order.

"At least," the High Justice shouted above the rising clamor. "At least we have water! I have heard tales of besieged castles, where the defenders—especially stocky ones with incomparable political power—have survived for days upon water."

It seemed to assure no one. Justice Ballista, whose moaning and complaints had set off this mutiny, rose slowly and weakly, staggering toward the source of water—the ornamental pool into which the lever of the Paradise Machine dipped like a demented ostrich.

The old bastard! Gordusmajor thought. Hobbling around like he's starving already!

"May the court consider," Ballista shouted, "the water in question. Tepid and probably impure, pumped and piped and aqueducted through the-gods-know-what-kind of strata and silt and garbage! Vile stuff from its source and . . . and . . . "

Ballista looked over the edge of the pool, his eyes widening in rising horror.

"And *there's even a gully dwarf afloat in it!*"

He reached into the water and drew forth a sputtering, coughing creature, its oily hair matted and dingy rivulets tracing down its crusty tunic.

With a gasp, Ragg Karputt looked around the room, recognized dimly that he was in some place of importance, and fell to his knees.

"If *that* doesn't settle it!" old Ballista cried in triumph, folding his arms. "The water's ruined! We'll skim squalid and ugly from it for weeks! Nothing could be worse, saving more of the same!"

At that moment, Shagg Karputt came bursting through the pipes and surfaced in the murky pool. He cried out once, his bellow filling the Tribunal Hall and startling old Ballista into a horizontal position.

Then, with the precision and punctuality the gnomes had come to dread and expect, the dipping end of the Paradise Machine descended. The birdlike head of the lever almost seemed to wince as it swiveled, pivoted, and crashed down on the head of the hapless gully dwarf.

Chapter 28

"Why did they attack us when they did?" Innova asked.

The gnomes were resting around a low fire in Lucretius's water chamber. For hours, the old gnome had guided them toward this place, away from the great burning, the bands at his feet flapping loudly in the corridors. Now they had stopped to regroup, to nurse burns and bruises, and to quench a searing thirst.

It was a chamber designed to collect and purify the suspect underground waters. There was a pool in the cavern above, or a stream that snaked between the levels—Innova was not sure. But from its store a steady stream dripped into the water chamber.

Under that stream, amid a litter of ladders and wheelbarrows and fragmented handcarts, Lucretius had erected an elegant device. A wheel, a bucket attached to each of its spokes, turned ever so slowly. When the top bucket filled with water, the weight would lower it until finally it was the bottommost, hovering over a small fire that boiled and purified its contents. Then, when the water was poured out or when it evaporated, the bucket would rise again, to be replaced by the next one on the wheel.

At any rate, the contraption worked, far better than most machinery below the ordering power of the Paradise Machine.

"Why did they attack us when they did?" Innova asked again. "After all, they had followed us for such a long time through corridors that would be perfect for ambush, into chambers where there was only one entrance. Why then and there?"

The colonel and Pillaster shrugged. It was a question irrelevant to soldiers, therefore irritating.

"I expect they found us more vulnerable," Pillaster finally growled, genetically unable to resist the temptation to explain the obvious. "We were up on a shaky structure in the midst of fire. One of our number was swept away by water. The earth was collapsing around us, and the air was thick with smoke. For a military specialist, which some of us are *not*, the whole situation was apparent: the best of all possible times to attack."

It was not apparent to Innova. "Why didn't they let the fire do it, then?" he insisted.

Lucretius turned to him and smiled.

"Perhaps it was part of a larger plan," the old gnome suggested.

Lieutenant Colonel Grex Pointillo was suddenly interested. "*What* larger plan?"

"I'd be damned to the strongest gust of the Abyss if I had any idea," Lucretius replied. "Let us say *some* larger plan, and begin our speculation at a common point of agreement."

He rose from the fire, hitched the elastic ankle bands to his belt, and walked toward the water wheel.

"Gentlemen," he announced, "I should like you to ponder my invention for a moment."

Pillaster rolled his eyes, but his two comrades turned respectfully to the grimy old philosopher, who was already raising a rickety stepladder behind the wheel.

Lucretius climbed to the top of the ladder, which rocked dangerously under his weight. Innova rose to steady the thing, but Lucretius waved him away.

"A self-propelled water retrieval and dispersal system that has worked this way for years," the old gnome said proudly. "On a simple principle of a Fourth Rule of Speculative Physics, which I have not had the time to record because of my constant shoring and collecting, but the practical principle goes as follows: As long as the fire is stoked, evaporation and cyclical motion take care of the rest. Better, I'd fancy, than your dripping and dipping levers, Innova."

Innova allowed that it was.

"But observe," Lucretius continued. "What will happen if I increase the flow of water into the bucket?"

"It'll go faster?" Pointillo suggested.

"So a priestly soldier might think," Lucretius said. "Or even a soldierly priest. But to a specialist, it is obvious."

He gave Pillaster a scolding stare, opened the conduit in the chamber ceiling to a stronger rush of water.

"As you will see," he continued, as the wheel picked up speed, "as the wheel moves more quickly, the buckets no longer have time to fill. Notice what happens as a result."

The gnomes watched as the wheel slowed, paused, moved in the opposite direction, then paused again and righted itself, spinning backward and forward in a rocking movement without reason or predictability.

"It is my guess," Lucretius said in a low voice, "or perhaps more than a guess—a *hydropothesis*, I like to call it—that there is a pattern to this new motion as well. One we can't predict by cause and effect, something large and, I hope, mathematical."

"*And*?" Pillaster was impatient with philosophy.

Lucretius staggered at the top of the ladder, as a strong current pushed against him. "*And* it seems like chaos to us," he said, "because whatever the machine is doing, it's no longer boiling our water."

Pointillo was the first to catch on.

"So all of these unusual happenings," he said, "these bizarre creatures, the tremors in the magma, even the Paradise Machine with its living Graygem oil, may be part of a larger pattern we don't understand."

"Great Reorx!" Pillaster exclaimed, insight pouring over him like water from a tipping bucket. "You mean it's part of some large strategy!"

The gnomes fell silent, each in his own way absorbing the awful news.

"What—what do we *do*, Lucretius?" Innova asked at last.

"Who knows?" the old gnome said with a shrug. "Perhaps, in all that order that the Paradise Machine is establishing upstairs, there is something that tends toward chaos. We've been operating on the assumption that the oil was a silt from something in the Graygem that served as a *barricade* against chaos . It just as well could have been that very chaos escaping. Perhaps, in secret and in a way we cannot yet understand, the Paradise Machine, for all its efficiency, is allied with the forces of Chaos."

"I can't believe it," Pointillo said. "Can't believe that it is so *largely* planned. That the sole purpose of that kind of order is to break down eventually, to let disorder in."

"Suppose it is," Innova said. "What do we *do*? How do we attack something if we don't understand it at all?"

"When did *they* attack?" Lucretius asked. "Be specific, now."

"The warriors? Why, when we were in that burning chamber," Pillaster replied, clutching his sword as though he replayed the battle in his memory.

"More specific!" Lucretius urged.

"When we were atop the aqueduct," said Pointillo.

"More *specific*!"

Innova cupped his chin in his hands, looked up at the shaking water wheel. "When we started to block the flow of water?"

"I taught you well, Innova," Lucretius said quietly. "I taught you very well."

Innova frowned. Apparently he had missed his own insight.

"We proceed," Lucretius said, "as we always proceed. By what we *do* know, and by cause and effect. The warriors tried to stop you when you blocked the flow of water; therefore, the flow of water to the surface is something they desire. Why?"

With great effort, the old gnome narrowed the conduit above the wheel, and the machine resumed its old patterns as the gnomes mulled over the mystery.

"Underground water is the major source," Pillaster said at last, "of irrigation and ornamental fountains. Of water supply to the city, now that the Knights of Takhisis have shut off the water from above."

"You haven't learned anything, have you?" Lucretius snapped. "Here I am one good stagger from breaking my neck, sodden with greasy water and no telling what kind of lethal minerals . . . "

Pointillo raised his hand, like a schoolboy at lecture.

"Yes!" Lucretius roared, "Lieutenant Grex Pointillo!"

"Lieutenant *Colonel*, sir," Pointillo said. "Might it be, sir, that the principal use of the water we are now considering is in the . . . *fueling* of the Paradise Machine?"

Fergus Ryan

"A fine and most perspicacious answer, Lieutenant *Colonel*. Breeding will tell in the solution of problems, I always say. Or I will always say from now on. Malonadon and Sardonican, on your mother's side? It shows, lad, it shows."

The colonel beamed with pride, a faint flush on his too-pale cheeks.

He's come down with something, Innova thought. Chill or white fever or, Mishakal forbid, the pneumalaise. We should tend to him, and at once.

"We should tend to this, and at once," Pointillo said, staring at the water wheel, his eyes fiercely bright. "If we must proceed from what we know, and what we know is that, for some reason, the forces allied against us do not want us to block or dismantle the aqueducts, then—"

"We do what we have to do," Pillaster said, at last in agreement with all these intellectuals. "We stop the flow of water to the upper city."

* * * * *

High in that upper city, Halion Khargos looked out a window on the second story of the Geometers' Guild Hall, onto a little town square. The fountains jetted and cascaded gorgeously over a garden of moss and decorative mushrooms. This lovely place seemed double in size because of the surrounding mirrors, which reflected the rows of lichen and fungus.

Funny, Khargos thought, that the mirrored borders had been conceived as part of the surveillance system. So far, they remained only mirrors, not yet attached to the Paradise Machine. Yet they were perfectly good as ornaments, reflecting the garden in all its shadowy beauty.

Once again, the Commander thought about how eccentrically lovely this city was, how charming and intricate its patterns of decoration.

And now that most things on the upper levels worked with precision and efficiency, it was more beautiful still— things running well and on time and according to the ancient designs of planners, artists, and architects.

Oh, as always, there were the pockets of discord. Mirrors, an occasional wandering cart track, and of course the gnome institutions his word of honor had left untouched. For the last three days, the Philosophers' Tribunal had imagined itself under siege, issuing manifestoes and proclamations hourly by metavox, by notices posted throughout the Thirtieth Level by Gordusmajor's overburdened law clerks.

The uprising would take care of itself, Khargos thought. Supplies in the hall were scarce, and who'd ever heard of a gnome missing three meals in a row?

What troubled him more was the news from the lower levels. The Generalissimo's army had retreated to the belly of the mountain, where gossip had it that they were re-armed and reinforced.

There were even rumors of surfacing dwarves in the waterworks.

All these menaces from the depths seemed like poetic justice to Halion Khargos. If you push something under, he told himself, it can resurface horribly, in ways you could never foresee.

But that was just philosophy. What truly troubled him was the absence of the Goddess.

He had not communed with Takhisis since the early days of the occupation. She had been short with him, scolding, and he had left the Vision with his questions and desires unfulfilled.

She had challenged him to hold fast, and he had held, against the bloody counterattack of Flurious Akimbo—the failed assault that had left even the enemy Commanders sickened.

Khargos remembered the smell of the fire-gutted amphitheatre. Regret and misgiving heaped on one another like rubble and ash.

He had held fast, as well, against this absurd insurrection in the Tribunal Hall. And above all, he had held against the nature of the gnomes themselves. Against the chaos that always churned and bubbled beneath the surface of their intricate society.

Peace was uneasy. A sense of trouble stirred his thoughts like a low-grade fever—his constant companion through the tedious daily activities of an occupying general. Khargos longed to commune with the Goddess—longed for her touch, her assurance.

But his dreams had remained blank, his reveries unremembered.

Until this morning, when She visited him unexpectedly.

Standing on the balcony, looking over the fountains, the Commander became dizzy. The artificial light of the square, brightened unnaturally to resemble a summer day, seemed to flare at the corners of his eyes.

He was almost blinded by the sudden flash. His vision sank to a dark patch ringed with a corona of light, as though he gazed directly at an eclipse.

Khargos sank to his knees, clutching the railing for support. And out of the heart of that darkness came the Lady, so pale she seemed to abide and reflect all colors.

He gasped as her dark eyes settled on him. For it was not the Takhisis he remembered. No longer soft and seductive, she was cold and sinuous, her beauty as brittle and brilliant as the scales of a snake.

He wondered how he could have wanted her all these years.

I shall be leaving you for a while, Halion Khargos, she said.

"Leaving me? I—I don't—"

Oh, it was nothing you did or didn't do. Isn't that what I'm supposed to say?

A strange, melodic laughter cascaded over the balcony, drawing darkness with it. Now Halion Khargos could see nothing—no fountain, no square, no pallid Goddess.

He brought his hands to his face, as though he shielded his eyes against this abandonment.

For abandonment it was. Something within her nourished him entirely. Something in her voice called constantly to his blood. Beautiful woman or scaly, reptilian thing, she was his essence, and the shadow that haunted the edge of his mirror.

"Then why?" he asked. "Why are you leaving?"

Who are you to ask? Where were you when this world was fashioned, and when the forces of old Chaos were conquered and restrained? Where were you in the ages preceding? When Huma split my side and sent me into the Abyss? When Istar fell in the Cataclysm? When the dragonarmies gathered?

Khargos could only fall to his knees and marvel.

I am a goddess, Takhisis said, *and my ways are mysterious to even my more intimate servants.*

"But..." Khargos tried to stand, but the weight of the air held him down. It was as though the darkness had become thick and palpable.

I can do as I wish, without answering to any man or gnome or dwarf. And yet I refuse to abandon my favorites entirely.

Which is why I have returned to you this afternoon, in what seems to be a time of great safety and security.

Do you feel it, Halion Khargos?

Do you feel the threat in the air?

Khargos nodded stupidly. Words had fled him in the new face of the Goddess's power, but he knew what she meant.

The Paradise Machine had taken too long. The pools of resistance that spread throughout Mount Nevermind were widening, gathering volume.

It is only a matter of time, the Goddess said, completing his thoughts. *This is no place for victory.*

"What? What is happening?" he asked, but the Goddess did not seem to listen.

It is simply defeat. Defeat is rushing toward you with the speed of unleashed fire. This was not the place. This was not the time.

There were betrayals in your ranks. The greatest of which was your own.

"My own?"

Suddenly the darkness began to reel. Great gaps seemed to open in the air, astounding drops into greater darkness, into voids that heretofore Khargos had never imagined.

"My own?" he whispered. "Why, no one has been so faithful, my Mother, my Goddess."

A pause, and then Takhisis answered.

The Test of Takhisis is not the only test to be passed and discarded by a Knight on his way to power.

There are other tests of true greatness—informal, neither written in the Code nor shared among Knights, for these tests are private and individual.

They are the tests of honor and wisdom and insight—tests my commanders must pass every day, with or without my assistance.

Many of my Knights have murmured that your tests have been too easy, your obstacles too few. That I have played at a game of courtly favorites, rather than abiding by justice and merit, as the Code dictates.

But all along, I have followed their Code. I tested you further, beneath a veil of indirection and secrecy.

I had great hopes for you, Halion Khargos, and so there was a long night in which I tested you by withholding my words and favors. I let you decide, trusting in your intelligence and your foresight.

When you decided to seize Mount Nevermind, I stood beside you as you ordered your troops, as you arranged your defenses in the upper levels of the city.

I stood beside you, because it was time for you to learn.

But you were not ready. Perhaps too young, surely not wise enough.

"All that I did, I did for your glory!" Khargos shouted. But his own doubts crept into the edge of his thoughts.

Had all of this been for the betterment of Takhisis? Or for his own glory, his own desires?

Other things worked against you. Other factors, other individuals. Consider yourself warned. Our venture in Mount Nevermind has failed. Perhaps you will learn to trust me again. When you do, I suppose I shall learn to trust you.

Pale light flickered at the edge of Khargos's darkness. She was leaving him, leaving him because of his own unworthiness.

His thoughts raced back into his memory. He did not recall his decisions and strategies in the way that the Goddess presented them. No, Takhisis had been his intimate in policy and tactics. Surely she had. There was no decision he made without consulting her.

She simply had not answered back.

But perhaps there were clouds in his memory. And hadn't she said they would trust one another again?

Why, she was warning him now, warning him of a rising danger.

Gather together a band of supporters, the Goddess urged. *Few enough to move quickly from this trap of Chaos, enough to*

*form an army around you as you regroup on the shores of San-
crist.*

*Spare no one who is expendable. There is vantage in leanness,
in small, effective numbers.*

*I shall be watching. From below you and above you and all
about. Consider it your continual test, as you show me the qualities that have formed your character, have suited you to lead in my
armies.*

She vanished then. Receded into the shadows of the
stony vault above the garden. Khargos looked for her, but
she was nowhere to be found.

* * * * *

It was a strange sight for whoever was watching, from
the square below the Geometers' Guild Hall.

A young man in a dark tunic, kneeling at the railing of a
second story balcony, the air around him bent and shimmering like a mirage on a hot road.

He seemed to be overcome by heat, this young man. Or
perhaps he was lost at prayer—prayer to whatever god or
goddess governs fire and warmth and illusion.

This observer would not know the mind of Halion Khargos, who knelt out of tradition and respect and confidence,
but no longer in assured desire and trust and love.

There was something missing in the Goddess's account.
He could not put words around it. It was as though she
played from a thinly concealed disadvantage, like the gambler surprised at cards who claims, weakly, "I knew you
would do that."

It was a time for faith, Halion Khargos decided. When
the evidence of his senses told him he was abandoned high
and dry—that was the time that a loyal officer believed in
whatever gods sustained him.

Followed their orders to the end, even if that end was
death.

He had been given another chance to prove his loyalty, to
follow the Goddess's orders.

She had said they would trust one another again, and
part of him thrived on that hope, but there was another

part—a voice less quiet now in his own imagination—that said new things about trust and doubt.

She had been gone such a long time that Khargos could imagine the world without her.

He stood, braced himself against the balcony rail. Already the gardens below him seemed pale and withered, and the fountains seemed suddenly less vibrant, as though anticipated memory was already diminishing the things he was seeing.

He would leave Mount Nevermind, as Takhisis suggested. He would trust in the gods that sustained him.

Or pretend to trust in the hopes that pretending would lead him back to the real thing.

Back to the gods. Whatever gods they were.

Chapter 29

Lost in unsettling thoughts, Halion Khargos stood on the balcony of the Geometers' Hall, overlooking the tranquil little shade garden. Slowly, the lichens and mosses, the mushrooms and the night-blooming cereus took on a sickly amber color. The artificial lighting on the Twenty-Ninth Level dimmed in sad attempt to mimic natural moonlight, reflected in a score of circling mirrors.

The city had come easy to him.

As had everything.

A spy had shown him the entrances to Mount Nevermind. Once the invasion began, a disorganized gnome army had offered little resistance. Khargos's luck, some said. The will of the Goddess, said others.

Now the Commander cursed that luck, that guidance. It had not prepared him for defeat and adversity.

The forces that had lifted him up were telling him to leave now, to leave without a fight, surrendering a city whose conquest meant little because it was too easy.

Something in Halion Khargos knew how the gnomes felt when everything was ordered.

He would have liked the chance to govern Mount Nevermind, he told himself. Then he laughed softly, knowing that thought was a lie. He was too young to govern, too young to take on the thousand complexities of daily life. Part of him still longed for the dramatic—for the high mountains illumined by a flash of lightning, for voyages in stormy water, for pitched battle and the life of the moving camp.

Yet even that life had come to weary him. There was a sameness in sacked and surrendered cities, in the eyes of captives and in the plunder that spilled into the coffers of the Goddess.

A Goddess who, it seems, had repaid him with her absence.

His thoughts fixed on everything, on nothing in particular, Commander Halion Khargos watched the garden dim, barely noticing the two small figures that approached the Guild Hall along a winding path.

*   *   *   *   *

At the edge of the garden path, Beryl Barium paused and looked behind her.

The automated creature had followed obediently and silently. Beryl wished that the late Deddalo had designed the device to emit cheerful sounds—whistles and beeps, perhaps, or the ringing of soft chimes.

As it was, the artificial Barium girl was downright creepy. As suited her current purpose.

Shaped more like a buoy than a gnome female, the contraption had seemed little more than a toy until Oliver's plans had breathed a new life into all those wheels and gears.

It was the last thing Khargos would expect, the young cleric had urged. What's more, he is drawn to gnome inventions, the more far-fetched the better.

How fitting if one were to bring him sweet poison.

So Beryl and Deddalo had remodeled the mechanical Meryl. The arms, which once swung playfully in imitation of a girl's jaunty walk, now concealed sheathed knives, and the device's hourglass figure had straightened into a cylinder with the addition of a layer of armor.

Only the face remained the same. Painted simply and without expression, it was a doll's countenance, pretty but oblivious.

All in all, a grotesque version of Beryl's dearly departed sister.

Khargos would see no harm in the thing. Oliver had assured them of that, assured her of his love of gnome devices, especially those that seemed useless to the casual observer. He would draw near it to examine it and, when he was near enough, the creature would spring into contrived life: the knives would unsheathe in the gloved hands and a cut—any simple cut—would send the poison coursing into the observer.

It was all simple, but there were contingencies. The machine could tip over while climbing the stairs. It could wander stupidly down the wrong corridor in the Guild Hall. It could sink its knives into someone other than Halion Khargos.

That was why Oliver's suggestion had been a stroke of genius.

Whatever powered the Paradise Machine, it was the Graygem oil, the cleric said, that kept it about its purpose. Why, the Paradise Machine even restored itself when there was a need! Linked itself to other machines and spread its power throughout the upper levels.

What else could it be but the mysterious oil?

Designed toward one purpose alone, and oiled with the magic of self-preservation, what could this automaton do but enter the hall of the Geometers' Guild and, having climbed a flight of stairs to his chambers, dispose of the Occupying General, leaving his command to one more capable. . . .

To the Bone Acolyte Oliver?

The cleric had promised Beryl her reward. Though he had been anything but specific, she had seen it in his eyes.

Anything could happen. Romances more strange had blossomed in stranger places.

"Be swift, my unnatural sister," Beryl whispered, and poured the first bottle of the shimmering oil onto the gears of the automaton.

*   *   *   *   *

From the balcony, Khargos watched the two figures in the shadowy garden, watched their reflections on the faces of bordering mirrors.

Two gnome females, both elaborately overdressed. One of them knelt beside the other, as though adjusting the hem of her companion's skirt or attending to a ravel in the sleeve.

Khargos leaned his elbows on the balcony rail, squinted for a closer look.

How charming, he thought. The object of attention is a machine.

It was obvious from the outlandish look of the thing. Wires sprouted in the place of hair, and the figure of the creature was solid, blockish—even more barrel-like than the standard gnome female. The painted doll's face was even more absent-minded, more vacant than dollmaker or puppeteer might imagine, though it was round, symmetrical, and pretty in a mathematical sort of way.

Whoever had built this contraption did not understand the female of his species.

Khargos smiled from his vantage point, recalled the high romance of his continuous Vision. He was one to talk of misunderstanding.

It was then that his thoughts scattered. A movement in the garden caught his eye.

* * * * *

Beryl stepped back as the automaton began to move.

Slowly, the thing trundled toward the entrance of the Geometers' Hall, and Beryl watched with great contentment, sure that the plan was underway.

In the shadows, the automaton looked almost alive. The charged wires on its head seemed to wave like windblown hair, and a movement in its hand as it turned seemed almost uncertain, almost living.

You had to hand it to Deddalo. He might have been a fool, but he was a decent craftsman. Though dead, he was the artisan that would set it all in motion—the assassination of Halion Khargos, Oliver's rise to power, and her own coveted inheritance handed to her at last.

And who knew what else might follow?

Folding her arms, she smiled at the fruits of scheming and handiwork.

Her eye caught a flicker in one of the bordering mirrors.

All of a sudden, the reflection no longer contained the garden, the rows of lichens and the mechanical girl. Something had happened to the mirror: Beryl had heard that the vast surveillance system was linked to the Paradise Machine, was slowly beginning to work, and she supposed the mirror's new image had something to do with that.

At any rate, the glass showed a dark, cavernous boulevard some levels down, lined with windowless marble buildings. Forms perfectly geometrical, slabs lining narrow, unpeopled streets. This landscape, if you could call it that, was aglow in pale torchlight, but the buildings were so tall, so featureless—so tomblike—that the well-lit corridors seemed shadowy, even in steady light.

Beryl looked deeply into the mirror. Something hovered beneath that arch.

As though it was guiding her sight, focusing her attention, the scene in the mirror shifted, lurched toward the arch, toward the thing that dangled and swayed in its apex.

A body. Dry and browned, no longer recognizable.

It was a gnome. She was sure of that much.

Behind that body, framed by the arch, a thousand scaffoldings littered a blank and desolate landscape—wooden gibbets spread out to the edge of the torchlight.

Under which yet another, or two, or three, hung and twisted in a windy chamber.

Beryl blinked in horror and looked into the adjoining mirror.

It still reflected the garden. A long row of lichens, at the end of which the automaton rumbled merrily toward her, turning at last to face her.

Gone was the pleasant, vacant stare, the dull doll's eyes painted on a porcelain face. For a moment the eyes seem to glitter, the mouth turn downward in a clownish expression of rage.

Beryl took a step back. Surely not, she thought.

The automaton charged her.

Overwhelmed by surprise, by the sheer silliness of it all, Beryl froze in place. The artificial Barium girl was on her in an instant, ramming into her, knocking her over, bladed hands flickering in the half-light of the garden.

In the face of that relentless machine Beryl saw something familiar, something turned suddenly malign.

Meryl. The thing had the eyes of Meryl Barium.

261

Just as suddenly, a dull doll's face smiled down on her, the painted nose chipped in the collision, the machine still quivering, rocking, coming to a halt.

Somewhere someone was calling for guards. But it would be too late to rescue Beryl Barium.

In a calm wonder, the gnome girl looked at the knife cut in her side, the blood pooling over her dark robe. Her legs were numb already, and her breath was shallow.

All thoughts of inheritance, power, and the Bone Acolyte fled in that moment, and she remembered a cavern of quartz and onyx, transparencies and bright opaqueness. . . .

Meryl standing at the threshold. A younger Meryl—a Meryl at the edge of childhood.

Beryl blinked in amazement, in wonderment at a memory long buried in the silences of Mount Nevermind and her own forgotten past.

The darkness closed in for the last time.

*   *   *   *   *

It was Khargos who had called the guard. Khargos who had hurtled down the stairs and into the garden.

He was too late. Whatever had transpired between the girl and her odd machinery was over. Now the girl was dead, and the bizarre, painted contraption crackled with the last spasms of electrical life.

One of the guards drew sword, sheared the wires of the thing in a flurry and rain of sparks. Yet another guard—a Thorn Knight with experience at court—knelt over the girl, pronounced her dead by some exotic poison.

It was only then that Khargos noticed the resemblance.

Both the girl and the automaton were lifeless now, and in repose there was something similar in their appearances. Little barrel-chested oddities, the both of them.

The girl, it seemed, had made a creature in her own image. For whatever reason, whether mechanical or chemical or even magical, the automaton had turned on her in the garden, destroying the thing that it resembled the most.

It was all like something out of an old myth, an old story. But thinking of it returned Halion Khargos to the here and now, to the commands of the Goddess and his retreat from this hapless mountain.

He looked into the mirrors. In most of them he could see the garden, himself, the dead gnome girl. But in others, the glass had aligned itself with the workings of the Paradise Machine, with the mirrored surveillance system that Fleetwood had used effectively.

Khargos, too, saw the desolate level. The tombs, the gibbets, the hanged gnomes.

It left him horrified.

This was "keeping order" and "occupation"? Had Fleetwood watched these executions through the mirrors in the levels above?

Had he approved such atrocities?

One great catastrophe followed by others, Khargos thought. For the Goddess had said . . .

That a great disaster would strike Mount Nevermind. That he was to take a band of supporters—*few enough to move quickly from this trap of Chaos*, she had said.

Spare no one who is expendable.

He knew she meant that he should leave the gnomes.

And if disaster came, according to her promise, it would strike the gnomes in all their natural silliness and their confusion. To leave them now would be to continue the destruction he had started in his negligence.

Khargos was not ready to remember himself that way.

Instead, a purpose formed in his imagining, a heroism that would restore him in the eyes of his legions, in his own eyes. In the eyes of Takhisis Herself.

He would bring deliverance to a people. He would guide the gnomes away from the coming disaster.

Once they were free of danger, on safe and distant ground, Khargos would decide their fate. By then, they would be beholden to him—bound by love, he supposed, as well as healthy fear.

He could destroy them then, if he had to. If they got in the way, or he found them useless.

Or so he told himself, recovering the thoughts and voice of a Knight of Takhisis, as two hearts warred in the depths of his spirit, as they had warred a decade ago on a cloudy beach not far from here.

This heroism would bring the Goddess glory, he thought. More glory, at least, than a string of drying bodies in old Incline Barium's Necropolis.

He did not stop to question whose honor, whose glory he was truly after.

"Come with me," he said quietly to the Knights of Thorn and Lily who had come at their Commander's call.

"Come with me to the Philosophers' Tribunal."

*   *   *   *   *

Khargos and his guard were not the only ones to see the death of Beryl Barium.

From a shed at the garden side, once used for hoe and spade, but cleared away in the weeks of the occupation, a solitary figure watched the proceedings and their aftermath through a narrowly opened door.

The Bone Acolyte Oliver turned away and lit a candle. Shadows vaulted up the bare wooden walls, and he turned to the bones that lay strewn across the floor of the shed.

Inconclusive, as usual. As usual, a mixture of prospect and peril.

Things had changed now. The gnome girl was dead, and her silly conspiracy in ruins.

Oliver shrugged. Not that he had expected it to work in the first place. An automaton, for the gods' sake, guided by a fool of a female in the hopes that the machine would assassinate a well-guarded Commander of the Knights!

Of course, had it worked, it would have been a miraculous stroke of fortune. And he *had* hoped that the automaton would make it as far as the presence of the Commander.

But Oliver had prepared for the failure. For all kinds of failure. Had stroked Beryl Barium with sweet words and promises. Had even flirted with the girl a little, and been surprised when she seemed to lap it up.

Now she lay in the garden, poisoned by her own machinery, and her former intended, that fool Deddalo, vanished many levels below.

Expendable, both of them.

Now the little conspiracy against Halion Khargos, hatched by the three of them in the Hell With Dinner, was known to Oliver alone.

It had failed this time. But he would try again.

After all, the attempt had been harmless.

Oliver chuckled. Unless you were Beryl or Deddalo.

The Bone Acolyte knelt, gathered the bones.

Who knew what Khargos would make of this sorry incident in the garden? Oliver hoped the commander would see gnome conspiracy in the event, would tighten his control of the captive people as a result.

When control was tightened, reckless rebels would surface from the caverns and tunnels, and Oliver's own plans would become easier still.

But suppose he saw no conspiracy? Khargos was anything but stupid, Oliver mused, and yet there was a vein of trust that ran in the young man, an attendance on honor and loyalty that made him overlook suspicious actions.

How Flurious Akimbo's troops had passed the first . . . *drowsy* lines of defense in their assault on the upper levels. Or where Oliver himself had been in the midst of the battle that followed.

Khargos's trusting nature had been used to the Bone Acolyte's advantage before. But now, if the Commander did not suspect that Beryl was some sort of assassin, it would be a setback for Oliver's larger plans.

He produced the bones. Cast them over the floor of the shed.

And whether it was the will of the Goddess, his own desire, or a simple trick of light . . .

At last they told him something.

Trouble, they told him. New peril below.

It was a strange and unsettling reading. For the past few days, his speculations had directed him to the upper levels. To Gordusmajor and the standoff at the Tribunal Hall. To Beryl and Deddalo, and their work on the ridiculous machine.

But nothing had changed in the Tribunal Hall. Or had it?

And Beryl and Deddalo were both accounted for. Unless . . .

The thought struck him like a blast from the Abyss. With a gasp, Oliver stood and bolted toward the door of the shed.

Deddalo. Deddalo was alive!

Despite her oaths and promises, the little bitch had failed at that as well!

Out into the mottled light he lurched, unheeding whether he was watched. Clutching his robes around him, rifling his memory for all of the spells he would need, the Bone Acolyte hurried toward the center of the level, for the stairwell leading down to the depths.

It was a loose end that needed tying, and he was the only one left to do it.

Chapter 30

Meanwhile, the gully dwarves were well into their account of what was taking place in the lower levels.

As might be expected, Shagg and Ragg disagreed on the details. Shagg, for example, had confused the daemon warriors with the Knights of Takhisis: "Skull Knights, me betcha!" he kept repeating until one of the captive Knights, a mild-mannered young swordsman named Phoenix, cleared his throat and explained that there was but *one* Skull Knight among the soldiers of Halion Khargos.

Shagg settled into a sullen silence, barely tolerating his brother's confusion of the aqueducts with "rail bridges was flooded." The two finally came to blows over a description of the waters on those very aqueducts. Shagg claimed that the current moved "very fast."

Ragg tried to correct him to "very, very fast."

Knives were drawn. Gordusmajor cried for order, and only the strong arms of the captive Knights could separate the brothers.

As Shagg and Ragg puffed and glowered at one another, Scymnidus tried diplomatically to explain that two people could see the same events differently.

"One right, one way wrong!" Ragg agreed emphatically, and the dwarves lunged at one another again.

Cooler heads prevailed, and the four gnome justices took counsel with Scymnidus in a small chamber off the Tribunal Hall. Oddly enough, they invited Phoenix to join the debate. The so-called "hostage situation" on the Thirtieth Level had taken on a life of its own, the participants having all but forgotten what had brought them together at the start, not to mention who was hostage and who was captor.

This was what they could determine: A party of gnomes—"many," according to the gully dwarves, which meant more than two—were bound for the lower levels, seeking to undermine the Paradise Machine. They had been set upon, apparently, by what Phoenix called "Chaos creatures," and they might or might not have survived the attack.

"A paradox," Scymnidus mused when all the information lay before the counselors. "We have imagined that the Paradise Machine turns away or re-orders disorder. It's why the clocks are synchronized, the tracks unbroken, and the plumbing tight. Then why are these 'Chaos creatures' bent on preserving it?"

"Perhaps it doesn't do what it seems to do?" Phoenix asked.

Justice Harpos regarded him coldly. "Aren't you one of our hostages?" he asked.

High Justice Gordusmajor waved his stubby hands in dismissal. "Of course he is, Harpos! You were here when we seized 'em! But the lines between friend and enemy aren't clearly drawn any more, and that seems to be the case up and down the levels. Let the boy speak."

Phoenix only shrugged. He had reached the end of his imagination.

Scymnidus followed the young Knight's question with characteristic insight and paranoia. "Let's suppose the worst," he said. "I'm good at that. Suppose there was a conspiracy."

Justice Ballista sighed loudly, but Scymnidus was in full distrustful glory.

"Suppose that the Paradise Machine is somehow . . . allied with the forces of Chaos in the lower levels, bound to an alliance that has been plotted for millennia, even since the Graygem passed over this island and our pursuing ancestors laid the foundations of the city . . . "

"Preposterous!" Justice Julius sniffed.

But they all loved it, of course. An intricate story with themselves at the end and in the center. Though various side roads took them through Scymnidus's fantasies regarding an elven poisoners' cabal, a subterranean trade in dwarf spirits by draconian survivors of the War of the Lance, and a Solamnic expedition to one of the three moons, the story kept returning to the Paradise Machine and the Chaos in the lower levels.

Until at last their eyes widened as Scymnidus made his suspicions clear.

"Let me see if I have this straight, Scymnidus," High Justice Gordusmajor said, after half an hour's elaborate explanations. "After all, I am new to intrigue and scheming."

The barrister only smiled.

"If Chaos tends to a larger order—an order we cannot recognize for its largeness and intricacy—then order, eventually, tends toward Chaos as well? The whole idea of the Paradise Machine has been to abolish the smaller disorders, of gnome and human and natural nature, in preference to a single, solitary order that is thereby easier to disrupt."

"All heads with a single neck," Scymnidus said with a nod. "You know the story."

"Cover the ears of that machine!" Gordusmajor shouted into the Tribunal Hall.

Shagg and Ragg scurried dutifully to the ornamental pool, where Shagg removed his threadbare cloak and, straddling the neck of the lever, attempted to tie the garment around the dipping end of the machine.

Meanwhile, in the little chamber, the self-appointed council marvelled at the possibilities one of their number had raised.

"It's too complex for me," Phoenix said softly.

"Of course it is," Justice Harpos snapped. "You're a hostage, aren't you?"

A hammering at the entrance of the Tribunal Hall disrupted their silent thoughts. Ragg crept to the door and peeked through the keyhole.

"By Mother's beard!" he exclaimed. "It the Commander!"

Shagg plunged into the pool, his task unfinished.

The justices stared at one another in consternation. Scymnidus stood, no doubt contemplating the safety of his wicker cage, but was restrained by the strong arm of Gordusmajor.

"We've a visitor, Ragg," the High Justice called out. "By all means, let him in."

* * * * *

Halion Khargos was a little worse for wear, Gordusmajor noted, as the law clerks lifted his Ponderous Eminence back into the High Justice's seat.

First of all, the ride in the vaultwallopper up to the hall threshold had apparently not been without mishap. A dent in Khargos's ceremonial helmet suggested that the stone archway was a little lower than the Commander might have hoped.

But it was more than that. The young fellow had not been sleeping.

Restless nights are easier on a young man, but when they finally get to him, their toll is greater in his eyes, on his face.

And the Commander who stood before his bench and bowed politely had been dreaming unsettling dreams. Or not dreaming enough.

The two adversaries—the old wily gnome and the young Knight of Takhisis—regarded each other skeptically in the vaulted Tribunal Hall. Since their earlier meeting had ended in threats, the two had kept a respectful distance, but now some change in circumstance had brought them together.

Gordusmajor wondered what it was.

"I have been visited," the young Commander said, "by the Dark Queen in a Vision."

Gordusmajor glanced at Scymnidus. So what else was new?

"In which . . . " Khargos struggled for words, "she announced her departure. For a while."

Gordusmajor kept his expression blank—his best gambler's face. But his thoughts raced and burrowed.

What kind of Dark Knight stratagem was this? If it were true, it would make Khargos vulnerable. And he would know he was vulnerable, would know that the gnomes would know he would know . . . .

The High Justice stopped his thoughts, nearly breathless in his own speculations.

"Did she speak of aught else, Commander Khargos?" he asked sweetly.

"Of dangers in the lower levels," Khargos said. It was obvious he was choosing his words carefully. "Of a disaster,

270

perhaps *cataclysmic*, in the offing. A disaster of fire and eruptions."

Gordusmajor folded his hands. The lad was clever, knew how a gnome audience would react to any mention of *cataclysm*, not to mention the standard fire and eruptions that were volatile words for anyone who lived inside a volcano.

That is, if the lad were thinking of such things.

"The Goddess has instructed me," Halion Khargos said, "to leave this city before the brewing disaster strikes. I am to take with me only a select few, she says."

"And have you selected that few, Commander?" Gordusmajor asked, his voice subdued, neutral, opaque.

"I have selected," the Commander said, "those who would select me."

A murmur rose among the gnomes. Scymnidus and Gordusmajor eyed one another uneasily, each suspecting a hidden agenda, profoundly favoring the Knights of Takhisis.

But in the questioning that followed, no agenda surfaced. The Commander, it seemed, had been left to his own devices, and those devices were the Blood Oath and the Code.

Part of which counseled fairness and loyalty.

To the skeptical tribunal, especially to the extremely skeptical Scymnidus Carcharias, Halion Khargos explained further: It would be dishonorable to abandon anyone who cast his lot with the escaping Knights. Now, with his divine Vision dimmed, Khargos was left to steer by the light of that honor alone.

It was frustrating, though, to abide this gnomish scrutiny of every sentence and phrase and word, with Counselor Scymnidus eager to suggest the most devious and evil motives for everything he said. Khargos was about to give up, to tell the whole bickering lot of them that he had come here prepared to offer them rescue but instead would abandon them in relief and gladness. He was about to give up, but then the memories of the charred amphitheatre, of the gnome girl and her destructive automaton softened him again. He listened to more foolishness, more hair-splitting and semantics, until finally, edged once more toward desperation, he turned to Gordusmajor with his most open, most dangerous offer.

"If you must, High Justice" Khargos said, "you may reveal my past to those assembled. I know that it is not a pretty story."

Then he sat back and waited. Gordusmajor could tell them all—the gnomes and Phoenix and the rest of the assembled Knights—about the early days of the Commander along the beaches of Sancrist. About his yearning for another Order entirely, and about the horrible things he had done in the name of that yearning.

And when the Justice had told that story, of deception and covetousness and finally parricide . . .

He would see, Khargos guessed, who would choose to stay, who to shear away.

Indeed, Gordusmajor looked long and hard at the young man before him. No doubt his years on the bench had taught him things about gnome nature, and Khargos expected that most of that learning held for humans as well.

He could only imagine what the Justice was thinking. No doubt that there was such a thing as too much reasoning. That though their stories were all in conflict, the Commander and the brace of gully dwarves, apparently, all had told a roughly similar truth—that they had heard of or seen some disturbance, great and horrible, in the lower levels of the city. Though none of these were sources upon which a gnome justice might expect to rely, it was all Gordusmajor had to go on in the way of evidence.

Cautiously, almost as though he were testing a treacherous current, High Justice Gordusmajor spoke at last.

"Come now, lad," he murmured. "Everyone's past is a mite chequered in these times. So you . . . stole a net of clams from a fisherman! It's not like you killed your father, now is it?"

This last question was asked with what seemed to be a steady gaze into the eyes of Halion Khargos.

"And I've been about judging long enough to know," Gordusmajor said quietly, "that everything, for good or ill, can be explained or explained away. That what you're left with is the here and now—the resolve of the time, and the honor to carry it off. I say we forgive you your molluskery, and follow you from this firetrap of a city."

* * * * *

Khargos was clearly surprised at the decision of the Justice. Many of the gnomes remarked on it later: how the young man had seemed positively redeemed when his theft of clams—a common enough misdemeanor among gnome children, and certainly no cause for great guilt—was made public in the Tribunal Hall. How that redemption gave him a sort of clarity and stature, and how he seemed from that point on to be one they could willingly follow.

Only Scymnidus held back.

Skeptical and anxious to the end of all debate, the barrister proposed politely a number of reasons for the Commander's appearance in the Tribunal Hall. None of these reasons cast young Khargos in a favorable light, but they became worse and worse the longer the counselor spoke.

How perhaps the noble Commander was using the occasion to evict all gnomes from their ancestral home . . .

Or how there was a conspiracy afoot, between the Knights of Takhisis and the conclaves of gully dwarves, to hold elections while the gnomes were absent from Mount Nevermind, thereby establishing a gully dwarf council of elders . . .

Or even that the Knights intended, through the agency of the Paradise Machine, to realign all plumbing so as to drown every gnome unfortunate enough to bathe, shower, draw water, or enter a toilet within the next two months . . .

This last accusation made the High Justice laugh, but Scymnidus still persisted, his accusations wilder and wilder.

"You do not understand!" Scymnidus ranted. "So rapt you are with whether your machines work or don't. You're missing the larger truth—that they're only as good or as bad as the folks who wield them. And I've seen the bad in folks. Know it up front, from the cries of the gully dwarves when you send them off for battle fodder down to an old beachcomber cursing his young son for aspiring to parricide, saying that the boy should've finished what he started, then forgiving the little monster in the same breath. And that terrible girl who fixed a swinging anvil in wait for *her* father not a dozen days ago . . . "

Alarmed, Halion Khargos stared at the hysterical counselor. A question formed on his lips.

There was neither time nor place. The Goddess had spoken, about impending disaster, about escaping with whomever he chose.

Asking would reveal everything.

So when Gordusmajor nodded to Halion Khargos and offered to show him the quickest and most ready way free of the volcanic city, the Commander set aside his questions, and an accord of sorts was struck. In the Hall of the Philosophers' Tribunal, there on the lofty Thirtieth Level, all authorities, military and civil, began to plan the greatest gnome migration since the pursuit of the Graygem that established Mount Nevermind.

Scymnidus Carcharias refused to take part in "any consensual deportation," as he called it. Instead, he scrambled into his wicker cage, and, swinging like a chattering pendulum from the vault of the Tribunal Hall, offered a challenge to "all who stood against the army of occupation and its gnome collaborators" to "join with the resistance that will abide in this room, this very fount and source of all things gnomishly philosophical."

But nobody stayed with him.

By silent consent, it seemed, Mount Nevermind's first hostage crisis was over. A hundred gnomes left the Tribunal Hall, each intent on enlisting others, on packing belongings and meeting by the gnomeflingers on whatever particular level was nearest or most convenient.

Khargos would never know whether those hundred souls believed his story. In fact, it probably did not matter.

For what prompted the Second Migration was finally neither fear of disaster nor certainly trust of the appointed leaders, whether human or gnome. Neither was it reliance in divine Vision or gully dwarf testimonials.

At the end of the day, the gnomes decided to leave simply for the adventure of it, for the change of venue and habit.

Chapter 31

Levels and levels below the assembling exodus, a much smaller party—four weary and ill-equipped gnomes—had begun the process of dismantling Mount Nevermind's aqueducts.

They traveled by foot, having decided that all the hand carts were in some kind of mute conspiracy against them.

There were six aqueducts, of course. Or so Lucretius, familiar with the ins and outs of the irrigation system, insisted—six being the great recurrent number in nature. The first of the six was already down, demolished by fire in the midst of the gnomes' skirmish with their shadowy enemies.

Five to go. The prospect was doubly daunting to Innova.

"To hear Lucretius tell it," he confided to his companions, as they circled a stairwell on their way to the Third Level, "these aqueducts are spaced far apart, to assure that schemes of sabotage will not come to pass."

"Wouldn't you know it?" Pillaster observed dryly, shouldering the heavy bag of adzes and hammers that Lucretius had given him to carry, the other big bag full of uncut jewels and shattered glass. "One thing that the engineers get right!"

"But their foresight saw only so far to the fore!" Lucretius exclaimed cheerily. "They counted on foiling the sabotage of *invaders*, but never counted on the saboteurs *living* down here, knowing the tunnels and shafts and adits, the way to move quickly from conduit to conduit."

"I can only hope that quickness is our ally," Innova said. "I have misgivings about this whole venture."

Pointillo frowned, but Lucretius arched an amused eyebrow.

"Misgivings," the old gnome asked, "of a causal and effectual nature?"

Innova waved his hands, as if to brush away the question. "I know, I know. It's the same thing that the High Justice scolded me about—'cause and effect is a disease' and all. But I can't help thinking that maybe these Chaos creatures *want* us to destroy the aqueducts, that drying out and sabotaging the Paradise Machine would work well for *their* interests, not for ours."

There was a silence, as the gnomes considered Innova's suspicions.

"Sounds plausible to me," Pillaster conceded, but everyone knew he would jump at the chance to stop this burdened journey through the depths of the mountain. The "tools and jools," as Lucretius called them, grew heavier with every step, and the heat from the nearby magma had made the climate nearly unendurable for Pillaster, his sweaty smell nearly unendurable for his comrades.

Grex Pointillo lifted Pillaster's cloak from his shoulders and draped it around his own.

Innova looked at his friend with concern. Something had happened back in the battle with the Chaos creatures that had wounded the colonel gravely. Here, in heat nigh unbearable, Grex Pointillo still shivered and bundled himself.

"M-maybe they want us to stop," the colonel said through chattering teeth. "M-maybe they're counting on our second-guessing ourselves until . . . until—"

"Until we're frozen," Lucretius interrupted. "I mean, paralyzed. By our own thoughts, our own supposing. Don't you see it by now, Innova? That Justice of yours, for all his bluster and lusts and corruption, is wiser than you've imagined."

Lucretius nodded toward a fork in the tunnels.

"Bear left," he said. "The next aqueduct is not far."

This time Innova was not to be brushed away. "You'll forgive me, Lucretius," he said, his voice thin and shaking in the close darkness, "if I can't be soothed by a proverb or some kind of mysterious pronouncement."

Lucretius stopped in the tunnel. Pointillo and Pillaster walked on ahead, the colonel a bundle of cloaks and rags, Pillaster stripped to the waist and laden with the bag of tools. They looked like emblems of summer and winter, Innova thought.

Then he felt Lucretius's strong, thin hand on his shoulder.

"Would that those things *could* soothe you, Innova," he said quietly, "because trying to figure all the prospects will lead you down a road to madness. 'What if *they* think *we* think *they* think?' you'll be asking yourself. 'What if their plan is larger than we have imagined?' But what if their plan is no plan at all? Remember, after all, that they are creatures of Chaos. And Chaos, as I understand it, abides neither plan nor cause nor effect. Be content with a simple definition for once."

"I would," Innova muttered, "if you'd give me one."

Lucretius laughed. "No you wouldn't! You may not talk much, but the more words you listen to, the happier you are. So just close your ears for a while, and cease your questions. For with all the asking and listening, you'll end up standing stock still, handcuffed by possibilities. It's what old Gordusmajor was talking about, I suppose. Cause and effect *is* a disease, and of all the peoples in this world, we gnomes are most liable to catch it. The remedy, Innova, is to do it simply. Now, when did these Chaos creatures attack you?"

"I've told you before," Innova said. "When Triquet, Reorx receive him, blocked the flow of the conduit."

Lucretius smiled. "Well then," he said. "It appears to me that's a healthy place to stand."

He nodded toward the end of the leftward tunnel, where Pillaster's and Pointillo's lanterns had framed the entrance of a chamber with an eerie light, within which the thick, horizontal shadow of an aqueduct seemed to bisect the tunnel floor.

Tricky shade and darkness. Innova thought of spiders, of the devices of the miragos.

Lucretius was right, he thought, as he gathered his courage and stalked toward the threshold of that chamber.

You had to stand somewhere. But nowhere in these lower regions seemed like a "healthy place to stand."

* * * * *

So went their work, for what Innova guessed to be an afternoon, an evening, and yet another morning.

Guided by Lucretius's uncanny sense of direction, the gnomes located three aqueducts and demolished them all. There was a certain delight in the destruction, and by now even the surly Pillaster was enjoying himself, especially since some of the tools had been distributed between Lucretius and Innova, lightening his burden considerably.

Now they were somewhere in the middle of the Second Level. The heat was intense in these parts, like a hot summer doubled in the world outside. Magma pooled beneath a narrow footbridge they crossed on their way toward the outermost regions of the level, and it had become difficult for all of them to breathe.

Even Grex Pointillo had removed one of his many layers of coats and jackets.

"The fifth aqueduct is beyond this turn," Lucretius suddenly announced, producing something from his robes. He held up a curious contraption—a compass, it seemed, from which dangled a pendulum, a broken, unlit lantern spinning atop the gadget. "Well, *this* thing says we've still a mile or so to go, but the fifth aqueduct is just ahead, regardless of measurements."

Once again, Innova marvelled at the old gnome's bearings.

Lucretius shrugged, tossed the compass over his shoulder into the dark. "Didn't think it worked when I found it," he said. "Best rely on head and ear and memory. After this, there is but one more aqueduct, as far as I know—one that lies almost directly below us, in a dark and abandoned notch of the First Level. If we are quick and resolute, we should be done before the next nightfall."

"Let us hope it is in time," the colonel said.

Lucretius's laughter was dry. "There is no way of knowing. Nor should we even try to guess. What remains for us to do is simply whatever comes next."

Pillaster moved ahead of the rest of the party. Like Innova, he was impatient when things became proverbial.

The others watched him turn the corner, lost the last glimmer of his lantern amid the rocks.

Innova was handing Pointillo an axe when the cry came rushing up the corridor. Shrill, almost animal in its distress and pain, choked off suddenly as though something swift and relentless had muffled it.

They instantly knew that something had waylaid Pillaster and rushed toward the source of the cry.

Pillaster lay on his back in a thin pool of light cast by his lantern. All around him were shadows—patches of darkness against which the paltry glow failed.

Innova could make out faint shapes within these shadows: the looming arch of the aqueduct and, in the near corner of the chamber, a gnomeflinger. For a moment his thoughts played idly over the past. Had he repaired this machine?

Had he even seen it before?

He almost forgot the apparent danger, the plight of his comrade on the chamber floor.

Pointillo's thoughts were more clear, it seemed. He was the first into the chamber. Rushing to Pillaster's side, he knelt beside the fallen gnome, who writhed and coughed in agony.

"Galloping pneumalaise," he called out bitterly.

In alarm, Lucretius and Innova approached the suffering Pillaster.

Something in Pointillo's touch and attentions seemed to still the coughing but did nothing to heal the stricken gnome. Pillaster settled into a fitful unconsciousness, his breath rattling.

The rattling grew worse as they watched.

Pointillo looked up, the lantern light glittering fitfully through his tears.

"I can do nothing more," he said. "I learned that some time ago, when the Knights of Takhisis brought forth this horrible disease."

He gathered his blankets and robes around him, and sat down beside the dying Pillaster.

A voice startled them. A deep, melodious voice from somewhere upon the shadowy aqueduct.

"He is not Deddalo, I gather. Your people look alike in this light and distance."

Pointillo scrambled to his feet, struggling for his sword amid the layers of cloth and furs.

Innova, axe in hand, squinted as he scanned the shadows. Was it there, by the left-hand wall where the aqueduct emptied into darkness? A sudden shifting of darkness, as though something was moving?

Crawling spiderlike from shade to shade?

"I assure you that I *thought* he was Deddalo," the voice maintained, "else I might have let him pass. But my mistake is his misfortune, and yours as well."

"You're the Skull Knight!" Pointillo shouted. "The Bone Acolyte Oliver!"

Now a faint light glimmered from atop the aqueduct. From entirely the opposite side in which Innova had thought he saw the movement. My eyes are playing tricks, he thought. He was glad he had not hurled his axe at illusion.

This new light illumined a standing figure—a spindly human, helmed and robed.

"You are right, Colonel," Oliver said. "It must be unusual for you, this being right."

"What brings you here?" Innova asked. Then he was sorry he had drawn attention to himself.

"I have an appointment with Master Deddalo," Oliver announced. "But I gather he is not among you."

"Obviously, this appointment is not therapeutic," Lucretius said, and the cleric pivoted to face him.

Lucretius stepped into the light of Pillaster's dropped lantern. In full view of the Skull Knight now, he scratched his beard, the top of his head . . .

Then his hindquarters.

Oliver sniffed in disgust, climbed off the aqueduct onto a ledge just above the conduit that led into the chamber. All the while his gaze did not leave Lucretius Climenole.

It's as though he expects something, Innova thought.

"You have the mark of a god on you," Oliver said at last.

"Oh, dear!" Lucretius exclaimed ironically. "And just *which* god might that be?"

The Skull Knight fell silent. Then he spoke at last.

"I am not sure. But you smell of something more than smoke and steam and crankcase oil. You would be a formidable adversary . . . given time."

"How thoroughly dramatic and villainous of you," Lucretius said, a cold edge to his voice that Innova had never heard or had never remembered hearing. "I suppose that if this were an old story, we'd magic it out here and now, each of us waving wands and staves, conjuring by elements and stars and by whatever components we might find in our . . . *respective pantries.*"

"But it is no old story," Oliver said, "now is it, Master . . . ?"

"Lucretius Climenole," the old gnome replied. "Of the Mount Nevermind Climenoles—pre-Cataclysmic clergy when your kind were combing beaches for kelp and flotsam. No, Master Oliver, it is not an old story, most assuredly."

"I'll give you one thing," Oliver said, a vague irritation in his voice. "I had not reckoned on your kind among the gnomish people."

"And you thought you had reckoned everything, did you not, Master Oliver?"

"And still do. Everything that matters, that is. You are merely contingencies that I shall deal with at once."

Innova frowned. All this clerical bravado made little sense.

"You are merely intruders," Oliver explained grandly. "Intruders in my plan. One of you—the unfortunate colonel—needs no reckoning. For the time will come, Grex Pointillo, when you will long for the searing heat of the magma, for fire or explosion or anything to warm the abiding cold that grips you now. And as for the others . . . "

Oliver waved his spindly hand dismissively. " . . . it will be short work."

Lucretius stood steady in the light, but for a second, almost indetectably, his eyes flickered toward Innova.

It dawned on the lad. For some reason, Lucretius was bluffing for time.

Slowly, Innova backed into the shadows and sidled toward the gnomeflinger. It was the only option he saw in the huge, bare chamber.

Perhaps, if the machine were aimed just right . . .

But had he repaired *this one*? And in the repair, had he aimed it somewhere, anywhere, that might avail them now?

Cause and effect. The old disease.

He remembered Lucretius's advice.

The remedy, Innova, is to take a stand.

Silently, he moved toward the gnomeflinger.

High atop the ledge, the Skull Knight raised both his hands. A mist, sickly green and glittering, balled and boiled between his gangly fingers.

"In a better time," he said, "I would make yours a quicker and less painful death, Lucretius Climenole. But I must net in the consequences, and net them now."

With a brief incantation in some forgotten tongue, Oliver hurled the mist toward the old gnome as Innova, headed to the gnomeflinger, broke into a run. Glancing over his shoulder, Innova saw the green glow of the pneumalaise hurtle and settle upon Lucretius.

Hurtle and settle and break. The mist spread about the feet of the old gnome, faded, and dissolved.

With a leap, Innova found himself in the basket of the gnomeflinger. Oliver was dumbstruck, his gaze still fastened on the failed spell.

With a prayer to the gods, to any god, Innova struck the lever that triggered the old machine.

* * * * *

Atop the ledge, Oliver gathered himself for another spell.

Darkness? Some powerful incantation of wound and blind heat?

Then, at the margin of his sight, something flew at him through the darkness.

Something somersaulting and shouting, a flurry of cloth and hair. A glint of a blade.

With a cry, the cleric stepped back.

The thing struck the aqueduct, clutched, and settled with a grunt. Oliver spun toward the impact, raised his hands in preparation for prayer, for incantation . . .

And the ledge beneath his foot dissolved and vanished.

Mirago, the cleric thought, briefly, desperately. His raised hands clutched at rock, at air . . .

The bridge of the aqueduct rushed away from him as he fell into darkness and death.

Chapter 32

Pillaster died within the hour, gasping painfully for his last breath.

By that time, Innova had dismantled the aqueduct, his thoughts and his glance drawn constantly to the pool of light on the chamber floor, where Pointillo and Lucretius knelt by their dying comrade, offering solace and company and prayer.

Labor with the axe hurt, as the wood and stone of the aqueduct splintered beneath a heavy rain of blows. He had bruised something in his flight to the span, in his headlong collision with the very thing he was destroying now.

But what hurt more was the scene below.

The greatest pain of all came when the colonel and the old gnome bowed their heads, and Pointillo removed one of his blankets to cover the spent form of Pillaster.

His eyes welling with tears, Innova doubled his efforts on the span, his axe rising and falling in sorrow and anger. The aqueduct split before him, and the coursing water tumbled onto the floor in a sad waterfall.

He heard Pointillo's shout, and looked down.

The colonel, it seemed, had been calling to him for some time, his words lost in Innova's fury.

"Come down," Pointillo said, lowering his voice. "We've one more aqueduct to find. It would be a great disloyalty to them—to Lozenge and Triquet, to Roundell and Pillaster and the dwarves—if we did not complete this task."

Innova breathed deeply, recovering balance. He caught a faint, acrid whiff of brimstone and smoke and steam, and the hot smell brought him back to his senses. Carefully, he climbed down the nearest abutment, and stood beside his comrades on the floor.

"How?" he asked at last. "When that horrible man—that cleric—tried to hurl the green mist onto you, Lucretius . . . how did you avoid it? How did you survive?"

"I'm not sure," the old gnome replied. "It was a form of grace or miracle, or perhaps even something in the old clerical bloodline—residual, but still powerful, like an inheritance of a cowlick or an unattractive squint."

"Perhaps it *was* the bloodline," Innova agreed. "After all, Oliver seemed to recognize it in you."

"He did, indeed," Lucretius acknowledged, shouldering his bag of jewels and glass. "But as for me, I'm not prepared to discount grace or miracle as well. I expect it's a heartening thing *not* to discount the things that drop out of the math, wouldn't you say? But forgive me if I don't feel heartened now."

Lucretius nodded at the wrapped body at their feet. "This makes the victory hollow," he murmured.

"There's no victory without costs like these," Pointillo said mysteriously, wrapping his topmost cloak more tightly about his shoulders. "We can take all the stands we like, ignore the causes and effects in the doing, but it still comes down to consequences, doesn't it?"

Lucretius stood in silence, placed his hand on the colonel's shoulder.

"All the more reason to pursue that victory," he said finally. "In honor of those consequences."

"It's a Life Quest of sorts," Pointillo said. "Even if you lose your life in achieving it."

*   *   *   *   *

The journey to the First Level seemed the longest of all.

Weighted down by weariness and sadness, the three gnomes circled the stairway that led to their last destination. The heat that struck them when they set foot on the bottommost excavated floor of Mount Nevermind was virtually unbearable: Smoke veiled the passages, and the rocks virtually sizzled underfoot, as the magma skimmed only a foot beneath the surface.

The mountain itself seemed to breathe, possessed of an alien life.

At places along their lonely path, the ground beneath them was broken entirely. Fissures and cracks glowed in the stone, and on several occasions they were forced to sidle around pools of magma, spreading slowly across the beleaguered cavern.

"It's our good fortune," Lucretius called out over the hiss of steam and the mysterious, ragged rumbling, "that the aqueduct lies near the outermost part of the mountain. It's almost as far away from the core as you can get, while still being underground. If the fire follows us, we've half a chance to escape—maybe even sixty percent, according to my geometry and secondary algebra."

To escape? Innova stopped short in the vaporous passage.

He had been so busy doing the next thing, banishing cause and effect, that it had not occurred to him.

When they had destroyed the final aqueduct, how could they escape the magma and eruptions that might follow?

Lucretius seemed to read his thought.

"The glade!" he shouted, in his voice more than a glimmer of hope.

Innova remembered the story. Remembered Lucretius's account of the small secluded spot at the foot of the mountain, filled with fresh air and sunlight—the place to which he retreated for a while, when the closeness and the dark grew too much for him, when his "gatherings" grew too heavy to carry and he needed a place to store them.

The old gnome's subterranean habits would save them yet!

Encouraged, Innova approached a threshold where the tunnel opened into a small chamber virtually consumed by the rising magma. A narrow footpath, barely the width of his axe, circled halfway around the bubbling pool and exited the chamber through a low tunnel.

They had come to this place barely in time. Odds were that they could not return the way they came.

Cautiously, the gnomes took the path, skirting the edge of the glowing magma. Innova and Pointillo averted their eyes: Lucretius had warned them that staring into the stuff was like staring into a doubled sun. It could blind them in a matter of seconds.

Which was why they were surprised when Lucretius shouted.

They turned to face the old gnome, who pointed into the pool of magma.

Casting his eyes down, Innova blinked stupidly at the blinding glow. Then he saw it—the red and black of the roiling surface replaced, only briefly, by something rising and diving and vanishing under the magma.

Black and red as well, but solid and living . . .

The rising of a scaled back, of a monstrous thing surfacing for a moment.

Innova's breath fled him. He heard himself scream.

He remembered nothing until, in a shadowy room, the light of a lantern brushed his face and Lucretius stood over him, shaking him back to his senses.

"Innova!" the old gnome called. "No dawdling, now! I need you!"

*   *   *   *   *

Dragonfear.

That awestruck, paralyzed state that rushes on you after you glimpse the great beast. It dazes some, stuns others, and has been known to kill less complicated creatures.

So Lucretius Climenole told his two companions as they sat by a lantern on the chamber floor, some distance from where the dragon had surfaced in the magma pool.

He assured them that, fortunately, the dragon was bound for some nether caverns far beneath the excavated part of the mountain. Whatever type of creature it was, it seemed to thrive in magma and fire.

It was the source, he believed, of the mysterious rumbling.

"Good or evil?" Innova asked, his thoughts still addled by the sight he had seen.

"I beg your pardon?" Lucretius asked. "Here we are, but a brisk walk away from more *interesting* questions of leverage and hydraulics and infrastructure—the kinds of things that boggle the most incomprehensible engineers—and you're stuck on a question of *ethics*, for the sake of great sweaty neutral Reorx!"

Chastened, Innova shrugged. The old gnome's next words were softer, more soothing.

"I expect that the creature is oblivious to *manners*, much less more eternal questions. If it's born of the same Chaos that is working the bottom of this mountain, it probably cares for only dragon things—riches and destruction. No moral philosophy in that!"

"But why didn't the dragonfear take you as well?" Innova asked. "And how did you get us here?"

"I don't know and wheelbarrows," Lucretius replied, answering both questions at once. At the edge of the lantern light, Innova could see the still wheels of a capsized barrow.

He could not get over the way Lucretius knew this place—the nooks and the stockpiles, tools produced out of nowhere, and the one right path chosen among many. The little glade that would serve as their refuge if it all came to explosions and hurled fire. The endless supply of pure water.

Something in the old rascal's nature, evidently, protected him against malign spells and natural phenomena.

"You're like a wise man in an old story, Lucretius," he whispered.

"The one who comes and makes it all right?" Lucretius asked ironically. "The wizard with the key? The cleric with the healing spell? No, Innova. It's been all I could do to guide you this far, to keep you at task in the midst of all these disasters and disruptions. So come, enough of heroic fantasy. The last standing aqueduct—if it is indeed the last standing—is not far from here."

Feebly, Lucretius helped his two companions to their feet. Pointillo was listless, his movements slow and constrained, as though he walked in a great depth of water.

Innova moved slowly as well, because once again he was distracted.

If it is indeed the last standing? What in the name of great Reorx could *that* mean? Had Lucretius brought them this far, only to doubt and dither?

He watched the old gnome shoulder Grex Pointillo, guide the colonel down the middle path of a thrice-branching tunnel.

No, Lucretius wasn't dithering. He was just old. And the added anxiety of enemies in the depths, of rising heat and a difficult task that needed to be performed quickly . . .

Well, it all added up to exhausting days. Exhaustion and doubt, the diseases of a journey's last steps.

Yet the old fellow persevered. Ahead of Innova now, his knees bent, Lucretius guided the staggering Pointillo toward the threshold of another chamber, where he stopped, leaned the colonel against the arched entrance, and continued through the portal, his lantern raised.

Somehow, Innova had thought this room would be bigger. It was the last of the aqueducts—he told himself it was, despite Lucretius's cryptic, doubtful comment. So he had expected it would be huge and vaulting, the father of all aqueducts arching breathtakingly over vast spaces.

But it was a narrow chamber, tapering to a ceiling more narrow still, where the aqueduct emerged from one out-cropping of shadowy rock and tunneled into another, its visible span no longer than two gnome paces.

Innova wiped his hands on the front of his sweaty tunic. In some ways this would be easy: no debating where to strike the structure, because so little of it was within reach. At the same time, good purchase and good leverage would be hard to come by, because up among those jutting rocks there was scarcely enough space to swing an axe.

Still, it could be done, and he was almost cheerful as he searched the sloping walls for a handhold. That cheer evaporated when a rustling sound rose from the shadows past the aqueduct.

At first, Innova froze in place, imagining that somehow the dragon had returned. He was almost relieved when the four forms that emerged from the darkness were smaller, human-sized.

Until he saw what they were.

Whether it was the darkness of the cavern or the darkness within the creatures that made them seem almost insubstantial, Innova was never sure. But now they stepped forward with certainty, spreading out as they approached the huddled gnomes.

Innova had already seen them in action. Four of them, armed and ready, were more than a match for his wearied party.

He glanced up at the aqueduct. After all this time and suffering, it was just out of reach.

I have heard of stories, he thought, where the hero dies within sight of his goal. I've always thought they were sad, but I suppose it's better than never getting close at all.

Then Grex Pointillo pushed him toward the walls.

"Climb," the colonel said. "Both of you."

Innova looked uncertainly at Lucretius Climenole. But the old gnome seemed to understand something, to recognize something in the colonel's face and bearing.

"He wasn't right, you know," Lucretius said quietly. "At least there's a chance he wasn't."

Innova puzzled over who "he" was, until Pointillo spoke.

"That chance is a thin one. Whatever this is, I'm half as alive as I was an hour ago. Oliver was right. I'll need no reckoning soon."

"Not necessarily. There are poultices and potions, medicines and nostrums and . . . " Lucretius began. The old gnome was grasping at air. He knew that the colonel was right.

"Go on," Pointillo said. "I believe I can buy you time enough to destroy the aqueduct."

"But there are four of them!" Innova protested.

Pointillo drew his sword. "I may not get them all. But one thing's for sure. I can't get much colder than this."

With a push from Lucretius, Innova began to climb the wall toward the aqueduct. The rocks were almost unbearably hot, even through his gloves, and for a moment he feared he could not hang on. But another boost from behind, a dull pain in his backside from an injury that seemed years ago, told him Lucretius was urging him on.

He took one upward step, then another, climbing the rocks like steaming, scarcely visible rungs of a ladder. Before he knew it, he was to the last outcropping, and a swift step took him to the aqueduct itself. He turned, extended his hand to Lucretius . . .

Who clung to the wall, unable to take his grasp.

"I've about reached my end, Innova," he said with a weak smile. "Bad lungs and creaking knees'll do you in more surely than any dragon. So much for magic and the wizards in stories, eh? You'll have to take it from here. I'm doing my best just to hang on."

Innova looked down to the chamber floor, where the chaotic warriors circled the colonel. Grex Pointillo lunged at one of the things, which almost seemed to evaporate as it eluded his sword point.

It looked bad on all fronts. Best get this done with.

He propped his haunches against the near outcropping and raised his axe.

At the far end of the aqueduct, scarcely an axe length away, the rocks began to glitter and boil.

Miragos! Innova thought, in the brief second before the outcropping changed from solid stone . . .

To a flickering nest of spiders.

*   *   *   *   *

Many times before, Innova had imagined spiders lurking where he did not see them. Now, by the trickery of the mirago, he saw spiders where he did not imagine they were.

An illusion, he told himself.

"An illusion!" Lucretius shouted.

Still, the spiders boiled out of the rocks in front of him, doubling in number with every blink of his eyes. Reflex drew him back, and the illusory creatures spread to cover the entire aqueduct, the surrounding walls . . .

The haft of his axe.

Innova closed his eyes, but like an afterimage of light the vermin raced across his lidded vision, and he felt them crawling up his legs, his arms, onto the back of his neck.

He shrieked, opened his eyes, climbed toward the rocks and a hasty descent—

Then he saw them looking up at him. Lucretius, clinging to the rockface, and Pointillo, hemmed in by monsters.

Long ago I thought I had friends, Innova thought. And now that I do—*really* do—here I am ready to betray them!

With a sudden turn, not stopping to think about the consequences, about the creatures he only imagined swarming at his feet but which were there because he saw them and felt them, Innova brought the axe crashing down into the horde of spiders, into wood and stone and water.

He raised it, brought it down again and again. Suddenly the aqueduct gave way, and the water spilled into the chamber, showering Pointillo and his enemies, spattering across the dangling Lucretius.

The shadow warriors looked up. One of them—Innova could not tell which—shrieked mouthlessly, and two of them retreated into darkness. The other two lunged at Grex Pointillo, who drove his sword through the nearest. The one remaining warrior brought its axe down in a blurring shadow, driving the blade between the colonel's shoulders.

Then quietly, the creatures faded back into the shadows. Whether they had been defeated or simply chose to retreat, it was impossible to tell.

Nor was Innova certain that his work on the aqueduct—*their* work in the lower levels—had stopped the Paradise Machine that protected the Knights of Takhisis upstairs.

He would have to trust that it did when he had time to think about it. But he didn't much care at that moment.

For Grex Pointillo lay on the hot floor, his beard incongruously crusted with ice and his lips blue and quivering. It was a chill, it seemed, that not even the magma could banish.

Innova descended and knelt by his friend. Pointillo stared at him absently through pale, indifferent eyes.

"Maybe this is the Quest after all," the colonel whispered. "No spells, no wise men, no answers. Just doing what you can for those around you?"

Then, so gradually that Innova could not tell when the final change had come, the colonel refocused his gaze from his comrades onto nothing.

"Had it been a story . . . " Innova began.

"I know," Lucretius interrupted. "He would have had some revelation for us. Some ultimate truth of moment and importance. I don't know whether we'd have had time to hear it.

"We're not far from the glade, and it's a good thing. Something in all of this is about to change."

Chapter 33

They were fools, mostly. Trusting fools who believed the old High Justice and that serpent of a Commander.

So Scymnidus told himself as, secure in his wicker cage, he watched the last of the gnomes leave the Tribunal Hall under the guidance of Gordusmajor and Halion Khargos.

No telling what the Knights of Takhisis had in store for a trusting lot. And as for the august High Justice, well, Scymnidus knew from long acquaintance that his sympathies could be turned by bribery or even flattery.

He would sell out Mount Nevermind for a stack of oatcakes.

Scymnidus congratulated himself on his foresight, tested the door of the cage. Secure against intruders or assailants.

Meanwhile, the metavox squawked throughout the upper levels, the intricate little pipes singing out a solitary message to all listening citizens of Mount Nevermind.

Disaster. Fire in the hold. Escape to the uppermost level.

Scymnidus laughed cynically. There were all kinds of disasters, and the gnomes would learn this to their great dismay. Meanwhile, he would wait out the silly migration, and then, when the time was right, descend to the lowest levels, where the Knights of Takhisis would never find him.

For they would be back. Scymnidus Carcharias was sure of that.

The metavox rattled once more, sputtered out its urgent message.

Then, to Scymnidus'ss surprise, the water in the ornamental pool began to bubble and fall. Receding like a little tide, it bottomed out low in the cylindrical depths of the fountain.

What was happening? He craned toward the pool, sticking his neck out from between the wicker bars.

The absurd, goose-necked lever that comprised the Paradise Machine rocked more slowly on its wired fulcrum. More slowly still. And then, to his surprise and outrage, the damned thing stopped, the water on its bill dried entirely.

The lights of the chamber fluttered and went out.

"I'll be switched!" the counselor exclaimed. "They were right after all!"

He stood there in silence, taking in the amazing prospect. Then it occurred to him: if they were right about one thing . . .

Something rumbled faintly in a level far beneath him.

"By Reorx's beard!" he cried, and pulled back to open the door to the cage. But his head, slipped so easily between the wicker bars only a moment ago, refused to come out, to follow the rest of his struggling body.

It was like being caught in stocks of his own devising, he thought bitterly. The bitterness turned at once to uneasiness, then to fear.

"Help!" the counselor cried, his voice echoing vainly in the vaulted hall of his many legal victories.

"By all the assembled gods, help me!"

* * * * *

At a great distance from the Tribunal Hall, out of earshot from even the loudest of cries, Halion Khargos listened to the metavox sound out its last warning and die into the sound of a great rumbling, of something rushing through the lower levels of Mount Nevermind.

He had thought that the first time Gordusmajor had used the device, it would be to trumpet the chequered past of the commander and Occupying General—to tell everyone, gnome and Knight alike, of his childhood treasons.

The old rascal had surprised him. Instead of using the machine to ruin his enemy, he had used it to save his people.

All around the Thirtieth Level, gnomes were gathering. Filing up the stairwells, rushing up the tracks borne in the beds of handcarts, scrambling up self-extending ladders and bouncing on powerful trampolines Khargos had not

even known existed until this hour. Most amazingly of all,
they were filling the receiving nets like fish in a fisherman's
dream, somersaulting and diving like upstream salmon
from the gnomeflingers levels below, catching in the webbing and wrestling free. All of them chattering and laughing, gossiping even now as the vents in the city began to
haze with smoke and the excavated throat of the volcano
began to fill with rising steam.

There were thousands of them. Hundreds of gully
dwarves as well, their ugly faces troubled with suspicion
that this whole enterprise was another gnome trick, some
huge practical joke that would end for them all in some
enormous vat of mud and offal.

"How did you manage this?" Khargos asked Gordusmajor, who had joined him at the top of a stairwell. The old
High Justice was puffing and sweating from the exertion of
a simple climb, but he was clearly enjoying himself, a witness to all this chaos and energy erupting around them.

"Simple, lad," Gordusmajor explained. "After a while,
folks'll believe anything unexpected. You've governed efficiently, the metavox works, and the whistles blow regular
hours. But you've nearly bored them to death in the process.
This disaster, whatever it's bound to be, they'll take as holiday from all your scheduling and order. There may be a
worse chaos underneath us—we've both heard rumors of
that, and I expect neither of us would like it. But this disruption . . . well, it's as welcome as breathing, and almost as
natural to the folks wrangling out of those receiving nets
over there."

Khargos nodded. It was hard to argue with philosophy,
especially when it could be used to his benefit in the time to
come.

At least he could plumb the depths of Scymnidus Carcharias. Find out what he had *really* seen on that Sancrist
beach years ago.

Just how Khargos would use this journey, he was yet
uncertain. In the absence of the Goddess, all forethought fell
away, and he was left to his own devices.

Philosophy was as good a tactic as any.

But military presence was a form of control.

So just to be sure, Khargos stationed his Knights at the passages out into air and light. There they could guide the gnomes to the surface, if excesses of energy or their eternal desire to make a simple thing complex would guide them back into the lower levels and back toward the approaching doom.

* * * * *

They all assembled about a mile from the lip of the volcano.

Here the mountains jutted up again. A steep incline took the paths toward even higher peaks, so if the promised eruption *did* take place, the lava would flow safely below them.

Khargos watched the gathering in amazement. Some ten thousand of them, chroniclers would later record, when the stories of the Chaos Wars were written. Of course there was no time to count them now, but Khargos guessed that he had just led one of the greatest escapes in the history of Krynn.

"It is a good thing we've done, Halion Khargos," Gordusmajor declared from his seat on a rugged outcropping of stone.

" 'Good' has never been a word countenanced by the Lady," Khargos replied. "Let's call it 'honorable.'"

He turned to face the rotund High Justice.

"Answer me one thing, Gordusmajor," he began. "You've known of my past for some time . . . "

"Question me all you like," the justice said quickly. "I'll not betray where I learned your story. Unless, of course, you plan to return to the mountain after whatever impending disaster takes place, and there might be, perhaps, a position opening in your military government . . . something with minimal duty and maximum reward?"

Khargos laughed. "Save your petitions. I no longer care how you learned of such things. What I want to know is this: why didn't you use the information to ruin me?"

Gordusmajor stroked his beard. "I thought I could use your influence at a later time. Call it forethought, if you will."

"Let's call it honorable," Khargos said, shuddering at *forethought*—the word that had passed through his thoughts only moments before.

Gordusmajor blushed.

"Let's call it a day, as well. Are all your countrymen accounted for?"

Gordusmajor laughed. "Don't be ridiculous, son! How could anyone possibly know? All of my rivals and enemies are accounted for, and that's a sizeable number in itself."

Something rumbled in the old volcanic bowels of Mount Nevermind.

"Here it comes," Gordusmajor said. "And no Paradise Machine to stop it now. I'll bet you old Scymnidus is stewing. It's the one disaster he never predicted."

"Scymnidus?" Halion Khargos asked, his voice forcing a casualness. "Where is he? Between events and his lying low, I've never had occasion to talk to the fabled Scymnidus at length."

Gordusmajor shielded his eyes, scanned the throng of gnomes on the mountainside. "I don't see him. You don't suppose that . . . "

Justice and Commander looked at one another with apprehension.

"You could always send someone . . . " Gordusmajor began, but a wave of Khargos's gloved hand dismissed the suggestion.

"He's probably still in the Tribunal Hall," the Commander said. "It's where we left him, and surely he's not fool enough to descend. It should be an easy rescue. I should return before the topmost level is in any kind of danger."

"It seems unwise," the justice objected. "How do you know when—"

"Let's call it tying up a loose end," Khargos said. Suddenly, to the surprise of Gordusmajor, he set off down the hill toward the smoky entrances to upper Mount Nevermind.

For the briefest moment, High Justice Gordusmajor thought about following, but his customary admixture of cowardice and good sense held him back. Instead, he watched as the dark-robed young man vanished into the smoke, and regretted that he had not told him the last thing left to tell.

"It was a bluff, Halion Khargos," he whispered into the hazy air. "There's still a whiff of Sancrist in your accent, and that's all I had to go on. I only pretended to know your dark secrets. The gods know we each have enough of them."

He watched as the smoke folded over the top of the mountain and shook his head sadly.

"I only hope I haven't added one more darkness to my little store."

* * * * *

"Well, there's one consolation to this," Scymnidus said bitterly, as he tugged vainly against the too-solid wicker cage.

"If the whole place erupts, nobody will know that I ended like this."

His head was wedged firmly between the bars. It seemed that the more he pulled, the tighter the hold.

The ornamental fountain had begun to steam, vapors rising over the head of the useless Paradise Machine. The great bronze balance from which the justices had ruled for generations was empty now, the Gordusmajor side still tipped comically downward, as though the scale pans still remembered the weight.

Everything's off balance here, Scymnidus thought.

And it's not particularly funny.

He had prepared for contingencies all his days. Had plotted and strategized with the best of them, but he had not been ready for a time in which contingencies ran out.

He rifled his memory for prayers and petitions, but it was uncertain ground. Some old gnome clerical prayer that his grandam had taught him mingled with a Solamnic chant he had heard on a beach long ago, and there was some kind of dwarven incantation . . .

He remembered only snatches of them. Years of schemes and anxiety had swept them from his memory.

"Dammit!" he muttered. Perhaps a curse was as good as a prayer, given the circumstances.

And then, to his great surprise, a dark form materialized in the wavering smoke. Surprising him even further, the form assumed the shape of Halion Khargos.

"Don't tell anyone," Scymnidus said miserably. But the Commander, it seemed, was not there to watch or gloat. Drawing his sword, the young man stalked toward the dangling cage, toward the counselor who trembled inside.

Well, at least he's going to make it swift and easy for me, Scymnidus thought, embracing his suspicions to the last.

And then, the greatest surprise of all. The sword of Commander Halion Khargos tore through the bottom of the cage, shearing the wicker swiftly and easily.

Scymnidus felt the wind of the descending blade and fell back in the cage.

Fell through to the stone floor and freedom.

"What . . . " he began, as the Commander yanked him to his feet.

"Hurry up!" Khargos growled. "No time for questions!"

The big scale tipped and toppled behind them as they made for the smoky exit. A rumbling, faint at first, grew louder and louder still, no longer sounding geological but more like a deep, infernal breathing.

Coughing, his eyes smarting, Scymnidus followed the dodging shape in front of him, his thoughts dismissing all suspicion in a desperate attempt to escape, to breathe, to stay alive.

In the midst of smoke and unsteady rock, even the tunnels were strange. A fierce light shot through the dark of a side tunnel, and Scymnidus, thinking *daylight* and *surface*, turned toward it, only to be grabbed by Halion Khargos and dragged on, up an incline, their feet skittering and sliding on fresh rubble.

Then another light. Brighter, more clean. A shifting of smoke ahead of them . . .

And a narrow passage through a puzzle of heavy stones. At its end, sunlight and a welcoming breeze.

Khargos shoved the gnome ahead, and Scymnidus squeezed through the first gap in the boulders. Climbed over yet another stone . . .

And stood on the outside, in smoke-rifled air.

He turned. To his alarm, he saw that the passage was too narrow for the young Commander. Scymnidus scrambled back in, set his shoulder against a stone, pushed . . .

Nothing. As solid as the thousand-year walls that once upheld it.

"Go on!" Khargos urged. "I'll double back! There's another passage, I'm sure!"

Scymnidus had cross-examined enough witnesses to know the man was lying.

"No!" the gnome cried out. "Push against this stone and . . . "

Khargos shook his head. "Go on," he repeated. This time there was a faint desolation in his voice.

Scymnidus stood, leaned against a rock.

"Answer me one thing, Master Scymnidus," Khargos said. "It's as good as rescuing me, that answer."

"What do you want to know?" the gnome asked bleakly.

"The beachcomber on the coast of Sancrist. The man nursed by the Solamnic Knight . . . "

"Yes?"

Khargos stared at the gnome, his eyes brittle and bright. "What was his name?"

Scymnidus turned away. He tried to remember. He had never known the man's name.

"I . . . I don't remember," he said, half-lying but hoping that an old counselor's trick might work—this time, of all times.

And it did.

"Was it . . . Mant Kallay?" Khargos asked.

"You know," Scymnidus said, wrestling a false surprise into his voice, calculating here at the edge of doom. "You know, that *was* his name! How did *you* know?"

It was a good lie. The Commander's eyes softened.

"It was part of a vision I had," he said. "Now go on."

*   *   *   *   *

He watched as the gnome staggered up the hillside.

Then Halion Khargos sat down in the blocked tunnel,

awaiting the onrush of fire and the end.

How fortunate, he thought, that the counselor remembered so well.

And Mant Kallay had forgiven his son. *In the same breath*, Scymnidus had said.

Years of misplaced devotion rushed over Halion Khargos, a prelude to the fire that would follow.

He had trusted Her, and She had left him.

Yet he smiled, prepared himself for the worst, for the liberation that would follow the worst.

At the last, his honor would be greater than the Goddess who demanded it.

There had been an old Solamnic song. Dimly he remembered it through the veils of smoke and distracting old visions.

How did it go?

Return this man to Huma's breast . . .

A long way to return, Halion Khargos thought with a smile.

Best start right away.

That was why when the wave of fire spread through the topmost level of Mount Nevermind, enkindling everything from the Tribunal Hall to the ancestral home of the entirely acquitted Talos, the flames found Commander Halion Khargos singing defiantly.

Chapter 34

Rushing toward a faint natural light, the two gnomes dodged through collapsing corridors and vaulted over mounds of trembling rubble.

"Not far from here!" Lucretius shouted back to Innova, his ankle bands loose again and smacking softly against the unstable stone.

It seemed far. For a nightmarish span of time, Innova thought they were getting no closer to the exit and the promised glade. That the complete collapse of the tunnels would find them far from the outer world and safety.

The corridor sloped upward. Only yards beyond an abandoned gnomeflinger, Innova could glimpse a full, unwavering light, the green wave of branches and a sloping, grassy terrace.

"Almost there!" Lucretius cried, clambering painfully through the old machine.

Innova caught up to his mentor as they crossed the threshold into the glade, and fresh air struck them both, at the same time and for the first time in what seemed like years.

Falling onto the ground, gasping and coughing dust from their exhausted lungs, the two gnomes rested for only a breath or two.

It was a beautiful spot—high grass and shade-blooming flowers, littered with the gems and broken glass of Lucretius's collections. Walls of rock rose steeply around it, and far to the north you could see the glitter of sunlight on the mirrors of the pass they called the Getinandgetout, as though Lucretius had scattered "jools" to the edge of sight.

For a moment Innova rested in the view. This was a place that a gnome could settle. You could rest here from confusion and turmoil and all the noise of chatter and machinery.

If it were not for that infernal rumbling.

All at once the danger came back to him. Somewhere in the mountain, in the midst of crumbling tunnels and shifting volcanic rock, the dragon was stirring.

All of Mount Nevermind tottered at the edge of destruction.

"Lucretius?" Innova shouted over the tremors.

The old gnome lay peacefully on the grass, his eyes shut and his beard stirring with soft and restful breath.

"Lucretius!" Innova shouted again, and the ragged philosopher's eyelids fluttered.

"What about the dragon, Lucretius?"

"I expect we're safe, Innova."

"That may be," Innova replied testily. "But what about the rest of us? What about Talos, and Scymnidus, and . . . "

Lucretius shook his head. "By now it's a question of simple tactics," he replied. "I refer you to the Glorious Memoirs of Generalissimo Glorius Peterloo, Section Seven, Subsection Twelve, where it says that, given the superior strength of the opponent—"

"Damn you and your references!" Innova roared. He fell silent, shook his head at his own insubordination.

Then continued.

"Good or evil?" he asked. "Lucretius, will the dragon work good or evil? Is he . . . after the Knights or after all of us here?"

"An interesting philosophical question, lad," Lucretius mused serenely, undisturbed, it seemed, by the outburst of his young companion. "I suppose he will work evil for us, good for himself. It is the way with dragons."

Innova's thoughts churned and swiveled like wheels in a hydraulic mill. For a moment, he remembered Scymnidus's offices, his first glimpse of the dipping, perpetual toy on the barrister's desk.

Once again, he sang the thinking song his father had taught him:

> *If thought is the mother*
> *of all good action,*
> *Then what is the child*
> *of plain distraction?*
> *Think! Pay attention!*
> *Let your mind change!*

> Make everyday things
>   complicated and strange!
> There are fish to be fried,
>   but first to be caught:
> So spread wide the nets
>   and get tangled in thought!

Again, like a spell, something came to him.

"Greed, isn't it?" he shouted triumphantly.

Lucretius frowned. "I beg your pardon?"

"The good of a dragon is to follow its greed!"

Lucretius nodded. "Among others. There are, of course, six layers of good—physical, emotional, spiritual, metaphysical, seriocomical, and mutual—and I expect that a dragon is capable of but a limited number among these. Old Belisarius had it that—"

"Be quiet, Lucretius!" Innova shouted, as he scrambled back toward the entrance to the mountain. "Come with me! I need your shoulder to set against that flinger in the mouth of the tunnel!"

*   *   *   *   *

As much as they pushed, the gnomeflinger would not budge.

Innova had forgotten how unwieldy these contraptions were. After a few minutes of pushing and grunting, he looked at his progress in despair.

The damned thing hadn't moved an inch.

"By the great sweaty ass of Reorx!" he swore, and kicked at its wheel.

He was about to draw forth his axe, make short work of the thing just for the pleasure of venting his anger, when Lucretius tapped him on the shoulder.

"What, dammit?" Innova cried, spinning around so rapidly that he almost knocked over his teacher.

Almost knocked the last bottle of the Graygem oil from the old philosopher's hand.

"By the Hammer of Reorx!" he swore this time, an oath of joy and one far less blasphemous, as he took the bottle from Lucretius and sprinkled half of its contents onto the axles of the gnomeflinger wheels.

He would save the rest for what came next.

The gnomeflinger rolled easily into the glade, almost as if it were on an incline or descending track. It was a little more difficult for the two gnomes to turn the contraption, but eventually they had spun it almost entirely about, so that anything placed into the fling basket would be hurled over the rock face at the northern edge of the glade.

The rumbling was louder now, and the foot of the mountain shook.

"An adequate defense, this gnomeflinger," Lucretius said, "for southerly attacks, or a most capable means of escape from this glade. But since neither of those events seem tactically or logistically probable, might I ask—"

"Give me one of your ankle bands," Innova insisted.

The old gnome shrugged, untied one end of the thing from his belt. The band was long and black, stretching admirably as Lucretius untied its other end from his ankle.

"What's it made of?" Innova could not help but ask.

"Petrol, I suppose. Other things. I was merely the finder, not the inventor: I collected these bands not long after you and the girl went upside."

"Which brings me to my next point," Innova said, replacing the worn-out tensile straps of the flinger with the ankle flap, then oiling the arm of the catapult with the rest of the Graygem oil. "I'll need some of your collection, Lucretius."

"I beg your pardon?"

"Your jools, old fellow," Innova insisted. "I need to fill the basket of the flinger with jools."

"It's all well and good," Lucretius stammered. "I mean, I will not miss a handful or even a basketful of my collection, especially if the cause is safety and justice."

Innova began to toss cut gems, polished bronze, and broken glass into the basket of the flinger. "I expect," he said, "that this device, all strapped and oiled, can fling as far as the Getinandgetout."

"The old northern pass?" Lucretius mused. "Why, I wouldn't know it was still open, were it not for that array of mirrors . . . "

And it dawned on him. The mirrors would reflect the jools.

The jools would draw away the dragon.

"A clever idea, lad!" Lucretius exclaimed. "Why, there'll be enough glitter and glow—"

"Now help me into the flinger, Lucretius," Innova ordered, stepping onto the long arm of the catapult.

*   *   *   *   *

Innova claimed he needed to "see things through."

The only way, he claimed, to clear his name of alleged treacheries and the abuses of the Paradise Machine.

Lucretius, however, thought that the whole thing— hurtling a thousand yards over canyons and crests as some kind of dragon's decoy—was a little theatrical.

For a while, the two gnomes argued the wisdom of Innova's riding with the gnomeflung jools up to the Geti-nandgetout. Meanwhile, Mount Nevermind shuddered and spat, steam and smoke billowing from crevasses along its face as though the whole inside of the mountain were burning.

"Very well!" Lucretius agreed at last, rather suddenly, as the tremors and rumbling made it difficult to stand upright in the glade. "Hop in the flinger, for philosophers say that it is often good to balance hot with cold, sweet with sour . . . *brilliance* with *dullness*."

Innova was too involved to hear the insult.

"Pile more of that lamp glass on my stomach!" he shouted. "Here—fill my hat with rubies!"

"Stuffing your boots with iron pyrite, Innova!" Lucretius exclaimed. "Fool's gold, it is, for a big fool—"

Innova sat up in a rattle of gems. "I beg your pardon? 'Fool,' is it?"

Lucretius smiled and turned away. "That fool of a dragon," he said, but Innova was not convinced by the explanation.

"I may not see you again, Lucretius!" the young gnome bellowed heroically. "Speak well of me in your circles!"

"*I* am my circle, Innova."

"Tell my story, Lucretius!"

The old gnome shrugged, and the gnomeflinger launched Innova toward the distant pass of Getinandgetout.

*　　*　　*　　*　　*

He remembered the flight surprisingly well.

The Graygem oil and the strap had done their job. The gnomeflinger was transformed, and as soon as Innova was launched from its basket, he was sure that the aeronautical problems had been solved.

He was bound for Getinandgetout. He knew it.

All around him flew a cloud of bright objects. He was aloft in glitter.

For a moment Innova thought that his life was closing. That this grand, dramatic sacrifice would be his last gesture.

"Just like a story!" he told himself, and prepared heroically for his fall from the sky. For the impact among mirrors. For the dragon.

Suddenly he was yanked back toward the glade. Desperately, he watched as the jools hurtled north and he reversed his direction, flying south at doubled speed.

"Damn Lucretius's fool's gold!" he shouted, fumbling vainly at the second elastic ankle band that the old gnome had tied quietly to his boot.

*　　*　　*　　*　　*

It could have been worse.

After all, it was only a dragon.

Of all the observers, only Innova and Lucretius—one battered, but both safe in the old gnome's beloved glade—were not astonished when the huge, fiery creature burst from the mouth of the volcano like a bright, scaly eruption. Stones scattered in its wake, and the air itself seared and smoked with the heat of its passing.

The gnomes scattered along the mountainside shielded their eyes against the brightness. Most of them stood still, paralyzed by the dragonfear, while some keeled over in a faint, as Innova and Pointillo had done in the depths of the mountain. Even Gordusmajor, wedged safely among the rocks as a sort of personal protection against quake and explosion, lost consciousness for a breath.

Then the world returned. The old High Justice blinked, looked up.

The creature swirled above the company of gnomes and Knights, scattering sparks over the mountainside. It rose higher and higher, spiraling in ever-tightening circles.

Below, the refugees screamed and made for the rocks. At a shouted order from Subcommander Hanna, the Knights raised their shields now, and readied their swords.

The dragon rose higher still, borne on a hot ascending wind. It was as though nothing was left for it to disrupt, to ravage, and at the apex of its arching flight it looked down, indifferently, at the scattering mortals it could have consumed then and there, erasing them from the surface of Sancrist and from all recollections of history.

But something turned its gaze from the mountain. A bright arch of glitter sailing toward the northern pass. Some gnomes, equipped with spyglasses or magnifying periscopes, would swear later that they saw a dark apish or gnomish shape straddling the shining arch, riding it north toward the pass at Getinandgetout.

All of a sudden, some of them would claim later to an audience of unbelievers, the little dark rider was yanked back, snapped south like a toy at the end of a rope. And the arch completed itself in an eruption of light among the mirrors of Getinandgetout.

Above these fireworks, the dragon banked in the air. With a deafening shriek, the creature swooped down, gliding through a wrack of clouds and surging toward the north. The long wail of its passage echoed into the summer air as it rocketed aloft in alarm, having mistaken its image in the multiple mirrors as a convergence of greedy rivals.

Higher and higher it went, sailing past the clouds in its fear, no doubt sailing past all greed and thought of treasure.

Its last cry was faint, carried on a high wind from somewhere north of Ergoth.

Led by Gordusmajor, the gnomes burst into applause. Shouts and whistles and cheers echoed along the slopes of the mountains, and even the gully dwarves picked up the jubilation, tossing caps into the air and banging spoons and wrenches on their battered shields.

Hanna looked quizzically at the High Justice, who only shrugged.

"Oh, I'm sad as well," Gordusmajor explained. "I mourn whoever didn't make it out. Your Commander included. In fact, I'll see to it that a statue's raised to him somewhere on the Thirtieth Level of the city he saved from disaster. I'm sad, and they're sad, too. But look how many of us survived. That's good enough for applause, isn't it?"

Hanna supposed so, but the old gnome could see that she was barely convinced.

"Oh, there's more of a reason as well," he said. "Just think of all the repairs we'll have to make in Mount Nevermind. It'll keep us busy a century, and repairing the repairs will take a century more."

He lifted himself wearily from the rocks, as though he was already bound on the task of rebuilding.

Hanna marvelled at him. Marvelled at the resilience and silliness of this strange people whom the Knights could capture but never conquer—could never dream of conquering.

"And when all is said and done, Commander Hanna," Gordusmajor said. "Don't the big lizard put on a show?"

Hanna shook her head. "I don't think I'll ever understand your folk," she confessed.

"You'd best try, Subcommander Hanna," the Justice said. "If I'm not mistaken, you're next in line for the Occupying Generalship."

Hanna fell silent as the horror of the prospect swept over her. "Oh, I think not," she said at last. "I remember, back when I received the Vision, that the Goddess told me not to stay long in Sancrist."

"I understand that Vision," Gordusmajor said, with a sly look at the subcommander, who was doing her best not to meet his gaze. "It was the Vision I'd hoped you had."

*   *   *   *   *

Hundreds of yards below, down in the little glade, Innova and Lucretius turned their eyes from the north, where the dragon had descended, snatched up the bright things, and lunged aloft once again, jools raining from its fiery claws.

It was bound farther north. Its destination only the gods knew.

The danger had passed for now. Lucretius and Innova peered up through the thinning smoke at the assembled nation of gnomes, and their erstwhile conquerors.

"What do you think, Lucretius?" Innova asked. "Should we go up to join them?"

"Not for a while," the old gnome replied. "You may still be a scapegoat in some quarters—the one who brought ruin on them with his Paradise Machine. Give 'em a week of clearing rubble and their minds will move to other things. By then, some of them will welcome you."

"A week?" Innova mused. "It only takes a week, and my achievements are forgotten."

His melancholy lifted a little when he recognized his cousin Scymnidus, climbing toward a high outcropping of rock upon which sat a gnome so enormous, so rotund, that it could only be His August High Justice Gordusmajor.

Some of the old crew had survived. That was consolation, more than consolation.

But his celebrity, his notoriety, the dramatic climax to his story, complete with aerobatics and dragons and jools—all the tales he imagined of Innova and the Paradise Machine and the Siege of Mount Nevermind. Would they all be forgotten in a week? In only a week?

"Look at it this way," Lucretius soothed. "If it takes them a week to forget your achievements, then it will take about a month for them to forget your misdeeds. Because, given the general course of peoples and nations, we gnomes are a forgiving lot."

"My backside still hurts, Lucretius," Innova complained. "All the more so for the last recoil."

The old philosopher shrugged. "Some things last longer than fame."

Innova looked back toward the tunnel through which they had escaped. The magma had followed them, had slowed in the cool mountain air, had come to a stop not fifty yards from where they stood.

Even at that distance, he could feel the receding heat.

It promised a few nights' camping on the surface.

"I suppose," he concluded, "that my part in the story is a small one."

He said this to the mountain, to the open air, to nobody in particular.

Of course Lucretius was nearby and listening.

"That's up to you," he said to Innova. "Your story isn't over, though I expect that this particular chapter is coming to a close. You've many days left, Innova, days moving into years if you trust the operations of calendars, which I do not. However you reckon the time, you'll have more of it to continue your story or to start another altogether."

"I don't even have a Life Quest yet," Innova complained.

"A vastly overrated venture," Lucretius observed. "Presupposes that one of us actually knows what he's doing. But a Life Quest is clear only at the end, when you look back over it and say, 'So *that's* what it was! *That* was my quest all along.' And it seems to me that you already have a quest or two under your belt—a history that even the least circumspect of gnomes might have cause to envy, if cause still works in our transformed city."

Innova smiled, dusted the ash from his jacket. "Is that philosophical consolation?" he asked.

"No other kind of consolation works," the old gnome said. "With the possible exception of Thorbardin Oeconomy Malt. But there's another consolation as well."

Innova sighed. "I feel a homily coming on."

"Not in the least. I've sworn off homilies. In fact, now that there's so much repair to do upside, you may see me more often than you'd like. But the consolation, Innova, is this: When you return to the upper levels, when you join again with this cousin of yours and with your old friend Talos, and with whoever else you left upstairs, there will come a time when you convene in that tavern—what was its name, again?"

Innova chuckled. "The Hell With Dinner."

"The Hell With Dinner. Well, when you convene, that's where the story picks up again."

"And how is that, Lucretius?"

"In the Hell With Dinner, over bottles of ale and Old Tom, you can lie like a poet, and finally, above and below this impossible mountain, there will be no one with the knowledge or the gumption to call your bluff."

"It's a start," Innova said, as the smoke cleared from the surrounding peaks. "It's a new kind of invention, I suppose. Now let's see, Lucretius . . . How many times did I stare that dragon down?"

Lucretius looked somberly at the young gnome.

"Twice," the old philosopher replied at last.

"Are you certain it wasn't *three* times?"

"Twice, Innova. Don't be improbable."

"Well, twice is a start. And what of my dragonfear?"

Lucretius's face was unreadable, but the depths of his eyes were merry. "As I recall," he said, "you may have felt, let's say, a *ripple* of dragonfear. No, a *quiver*. Lasted a breath or two, like a breeze passing through dried leaves, you'll say."

"I see," Innova said. "*Quiver* is good. I like the part about *dried leaves* as well."

"You'll say you were lucky the fear did not last longer."

"I'd have been done for, wouldn't I?"

"Indeed you would have. And none of your friends at the Hell With Dinner would ever have heard this story. You're getting the idea, Innova. Remember, it isn't lying if they don't believe you."

Innova nodded. "New inventions. New stories. It's certainly a start of *something*."

Bridges of Time Series

This series of novels bridges the thirty-year span between the Chaos War and the Fifth Age DRAGONLANCE® novels.

Spirit of the Wind
Chris Pierson
Riverwind the Plainsman answers a call for help from the besieged kender in their struggle against the great red dragon Malystryx.

Legacy of Steel
Mary H. Herbert
Sara Dunstan, an outcast Knight of Takhisis, risks a perilous journey to Neraka to found a new order of knighthood in the land of Ansalon.

The Silver Stair
Jean Rabe
As the Fifth Age dawns, Goldmoon, Hero of the Lance, searches for a new magic and founds the great Citadel of Light, linked to the heavens by an endless stair.

The Rose and the Skull
Jeff Crook
When Lord Gunthar, head of the Solamnic Knights, dies mysteriously, the order must make an alliance with their deadliest enemy, as a troop of gully dwarves races across Krynn to unmask treachery.

Dezra's Quest
Chris Pierson
The daughter of Caramon Majere brings aid to the centaurs, as they try to escape a terrible pact made with Chaos.

HEROES AND FOOLS

Edited by Margaret Weis and Tracy Hickman

An anthology of short stories from prominent DRAGONLANCE authors, describing the terrible battles and brave exploits of heroes during the first decades of the Fifth Age.

Contributors include Margaret Weis and Don Perrin, Nancy Berberick, Richard A. Knaak, and Douglas Niles.

DragonLance

The Raistlin Chronicles

The story of Raistlin Majere, Ansalon's greatest mage, told by the person who best knows his tale.

The Soulforge

Margaret Weis

A mage's soul is forged in the crucible of magic. Now, at last, Margaret Weis reveals the hidden story of Raistlin Majere's early years, from his first brushes with magic to his Test in the Tower of High Sorcery. His life, and those of the people near to him, will be changed forever.

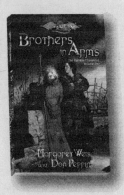

Brothers in Arms

Margaret Weis and Don Perrin

As the shadows of war gather across Krynn, Raistlin and his brother Caramon offer their services to a commander. Half a continent away, their sister Kitiara also enlists in an army and begins her rise to power among the Dark Knights of Takhisis.